I0602760

THE OPEN BOOK UNIVERSE

THE OPEN BOOK UNIVERSE

L. MARIE WOOD

FALSTAFF
BOOKS
WWW.FALSTAFFBOOKS.COM

Copyright © 2025 by L. Marie Wood

Cover Design by Susan H. Roddey

All rights reserved.

No part of this book may be reproduced in any form or by any electronic or mechanical means, including information storage and retrieval systems, without written permission from the author, except for the use of brief quotations in a book review.

PART I

THE OPEN BOOK

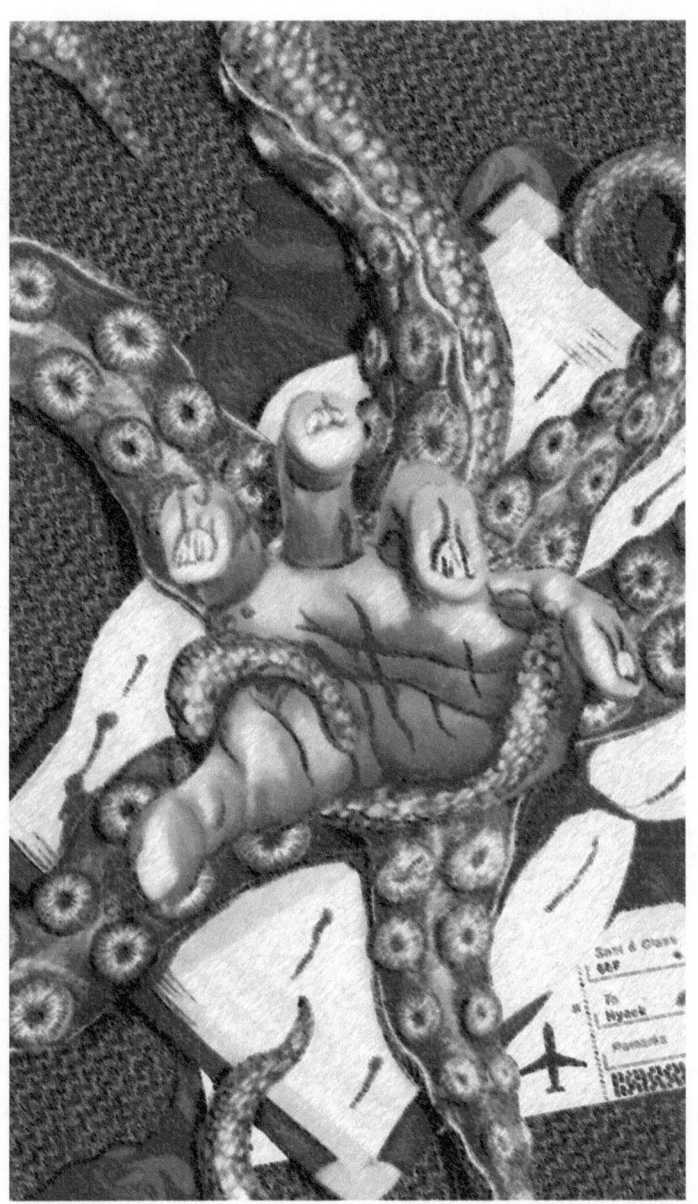

PROLOGUE

The tentacles had barely tucked themselves securely away before someone noticed the book lying open near the seat. The man had been the first one to ever resist, and his misstep proved delightful, at least for one of them; the other, not so much. Having the last thing ever seen in waking life be the gelatinous underbelly of a creature whose name can't quite be placed but that smells of the familiar, nonetheless; to know that the sound of sucking and slurping was the result of some other being's pure gastronomic ecstasy at the taste of one's own flesh; to understand, yet try to blot out the fact that one is breathing last breath number 5, then number 4, and so on, must have been hellacious. The effect was much like a tenderizer on tough meat; a sweet undertone of flavor infused in gracious quantity.

Innocent and tranquil lay the book, its pages open to the stale air of the airport terminal. There was no trace of the blood that had poured from the man's gaping mouth as his insides compressed, no residue from his eyes that had burst from the pressure. All of that had been carefully consumed, the contents fusing with the dexterous appendages as if animate themselves. There was nothing to see. Nothing to know. Its life was, indeed, an open book.

1

A woman pulling one of those wheeled carry-on bags approached. She was dressed elaborately, bright colors tangoing on her duster; knee-high boots adorning her calves and feet. She wasn't paying attention to where she was going—her smartphone possessed all her attention. Because of that, she stepped right onto the yellowed pages of the book and stumbled, surprised by the obstruction. The woman bent down to pick up the book and had every intention of placing it on a seat and continuing on. It was either that or kicking it under the chair, but that wouldn't be right, would it? It probably fell out of someone's bag, left there by a person who had already boarded their flight. Kicking it under the chair was wrong—that was littering, wasn't it? Wasn't she trying to do better about things like that? Wasn't the whole reason she was in the airport dragging environmentally conscious cleaning supplies around because she wanted to make a difference in the world? The woman frowned as much at the book on the floor as at the absurdity of her current situation (have toilet bowl cleaner, will travel) and picked up the book, deciding to take it to the people at the gate check-in counter. What they did with it then was up to them.

"I guess I'm doing my part," the woman said aloud to no one in particular. A little boy laying on his mother's lap stared at her as she reached for the book.

The woman pulled it toward her, noticing that it was open to a story.

Her eyes cascaded over the page, reading the first few sentences before she realized what she was doing.

Home Party

You gotta be kidding me.
The front of the trailer was barely visible beneath the overgrown bushes, if they could even be called bushes. They looked like the stuff that grows at the base of trees, wispy and vine-like, with pathetic little leaves that were more brown than green. They covered the front of the trailer in clumps, all camo green and switch bearing, growing wild. Where there weren't bushes, there were bins of empty beer cans. Four of them on the splintered porch and at least three in the tall grass that made up the yard. The place stank of beer, piss, and sweat.

The cornucopia of sound from the loudspeakers filled the woman's ears in a rush. She bolted upright as if she had received an electric shock. Her head whipped from side to side, her eyes desperately searching for something, but not finding purchase. Then as they landed on the little boy who stared at her from his mother's lap, the child whose eyes seemed to take up most of his face, she settled down. He pointed at the pool of urine that had formed below her. She felt the warm path it had traced along her leg before hitting the floor, felt her pants sticking to her. She looked at the puddle, the strangest smile forming at the corners of her lips.

In silence, the woman walked to her gate and got in line with the other passengers, cracking the book open as she did.

Carrie looked at the place, noting that two of the windows facing the front of the house were boarded up, and the window in what might be the kitchen was so tiny, it was hard to see into. But was someone looking out? She looked around the yard. Given the state of the house, she expected there to be a bunch of discarded, rusted out cars littering the lawn, but that cliché didn't fit. There was an older model Ford, but aside from faded paint and an ancient dent on the passenger side, it had been kept up. There was a sticker in the back window from the local college. There was also a brand new pickup truck. All this was odd, but not that odd. They could have needed a pickup for work and maybe it wasn't really new... just

new to them. The Ford made total sense—a college student paying for something herself. You get what you need. That explained the beer cans too, and maybe even the boarded-up windows. One party with college kids could produce half the number of bottles in those bins. And what's a good college party without a broken window?

But as she sat in the car, trying to rationalize everything she was seeing, she didn't believe it. The trailer didn't feel like a college hangout or a hauler's dive to crash in when he wasn't working long hours. It felt... wrong. It felt empty, but not because no one lived there. It felt lost.

Carrie swallowed, her mouth going dry while thoughts of crazy hill people of Texas Chain Saw Massacre *variety ran through her head. She forced a self-deprecating smile and got out of the car. It's no mansion, but it's someone's house, she told herself, and allowed for a hint of reproach to show in her inner voice. She had never been one to judge a book by its cover, as the saying goes, and she wasn't going to allow herself to start now. She straightened her smart blazer, red for the season and a perfect accompaniment to the new product line she toted with her to this afternoon's soirée. She has been excited about showing the new bags to this group of people. The lottery she posted in the local nail salon gave her entrants who wanted to have a home party and look at the new catalog items. Michele Davenport, resident at this trailer, was the lucky winner. After weeks of excited conversations, party day was here. And alone in the gravel driveway of a broken down trailer stood Carrie.*

It was quiet for mid-afternoon.

Carrie got back in the car, suddenly spooked. She looked at her watch. 1:30. She was supposed to be there a half an hour early and she was late. She got stuck behind Sunday drivers on the two-lane road leading to the place and got there with only ten minutes to set up. And she ate half of that time up staring at the trailer.

Maybe there was no one there. If there was, surely, they would have heard her car idling, would have seen her sitting there. As annoying as that would be (driving 45 minutes to get stood up was not her idea of a fun afternoon), Carrie didn't really want to go in the trailer. In fact, she thought, come hell or high water, I'm not getting in the trailer. There was something in the trailer that she didn't want to see. Something that was watching her, waiting for her to knock on the door, to look too closely at that little window in what might have been the kitchen. She could almost hear it breathing; a wet, phlegmy sound that made her skin crawl. And it was watching her. It had been watching her the whole time.

Carrie turned the car on and put it in gear without looking back at that window. She didn't see the front door open, didn't see the college student's odd, slow gait toward the car. She didn't see what trailed behind her, coloring the high grass. Carrie threw her arm over the passenger seat to back out of the driveway, but a car parked her in. Laughing ladies in the front seat smiled at her, excited about the party, the games, the goodies. She didn't see the larger of the two lick her fingers as she pulled herself out of the car.

∾

The flight attendant noticed the book laying open when she moved through the cabin after the passengers had disembarked, the pages facing the seat. She sighed, irritated that there never seemed to be a flight where people just did as they were told. Take all your stuff with you when you leave. Do not leave wadded up napkins containing god knows what in the seatback in front of you. Do not stuff garbage between the cushions or leave things behind. Seems simple, but there was always something left.

She picked up the book and prepared to throw it out, already catching a glimpse of sandwich wrappers and—what is that, chewed up gum?—wedged under the window shade, but the cover caught her attention. The intricate design, elegant and ornate, was breathtaking. The lettering appeared to be gold done in the finest calligraphy. *The Tales of Time.* A smile played at the corners of her mouth as she imagined a fragrant wind mussing her hair as she stood on a beach with the book in her hand. She could almost feel the breeze cooling her skin; could almost smell the ocean air as if she stood directly on its shores. She opened her eyes to look at the cover again, not realizing she had closed them.

The Tales of Time.

The wonderfully winding lettering reached up like vines to caress her skin. She inhaled luxuriantly, the memory of the sea making the moment surreal. With a decisive grunt, she put the book into her apron.

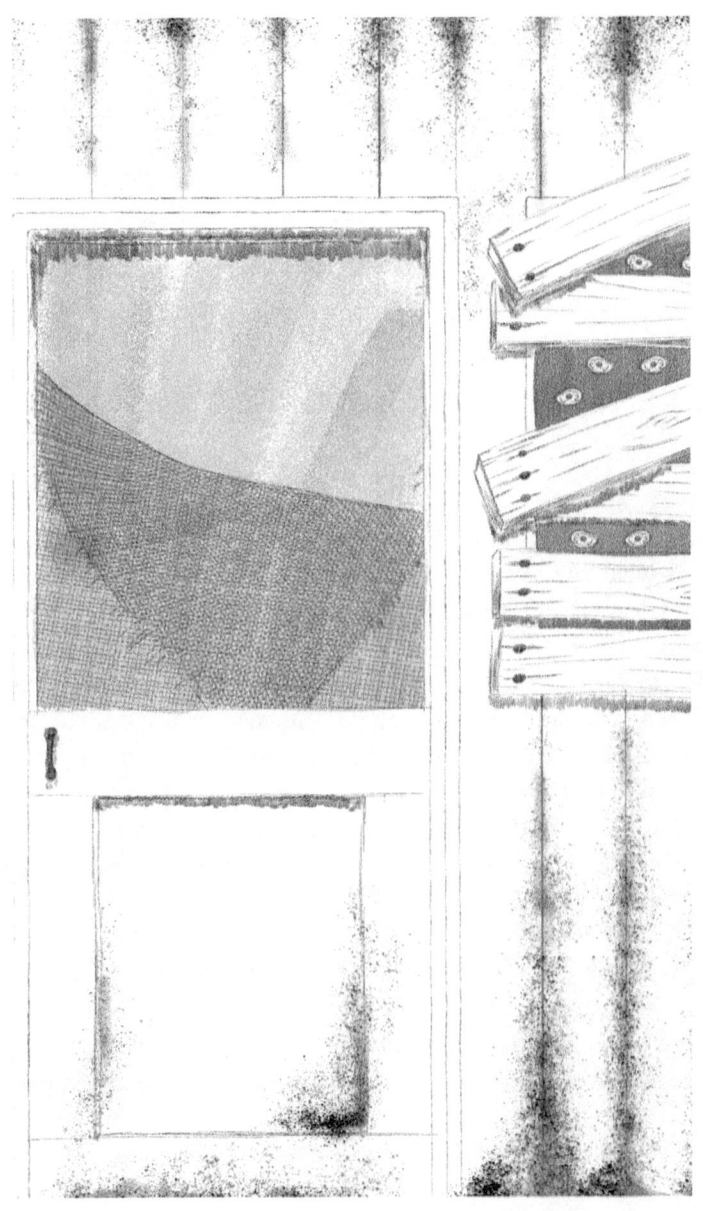

2

The flight attendant walked into the coffee shop near her house and sighed at what she saw. The line was almost to the door. She shook her head and leaned out to look at the barista, a young girl with purple streaks in her hair and a discreet little nose ring that was still visible even though she probably thought it was concealed. The other two people behind the counter were working frantically in a cloud of froth and steam, the look of barely-contained panic showing on their faces.

This could take a while.

She put her hand into her bag to pull out her phone, and it brushed against the book she had found on the seat of the plane. She took the book out and examined the cover again.

The Tales of Time.

She felt windswept all over again as she opened it and thumbed through the front matter, looking for nothing in particular, but noticing that there was nothing to find either. No dedication page; no copyright page. No author name listed anywhere. Just blank, yellowed paper.

The line moved.

Her brow furrowed as she stepped forward to keep up.

When she found the first page of type, she breathed a sigh of relief. She had been holding her breath without realizing it, afraid the pretty little book she found was really just a journal some wannabe introspective passenger left behind. But no, the book had words and lots of them. She flipped through it as she stepped forward; another sweet and foamy drink delivered to a happy customer. There were several short stories inside. She turned back to the beginning of the book in search of a table of contents to see if any titles jumped out at her, but there was none to be found.

"Humph," she said under her breath. The guy in front of her turned, doing that passive-aggressive thing we are all guilty of—the one where we turn to the side like something important is happening over there but really we are glaring at the person behind us out of the corner of our eyes —showing her his chiseled profile and a mildly disapproving expression to go along with it. She couldn't help but thinking that he would be really hot if he would dislodge the stick that had wedged itself in his ass so firmly. She smiled at him coyly, thinking she'd happily help him with that, if he wanted.

The line moved.

She stepped forward, almost banging the book into pretty boy's back.

She leaned out to see how many more people were in front of her: four.

Great.

She started reading.

Impure

He sat in the shadows watching her as she moved, savoring the way the light caught the red in her hair, the way her chin dipped slightly to the left as she thought. He was tempted—that went without saying. But it went beyond the innate desire to satisfy the burning in his lap. Indeed, his hand resting there, absently stroking, was far removed from his thoughts. Instead he spoke to her, told her exactly what he wanted to do to her. He caressed the words, leaving them silky and smooth. He reached for her and felt her rise to meet his—

"Miss?"

The flight attendant looked up from the book in a daze. She felt hot, flushed, like she had been running, or...

"Ma'am, do you know what you want?"

The flight attendant looked at the barista waiting impatiently behind the counter. The line had depleted, and she was next. She was still standing yards away from the counter, where she had been when she started reading. Surprised, she looked back at the barista.

"I-I-," she stammered.

"Do you need a minute to decide?"

"N-No. I know what I want."

She walked toward the counter. One, two, three strides. She caught sight of pretty boy waiting for his drink at the pick-up counter. The smirk he wore made him look even more appealing than before.

She smiled at the barista, ordered, turned on that charm she reserved for work, and diffused the situation. She paid awkwardly, fumbling with the book and the credit card and her purse and her phone and all the crap that ended up in her hands as she stood at the counter. Laughing self-deprecatingly, as the situation called for, she put everything on the counter, the book included, which she did reluctantly.

'A woman fitting the description was seen driving the car toward Eel Road in a rural Virginia neighborhood this morning, sources say...'

The flight attendant heard the news in the background. She gathered up her things not realizing that her mind was picking out bits and pieces of the news story to focus on. Eel Road Didn't she know where Eel Road was? Maybe. Maybe not.

'... the body was discovered by a neighbor who didn't recognize the car...'

The flight attendant turned to the screen to look at the news story rather than listen to it.

'... we heard somebody knocking on the door, but nobody's lived there in years.'

"Ma'am? You can pick up your drink at the pickup at the end of the counter."

The flight attendant looked at the purple-haired barista who was clearly losing patience with this distracted routine. She flashed another winning smile, grabbed her purse, and went to the pickup counter, where her drink was already waiting for her.

Pretty boy was gone.

It took her almost two hours to realize she had lost the book. After going to the gym, the cleaners, and the grocery store, she almost didn't care. Except she did. She wanted to know what happened with the weird stalker guy she was reading about. She wanted to feel the way she felt in line again, wanted the sensation of someone telling her what they wanted her to do... where they wanted her to touch...

The flight attendant called the coffee shop to ask about the book. She could almost hear the laughter in the girl's voice. It was Purple Hair, she was sure of it. Purple Hair thought it was funny that someone could be that desperate for a book that they would call about it like it was a precious jewel or something. How did she know the flight attendant was desperate, she wondered? Could it have been how fast she was talking when Purple Hair answered the phone? Maybe it was that harsh intake of breath when Purple Hair said the book was gone. Even more likely, Purple Hair heard the sadness that she couldn't keep out of her voice when she realized the name of the book had escaped her. Maybe it *was* funny. Maybe Purple Hair was right.

The flight attendant went online and researched the book, describing the cover the best she could, but the memory of it was hazy now. Was there water? A horse? Words on the cover? Sher couldn't remember—it might as well have been a rainbow and unicorns.

The flight attendant felt tired all of a sudden. She lay down with thoughts of pretty boy from the coffee shop in her head.

3

The barista, better known as Purple Hair, struggled to wake up. She felt as if someone was sitting on her chest, crushing the bones there, compressing her lungs. She tried to tell herself it was just that thing that happened to her sometimes, that feeling of trying to wake up but being unable to move. Sleep paralysis? Yeah, that had to be it.

Screaming.

She was screaming.

It sounded like her voice was coming from under water, low and muffled. Frantic.

Quiet... no. Silent.

Could anyone hear her?

She thought she was hyperventilating, thought she was using her full voice to scream for release, but she wasn't so sure. Was she moving? In her mind she was, arms flailing, hands grasping for purchase. But was she?

She raised her hand in front of her face—sent that very signal to her mind and willed her hand to rise, but it didn't. It didn't and she wasn't screaming, wasn't moving, wasn't hyperventilating. Was she breathing at all?

There was something at the foot of her bed.

Dark and shadowy, floating above her feet, its toes aligned with her own, one cracked and yellowed claw reaching toward her chipped mani-cured big toe.

Shit.

She blinked—it was still there.

She tried to move her toe away, but she couldn't—she didn't even flinch.

She screamed louder still, begging the thing over her bed, the thing clad in black rags that billowed around its form and was carried on an unseen wind—the thing that was lifting its head to look at her ever so slowly—to leave her alone. She cried, her voice cracking, her sanity fracturing.

And then it was gone, and she was screaming her most blood-curdling horror movie scream aloud in her bedroom, the sound reverberating off the walls like she was in an echo chamber. Soon her mother would rush into her room, terrified by what she might find after a scream like that, but for now she was alone, lying in her bed staring at her foot, the chipped manicure seeming to glow from her big toe.

Her chest heaved.

A sheen of sweat cooled in the morning air.

Her throat was raw before she finished. When her finger twitched beside her, fluttering against her leg gently, much like the touch of eyelashes in a discreet butterfly kiss, her heart nearly stopped.

The book lay open on her nightstand, marking the page she had started to read but had fallen asleep on. When had she placed the book there? She could remember falling asleep on it, the book slipping out of her hands and landing... where? The floor? The bed? Her legs? She didn't know. But there it was, waiting for her to pick it up, to read it; to finish what she started.

She wanted to get up, wanted to splash water on her face, maybe go downstairs and talk with her mother, ask her about her day. Funny how that's what she was thinking about right then—talking with her mom. She hadn't been interested in just having a conversation with her in a long time—longer than she could remember. She didn't think about that normally—didn't think about her mother at all, really. She was 19—it was normal. That's what her mother told her, even as her eyes showed the sadness that her voice denied. She hadn't thought about doing it, just sitting with her mom and talking maybe over a cup of coffee, the way they used to, before school and work and boyfriends and parties had taken over her life, but it was all she wanted to do right then. She sat up, intent on doing just that, swinging her legs off the bed with less effort than she expected and moving to stand... but she couldn't. She couldn't roll herself off the bed either as she attempted next, her panicked mind telling her she'd better get off the bed or she would die there.

She was stuck.

She didn't know if the book floated in the air, moving of its own volition, to rest in her open hands, but somehow it was there. The words on the page seemed emblazoned in gold.

Pretty.

As her mind begged her to shut her eyes, to throw the book across the room, to get up and burn it where it landed, she read the title of the new story, her eyes tracing the words as if they were sacred. With a sigh that was both fearful and expectant, she settled into the tale, her purple hair falling into her eyes as she read.

The Garage Door

There's something to be said about the stamina of a 4-year-old.

People are always saying, 'I wish I could bottle some of that energy,' or some other annoying little comment that always strikes me as hollow. Those cute little one-offs always made people sound like they are just trying to find something nice to say to draw attention from the fact that the kid in question is acting like he's hopped up on something. The 'I've been where you are' comment that older ladies say to young mothers when their children run wild in the aisles of department stores, or when they eat all of the grapes before they are paid for, or, and this is priceless, when Junior decides it's time for American Idol *tryouts at the deli counter, is really judgment thinly-veiled as commiseration. 'Tsk tsk,' that seemingly understanding smile really says. Get your shit together, Miss. But of all the offhanded comments made by spectators of the parental variety show, that one rings true. Now, as the mother of three, shall we say, spirited children, I do want to bottle that energy. I'd sell it to folks in their fifties who are just starting to realize that the flexibility from their youth is never coming back. I'd sell it to people trying to lose weight; jumping around like the Energizer bunny from sunup to sundown will surely do the trick. I'd sell it to anyone who wanted it and make a mint. Even at $1 a bottle, I'd be a millionaire within days. But one of life's cruel jokes is that you can't bottle it. You can't put it in the freezer to defrost when you really need it. All you can do it use it when you have it.*

My 4-year-old understands that concept really well.

I thought maybe we could watch a little TV after music class and a play date at the park. Thought just maybe we could relax a little before naptime when I would, inevitably, fall asleep too, missing my chance to get something done. There's only a short window between having one wild thing in the house and three—just about an hour and a half. I try to vacuum, do some laundry, clean up, start dinner, and sit down for 10 minutes in that time. Sometimes I can get one or two things on the list done, but on days like today, when Mr. Baby is excited about everything he sees, I don't do anything but sleep. So I sigh, as my eyes get heavy, and settle in to a nice recline on the couch, watching Nick wind down like a top losing its juice. I didn't realize I was lying down until he climbed on top of me and got comfortable, his head on my chest, his soft hair tickling my nose. Maybe we'll just stay here on the couch for our nap instead of trudging upstairs to the bedroom. The TV's on but that's ok. It's on a kiddie channel, so there's no chance of us waking up to a mob movie or something like that. As Nick put his arms around me, his clammy skin sticking to mine, feeling good in a way that only moms know, I decided that yeah, a nap on the sofa with my little guy would be perfect.

The sound of the garage door opening should have woken me up, but it didn't.

Oh, I heard it (its low hum is unmistakable through our paper-thin walls), but I didn't wake up. I should have—the door opening in the middle of the day is unusual to say the least. My other two kids don't get out of school for hours and Chris isn't due home from work until after six. More disturbing is the fact that knowing these things, I still didn't get up. Someone could be breaking in. Or what if we overslept and the kids were opening the door with the keypad? What if someone was making them open the door with the keypad? For some reason, in that place between deep sleep and awake, I didn't think either of those things was happening. I just figured it was Chris. He was home early, and that was all it was. Some part of my subconscious wondered why he was home early—slow day at work; playing hooky; laid off?—but didn't care enough to wake my body up to find out.

At first.

Chris took a long time getting into the house. In fact, I never heard him come inside, but I heard him moving around. That was weird because I could hear Nick's rhythmic breathing, could feel his hair under my nose if I reached for the sensation like a swimmer coasting to the surface for a breath of fresh air. But the door didn't unlock, and the alarm didn't announce his arrival with a beep. He was just there all of a sudden, puttering around in the room. I heard him drop a bag, then unzip it and rummage around inside. I heard the volume on the television turn up—one of those incessant cartoon jingles blaring suddenly; ramming the sugary-sweet lyrics about a being four and, each day, growing some more down my ear canal, as if I couldn't already recite them in my sleep. I heard footsteps, Chris' socked feet approaching Nick and I on the sofa to kiss our heads like he always does when he finds us asleep on lazy weekends. I could feel myself straining towards his lips, expectantly reaching for his touch. But none came. Instead I heard raspy breathing overlaying a sickening whine—barely audible, but there, persistently there. It was so primal it affected my soul. I felt the heat from his skin as he stood over me, leaning in to peer into my face. I heard him lick his lips, his tongue flicking out like a snake's over dry lips.

That was enough to get my attention.

It wasn't that I hadn't heard ragged breath from Chris before. It had been a while, but not that long. Something about this sound, the base desperation in it, made me feel different. The usual butterflies in my stomach followed closely by warmth cascading down past my navel didn't happen. Instead I felt a sensation that I couldn't really put a finger on. Edginess? Maybe. Fear? I didn't want to admit that.

I tried to open my eyes, ready to tell him about the weirdness that started the moment he came home. He would appreciate it for what it was—an overactive imagination going full tilt. I felt. It was obviously because of Nick's clammy skin and the drool that had slipped out of his mouth and onto my skin. That's why I was thinking about a wolf or a dog that we don't have, or some other panting, heavy breathing thing. He would laugh and hug me the way I like and everything would be fine. If I'm lucky, maybe I can slip out from under Nick without waking him and have a little play date of my own. But I couldn't get my eyes to obey me. They were stuck together so well, it was as if they had been glued. I couldn't stop my mind from going to a place I had hoped I would forget. When in the dim room blanketed by humidity so stifling it was tangible, and surrounded by the sickeningly sweet-smelling combination of fresh flowers and cheap perfume, I must have been the only one to see the glue giving way on Uncle Wally's eyes, the whites (well, grays considering his state of repose) winking out at me. But this time my memory of that day distorted into something far worse. Uncle Wally's right eye opened all the way, blinked, and then he turned his head toward me, his neck popping and cracking as he did it.

I tried to scream. I knew I would scare Nick and ruin any chance of having a little afternoon happy, but I needed to wake up and in a hurry. Before Uncle Wally decided to get out of the coffin and come see me. But I couldn't. I felt like my mouth was open, but there was no sound coming from my stretched vocal cords. I tried to sit up, to shake myself out of this crazy vision (oh God, why is Uncle Wally smiling?) but I couldn't move. I started to panic. I could still hear that feral breathing over me, like an animal waiting for the right time to pounce.

I could see Uncle Wally lifting his head out of the coffin, his body slow to react, but moving, nonetheless. I imagined that Nick, my sweet little boy, was staring at me as I struggled, his face unreadable, impassive... cold.

I screamed.

I screamed long and loud. But that's not what I heard. The smallest, weakest crescendo emitted from my lips, building to a faint whimper, before all my limbs jumped to attention at one time. The jerk snapped me out of whatever spell I was under. It also woke Nick, my beautiful, still asleep and not staring at his mom like she was an experiment boy, up.

"Mommy! No!" He protested groggily. I kissed him on his head, the action making me acutely aware of the fact that we were alone in the room and laid him down on the sofa. Children have an uncanny ability to fall back to sleep right away as though nothing happened. I was grateful for that today.

The room was still. I don't know why, but that made me uneasy. I mean, it should have been still if there were really only Nick and I at home, but just seconds before, I knew someone was in the room with me. Knew, not felt. And now there was no one here.

Was this a game? I almost let myself buy into that as I stood tentatively and peered into the kitchen. Hide and seek maybe? Come find me, and quick so we can steal a couple of minutes to ourselves? I wanted to believe that. But as I saw the red Virginia clay on the floor leading from the family room—from the very sofa Nick and I were on—to the garage, I knew it wasn't true.

I thought I had shut my eyes. I imagined I was standing in the family room, facing the dining room, imagined I was still waiting for Chris to pop out and whisk me to the bedroom. It was safer than where I ended up. But the door handle beneath my outstretched hand couldn't be ignored. Neither could the hot air that hit me in the face like a blast from an oven when I opened the door. I tried to shut my eyes then, tried to will away the sight of it all. But I couldn't. Partly because it didn't make sense. Chris' car would have been in the place where his shoe lay on its side. It would have filled the space where his leg bent obscenely under his body if he had come home. But he didn't come home, did he? He was still at work.

Chris' eyes were cloudy, his beautiful brown covered in a white film. That doesn't happen right away, the part of my mind that was fighting off the paralysis that fear was trying to impose, rationalized. It takes at least a couple of hours for that to happen, right?

I stood there trying to figure out what I was looking at, my mind flitting back and forth between thinking it was an elaborate dream or if I was standing on some alternative plane, where reality was just a little different than the one I am from. I was in the zone; sweat coating my brow as I tried to make sense of the scene playing out in my garage, when the shuffling of feet brought me back to reality. And Chris was still there.

"Mommy, I don't wanna be 'wake," Nick said rubbing his eyes, the beginnings of a major pout sprouting on his lips. I looked at him, his hair all over his head, his eyes squinted against the light, and then back into the garage at the man I planned to spend the rest of my life with, and bit my lip. I wanted to keep biting and biting until I drew blood. Maybe that would snap me out of it. Maybe the dead Chris would disappear.

I didn't want Nick to see anything, so I closed the garage door. With any luck I could keep him away from the garage until everything was said and done and Chris had been moved.

Uncle Wally's joyless smile nagged at me.

I bit my lip a little harder than usual (just in case) and let the sob that was rushing from my throat turn into a yawn.

"Me either, baby. Me either."

~

"Honey?"

Leslie was so tired of yelling. She yelled up the stairs, yelled through doors, yelled into other rooms because her lovely daughter always had headphones, earbuds, AirPods—whatever they were called—jammed into her ears, blocking out all other sound She was always in another world... a world Leslie wasn't sure how to navigate anymore.

She needed to go. The longer she waited to get on the road, the longer it would take to get there. Traffic was horrendous these days—one of the only things that hadn't changed in the past few years... her commute sucked then, and it sucked now. Normally she would have just left, but she really needed her daughter to answer her, to acknowledge her request this time. She needed her to take the dog to the vet on her way to work. Leslie couldn't do it herself—it was too early. She had written a note, but Leslie wasn't sure that was enough.

"Ok?" Leslie tried again, "I can't take her, and she has to go today. If you leave her there, I will pick her up on my way back home, ok?"

Nothing.

Not a peep.

Damn it, Leslie thought. *This girl is going to make me climb the stairs and look her in the eyes.*

Leslie went upstairs again and knocked on her daughter's bedroom door.

"Babe?"

No reply.

She turned the knob and pushed the door open. She couldn't help the smile that spread on her face as she spied her daughter's purple hair splayed on the pillow. Purple hair, she snickered as she walked toward the bed. If she's not careful, she'll burn all the ...hair... out of her...

Leslie's mind almost didn't process what her eyes were seeing. There was too much red where there shouldn't have been, too much all over her chest, all over the bedsheets, all over. Her nose had bled, that's all, right? It was just a nosebleed; Leslie could see the stream as it trailed from her nostrils. So, why didn't she just get up? Why didn't she just wipe her nose and get up from that dirty bed and change her clothes?

Leslie couldn't move, couldn't breathe... couldn't think.

She never heard herself wailing, never saw herself clawing at her daughter, yanking at her arms, shaking her shoulders, begging her to wake up. Leslie never saw the book that she tripped over, the one that sent her careening into her daughter's headboard, splitting her own skin and letting blood to mingle with her child's. She only felt the purple hair beneath her fingers, purple hair made brittle from so many dye treatments, purple hair that would fade underground, where no one would see.

4

She hated going to those things.

Picking through someone's garbage, like a homeless person looking through trash cans for scraps.

So what you could get good deals?

So what people let go of perfectly good stuff—unopened stuff—that you might never have bought new yourself.

So what?

Yard sales were not the way she wanted to spend her Saturday mornings, but also, so what? This is what the senior center director told her to do. That and teach the old girls how to make jewelry—beaded rings, bracelets, and necklaces to accessorize their brightly colored outfits from Chico's.

It was hot out. She could make a case for them cutting their yard sale hopping short because of it.

Jenn got out of the van—the standard issue senior center go-mobile—and called to one of the women in her little group outing.

"Carol..." Jenn tried but realized mid-yell that the poor dear wouldn't hear her; her hearing aid was a bright fuchsia that seemed to glow against her silver hair and was definitely out of range.

Jenn started to approach Carol, feeling like she might melt in the early morning heat, but doubled back to the van to grab the ladies some water. Surely they were feeling it too. With five bottles in hand, condensation sweating off of them immediately and wetting her pants, Jenn started out again, this time seeing Samantha nearby as Carol had moved on to another table. Samantha, her southern belle, the leader of the crew, the one who called the shots. She was holding a book gingerly, rotating it in her hands, running her fingers over the gilded lettering.

"Samantha... you thirsty?"

Jenn held out the water to the woman who didn't pay her a second glance. She had shrunk as old people often do, standing about shoulder height to Jenn's 5'5" frame, but anyone who saw that and assumed her diminutive stature equaled weakness had another thing coming. Samantha was cunning and sharp, ready with a response that would cut you down and make you want to sit in a corner for a while. She had heard Jenn perfectly. There was nothing wrong with her hearing unlike many of the others. She just deigned not to respond.

Jenn smirked. It was too hot for this shit.

She retracted the arm holding the water like a good little girl and stepped closer to look at the ornate cover.

"Whatcha got there?"

"A book, dear," Samantha said, condescension lacing her words.

"I know *that*, but..." Jenn's eyes cascaded over the cover, swirls of gold atop hues of cinnamon and nutmeg. "What kind of book?"

Samantha looked up at the girl. She was a nice enough sort, unremarkable, but that was ok. She did her job well enough and stayed out of everyone's hair, her nose stuck in her phone when her tasks were done. She let them alone, and that was precisely how Samantha liked it. At least she didn't have to battle with her tooth and nail over everything like she had the last one. Samantha snorted quietly at the thought.

Samantha handed her the book and pointed at the title. "*The Tales of Time*," Samantha read aloud, almost irreverently, like she was holding some cherished tome from before her time. Truth was, she had never heard of the book, and reading had been her favorite pastime for most of her 83 years. She had been ready to crack the book open, to turn the yellowed pages and find out what the story was about, but she opted instead to let the girl do it. Infusing a little awe in her voice for the hell of it, she continued, "I've never seen one quite like this before."

It was true. She hadn't seen one quite like that before. She hadn't *ever* seen a book so beautiful and delicate like that one before.

Samantha looked at the girl with wide eyes for little added drama—the icing on the cake—before shuffling down the table to look at other things.

She laughed under her breath as she saw the girl turn the book over in her hands, water bottles forgotten on the edge of a table crowded with baby clothing and toys. *Maybe she'll buy it, read something she can hold her in her hand for a change*, Samantha thought. These kids and their smart-phones—no wonder everyone's eyes were going bad. She adjusted her glasses on the bridge of her nose. It had taken her until age 70 to need to wear them all the time, even with all the reading she did. She was proud of that fact. At the rate most young people were going, they'd be wearing glasses before they even turned 40.

Jenn ghosted her hand over the cover of the book, her fingers tensed in anticipation. In a distant corner of her mind, she was aware of how strangely she was behaving. She had never cared much for books, never read for fun at all, really. It was always part of a requirement for school or work. But for some reason, this book intrigued her. The look of it, the feel —soft in a velvety kind of way. She felt compelled to open it, like she really had to do it… Like she really had no choice at all.

She opened the book. Flipped past all of the blank pages until she found words. She settled herself to read as the sweat slid from the nape of her neck and down her spine.

The notification on her phone dinged so loudly, Jenn's knee jerked, slamming into the table, knocking over the bottles of water she had brought for the ladies and some of the baby clothes too.

"Oh dear," Samantha fussed, coming back to the flustered girl's side, bending to pick up the water bottles before Jenn snapped out of her surprise and stopped her.

"Don't Samantha; I've got it. You round the girls up and let's get out of here. It's hotter than Hades out here."

Samantha made agreeable *mmhmming* sounds as she walked towards her friends, more tickled than she should have been about the scene that had played out before her. *It's the little things*, she had always said, and that mantra still rang true.

Sun-ho posted a video.

That's what the message said.

Jenn couldn't help the smile that crossed her face as she penciled in time to watch it later, once she got the girls situated back at the center. She couldn't wait to see if he was going to talk about his upcoming concert. Maybe he would sing for them a little or show them a dance routine that would be in the show…

The book felt substantial in her hand.

"Excuse me," she called out after picking up the baby clothes and folding them in a way that hid the dirt she had put there when knocking them to the ground, "how much for this book?"

Idol

"How can he be that beautiful?"

Millie stared in awe at the image on her smartphone, enlarging his lips, his eyes, even his undercut for a closer look. The sigh that escaped her lips was heavy with sweet admiration and laced with feels she hadn't been aware of before finding K-Pop. It didn't take long for her to become entrenched in the mania. She found her favorite group almost right away, their luxurious voices caressing lyrics she didn't understand, creating an exotic, taboo-like aura in her room when she put on their songs... which was every day, for most of the day. She bought all the stuff: the summer video packages, the CDs with special photo albums inside, the swag featuring her bias and the one showcasing her bias wrecker (then, guiltily, something with the faces of the other members too because how could she truly be a fan if she only supported a few of the members, right?). Millie had it all. They were going to be performing in the US later that year and Millie had a great idea to pitch to her mom about travelling to LA to see them. LA is a lot closer than South Korea, she would say. I can work during the summer to help out on costs, she would add. Maybe her mom would understand. She'd had her own entertainer crush, right? I mean, what were all those tears about when Prince died if she didn't? Millie thought she probably shouldn't go there, not unless she really had to. Mom hasn't listened to Prince since he died—the mourning was real.

His oval eyes looked out at her from behind a fan of periwinkle-colored bangs (oh, how her bias loved to change his hair color!), giving all the fanservice he knew she and the millions of other screaming teenage girls around the world liked. He had just woken up in some other place on the other side of the world from where she sat and decided to go live on YouTube just because. Millie grinned from ear to ear when she got the notification and left the dinner table without warning. Her father said, "Don't forget about the movie," or something like that as she passed by him. Millie had shoved earbuds in her ears before taking her plate to the sink and had turned the volume up high so that she could hear every nuance of his voice before reaching the stairs.

She thought she grunted a response to her father but wasn't sure.

His face was filling her screen before she had gotten out of the room; his perfect pink lips parted suggestively as he worked to get the camera situated just right. She never saw her brother Chris smirking at her from the kitchen as she raced by, never saw her cat dodging her legs as they scissored wildly up the stairs. She only saw him, only heard his groggy voice speaking in his hypnotic foreign tongue.

He yawned.
Millie smiled.
He chuckled.
Millie blushed.

~

"Millie hasn't come down yet?" her mother asked of no one in particular. The kitchen was clean, and the leftovers put away. It was time for movie night, and three of the four of their little family were ready to get started.

Chris looked up, shrugged, and turned his attention back to the game he was playing on his smartphone. Millie's father sighed and said, "No, not yet."

Millie's mom looked up at the ceiling, a move she swore helped her to hear what was going on upstairs better, and listened intently. The muffled sound of a male voice speaking quickly could be heard. She didn't notice the staticky hiss that was deliberately, persistently there, but inconspicuously so. Like the assumption of crackling on the wind after an electric shock, the sound floated among the waves and pitch to mingle with his rich baritone. She strained, trying to understand something of what was being said, trying to determine whether the broadcast was almost over or not. She wanted to give her daughter a chance to join the family activity on her own. Choosing her battles these days, Millie's mom didn't relish the idea of pulling her away from something she wanted to do. On any given day, Millie might as easily bite her head off as give her a smile, and if the guy that was talking was the one from that K-Pop group she liked, and Millie tried to interrupt her...

"Go get your sister," their mom said to Chris reluctantly.

Chris' nose was stuck in the game. He was oblivious.

She looked at Chris and then over at her husband incredulously.

He cleared his throat first but got no reaction.

"Chris!" His voice boomed in the room.

Chris looked up, surprised.

"Your mother told you to go and get your sister."

The protest that rose in Chris' throat died on his lips when he saw the frustration in his father's eyes. He got up without a word, leaving his phone behind as he knew they wanted him to. Chris didn't want to fight. He wanted to watch the movie. *This week had been his choice, and he couldn't wait to rub it in Millie's face. He had chosen Child's Play, mostly because he knew Millie hated Chuckie. Crazy little demon doll, here we come.*

Chris bounded up the stairs, talking all the way. "Time to say goodnight, sweetheart," he parodied, trying to sound lovey-dovey. "It's time for the movie." He stopped outside her door, hearing a male voice speaking in a language he didn't understand. "You don't even know what he's saying, Mil." Chris turned the knob and opened her door, still talking. "He could be telling you to take off your clothes in front of class and do the dance from his last video." This struck Chris as incredibly funny.

Chris' hearty laughter turned shrill, like the scream of a siren, when his sister turned toward him slowly. It wasn't the saliva that spilled from the corners of her mouth that frightened him most, nor the milky white veil that covered her chestnut brown irises. It was the way she spoke that sent chills down his spine; the monotone delivery of a question he could not understand,

"Eotteohge geuleohge aleumdab ji?"

5

They didn't tell them much about what happened to that poor girl—really only said that she died as a result of natural causes, some kind of brain aneurysm or some such thing. But Samantha knew better. Even when the women who took her jewelry class said they thought something was off about her that last week, thought maybe she wasn't feeling her best (they said she looked a bit peaked in class, especially when she was trying to thread the clear beads for the crochet rope bracelet she was planning to teach them to make that day)—even then, Samantha didn't buy it. She tried to tell Clarise about it, tried to remind her that aneurysms didn't show themselves like that. Jenn wasn't sick, wasn't tired, wasn't anything. She just up and died, and none of the people who saw her making bracelets or serving juice or tapping her foot in the back of the room during country line dance class saw it coming.

Samantha hadn't gotten to be 83 years old being stupid. She knew better than to believe what the staff told her about Jenn. Whatever happened to Jenn wasn't natural at all.

Samantha saw the book among Jenn's things as she was leaving the center for what would be the last time. It was sitting there, propped on its side in a box alongside a coat, a picture of the girl with an older man, and all the knickknacks that seem to follow people from desk to desk, job to job. She reached towards it, wanting to touch the cover, lured by that gorgeous gilding work she had so admired that day at the yard sale. How intricate it was, how detailed. Such craftsmanship didn't exist anymore, it seemed. Samantha hadn't realized how much she missed it. It was like art inasmuch as the words themselves were and the creation of beautiful things seemed to be in short supply. She had woken up with that very notion in her mind that day, the fragment of a poem on the air that swirled between sleep and consciousness,

My darling, what speak you,
a voice
his voice
yet not
asked thunderously,
for I have not gone

Lyrical words. Pretty words chaperoning her from sleep from a poem she couldn't place—at least not yet. She wanted to think about it more, maybe search for it online as they say—put technology to good use. Thoughts of white horses on a backdrop of the blackest of nights filled her head.

"It's beautiful, isn't it?"

The voice, belonging to the prune-faced lady that sat at the front desk, surprised her. It wasn't only that she was speaking in a kind voice that Samantha had never heard from her before in all the time she had been going to the center that threw her for a loop. It was that she was speaking at all. That woman, whose name Samantha had never bothered learning, seemed to prefer frowning to smiling as she sat in the air-conditioned front office, the same papers scattered on her desk from one day to the next. That she nodded her head hello and goodbye was the only indication any of them had that she was still alive.

"That it is," Samantha responded belatedly. The woman had moved behind the desk upon which the box sat, standing opposite Samantha expectantly. What was she looking at? Samantha found herself more irritated than she expected to be at being observed.

Where the hell was the shuttle?

She decided to grab it, to pick the book up and feel it before old prune face moved the box away.

"These are Jenn's belongings…," the woman started.

"I was with her when she found it," Samantha countered, feeling the lie forming on her tongue. "I am so glad I saw this—I didn't want to have to contact the family for it."

"Contact the family? For what?"

"This book," Samantha continued settling into the story. "I bought it for her, well not really *for* her… but I let her read it first. When she was done she was going to give it back to me, but now…" She ran her hand over the velvety cover and had to suppress an appreciative moan.

"Oh," Prune Face said, unsure what to do.

"I guess I might as well just take it with me tonight," Samantha said, tucking the book under her arm and taking a step toward the door, silently hoping the shuttle would pull up and whisk her away with her stolen goods. "Doesn't make sense to do much else."

The woman nodded with Samantha, going along with whatever she wanted. Everyone knew Samantha, knew how she was… it was easier that way. Samantha continued to shuffle toward the door, decision made, will imposed. The woman sat down behind the desk and watched her go.

6

They met every week but it hadn't gotten any easier. Not for Karli. Not for Kevin either if the way he always leaned on the wall, backing himself into a corner so that he couldn't be surprised by someone coming up behind him, tapping his shoulder, singling him out was any indication. He never volunteered, always remained in the shadows, made himself as small as he could with his almost 6'0" tall frame. She'd talked with him once when they were on a break, everyone immediately crowding the snack table hoping that the food would chase away the jitters, and he told her it was his nerves that kept him quiet. Karli had responded with something nice enough, something people said when someone they didn't know well seemed to be teetering on the edge of sharing too much, something like, 'Yeah, we're all pretty nervous' or 'the struggle is real' – noncommittal, perfunctory, placating. He nodded and fell silent again, filling his plate with the lukewarm cheese and stale crackers that had been left out since they filed into the space, a backroom at a rec center that had seen better days. Karli remembered when the rec center had a preschool in it, a Tae Kwon Do class, senior citizen dances, and, of course, the requisite Bingo. But none of that happened anymore. Now the activities were comprised of AA meetings and support groups, self-help seminars from people who had gotten on, fallen off, and gotten back on a myriad of wagons. Instead of smiling faces glistening with sweat, high on endorphins or sugar, determination etched lines in the countenances of the people who exited those doors now. And then there was the ragtag group she was involved in, many of whom looked like they had wandered into the wrong room.

The fluorescent light in the hallway flickered. It always did. One day it was going to go out, and they'd be stuck back there, in a forgotten room off a dark hallway.

Karli wondered if she could write something about that.

The quiet man floated away, gliding as if he were carried by the wind, not making a sound as he moved – barely shifting the air at all, as if he were never there to begin with. He settled back into his corner then much like he had that day; the only difference was that now there was a sizeable printout from Ms. Watson in his hands. She had spent some bucks on that thing: she had made copies for each one of them – 12 in all. Karli was lost in thought about how she must have gotten hold of the copier at work and run them off because she couldn't see the woman who brought them stale crackers every meeting actually paying for copies. Karli thought about how the crackers really were stale every single time, how she must have dug into the back of her pantry to find ones that were out of date and taking up space to give them. She wondered how much Ms. Watson got paid to run the workshop, wondered if it had a stipend in it for snacks, because if it did, she was definitely not using it on them. And the light in the hallway kept flickering.

Ms. Watson said she used to worked mostly off-off-Broadway, but unless "off-off" meant outside of New York, she was full of shit. The lady who ran the Nicotine Anonymous group said she remembered seeing her in a show somewhere in Virginia back when those were her stomping grounds. She said she was pretty good if you liked the melodramatic type. Karli laughed and asked her if there was any other kind of actress which earned her a smile from a mouth not used to contorting in that way. Still Karli enjoyed the class for what it was worth, which was about $25 a month at present. She went every week, projected her voice, and tried to 'find her presence'. Whatever. It was a way to spend a few hours. So if the heavyset lady who looked less like an actress and more like a school-teacher who should have retired five years before wanted to make up stories about having been on the big stage, so be it. Karli didn't have the energy to call her on it.

Once everyone settled – she always waited for people to quiet down before she moved to the center of the room to speak, commanding an audience at all times – Ms. Watson made her way to the middle of the makeshift circle they had constructed to mimic a stage using rickety chairs, desks, and empty garbage cans to affect the look. She took a deep breath as she looked around the room, and then another, her way of urging everyone to follow suit. And they played along – there wasn't anything else to do other than that. After her third breath where she almost swooned as she let her eyes flutter closed and her chest heave with the effort, she began.

"OK. Today is going to be special. Today... we are going... to act!"

She swung her arms in grand fashion to indicate that acting was this massive undertaking that we, her lowly students, were now ready to embark upon. It was grand – like Yul Brynner in *The King and I* grand, big and bold and loud and gaudy. Theatrical at its most melodramatic, and it was then that Karli knew that every single thing the nicotine lady had said about Ms. Watson was true.

"Today *you* will take center stage. You will stand where I am standing right now and deliver emotion like you never have before. This goes beyond delivering lines. It's passion that I'm looking for here. You should be able to make us cry, laugh, feel pleasure and pain just by the look on your face, your posture, your body language."

She punctuated her words by moving her short arms through a series of pushes and pulls, stretches designed to look fluid and graceful but most decidedly did not. But she believed in whatever she was doing completely; in her mind her display, her garish gesticulations were as poignant a those seen in the best of performances - *Les Misérables* at the Barbican or *A Raisin in the Sun* at the Barrymore. Karli sniffed her inner stage snob – the one from another life where she collected playbills in shadowboxes that lined her walls and recited lines to imaginary cast-mates... the one she would never admit to – back inside herself, forced it to quiet down and go back into its cubby.

"You hold your performance piece in your hand," Ms. Watson continued, thumbing the side of the packet. "All you need to do is pick the one that speaks to you most."

People started to look at the papers in their hands like they were a new type of animal, unnamed and wild. They looked at the packet in reverent silence and something about that made the hair on the back on Karli's neck stand on end. It also caused a tickle to form in her throat... a tickle that would turn into full-fledged laughter if she wasn't careful. She watched them, this timid bunch of misfits that came together to find some way to spend their time other than on the streets with a bottle in their hands or a dime bag in the pants, awed by the experiment in human nature she was witnessing. Some braved their consternation enough to raise the cover a little, just enough to peek inside. Most just stared at the blank cover, caught in a strange limbo.

The girl with oily hair and a dirty nose ring spoke first.

"These are just a bunch of stories," she said, her voice thick with mucus before she sniffed it back into her nose. "How are we supposed to act something out if there are no lines to say at all?"

"As I said, Mara," Ms. Watson said exasperatedly, and Karli started to wonder if she was right about that name or if she had just pulled it out of the air, "the lines themselves are less important than the emotions you act out. Draw us in with your body language. Did you know that there is a Danish actor who can make you feel five different emotions in the span of fifteen seconds, all without moving his body at all? It's all in his eyes, his facial expressions," she looked away at nothing the way that theater folk often do, the look on her face nothing short of rapturous. "It's absolutely brilliant."

Ms. Watson turned her attention back to the group with obvious effort and looked each of them in the eye.

"Do that. These stories are all in first person. Do you remember what that means…?" Crickets.

"Neil?"

Neil should have cleared his throat before he started speaking; the gravelling, phlegmy thing that came out made Karli want to gag.

"Um, yeah, it's like when you use I and me," he said, the unspoken question raising his voice a few octaves indication that he wasn't at all sure that he was right.

"That's exactly right. They are all told from the character's perspective. You need to *become* the character. Make us feel what *you* feel. If your character cries in the story, then you should cry too. If you want to be great, you have to master this."

Pause. Indeed, a *dramatic* pause during which the class looked back at her with vacant eyes. They didn't want to be great, their expressions should have told her. They just wanted to exist. If she saw the messages written on most of their faces, she ignored them.

"Ok! So, go find a seat and read the material in the packet and-"

"All of it?" an older Latinx man said, the irritation at the prospect of having to go through all of the stories in that twenty-page packet written on his face.

"If you want to pick a story that you can embody, one that speaks to you and only you, yes. If you don't care, well," she shrugged one shoulder in that aloof way that dismissed the intended recipient and cast a cold pall over the others in close proximity, "I guess that will show in your performance, won't it?"

He sighed and so did someone else sitting behind Karli but she didn't turn around to see who it was. She was too busy looking at the light in the hallway, the way it flickered on then off, on... off...

Maybe she'd write something about that sooner rather than later.

"I would urge you to look at all of the stories. If you pick one of the stories in the beginning of the book simply because you want to be done with the assignment, you might miss a gem waiting for you at the back of the book."

Ms. Watson nodded at each of them, expecting reciprocation. Most acquiesced as people always do. Even Karli found herself nodding back in agreement even though she had no intention of reading the stories in the no-name, photocopied book, not when the light kept calling to her the way it did. If she couldn't finish writing the story before all the ones in the book were chosen, she would act out whichever one was left. How hard could it be?

"Ok, so let's get started," Ms. Watson finished. "With any luck, you'll have selected your stories and we can have a few run-throughs tonight, before all is said and done."

Ms. Watson turned on her heel and went to the snack table. For a while her work was done, and she could indulge in the old cheese and crackers left to decompose in the stuffy, heavy air that always seemed to hang with them there in that backroom, no matter how they tried to ventilate the space. The misfits found places to sit and pour over the stories, the strain of the exercise showing in their furrowed eyebrows and tense shoulders before even starting the first story.

Karli dug out a pen from the bottom of her burlap bag, flipped the book over to the back, and started to write.

The light flickering down the hall blinked like a strobe light. I felt like I would get dizzy if I kept watching it, but I couldn't pull my eyes away. It was pretty. I want to touch the light to see if it was hot because maybe it is hot and then

... And then?

Stuck.

Karli got stuck in the first 5 minutes and couldn't see a way out, couldn't figure out her next steps. Why would she touch the light? Of course it was hot! She would burn herself and then what? She tried scrapping the whole thing and starting again, this time without the detour of touching the light. She got to the point where her character flicked the light switch on then off, but the fluorescent light kept up its own beat anyway, and got stuck again.

She bit the cap of her pen.

She crossed out whole sentences and tried to rewrite them but nothing came.

Damnit.

Karli guessed she would be acting out a story from the book after all.

She opened the book and read the first page.

I Have Nothing to Wear

How does this go?

What do you wear to something like this?

Choker, accentuating the neck? V-neck to show more skin? Tight dress, short dress, loose dress, long dress, no dress, maybe pants instead?

Do you wear a jacket, a vest, ruffles, lace?

My hand lands on a crushed velvet top with buttons and strappy things, none of which I remember. When did I buy this?

Sequins?

No.

Burnout? That paper-thin material that always seems like it will rip and show off the things it barely concealed in the first place?

Maybe that. Yes, maybe so.

Do we dance or is this one of those drinking and smoking parties? I wouldn't mind feeling a body next to mine, pressed up close, hot breath on my neck –

Yeah, I'd better make sure my neck is out instead of in so I can feel all the sensations I am supposed to feel.

So...

Flower or stripes? Polka dots? Midriff shirt and leather shorts?

Damn, it's been a long time since I went out.

But he called and he's hungry and I want.

Karli turned the page before finishing, not wanting to waste too much time on one that she knew she wouldn't pick. She had spent enough time trying to write her own story and came up empty; she didn't want to lose any more precious minutes.

Because there really was a story in there for her – suddenly she could feel it.

The Cleansing

The flames licked, danced, engulfed the wood eagerly like a hungry beast. She watched it flicker then build, climbing the walls like vines on the side of a house, undulating against the wall like lovers.

Next.

She

It turned my stomach.

That from within the cabin I could still smell the eclectic perfume, a mix of fried chicken, wet pennies, and Eau De Toilette that only she could make sweet, made me weak-kneed. The scent, long cleared by earth and element, filled my nostrils as my mind first commands, then pleads, "You don't recognize, you don't recognize, you don't, you can't...."

Out of Time

Blind, aimless movement, like a wave crashing onto the shore, rolling over and flattening the sand, removing all distinguishing marks: the hearts carved by fallen branches, the initials inside.

K. T.

+

L. M.

4 eva

Or at least until the tide came in and wiped it all away.
Wiped away.
Obliterated.
Razed.
Like Gomorrah and the Arc.
Starting over.
Starting again.
Hands pushed and grabbed. Legs pedaled, propelling men, women, and children toward the back of the store. The sweater she had been looking at seemed to

disappear into thin air as if part of a magic trick - now you see it, now you don't - the garden variety activity provided for the very old and the very young at resorts when the parents go off to play. It had been ripped out of her hands by someone running by, face a blur. The tag came off in her hand, one of its corners puncturing her skin to draw blood. She thought to put the wound to her mouth and lick at it in that vampiric way that people did when they saw their own blood in the open air, selfishly recalling it into their own bodies before anyone else could partake. She thought to do so, to taste the metallic notes, but as the next person to barrel through the racked space nearly bowled her over, taking that route instead of the tiled path that was mobbed with runners from the café at the front of the store, the customer service section, and the bathrooms, she thought better of it. If her hand was in her mouth and she took another hit she might knock her own teeth out. She might bite so deeply into her flesh that the soft lapping of her tongue wouldn't be enough to assuage the pain.

Running.

Everyone was running. Yet their feet made no sound.

Because of the siren.

The siren started up, crescendoing to its highest point within seconds, its tone even and persistent. It sounded like an old-time ambulance, deep and full, not shrill even though the hair on her arms and the back of her neck stood up, responding to it the same way it did to high-pitched noises. She had always thought the gooseflesh came because of the shrieking nature of it all: babies crying, nails scratching on a chalkboard, the undertone of a fire alarm – that shrill beeping that seems to ring in the room even after the alarm has been turned off: all of it was enough to set her teeth on edge.

But that wasn't it.

That wasn't all.

The siren was going off.

The one that most people living there had never heard before, including her.

The siren that meant it was over.

Everything they knew was unequivocally, irreconcilably over.

Because They were there.

She watched an old man fall to his knees a few rows over from her. He had been in the toddler clothing section, perhaps shopping for his grandson, the one he would never see again because he would never get out of that store. She saw him drop to his knees because the racks that had separated his body from view just seconds before had been pushed aside, toppled, fallen upon. And there were bodies. Arms and limbs tangled, twisted, bent under the weight of their own bodies. Still.

She felt her mouth open, felt her jaw unhinge as her eyes fell upon some of the bodies stacked on top of each other: big, small, tiny.

Tiny.

And there was blood.

THEY were there.

She tried to take a step, to run with the rest of them, to succumb to the under-standing, the stark reality the older man had already allowed, to move, but she could do nothing, nothing, nothing at all as she thought of her parents probably trying to get into the basement, to get into the tub, to hole up like it was a tornado. She could do nothing as she thought of her dogs running around her house, ears flattened to their heads to block out the sound, whimpers escaping their throats – could imagine them bouncing nervously as they peered through the sliding glass door into their familiar yard, though that space likely didn't look so familiar anymore. She thought of her colleagues running into the storage closet like she would have if she hadn't gone out to lunch, pressing their bodies into a space filled with things that could kill them if turned into projectiles, but having nowhere else to go. And it wouldn't matter. Because this wasn't a hurricane; this wasn't a tornado, or a tsunami, or dust storm, or any other kind of storm. It was Them.

It was THEM.

And it was time.

Awakening

Night when I thought it was day.

Cold, but unnaturally so, or so said the daffodils that had pushed through the ground already, showing their brilliant yellow. Unlike the pinks and reds and yellows of the azaleas that bloomed in my neighbor's yard, the ones she fussed over and pruned, the ones I vomited into over the fence before I fell... fell while we were talking about summer vacation and watching each other's dogs: fell and never got up again.

Days?

Weeks?

Years since that day, the world cycling on without a care while I lay in my grave, cold and dank, trying to get out.

To get out.

Because I shouldn't be there... I shouldn't be in the ground.

Locked away.

Forgotten.

Because I am here and I can remember the way the sun kissed his hair while we sat on the deck, how the night sky looked when it was full of stars.

Because I can remember what it was like to laugh and walk and run, yes run, so I did run because I could and my legs could still carry me. They carried me right back to where I should be. Right back home.

Cold.

Unseasonably cold for April or May or whatever month it was. Killing my daffodils. Killing my follower that would come up even if I wasn't there to see them.

So yellow. I want to touch one but I am afraid to ruin it. When I see my fingers in the moonlight, gnarled and discolored, bloody because I had been clawing, clawing, clawing at the lid of the grave, beating against the cement enclosure, kicking my way up through the dirt, dirt that fell into my eyes to blind me... dirt that slipped into my mouth and down my throat to choke. I was afraid to touch the daffodils, not because I didn't want to make them like me because they were already like me – dead and revived, awakened, denied rest. No, I didn't want to touch the daffodils because I would soil them with the dirt from my grave and the dirt was my own.

Happy.

Laughing.

Music in the night.

They were probably dancing, maybe watching a TV show, the kids might be playing a game and maybe cooking together in the kitchen, maybe...
A new car in the driveway.
A new car where mine used to be.
They were probably loving anew.
The wind guided my steps and for that I was thankful because it meant-
Close.

So many of the stories were close, but they whispered her name instead of screaming it, and she knew there was something else, something more just waiting for her to find it. Something inside her wondered why she cared, why all of a sudden, finding the right story was so important to her... why she was able to shut her eyes to what she saw happening around her: the cutter scratching at her scars, the alcoholic rubbing his mouth. That thing inside her wanted to ask if she was paying attention, if she had noticed that the guy who hung out in the shadows was suddenly not doing that anymore, that Kevin had, in fact, moved closer in to the group as if in search of kinship. It wanted to ask if she smelled the excitement coming off the middle-aged woman whose story Karli had not worked out yet. It wanted to ask her why she wasn't afraid. But it didn't. It stayed in the back of Karli's mind, circled in on itself, folding, tucking, receding... trying to disappear. Because Karli wasn't Karli anymore... not like she had been before opening that nameless book with stories copied off center on recycled paper. Karli wasn't who she needed to be to hear that part of herself anymore.

Because Karli was on the hunt. She wanted something she could sink her teeth into, something that had teeth of its own.

Another Day

It rained the day I took them, trapped them, kept them inside – clear, where I can see. I took them all, let them settle, mingle, comfort each other as they rippled, moved, fought against the confines, their pretty little place, until they stilled.
No, not all of them.
Some I sampled. I couldn't make myself wait, not knowing when the day would come when I could visit with them again. So I tried them – I tasted them. And I loved them.
I looked at them, those from that first day, that rainy day under a sky that seemed to hate me for what I was doing, sought to stop me by growling and clapping its hands. I looked at them every time I added another, even if I never looked

at the other so often, never so intensely. I looked at them and they saw me too. They called my name and it made me smile.

Model Home

The light turned on in the darkness, a faint red glow indistinguishable in the unnatural greenish haze of night vision. Cabinets look creepy in the dark. So does the stillness of a sleeping house. Watching for too long can be terrifying – the feeling that something will show itself in the shadows is enough to drive someone mad.

Still, the camera came on for a reason...

Something floats before the lens. One would dismiss it as backscatter – indeed, most did that very thing – there is always dust in the air so the camera catching glimpses of it wouldn't surprise anyone except that shouldn't set off a motion sensored security camera. If a camera can be calibrated to ignore a 25-pound cat, then surely it should be able to discount a speck of dust. If they watched long enough they would see the orb take a decided turn and cross in front of the camera once more before travelling deeper in the room and disappearing into the shadows. Another speck of dust? Not likely.

But they wouldn't look that long – most people didn't. Because that's not what they would be looking for if they turned on this feed. There were countless other feeds of this very room when the demons came out to play, their forms sometimes translucent when wandering specters entered lost or angry; sometimes solid flesh and blood as looters lifted and squatters broke, but none of those recordings would be important if anyone found out about this one.

If they noticed.

It's there, just a little bit of heel, but still there, in view if you looked hard enough. But would they? Was anyone ever really looking anyway? It's late - past 3:30 a.m. Who would be looking at this hour anyway?

They wouldn't see in time, wouldn't be able to save him, this man whose heel is the only thing in the recording. A dark, solid colored sock – Black? Blue? - still covered the toes, but the heel was bare... brown skin against a backdrop of shadows in a darkened house in the middle of the night. Infrared will pick up something, make the heel more visible if nothing else, but what good would that do? From such a distance and without the benefit of the toes it won't look like much of anything – it could be a Styrofoam cup just as easily as the only thing visible of a dying man. And no one would think a Styrofoam cup suspicious, not with as many people that come in and out of this place every day. People were always in and out, picking up things, stealing things, chatting up the agent but never intending to buy. Sometimes the realtor invited her boyfriend over to have sex. Sometimes she hooked up with one of those people who had entered the house that day wandering, wandering, just like those wayward spirits. But the camera was never on then, so nobody ever knew. But it's on now – does it make a difference?

They brought him here to dump him, did away with the alarm before any notification could be sent, but not the camera sitting inconspicuously on the hutch, the one that had the broadest arc of the room. Different system – one of the really good ideas that the team designing the newer model homes came up with, because petty thieves wouldn't think outside of the box about a thing like that. As far as they were concerned, the place was empty at night which made it prime pickings. Snip, snip on the wires, use some computer geekery to screw up the Wi-Fi and you're in.

But these weren't thieves.

They brought him there to dump him, but he wasn't dead yet. They carried him in, left him there on the floor, and walked out, never realizing that he would squirm a little before he died, moving just enough to bring his heel into view, never realizing that he would add his low moans to the sounds of the house settling.

If the design team had thought about manning the camera, periodically watching live, they would have seen it. But they never would have saved him.

"Wh-where'd you get these stories? They're… there's…," someone started from the back of the room but Karli didn't look up from the book to see where the question came from. She didn't hear the answer either or if there even was one; she was engrossed in the next story in the book, each story getting closer and closer to the one that was written for her.

Even so, something in the back of Karli's mind reacted to the tone of the woman's voice and grew cold.

I Know

Shadows playing with the moon, making finger puppets on the wall and yes, I know that it's him and not me, that it's him come for me because he loves to play even if he has no hands to do it with anymore.

Cold.

Cold as the ice that encased him, trapped him, blanketed him below, down under, deep in the frigid blue. It's like that outside when the board creaks, and I feel it.

Beyond the Chain

I used to want to hear dogs barking, hear the laughter of children, get hit with the sprinkler every evening at dusk, and hope that baseballs didn't do any lasting damage. I wanted that, but what I got was a patch of grass hardly long enough for a grown man to lie down in heel-to-head, and trees so tall you could only see me in in the dead of winter, and then only if you squinted.

No dogs bark, no children play, not after they chained up the gate and took him away, not after what they found inside.

Gerald.

They never listened to him, not even when he swore he didn't know they were there, playing house in his shed, sitting around the table waiting for him to get home.

I knew they were there, but I couldn't tell.

I wouldn't tell.

They couldn't make me. Nothing could.

I knew they were they there, but they shouldn't have been. They were trespassing. They weren't invited. They didn't belong.

He said he didn't know, but that was a lie. He had to have known. I secretly think he put them there. For me. I fancied that for years, imagining that he had brought them there for me to see, for me to play with. I thought of what his voice might sound like when he told me to do what I wanted with them, that they were mine to do with what I would. He would sound strong and confident, nothing like the whimpering imbecile they dragged away that day, wide-eyed and pointing at me. I fantasized that he lied to them to make them stay, and oh, what a good liar he turned out to be! Maybe he told them that everything he did was for them, and that they had nothing to worry about because he cared for them and always would. Maybe he told them that my soul spoke to him and that I loved them too and that I wanted them there as much as he did. Their stench still sits in the wallpaper they had lined the walls of the shed with, trying to make the place look like a proper home.

He lied to himself about them, about me, about it all. Even as he set fire to the weeping willow that had been my friend, the massive thing that had sheltered cardinals and bluebirds over its 250-year life—even as he tried to use to it to burn away everything he ever knew, he couldn't murder the truth, couldn't clean away the stain. Even as he sits in his cell, far away from me now, still he knows, he remembers, he feels.

The table is still set for dinner, modestly, for three servings instead of five.

The pitcher upon the table, with the painted rooster on the side and the chipped spout, is empty now, but that can be easily remedied. All one need do is ask.

No one comes past the chain or ventures into the woods to peek anymore— that time has long gone. Now they pass by without a second glance at the over-grown driveway, the cracked asphalt barely visible beneath layer upon layer of dead leaves and weedy undergrowth. Someone left candy once, had thrown it past the chain and into the gaping maw that yawned behind it.

Glasses

I went back for them.

I went back because I knew he dropped them and someone would see.

I saw them fly off his face and land in the mulch, one frame obliterated by the blast and the other cracked and splintered – ruined beyond repair. They wouldn't need to be repaired, though; his blood smeared on the rim, on the lens, all over his face and hair, doubling back to mingle with what pooled in the gash at the top is his head told me so.

I went back for them.

I went back for them because I knew he'd want me too. I knew he'd like to have them with him wherever his body ended up, likely at the bottom of the quarry past the old farm because it was abandoned and the water was murky, filled with old shit that had sunk there decades ago – not even the sex-crazed idiots over at the high school used that spot for a romp because it was... there was just something off about it.

He'd like that.

If he had to die, he'd like to make a difference, and so I would put his body there. There he could be part of the lore, be one of the ghosts that haunted that old, shut down place.

Plus nobody would think to look there because nobody would have the guts to.

I went back for them, and they were there, right where he left them, right where they landed when they fell off after his eye was ruined and his face collapsed, little bones poking through the skin, piercing, cutting, flaying.

Except they were different.

They were bloodless.

The temples – arms, I called them, but he knew what the real word was... of course he did – were folded as though he had taken them off on purpose and laid them down.

But he hadn't.

He hadn't had the chance to do anything, least of all set his glasses up nice.

I went to pick them up but didn't because somebody must have done this, and the realization washed over me like a cold breeze. Ok, an animal could have come and licked the blood clean, got a little appetizer before its main course. That made sense. But no animal could fold those arms – temples, shit – that way. Not a single one.

I went back for the glasses alone, in the dark. Nobody knew I was coming because if they did, they would know I had a body in my trunk and maybe even how that body got there.

I was alone out there, and now it seemed darker than it was before, darker than when I let loose the shot that lit up the sky and blew up his head, darker than I've ever seen it before.

Was he still there... watching me?

Why did we always think it was a 'he', anyway? It could be a 'she' just as easily because there's some sick bitches out there too – just as sick as some of the dudes I know. It's ridiculous to just think men-

What the fuck? I hate when I got off on a tangent, thinking about something stupid instead of paying attention to the shit happening in front of me. Because somebody fucked

Karli ached. She flexed her fingers, stretching them, moving them out of the death grip they had been in as she squeezed the papers in her hands so tightly her fingertips turned white. The people around her seemed to have chosen their stories already, were starting to play with movement and work through the performances they were going to give center stage, yet she still sat flipping through the pages, looking for the one. She almost gave up and just picked one, wanted to so badly then because she wanted to have at least a few minutes to practice, but she couldn't do it. There was a story in there for her – she knew that as well as she knew her name. Karli also knew deep down that if she didn't find it, if she just went with something – anything – else, there would consequences.

Hypnopompia

The numbers spun – they spun! – right before my eyes and I know I'm groggy, I know I'm having trouble waking up this morning, but I know that's not right. When I woke and looked at my alarm clock, bastard that it is, beeping incessantly like a truck backing up, high-pitched and monotone at the same time... when I woke up and looked at the time, it was steady. 6:33 – I might have tried to ignore it for a few minutes and that's why it was 6:33 and not 6:30... sue me. It was overcast, but the sun was trying to peek through the blinds. I know that because I saw it. Everything was the way it usually was. Me not being able to haul my ass out of bed was normal too. Nothing to see here, folks, just your average Monday morning.

But I did get up. I didn't hit snooze this time. I trudged across the room like the walking dead, my eyes mere slits as I made my way to the bathroom, the commode, the sink, and then back into the bedroom. I sat down on the edge of the bed and put on the TV. A little news was what I needed, I thought, other voices in the room to coax me along. The distant thought I'd had last night about working out this morning was like a joke that some comedian had tried that fell flat. I had a moment to consider that I could dial my wake-up time back an hour if I was just going to let that fantasy go, felt the corners of my lips twitch in the beginnings of a smile at the thought before all was blank again. I fell asleep sitting up, remote in hand, and mouth wide open. I know that because I woke up that way too.

It couldn't have been long – couldn't have been. I would have fallen over or dropped the remote if it had been, right? Neither of those things had happened so I figured it had only been a few seconds, one of those moments where you doze off, are out of it so completely that you're disoriented when you wake up. I rolled onto my side, deciding to just give in, get another hour of sleep. I have a meeting in a few hours that I need to be sharp for and I was anything but that then. I laid down. Got into position to shut my eyes. That's when I saw it.

The guy on camera was talking about the weather – some storm system coming from the north that will cool temperatures and make it feel like Christmas in July. His back was turned, so I couldn't see his face, but what I did see made me sit bolt upright. His suit jacket was slit up the back and so was his shirt. There was raw, pink flesh peeking out beneath all of it. I could see a huge blister between his shoulder blades.

The temperatures showed on the map. At first it was just local, but then the map expanded to the United States, and then to the world.

"It's 90 ºF in Calgary, but we're working on that. Parts of the US are hitting 175 ºF and temps in Nigeria topped 325 ºF last night. The Seine in Paris as well as the Canale Grande in Venice began to boil in the early morning hours. The Nile has boiled off completely, leaving lungfish and bolti to cook in the sun."

My mind couldn't process the words he was saying. I was distracted by the other data that was posted in the corners and running along the bottom of the screen:

Birds take flight in Florida only to burst into flames in the sky.

Woman fused to her car in Leeds.

Fissure opens in the ground to reveal lost ancient civilization beneath.

My mouth is open. I can hear myself panting.

The time on the screen, the one that I usually look at to confirm that I need to get up off my butt, get in the shower, and get going, was broken. The digital numbers were rolling, spinning, flying by. It was 6:45, then it was 7:22, then it was 3:14, then it was 5:58. It changed every second and it was driving me crazy. Every time I tried to look at it, pin it down, see it clearly, it was something different.

And the world boiled.

"Do you want to go back to sleep? It might be best to stay in bed, sleep it off and wake up dead."

Stuart knocking the chair over was so loud, it pulled Karli out of the book, ripping her eyes from the words so forcefully that she wasn't sure she wasn't bleeding. She was irritated – beyond that... outright angry. She had finally found the story that spoke to her, the one that called to her from the pages. She wanted to keep reading, wanted to read to the end, felt like she had to or else... or else... she didn't know. Her fingers caressed the page she had been reading as her eyes searched the room for the cause of the noise, a veritable din seeming to rise from inside her as much as within the room.

Stuart was stumbling into the middle now, having righted himself after tripping over the desk chair combo that some school had donated to the cause. He had twisted his ankle in the fall, maybe even broken it, and it had blown up almost instantaneously, the swelling pushing straight the folds of his dingy sock, but he didn't seem to notice. He had announced his story title and then started acting it out right away, never waiting for the go ahead that Ms. Watson so loved to give, a practiced nod that was pretentious and demure at the same time. He barked the lines as if they had offended him and no one said a word.

The Conversation

"I don't want to go."

"What? Come on... you have to."

"Maybe I-"

"Maybe nothing. You already said you would – you can't just-"

"I said that years ago. I was a kid. He shouldn't have taken it so seriously. How could I say I would-"

"Wouldn't you?"

"Wouldn't I what?"

"Wouldn't you take it seriously? If you were getting everything you ever wanted, wouldn't you take it seriously?"

"How can he hold me to that, though? I was too young. It's-it's not..."

"Fair? Stop being ridiculous. There's no-"

"What are you talking about 'ridiculous'? How is it ridiculous? This is bullshit! I was too young to agree to something like that! No one in their right mind would hold me to-."

"- stupid."

"What? Why..."

"Are you kidding me right now?"

"I'm fucking serious. I'm not go-"

"And that's why I said you're stupid. He'll never go for it."

"Wha-"

"I mean, you know that, right? You can whine about how unfair it is and how you were too young, wah wah, but it's not gonna matter."

"You don't know-"

The girl with the oily hair and the dirty nose ring, the one Ms. Watson called Mara but whose name wasn't Mara at all, started shouting her story, her voice intermingling with Stuart's, not quite drowning his out, but matching it in volume and expression. And Stuart was doing what Ms. Watson told him too; he cried when his character cried. When he couldn't make real tears flow he made due, scratching at his eyes so that the blood would wet his cheeks just the same.

Stuart and Mara screamed their tales to each other from across the room, rupturing their vocal cords in grotesque harmony.

Penny candy loosely wrapped in dirty parchment paper. Lined up on a counter so caked with grime I could write my name in it. I did write my name in it after all, feeling like I had to, like it was the last thing I would ever do.

Stuckey wuz here.

I sighed as I looked at the parchment paper covering something that didn't look like candy at all. Too big. Too long. Too lumpy to be peanut brittle, like the man said it was. The man who was sweating and breathing heavy as he looked at me. The man whose fingers twitched as I watched. The day's special, he said, when I came into the store looking for some sunflower seeds. Try it, you'll like it. Something about the way he looked at me, about the way the door clicked when it closed, like it was locking me in, something about the haze in the dingy old everything store made me think I'd better try it if I knew what was good for me.

Penny candy loosely wrapped in dirty parchment paper. Waiting for me.

Mine to eat. As much as I wanted. But I knew as my dry tongue tried to retreat down my throat, I would only be able to stomach one.

The floor was slick with things Karli didn't want to think about, couldn't let her mind linger on, not if she was going to get out of there alive. She could see the fluorescent light in the hallway flickering on and off, on and off, and she wished she was there under its artificial rays, skin turned sallow under the blue hue because if she was out there it would mean she had made it. It would mean she had escaped the orgy of death surrounding her and made it out, out of the room, out into the real world again where tentacles didn't caress the faces of the smitten and the ground didn't open up to swallow people whole. But Ms. Watson was between her and the door. And she had picked her story too.

7

She remembered everything about that day. The words, the gestures, the look in his eyes. None of the haze that covered old memories descended upon her, upon it. The day and everything that happened within it remained as clear to her as if she were living it that very moment.

"You can't show anybody the tape," she'd said when Riley walked into the living room holding the 8mm camcorder tape gingerly by its corners. He dangled it over her head where she sat on sofa, teasing her as she swiped at it. Her book fell off her lap and hit the floor, the thump sounding like a protest at the disruption. She had been reading the book they picked up at the used bookstore around the corner from their condo, the corner store that had just opened in the middle of their chic little created city in the burbs. He remembered that she had fallen in love with the book the moment she saw it, running her fingers along the cover as if it was some cherished family heirloom. She had opened it gingerly, turned the pages slowly, handling them only by the corners. It had gotten her a nod of appreciation from the owner who was running the checkout.

"You seem to know your way around old books," he had said, gesturing towards her with the practiced chin thrust of a Southern native.

"Not really," his wife had said honestly. He had never known her to own a book that she hadn't bought off the mass market paperback rack at the supermarket. "I just feel like I should be careful with this one. It seems... delicate."

"It might very well be," he mused, appraising the book from behind the counter as she held it out to him. "But I don't rightly know."

His wife had raised her eyebrows. It made him smile then as it did now.

"I got this from an estate sale," the kindly older gentleman continued, "I get a lot of my books that way."

"The person who owned it died?"

The man nodded. "And usually the family doesn't know what to do with all the junk that gets left behind. You'd be amazed how much we pack away over the years. So many books come from the recesses of someone's attic."

Riley had nodded along with them as he shopped, listening but not closely, enjoying the sound of the older man's voice more than he expected to.

"I buy them in bulk without ever looking at the titles. Truth be told, I enjoy the surprise when I go to unbox them and put them on my shelves."

The shopkeeper giggled.

His wife giggled.

He couldn't help but giggle too.

"You wanna give this one a whirl? It's beautiful, whatever it's about." The older man adjusted his glasses but saw no better for it. "*The Tales of Time*... catchy title, that one."

She had looked at the book in awe then—that's when he knew it was coming home with them.

"What's it about?" he asked, walking up behind his wife and smiling at the shopkeeper. He had a few books of his own to buy and he laid them on the counter. Picking up the one on top, the shopkeeper mused, "Ah, one about Satchel Page... baseball fan, I assume?"

"That and history," he affirmed and kissed his wife on the cheek.

She was still holding the book when he asked again, "So, what's this one about?"

"I don't really know," she admitted, turning it over in her hands to find a back cover as empty as the front. "There's no information about what's inside anywhere."

"Maybe it *is* old. They didn't do summaries and such way back when," the shopkeeper supplied.

His wife thumbed the pages gently, looking for what, he wasn't sure. He started to ask her if there was something specific she was checking for when her voice filled his head. It was quick, fleeting, really, but he heard it. He toward her, a question on the tip of his tongue, when she spoke words that took shape in his own head as an echo,

"I saw him standing there
poise slightly mistook.
Stay away, my head tells me
but my heart beckons me look."

He felt the crease forming between his eyebrows, felt his lips purse as he formed the question, but he never gave it voice. Because it was gone... the words, the sense of déjà vu; it was completely gone. Riley tilted his head as he looked at his wife's unperturbed profile.

"How much do you want for it?"

The shopkeeper smiled, giving her a sum that he knew she would be happy with, and received the offered book to pack on top of the stack. She had smiled at him, then at the book now sheathed in the plastic bag, the unabashed excitement coloring her cheeks, making her look like a schoolgirl.

But she was no schoolgirl now.

Now she swatted above her head, grabbing at the videotape he held just above her reach, like a hungry little bunny going after the perfect carrot. She raised herself from the sofa, once, twice, three times, trying to snatch the tape out of his hand. He loved the rise of her breasts against the cotton undershirt she donned on casual weekend mornings like that Saturday. They pressed against the shirt, her nipples hardening from the excitement of the game, the desire to win. They, unfettered by a bra, kissed when she dropped back onto the sofa, resting against her ribcage without argument. He dangled the tape again, a fourth time, longing to see the forbidden dance once more, but she didn't bite. Instead, she pouted playfully, her sensuality almost brimming over.

"Why can't I? We might be able to make money with this thing. Picture the ad: Hot, steamy amateurs play their naughty love games for all eyes to see. On sale at your nearest sleaze shop."

Melissa threw a pillow at Riley as he sat on the ottoman, hitting him on the side of his face. "You'd better not, if you know what's good for you," she said, turning her eyes back to the book waiting for her on the floor. Picking it up, she plucked an apple from the basket on the sofa table and settled back into her reading.

"I don't know, Mel. This might be a huge moneymaker for us. Can't you see the potential?" Riley asked slyly.

"Well, I don't know. I guess I'd have to see the tape first."

Riley made a spectacle of standing, bowing, and exiting the room, saying something like, 'Your wish is my command.' Melissa wondered why she couldn't remember exactly what he said. His exact words, that minor detail remained elusive to her, even though she had tried desperately to recall them over and over again. Their disappearance from her mind troubled her somehow, as if the answer to the question, the reason for the insanity that ensued a mere twenty-four hours after he spoke those words, was hidden within them. She became obsessed with them in the hours after his death, trying to conjure them up, to call them from the recesses of her mind. They held the secret, the knowledge. She became so sure of it that she could hardly think of anything else some days. Without those words, she felt the walls closing in around her, the air in the room thickening, constricting her throat, confining her. Without them, she felt the coldness of death on the back of her neck.

Melissa remembered, could visualize Riley bounding from the living room into the bedroom to retrieve the camcorder. He connected the cables easily, faster than she expected, so that the contents of the tape would appear on their television screen.

"I can't wait to see how this looks," he said, excitement seasoning his voice.

"You haven't even looked at it yet?" Melissa exclaimed as she rose to her knees on the plush sofa, her right hand wielding another pillow.

Riley covered his face with mocked terror as she threatened to throw the pillow, playfully imploring, "No, I haven't seen it yet, but I know it's awesome. I mean, you and me au naturel, our bodies entwined, in the throes of making love... It couldn't be anything but great. Now put the pillow down. You've got the arm of a major league baseball pitcher!"

...

Riley's laughter had been infectious.

Melissa let herself daydream, slipping into that formless bliss with the memory of it in her mind... a sound she hadn't heard in years... one she would never hear again. She came to wanting something. She went in search of it, knowing it was there, it hadn't left her, would never leave her. With a genuine pleasure that she hadn't felt since Riley, Melissa moved back to the sofa, treasure in hand. The same book she had been reading back then she had decided to start reading again that day, finding it in her closet waiting, just waiting for her to stumble upon it, to be enamored by it again.

The Tales of Time.

Melissa opened the book, savoring the smell of the old pages, warm and earthy. She felt the paper, like parchment, beneath her fingertips. She let it comfort her, reading the first page and losing herself within it.

$5.99

The movie went off and cycled back to the main screen, burning the stationary main page into the plasma TV more and more with every passing second. Carla had fallen asleep in front of the television again, as she had most nights since she got the DVD, unable to pull herself away from the screen to make it to bed. That really wasn't true though. She hadn't made it to bed because she didn't want to go to bed. She was right where she wanted to be.

Her sister thought she was crazy. Not literally, but she would have if she knew—if she believed. It wasn't like Carla hadn't tried to tell her, hadn't tried to share him with her... once... in the beginning. But Carla's sister didn't see it. He didn't speak to Tami the way he spoke to Carla. It was only right, really. He was Carla's, after all.

There wasn't anything special about the DVD, just a B-level movie with a cast that you think you might have seen before, but if so, you can't remember where. Carla got it out of one of those bins full of surplus movies discounted to $5.99.

But that wasn't all it was. Not to Carla.

The storyline was slow-paced and didn't really go anywhere, but Carla wasn't listening to the lines. The actors either never really "made it," were over-the-hill has-beens, or were newbies, but Carla recognized one of them. She should. She had seen him in her dreams for years.

Well, not him specifically, and not in the dreams like the ones you have when you're sleeping. But in her fantasies, in her daydreams, he was always there. He looked like a combination of her first love, a guy she knew from work, and the last guy she slept with. Such an odd mix, with unkempt hair, deep, penetrating eyes, the most sensuous lips. Carla could hardly tear her eyes away from the screen when he was in a scene and found herself reaching for the remote to fast-forward to his next one even if it meant she'd have no idea what was going on in the movie when she got there.

After her second time watching the movie all the way through he started talking to her.

At first it was just a look—he would look at the screen, seemingly at her, when he should have been looking at the actor opposite him. The first look was just a peek, just a glance; Carla almost didn't notice it at all. His second look was so much more meaningful. There was a playful twist to his lips that was endearing. His third look was downright obscene, the way he licked those luscious lips of his and lowered his eyelids. It gave Carla chills. The good kind.

Twenty minutes into the movie he spoke to her.

"Carla."

She felt as though she was waking from a dream when she heard her name. He was looking at her again, full on, shoulders squared to the screen—watching her. He was smiling just enough for her to see a hint of white from his teeth. She felt herself respond though she knew she shouldn't. He didn't have many lines in the movie; he was nothing more than a glorified extra, really, yet he had spoken her name as clearly as if he was sitting in the room whispering it in her ear. Carla spun her head around, looking in all corners of the room to be sure that he —that someone—wasn't there making fun of her, laughing at her expense. But she was alone.

With him.

She watched the movie three more times that day and more that weekend, blowing off shopping with her sister, a date with a guy she had been interested in for months, sleeping in her bed, and eating. With every viewing he said more to her, sometimes telling her how beautiful she was, pouting his lips as he spoke, letting her see all the curves and contortions they went through as they formed words, other times asking her to remove garments so he could see more. She felt silly and excited at the same time. It was weird, strange all of those things, but it was the best fantasy she'd ever had.

As Carla snored, catching her first reluctant winks in 30 hours, the screen flickered and blinked before finally catching again on the beginning of the movie. For a second, gone faster than Carla's eyes could have deciphered had she been awake, a roiling sea of red bubbled to the surface, washing Carla's face in blood as a tentacle reached out to stroke her cheek.

8

Upperville

Upperville. The town where all the inhabitants are family. The town where nobody leaves because the world doesn't exist past the city limits. The town I'm from.

Getting out was always a priority for me. The streams that border the town, the well that stood in our backyard, all smelled stagnant to me. Like rot. Like death. I didn't want to be consumed, to be sucked into the very ground like it was quicksand or the hungry mouth of a Venus Flytrap. I didn't want to live and die only knowing Upperville's monotony, with its white picket fences and its picturesque winding roads. "Upperville, the sleepy hollow less than an hour from the city," it had been called in some magazine years ago. To me it was more like "Upperville, town of the damned." So I left. I jumped on 66 and made for the city. Washington, DC.

I even wrote an article about it, one of my first features at the paper before I got moved up. "The Decline of Rural America," I called it, proudly typing Susan McCoy in the byline. I had to rewrite it so it didn't smack of Upperville bashing, not because I cared what the people back home thought—I didn't think they would get the paper anyway, and if they did, they wouldn't read it—but because I wanted to make a good impression at my new job. When the paper came out there were grumblings, Mother said in her usual, I-just-happened-to-hear-it way. But there were always grumblings, at least, as far as I was concerned. People never seemed to like me or the things I did. Mother said it had more to do with her than it did with me, but she would never explain it. And she would never leave, no matter how much I begged. She said she was bound to the land just like my soul was bound to be free. I never listened when she started talking that way. Instead it strengthened my determination to get out. If that's what Upperville did to you, I didn't want any part of it. Sometimes Mother acted as kooky as the rest of them did. I wasn't going to let that happen to me.

I hate Upperville with a passion. Fucking Suckerville.

And now I'm going back.

Even my mother's death hadn't brought me back to that place. I had her body shipped to DC and forced anyone who wanted to pay their respects to leave their comfort zones and come to me. No one did. I found out later they held an informal service over my mother's body at the morgue. The coroner had lived in Upperville all his life, so even though it was against the rules, he lit a candle in front of mother's body on the slab along with the rest of them.

But now Bobby Zucker was dead. I had to go back.

The drive was over before I knew it. Memories of Bobby and me stealing kisses behind the school and copping feels in the cab of his father's pickup flooded my mind, wiping away the road and replacing it with his face. He was my first kiss, my first lover, my first love. I lived and breathed him until I left for college. He stayed behind to work at his father's hardware store. I begged him to come with me, to leave Upperville and start a life with me in the city. But he didn't. As the years passed and mother told me about Bobby's life—sending me the invitation Bobby gave her for his wedding to Mary Lou Kramer, (a cowgirl if there ever was one), giving me baby pictures when his children were born—I couldn't believe I had been so wrong about him. He wasn't the person I thought he was, wasn't the free spirit who thought for himself and did what he wanted to do in life. He was just like the rest of them in Upperville: a drone.

But I never forgot about him.

Even with all the dating I did, all the near misses, I never forgot about Bobby. I always wondered what it would have been like had he left Upperville and come with me. He might have been a lawyer, like he wanted to be. He might have had a successful practice in Northwest, DC, might have been a real player. We might have been happy.

But now he's dead.

Carlene, my mother's best friend and the only other person in Upperville who knew how to reach me, said that he fell from a ladder and hit his head. She said he never regained consciousness, using a sympathetic tone that made it seem like that was for the best. But it wasn't. The Bobby I knew would have wanted to

61

wake up and say goodbye to his family and friends, would have wanted one last moment to see the sun from his window. But I kept that to myself. There was no sense in upsetting Carlene's 'Uppervillian' logic, her untested, all-knowing sensibility.

Damn him for making me come back.

Damn him for not coming with me.

The main road—aptly named Main Street—looked the same as it had when I took it out of town twenty-one years ago. Same old stores, looking the worse for wear in the diminishing light, the same old church at the end of the badly pocked street. People went about their normal routine as I drove by, talking with each other in the entrance to the post office while scratching at their oversized, dirty overalls and plaid shirts, tipping their hat to the old woman who strolled past. Doing nothing. I've seen it all before. It hurt to think that Bobby had become one of them.

The funeral home was off a side street with even more cars lined up than on Main. People had come to pay their respects. Bobby must have been well-liked, and why wouldn't he be? He was one of the most handsome kids in school, one of the most grounded people I had ever met. I bet he was a magnet, someone who the cowpokes wanted to be around. It made them feel better about themselves. And now that beacon was gone.

That's what he was, wasn't he? A beacon that had called me back to a place I swore I'd never step foot in again.

With a deep breath, I walked into the funeral home. It was suitably muted, as were most places like that—no sense in turning up the lights so you can see the death mask in plain view.

I didn't recognize Carlene when she approached me. "Susan? Is that you? My God, you look so different!" she cackled louder than she should have in a funeral home.

"Carlene. It's great to see you!" I lied. I didn't care if I ever saw her again. Bobby was the only person I cared about in that godforsaken town. And now he was gone.

Two other people milled behind her, openly listening to our exchange. "Well, you remember Karen Whitetower and Vern Glover, don't you?"

I nodded my greeting, desperately wanting to get away from them.

"I bet you're anxious to see Bobby, then," she said, her face twisting in a sly smile. "I know how close you two were."

Something about her troubled me.

"He's right in there," she said, turning my shoulders and nudging me toward the room where Bobby's body lay. "Go on," she urged, flashing her too-sweet

smile.

The whole drive there all I wanted to do was see him, see that Bobby was dead with my own eyes, but now that I was there, in the place where he was laid out, I was afraid. Seeing him would mean that it was really over. Everything we had ever shared was done, gone, finished. Even when he got married, I thought there might be a little something left, something we might grab onto later in life. But now that he was dead, there would be no chance of that. I was terrified.

"Go on, Susan," Carlene said, her voice more urgent this time. "Go in and see Bobby."

I started walking before I allowed my thoughts to register. Carlene's behavior, her expressions, everything about her bothered me. Why did she care if I went in to see Bobby? Why did it have to be so rushed? I brushed the concern away, chalking it up to my nervousness. I was, after all, at my first love's funeral. Maybe I was a little sensitive.

I heard the whispering among the people who ringed the corridor—

"That's Lizzie's girl, isn't it?"

"She ain't been back here for twenty years!"

"Not even for her mother's funeral."

I turned to see who made that comment, but no one met me eye to eye. Funeral? I had mother's funeral in DC. If they were talking about their cultish sendoff in the morgue, fine. But they said funeral. Had they held a service that I missed? Anger welled within me, swirling inside my stomach. How dare they not let me know about something like that? I'll have to ask Carlene about that before I leave, I thought as I turned their whispers around in my head. I approached Bobby's casket at a snail's pace.

It was open, with a yellowish light shining on the place where Bobby's head should have rested. But there he wasn't there. I didn't see the what I expected to see, Bobby with his eyes closed and the lids pulled a little too tightly over the eyes to look natural, Bobby with makeup dusting his temples to cover the greenish gray tint his flesh had taken in death, Bobby whose glued lips looked nothing like the soft ones I had kissed so long ago. I picked up my pace, ignoring the voice in my mind that insisted that Bob's body laid lower than usual, that his wife must have sprung for the deluxe model casket, high walls, plush satin and all.

No casket is that deep, a stronger, more resilient version of my own voice admonished.

He wasn't there.

The casket was empty, its silk bedding untouched. As I turned to ask the nearest Upperville moron what was going on, I caught sight of a stocky man, about six feet tall with dusty brown hair and twinkling brown eyes. Bobby. He was older, but I'd know his face anywhere.

"Bobby, what—?" I started to ask him. His smile spread into a wild grin as I shrank against the casket. I never saw who hit me in the back of the head, never even felt the blow. The blood running down my neck felt warm, calming as I rested my head on the pillow and looked at Bobby. I didn't feel them hoist my legs over the side of the casket, didn't hear them laugh and jeer, condemning me for leaving as I bled out. Only the touch of Bobby's lips on mine registered. When he parted my lips and put his tongue in my mouth I closed my eyes like I did when we were kids.

Morbid… that's what it was. Not to mention creepy and coincidental as hell. Casey didn't like that the story she had just read kinda sorta mirrored her life right now. But that's what she got for picking up a book that someone left behind and sticking her nose into it, right? It's just that the book was so interesting—so vintage looking—that she was drawn to it. The colors, maroon and gold, antique brushed or something. The feel of the cover was cool too—soft and velvety like the inside of those boxes that held chips and dice for a home poker set. Weird that she would compare it to that but there it was, her days of playing dealer at the kitchen table in her mother's house had been good for something after all. But it was exactly right, no matter how obscure of a reference it might be. That's how the cover felt under her hands. She couldn't stop herself from rubbing it one way and then the next just to feel the microfibers shift. Her boyfriend used to call her a hipster because of shit like that. Maybe he was right.

But he wasn't calling her shit anymore, was he? He wasn't calling anyone anything, and never would. He was dead. That's why she was sitting on that godforsaken bus heading into the hills of West Virginia. She was going back home to say goodbye to her first love, the first in a long string of assholes.

He had kicked off early, the bastard. He was supposed to wait for her to come back and make it right.

Casey wouldn't have even known he was dead if it wasn't for her cousin texting her on the sly. Nobody wanted her back in town; nobody wanted her near Len, even as he lay dead at Johnson's Funeral Home. She had taken off without saying goodbye and most people thought that was fine enough. Casey and her city ways had never been understood out there in the one stoplight town she was from. Her moving on was expected, and it was fine and dandy to them. She told them she wouldn't claim that po-dunk shithole when she made it big, and they nodded approval. The way things were going for her, no one would have to worry about that anyway.

She had moved on, sure, had her share of guys to pass the time. But Len was the one, and she knew it. Her cousin knew it. Len's bitch of a wife knew it, too. As soon as she could get her shit together, as soon as she could call herself fit to help raise Len's two little girls, she was going to go back and take what was hers. But the cancer got there before she was ready. And now none of that mattered anymore.

Casey fondled the book on the bus as she rode into town; she handled it as she watched the ceremony from the doorway of the little church, away from the eyes of people who would spit on her as easily as look at her. She kept it in her hand, rubbing at the velvet hard enough to wear it smooth as she looked over at the mound of dirt waiting to be pushed in the hole as soon as the stragglers left the graveside. His mother was still there, his sister too. And that bitch of a wife who would forever and always be able to call Len hers.

Ten.

Twenty.

Thirty minutes passed while she waited for everyone to clear out. She only wanted a minute with Len, just one last minute to tell him she was sorry she left him behind.

She opened the book in her hands, the only thing that had grounded her since she started on her journey back to Hell. And she read.

Cemetery Road

I've never been afraid of the dark, but I'm damned scared now. Donnie said the trees looked like legs in the dark, and he was right. My flashlight ain't helpin' things either, just makes 'em look like they're moving.

I don't know why I'm here but I am.

I know'd better than to come up here, but I dint use the sense God gave me. They was just talking so much shit about how I wasn't gonna do it and how I was a chicken shit, that I just had to. So I'm here, and I wish I wasn't.

I drove up to the corner, like they said to, and parked the car. They said they'd be watching to see if I would do it, so I followed every instruction. I dint want them to say I cheated. And I damned sure don't want to do it again. I started walking up the road and zipped up my jacket. It was cold as hell outside, no kind of weather to go playing around in a cemetery, but then again, when was? My footsteps sounded loud as I walked up the deserted road, not a car to be seen. I started to count the crunching of the rocks—made the time go by quicker. By the time I got to 150, I had made it up the hill and could see the headstones shining off my flashlight. The white ones seemed to glow.

Houses lined the street, every one of them with dark windows. Who the hell would want to live across the street from a cemetery anyway? Even if it doesn't spook you, it ain't nothing to look at. The only people ever outside are crying.

Six, maybe seven houses stood there and nobody in any of 'em. For some reason that don't set right with me.

I looked at the tombstones, trying to decide if I was going in or not. My granddaddy's stone was on the edge of the street, damned near paved over when they put up the new road back in '84. It leaned to the side, sunken in the ground, chunks taken out of it from the wind and rain. Just beat up. That's what's gonna happen to me, I thought as I stared at it sticking out of the ground like a broken tooth. Something about that made me want to run.

I looked back at the houses with their black eyes staring at me. I couldn't tell which one I felt safer having my back to. The cold made me decide quick.

I looked back to the cemetery and saw the same tombstones, the same trees, and decided to go in. Ain't no difference in a cemetery in the day or at night. Dead people there all the time, and they can't bother nobody. And anyway, Donnie and the guys're watchin'.

The first step inside was hard, but they got easier after that. I walked past granddaddy's grave and on down the Barlow line, ending up by my cousin who just got put in the ground a couple months back. I snickered at his grave and thought for a second about leaving that $5.00 I owed him on the grass, but nah. Why waste good money on someone who can't use it anymore? Poor sucker.

This shit is easy, once you get the balls to do it. I walked around like I owned the place. Thought about what it might cost to buy a place like this. Make money off putting people in the ground? You could stack three or four coffins on top of each other and charge for a single plot! Do that over so many acres, and you got a goldmine. Might need to look into it tomorrow when I get up.

I figured that was enough after I got to Sandy Laurelton's grave. Old biddy died back in 1837 at the age of, what was it, 96? I think that's what the cross said, but it was pretty splintered, so I could be wrong. Either way, old is old. I gave the back of Sandy's cross a slap like she'd probably never had on her ass when she was alive and started back the way I came, happy this shit is over. I dare them to talk shit about me now.

When I saw them coming I couldn't help but call out. And why did it matter anyway? Dead people don't care how loud you are.

"Hey Donnie!" I yelled, steam filling up the air like a white cloud. "I did it, dude! Smacked this little bitch on the ass, too."

I thought Donnie would get a kick out of that. Hell, he's the one who likes to fuck 'em when they're damned near dead anyway. But he dint say anything. Well fuck him then, the jealous little bitch. I probably stayed in longer than him, and he was pissed. So who's the chicken shit now?

I stopped walking and let them get closer, the cloud in front of my face going in and out as I caught my breath. They dint have a cloud in front of theirs.

9

"It's like it's the 60s or something, me asking for a house call," Justina said to the empty room as she rubbed the sides of her arms, but she couldn't think of anything else to do. Her son hadn't been eating- he hadn't been bathing... he had barely come out of his room in three days. He had been relieving himself where he sat for the last day, only moving enough to switch out sheets of paper after the yelling stopped. Once he'd spent himself, shouting about the candy that was waiting for him at the corner store, the candy he'd read about over the old lady's shoulder, he'd fallen silent, offering no explanation to his mother; just letting the words sit in the air between them, fat and pungent.

He was freewriting again, like he had when he was young and none of the words made sense. They didn't make much more sense now, not all of them. There was a poem about a woman looking for a black dress to bury her daughter in and an apparition visiting a young woman on the cusp on marriage. She couldn't figure out where it was all coming from: neither Justina or her son had ever written poetry before or even read it except in school, and even though that doesn't mean much of anything, all that eloquence surprised her. Her son wasn't that kind of guy, at least she hadn't thought so until she read his words. While it was nice to think he had been sitting on a talent like that all this time, doing something more than just playing videogames all day, the words didn't feel right. They didn't feel like they were his. Justina didn't know what that could mean.

And the way he looked while he was doing it… it had made her retreat from the room more than once. He was staring at something off to the right, his eyes upturned to see something in the corner, something invisible to her but that held his attention even when she called his name. His jaw was slack, and his breathing was slow and deep. She'd held her own breath once to listen for his, his chest rising and falling so infrequently that she became worried.

And then there was the mumbling.

As unintelligible as it was, more sounds than words, it was spooky to her, scary in a way that she couldn't define. Justina told the doctor about it when they spoke, deciding to call after the stench had made its way out of his room and into the hallway. He was too big to move—he had reached his full height long ago and towered over her, not to mention outweighing her by 80 pounds. He was a man now, and she feared that he would be mortified if he snapped out of his fugue to find his mother wiping his behind.

By the time the doctor got there three new sheets of paper had been filled, writings about an old woman who fell down the stairs and broke her neck; a man who stepped into oncoming traffic and had gone through the windshield of a car; a dog that ran circles on his person's grave. There were poems about people in the woods, lost loves in the distance, straddling the line between life and death. The words were all over the page, up one side and down another, front and back, spiraling in the corners to break out into pieces and fray at the ends. Red, red letters on death and dying and loss and darkness written in blood. There were letters left for her, penned in what spilled with a sloppy hand, and she couldn't bear to read them herself or even lay eyes on them. She screamed as the doctor read the first out loud, unaware of the inscription, the dedication, her son's final request ignored. The doctor read the words like he didn't understand them, not separately, nor in combination.

Peering into the darkness
I have a sense of one
with me
searching also
for themselves
but finding me.

And Justina screamed and screamed because the words made no sense, no sense at all, and they made complete sense and she was sorry, so very

71

sorry that her happy boy would never be like before again... that he would never be.

10

"Where are you heading off to looking like you just stepped out of *GQ*?" Charlene said. She always had a nice word for the boys, flirting with them even though she was pushing 70. Because 70 isn't dead... only dead is dead and she would look and flirt and pinch and get a taste if someone would let her until she *was* dead. Once you got there, there was no going back. She planned to enter the gates of Heaven with no regrets.

"More like *Popular Mechanics*, if you ask me," Walter said, coming into the office from the loud bus garage, scratching the dandruff off his balding head. He appraised the younger man for a moment and then, finding a legitimate spot on his face— a little grease from the garage that had worked its way into the skin beneath his eye, and taken residence there—he took joy in saying, "You—you might want to get that before you go out, lover boy."

Charlene and Walter laughed when he ran to the mirror and wiped frantically at his face. "You got a date or something?" Charlene asked as her laughter waned and she moved to refill her coffee cup. It would be her fourth of the day, and her shift hadn't even really gotten started good.

"Meetin' her parents today," he said, still checking himself over in the mirror.

"Well, don't forget this," Charlene said, her tone leaning toward fond. She held out the book he had put in his box, giving it over reluctantly. It felt good in her hand. The cover was velvety soft and the pages, they smelled good…old in a smart kid of way, not a dirty one. Even though she wasn't much for reading, she wanted to open the book and see what was inside. Were the words written in that old English script they used to use way back when? Were some of the letters embossed in gold?

He took the book and tucked it under his arm possessively.

"Where'd you get that, anyway?"

"My bus," he replied, hoping he didn't have to say much more. Keeping stuff they found on the bus wasn't frowned upon if you did it after a few days—as long as you gave the person who left it behind time to pick it up from the lost and found. But he saw the book after his morning route and snatched it up right away. It was the perfect thing to give her mother; he knew that right on the spot. It looked formal, proper. She would think he was smart. Maybe she wouldn't give him such a hard time about driving a bus. It was just a temporary thing, anyway…

Walter was about to say something stupid—something that would take the wind right out of his sails. Charlene knew that like she knew her own name. Guys like Walter, the ones who gave up on love and life and anything outside of the four walls they worked and lived in always tried to clip the wings of the ones who didn't.

She cut him off before he could say anything at all, talking too loud and not caring one whit about it, "I think she'll like it. It's fancy. Got a real nice feel to it."

"Yeah," the younger man said, hoping she could see the thanks in his eyes.

Charlene looked at him for a minute longer before shooing him out. "Don't want to be late to meet the Mama. Go on, get out of here. We'll see you in the mornin'!"

He left, and Charlene smiled at the door after he was gone. Walter laughed and shook his head as he left the office for somewhere back in the recesses of the garage.

When he got in his car he froze. He was nervous. As much as he wanted to tell himself that meeting her mother wasn't a big deal, he knew it was. He didn't know if he wanted to meet her—didn't know if he wanted to put himself through it all. She would ask where he was from, would ask what college he went to, would ask what he wanted to do with the rest of his life. He didn't have answers to any of those questions—at least not answers that he thought she would be satisfied with. *Where are you from?* Bumfuck, USA. *Did you go to college?* Yeah, I started up at the community college but just stopped going. *What do you want to do with the rest of your life?* Not drive a bus, I'll tell you that much, but apart from that, not sure. Bullshit, all of it—truthful, but worthless... except maybe that last answer. He didn't have a clue what he wanted to do today, let alone tomorrow. He knew that was true—did his girlfriend know that too?

He really didn't want to go.

He sighed and thumbed open the book, chuckling to himself about who he was and where his life was headed. Of course the mom would hate him. He was too cheap to even buy the woman a gift, had to steal one off the seat of his bus. Because that's what it was, right... stealing? Someone might come back for it—someone had obviously left it there, and whoever it was had taken care of it. It was obviously old, maybe even some kind of antique or something, yet the binding wasn't broken; the cover wasn't scuffed. He thought fleetingly of selling it—it could be worth a lot of money. But no. Someone riding the bus—especially his route today... the one that went to the sticks—wouldn't be carrying a book that was worth a lot of money. Someone owning a book like that was likely riding in a Rolls Royce and getting carted around by a driver wearing those fancy black gloves.

The book was worthless... just like him.

"Let's see what kind of impression we can make together," he said aloud to the book within the confines of his empty car. He went to close the book but caught sight of a story called "Family Dinner." He could almost hear his name being called from the yellowed pages.

Family Dinner

"You gotta be kidding me," Nick said as he turned onto the dark road... a road that looked just like the last one, and the one before. He had been driving for an hour into the deep woods and across state lines for a girl he had just met. Come to dinner, she had whispered in his ear the week before. Meet my family.

Already?

They had only been out on a few dates, had only spent maybe 7 hours together, but who's counting? She talked about cavern hunting (who can resist stalactites and stalagmites?) and great skiing when he got there, but that wasn't the reason he said yes. It was her. She wore such a sweet smile when she asked him to come, looked so perfect in her tight jeans and loose sweater. She felt so warm when he hugged her close and felt her form underneath all that knit, so he said sure. It didn't matter that her family dinner was the same day that he was celebrating a win with his buddies, sending him in the other direction from her folks' house and adding 45 minutes to an already long drive.

Amy.

All that mattered was the smile she would greet him with when she opened the door and the warm hug that waited for him.

Assuming he could ever get there.

The drive from Fairfax was the easy part. He knew his old stomping grounds well enough to make it most of the way out of Northern Virginia and over to Warrenton, where the city lights were a distant memory, but that was as far as he could go without help. It didn't help that there was no Interstate to get onto. The closest one would have put him a half hour out of his way, so he braved the side streets and back roads, relying on his GPS and, after a while, instinct. GPS, God love it. Such a great tool when it works. But like that early-adopt model he won at a casino in the late 90s, the one that had to be suction cupped to his windshield and that sent him into the Baltimore harbor every time he made a turn off Pratt St., the route his phone gave him was no use. It kept rerouting as if the mountains surrounding the sleepy hamlet grew up overnight, making a once usable road impassible. Nick had gotten so sick of hearing that unaccented, mild-mannered female voice telling him to make a U-turn, that he closed the app.

White's Taxidermy on his left. Margie's Good Eats on the right. Coincidence?

Nick would have laughed at his joke if he hadn't already told it before. He was sure he passed a similar combination a few towns back. Taxidermist Tull and Jake's Steak. Forever Pets Taxidermy and The Rib Shack. It was funny the first time, but not anymore.

Nick pulled into a gas station. He was happy to find one of those big chain stations like the ones he was used to at home. The drive itself was starting to look like one of those low-budget horror movies. He didn't need to add a broken down, one-pump station with the stereotypically grimy gas jockey to the mix. He and three other people filed into the brightly lit convenience store at the station. He listened as the person in front of him asked for directions to the ski lodge near where Amy's family lived—the same one that had a hot chocolate with his name on it waiting by a warm fire. The route sounded like the one he had just come off, long and twisty and dark. When it was his turn, Nick told the attendant—young and clean, thank you very much—that he was looking for directions to the same place.

"But where's the highway?" Nick asked after being given the same directions the woman before him got. "There's gotta be something that cuts through these mountains instead of sticking to the back roads." He picked up a candy bar and laid it on the counter. "I feel like I've been driving around forever."

The young man nodded imperceptibly, his eye twitching under the patch of oily hair visible beneath the rim of his red service cap. "I wish, but there's nothing like that," he said a little too eagerly. "This is the best way to get out to the ski lodge, especially since it's almost dark."

Nick smiled at him incredulously. That's why he wanted the highway! The afternoon light was fading fast, and he did not relish the idea of driving around the woods on winding roads in the dark. He did not want hitting a deer to be in his future.

"There's gotta be something. I mean, there's no way trucks take these narrow streets to deliver to you. What do they use?"

The attendant rang up his candy bar without looking at him.

Nick tried again. "I saw lights, but I couldn't get to them."

Giving Nick his change, the attendant said, "I don't know. But the directions I gave you will get you to the ski lodge in about 2 hours."

The attendant held out his bag with hands that looked like they could be shaking. Just a little, but it was there. Nick shook his head, thanked him, and got back in the car. Two hours? He'd been driving for an hour already, and the GPS said it was just about 2 hours away from where he started. Could he really be that far off course?

Nick looked in the direction that the attendant told him to go. Two of the three cars that came in with him headed that way. The other car, a guy in a button-down shirt open at the neck and dress slacks driving a non-descript black sedan that screamed company car, went the other way. Nick climbed into his own car and turned it on fast. He could feel the attendant's eyes on him, beseeching him to go the way he had been told, but Nick ignored the sensation as it crept up his back to caress his neck. He followed the company car even as the gas station attendant screamed, "No!"

Leafless trees.

Asphalt.

Dead grass.

Repeat.

There was nothing. Not even a boarded-up house to break up the monotony. Nothing at all. Nick had caught up with the other rebel and was right behind him. The man had even made a saluting gesture to him in his rearview mirror – just two compadres bucking the system. It was getting late. At 4:30, it was almost completely dark. There were no streetlights on the country road, but Nick could see some off in distance. The road traversed a lazy hill. If he could just get down to those lights, Nick was sure he'd find a way to cut through the spiderweb of back roads and take him where he needed to be. Amy's family lived in a college town—there were bound to be major routes leading to it. He just needed to find one.

Oh crap, Amy!

She had to be worried. Nick picked up his phone and noticed she had called twice already. When? He had the phone with him when he was in the gas station, and it had been sitting in the cupholder the whole time he was driving. It never rang.

"Technology," Nick said out loud, "Gotta love it."

Nick dialed Amy's number and heard nothing. No ringing, no beeping, no 'all circuits are busy' message—nothing.

He looked at his phone, taking his eyes away from the road for a second to see if he had missed a number somehow. He had just added her number to his favorites list, but now he wondered if he had put the number in wrong. Nick didn't see the front end of the company car disappear like it got sucked through an invisible portal. The man threw the car in reverse and it lurched backwards. The doors seemed to stretch, pulling away from the side panels as if running from a magnet. The metal pulled like saltwater taffy, stretching in long lines of silver and black. The back tires spun against the asphalt, digging for purchase but finding none.

Nick didn't hear the tires screeching on the road, nor the muted screams left behind like an echo as the man travelled through the barrier. He didn't notice the country road rippling as it engulfed the non-descript sedan, the facade rising and falling like paper in the wind to reveal a glimpse of a black core that seemed to pulse with life. He never saw how flat the landscape was, how it mirrored itself every few yards, like cheap floor tiles keeping pattern. Instead, he heard the unaccented, mild-mannered female voice of his GPS telling him to turn around to start route guidance, only this time she was screaming.

11

The movie was good.

It had been a long time since she'd gone to a drive-in theater, and she was loving every minute of it. She only wished they still had the tinny speakers they could put on the windows, all the cars connected by a webwork of thick cords attached to sound pillars mounted throughout the lot the way they did back in the day instead of the audio shooting through the car speakers. She remembered those days, when she and her mom would check to see what movie was playing—and by check she meant leaning their heads over to look at the screen that stood tall opposite the supermarket to see what was on. If they liked what they saw, they would drive over and buy tickets, park their station wagon in one of the spots, and share the pint of ice cream that was in one of the grocery bags. If they had seen that particular movie before but really liked a few scenes, well, they weren't beyond pulling up to the fence and watching the screen sans speakers… and sans tickets.

So what, she was retro, old school? There was something to be said for the simplicity of the world before technology ruled.

The scene onscreen was epic. There was a fire, one that the characters had somehow missed before it was raging, the smell of smoke, let alone the heat, not registering until it was too late. Kelsey stared at John with such sweet understanding that he wanted to look away. But he couldn't do it, not when he knew he was looking into her eyes for the last time.

She felt like she was part of the scene, on set, listening in: right there.

When he saw her last she was reading a book, a story about a zombie apocalypse or something—that much he had picked up from looking over her shoulder. They were closing in, people in the house were already dead, and the one guy left was running around, thinking about what he should take from the home he knew he would never return to. It was good, this story by some anonymous author, and John wanted to finish it, felt compelled to do so, to rush past where Kelsey was in the story and speed-read the remaining pages, but then his phone rang with his sister on the other end sounding frantic. John removed himself from the room where Kelsey remained with the book to find out what new hell his sister was embroiled in, vowing to come back to the story as soon as they were done talking. Because zombies were at the window and John had to find out if the kindly doctor would make it out alive. But when he got back, the room was fast on its way to being engulfed in flames.

"You wouldn't let go of the book," John said through the tinny speakers. "I—I couldn't pry it out of your hands."

His voice was filled with desperation because Kelsey's sundress had succumbed to the flames right away, leaving her skin bare and vulnerable. The yellow flames licked around her arms, seeming to cut through her, teasing as they devoured. Kelsey still held the book in her hand, clasping it to her chest even as the flames reached toward it... much like she was holding the old, dusty book she found under the seat of the car when she bought it at auction the day before. She had meant to throw it away—it smelled of something she couldn't place but that unsettled her nonetheless—but it was still there, had been lying on the passenger seat where she had left it. The only reason she was holding it now was because her boyfriend was sitting there watching the movie... more like sleeping there during the movie. The book had sat between them when he got in the car during the ride to the drive-in, but when he fell asleep and the movie started getting good, she reached for it where it sat perched on her gear shift.

She didn't think about it, not when Kelsey's infatuation with her own book bloomed in the movie; not when it controlled every aspect of her existence... not even when the flames licked at it but it wouldn't catch.

People onscreen were running and she could detect movement in her peripheral own vision.

Directions were being bellowed, seeming to surround the car, coming from inside and outside of it, impossibly amplified.

There was so much noise. The sound director must have gone all out on the mix because she could hear crackles, hissing, popping, sizzling. Combine that with the yelling and screaming, the crying and sobbing, the muted beating that sounded like water hitting glass, intermittent thumps that seemed to come from another world, and you had an idea of what she was hearing. Stellar work, this. She tried to remember the name of the movie and found that she could not. She couldn't remember what town she was in or whether or not she'd bought popcorn when she got there.

She had to pee, so she did.

On screen, Kelsey's lips were turning a painful red.

"The book said you would do this," Kelsey said, her voice on its way to a ruin John hoped he didn't have to hear. "Either that or—" Flames danced along her shoulders and reached toward her hair.

"Or I would."

Kelsey faltered, failing. Dying.

Her boyfriend woke up to the heat of fire burning his lungs. He found himself locked in the car with his girlfriend who was just staring at the movie screen like she didn't smell the smoke threatening to force them into unconsciousness, like she didn't know there was a raging fire in the backseat.

The heat was starting to irritate the skin on the back of his neck.

"Hey! Honey, what the fuck?" he yelled as he slammed himself against the door. "Unlock the door—we need to get out of here."

The flames blazed unexpectedly fast. He beat his fists, his elbows, his hands against the glass, but it wouldn't shatter.

"I finished it, honey," she started, her voice nothing more than an afterthought now that the flames had leapt into her hair, "I finished the story, and it was everything I could ever hope for."

He screamed, wailed, really, as he saw her go up in flames, eyes open, staring at the movie screen while speaking to him in a monotone voice he had never heard her use before, all the while clutching the book in her hands. He hadn't seen her toss a match into the jumble of clothes and bags and junk strewn on the backseat—things she had purchased from a day of shopping in her new-to-her car. He wasn't awake when the flames grew behind them as she watched the screen, burning the image of the movie into her head as she mirrored the character's fate. All he knew was that somewhere along the line the screw that he always thought had been loose in her fell out, and he missed it, missed all the signs—might have ignored them so he could keep enjoying her for a little while longer. And now... well, now his time had run out.

On screen, John hesitated—his body telling him to run, to get blankets and beat the flames away, but his mind forcing him to stay. He knew she was gone. It was his duty to stand with her and watch until the very end.

"Kiss me," Kelsey croaked and reached for her boyfriend on the screen. Inside the car, she reached for her boyfriend too, saying the same words Kelsey had in the movie. And she was beautiful. The way the flames haloed her head, the way the orange made her face look like it was glow-ing... only she wasn't glowing, she was burning, and he could smell her, and she was reaching for him, and how was that possible... how was it possible that she hadn't passed out yet? How the fuck was it possible that she was awake through all of this?

She always had the nicest lips, he thought. That was the first thing he noticed and would be the last thing he would ever think about once she had her way with him. He was thinking that when she picked him up to go to the movies. She had been reading the last few sentences of a story in the very book she clutched in her death grip—the book that didn't seem to be burning even though it was embroiled in flames.

"... wanting closure; wanting release," she had read out loud. "The orange glow, tinged with the faintest lick of blue, she knew, would give her peace."

The way her mouth formed the words, stretching, pulling, pouting—it drove him mad. That's why he could never look at her when she spoke, could never stop himself from pressing his own mouth to hers, capturing her lips in a worshipping kiss. But right then, as her lips were curling over the words she spoke, caressing them, savoring them as if a last meal, the flames licked into her mouth to dance with her tongue.

John was hypnotized by the scene—the flames, the smell of burning flesh in the air, all of it like the sway of a boat on the open sea. It was intoxicating the way Kelsey's visage seemed to undulate in front of him, to waver like the air over asphalt in the summer heat. He stood watching as Kelsey's arm rose to touch his face.

She was engulfed in flames—pretty much the whole car was—but she was smiling at him. Not smiling, no, not really, he noticed as he leaned closer, abandoning the idea of escape in lieu of moving toward her. She was smirking, one corner of her mouth pulling up knowingly as she stared at him... beckoned him. That one side of her face had burned away, the sinews and muscles drawing up to reveal the bone beneath, escaped him. He was too busy looking at the side of her mouth that had remained untouched, those lips he so loved to kiss, to nip, to suck... he was too busy remembering how those lips felt on his skin to notice that she was dying in front of him. Dying and reaching out to him. She closed the distance between her flaming self and his sweat-soaked shirt in a second.

He recoiled just a little too late.

Her burning hand touched her boyfriend's chest as Kelsey's touched John's face, leaving a flame that would devour his cheek. She was distantly aware that her mind had been taken over by something—some evil being that wanted this, that craved the destruction. She could smell her own flesh burning and knew she should have lost consciousness by now, but still she was awake, even as her boyfriend screamed and writhed. She willed it to happen; tried to exert power over herself just one more time and force her eyes closed. But she couldn't. The thing inside her—the thing that had forced her to read the book, to hold onto it for dear life as the flames enveloped her, the car, the wire connecting the tinny speaker to the sound post between the quad of spaces she was slotted in, the same one that short circuited from the heat and sent sparks into the now empty cars that shared it—was too strong. The thing... it always got what it wanted, and right now it wanted her to take her boyfriend with her, to kill him just like Kelsey killed John in the movie that would be the last thing she would ever see.

She ran her hand around to the back of her boyfriend's head and pulled him toward her as his shrieks and sighs died down and he succumbed. She latched on to him, needing to feel him close as she waited to die as well. Her voice, nothing more than a painful whisper now, broke free as she embraced him with one arm, still refusing to let go of the book, but she doubted he heard her. He was burning in earnest now, the fire having spread from his shorts to his shirt to his hair with immeasurable speed.

"I love you, baby," she said again, at last slumping against the seat as the fire ravaged her throat, burst her eyeballs, and stilled her tongue.

12

Sunday Morning

He stood on the steps, listening to the choir lift their voices, a last-minute practice before the morning's service. He wished he could plug his ears, blot out the sound with his screams, something. He didn't want to hear them thanking God for their lot in life, for the streets that stank like piss and vomit, for the bread and milk the government let them have for free. He didn't want to open those heavy doors and feel the oppressive heat greet him. It was cooler outside. He didn't want to smell the foyer, its odd mixture of incense, sweat, and sulfur ever present. He couldn't bring himself to bow his head in supplication again. He didn't feel anything when he did anyway—just the hot, sticky sweat that coated his neck cooling in the air that had been whipped up by the dirty fan propped in the window.

But he had to.

Just as sure as he knew his own name, he knew he had to enter that place, hear those sounds, and smell those smells again. The thick, glossy tenement paint that caked the walls had his name etched in it. The hymns that the choir wailed incessantly spoke to him this time... every time. At least that's what it felt like. He was afraid of what would happen if he didn't respond to their deafening call.

He opened the doors to the church—big hulking things made of dark wood with antique gold trim—and slipped inside. He didn't want to make a sound, didn't want to draw attention to himself. He just wanted to do what he had to do and leave. He might never come back if he could get away clean.

"Where you been, Caleb? You know he been looking for you."

The sound of the old woman's voice startled him. She was there, sitting on her perch like she always was, her Sunday outfit covered by a thick black shroud with her head bowed as if in prayer. A stack of fans advertising Bedman's Funerary Services sat on her lap, waiting to be handed to the parishioners that would fill the sanctuary soon. Everything was the same as it always was inside the church where he had begged for forgiveness all those years ago, his knees bruised and bleeding. This Sunday morning was the same as every Sunday morning, yet the scene frightened Caleb to the core.

The old woman didn't look up when she spoke.

He passed by her without responding. There was nothing to say anyway.

He had been gone for—

"Hey doc, you almost done?"

"What?!?"

Dr. Lee nearly jumped out of his skin at the sound of his assistant's voice echoing in the room. That was one of the things he hated most about the autopsy rooms in that facility: the ceilings were so very high—state of the art diagnostic equipment advancement the culprit—that everything echoed. Sounds bouncing off the walls in the dead of night with nothing but one's self and a freezer full of the dead was disconcerting, even to someone who spent more time with those whose souls had left this earth than with those still living.

It didn't help that he had been reading a creepy story... reading a story when he was supposed to be writing his final notes... reading a book that he found in the deceased's possession.

He saw it on his desk when he sat down to fill out the last few lines on the autopsy report for one Megan Carlisle, age 28, cause of death: respiratory failure due to fire. There wasn't much to this case, at least not from his perspective. He wasn't the one who had to figure out why a young woman would set herself and her boyfriend on fire in her car in a public place, risking the lives of the other moviegoers. If the car had blown up... Dr. Lee didn't like to think that way. Two burning deaths were already two too many. Let the cops worry about the rest.

He sat down at his desk like he usually did, getting ready to finish up his part of the work on the case and then maybe take a minute to eat. It had been hours since he had, not since morning, when he'd had breakfast with his wife. He was famished. It always made him feel just the slightest bit guilty feeling hunger, in that place, but that's how he felt, nonetheless.

His eyes fell on the clear plastic bag that held the victim's belongings.

There was nothing inside except a book. Nothing else survived the blaze. The car was consumed by flames; it took at least an hour to put out. The book shouldn't have made it out. It was old, nothing but brittle yellowed pages beneath a cover made of some kind of soft fabric. It should have gone up right away.

Someone said they saw her clutching the book to her chest while she burned...

Dr. Lee hadn't realized he had taken the book out of the plastic bag until he felt the cover beneath his hand. Velvety soft.

Impossible.

He opened the cover and took in the smell, old and welcoming, nostalgic, though he couldn't figure out why. Not the smell of burn he had expected to catch, not the smell of flesh succumbing to flame.

He turned one page, and then another, seeing nothing but blankness, as though the fire had stripped away all of the ink, leaving barren pages in its wake. And then, the beginning of a story... the sound of voices singing, lifting above his head, carrying on the wind as they travelled up, up up.

"Dr. Lee," his assistant said, standing closer now. He had already gone out for lunch, the smell of onions floating heavily in the air before him, "you almost done? You should probably run out and grab something before... well, you know how it can get around here."

He did. One night they had four motorists come in right after a jumper and a stabbing victim. And contrary to what people might think, the dead won't wait.

"Right," Dr. Lee said distractedly. He put the book down reluctantly, wishing he could finish the story before he left, but knowing he would have no reason to give for even touching the book if someone asked. What could he possibly say... the story was so intriguing, he couldn't put it down? What reason could he supply for opening the book in the first place, or the bag besides? Fingerprints, residue, bodily secretions, whatever else the authorities might want to test the book for had been compromised because he couldn't control himself. But he had been drawn to it, hadn't he? Called to open the plastic, to stick his hand inside... to take a look.

Dr. Lee finished the last field on Megan Carlisle's autopsy report, signed his name, and pushed himself away from the table. He picked up the book gingerly but quickly, holding it by the corners and thrusting it into the bag fast, before his assistant noticed, sealing it again and walking away as if he hadn't been holding it in his hands not a minute before.

With a sigh, he left the office, the building, the book, finding food and eating it mirthlessly, the fragments of the story he was reading flashing in his mind, showing him things. Maybe he would finish it when he got back. Maybe he could hold the book back when the police came to talk to him about the victim. No one would believe it existed, not after a blaze like that. Maybe no one would remember that it was in her arms, fused to her breastbone so completely he had to use the rib cutter to get it out.

He heard singing off in the distance. Probably from the square, he thought as he walked back to the office, though it was a little late for that. The sound followed him, voices twisting, turning, intermingling with each other as they lamented their dirge.

The assistant felt restless. He paced the space he shared with the doctor, puttering around, looking for something to tidy, to clean, to do. The office was quiet with the doctor gone, and that was ok. He didn't mind the silence, even in a room filled with the dead. Some people got used to the job and some never did. Him? He came into it being ok with death. And he had seen a lot now, enough to have made someone hoping to wake up desensitized to it one morning quit and find a new career. Death was part of life, and he was there to help the process along as best he could.

Megan Carlisle's report was still lying on Dr. Lee's desk.

The man was brilliant but absentminded, and the assistant had taken to following behind him, dotting his i's and crossing his t's, and that was ok, too. He was fine being an assistant, didn't want his name to be the one on the report. They were a good team, and he wanted it to stay that way, even if it meant he had to clean up the doctor's messes every now and then.

Plastic shuffled as he picked up the report, pulling the corner from underneath what looked like a book. He picked it up, protected in the plastic bag, turning it over to inspect both sides.

"Where did this come from?" he said aloud to the empty room.

He didn't notice the air rushing out of the top of the bag, the seal breaking on its own as he held the book in his hands. He only saw, with distracted curiosity, that his hand was reaching inside to touch the velvety soft cover.

OR...

12

Sunday Morning

He stood on the steps, listening to the choir lift their voices, a last-minute practice before the morning's service. He wished he could plug his ears, blot out the sound with his screams, something. He didn't want to hear them thanking God for their lot in life, for the streets that stank like piss and vomit, for the bread and milk the government let them have for free. He didn't want to open those heavy doors and feel the oppressive heat greet him. It was cooler outside. He didn't want to smell the foyer, its odd mixture of incense, sweat, and sulfur ever present. He couldn't bring himself to bow his head in supplication again. He didn't feel anything when he did anyway—just the hot, sticky sweat that coated his neck cooling in the air that had been whipped up by the dirty fan propped in the window.

But he had to.

Just as sure as he knew his own name, he knew he had to enter that place, hear those sounds, and smell those smells again. The thick, glossy tenement paint that caked the walls had his name etched in it. The hymns that the choir wailed incessantly spoke to him this time... every time. At least that's what it felt like. He was afraid of what would happen if he didn't respond to their deafening call.

He opened the doors to the church—big hulking things made of dark wood with antique gold trim—and slipped inside. He didn't want to make a sound, didn't want to draw attention to himself. He just wanted to do what he had to do and leave. He might never come back if he could get away clean.

"Where you been, Caleb? You know he been looking for you."

The sound of the old woman's voice startled him. She was there, sitting on her perch like she always was, her Sunday outfit covered by a thick black shroud with her head bowed as if in prayer. A stack of fans advertising Bedman's Funerary Services sat on her lap, waiting to be handed to the parishioners that would fill the sanctuary soon. Everything was the same as it always was inside the church where he had begged for forgiveness all those years ago, his knees bruised and bleeding. This Sunday morning was the same as every Sunday morning, yet the scene frightened Caleb to the core.

The old woman didn't look up when she spoke.

He passed by her without responding. There was nothing to say anyway.

He had been gone for—

"Hey doc, you almost done?"

"What?!?"

Dr. Lee nearly jumped out of his skin at the sound of his assistant's voice echoing in the room. That was one of the things he hated most about the autopsy rooms in that facility: the ceilings were so very high— state of the art diagnostic equipment advancement the culprit—that everything echoed. Sounds bouncing off the walls in the dead of night with nothing but one's self and a freezer full of the dead was disconcerting, even to someone who spent more time with those whose souls had left this earth than with those still living.

It didn't help that he had been reading a creepy story... reading a story when he was supposed to be writing his final notes... reading a book that he found in the deceased's possession.

He saw it on his desk when he sat down to fill out the last few lines on the autopsy report for one Megan Carlisle, age 28, cause of death: respiratory failure due to fire. There wasn't much to this case, at least not from his perspective. He wasn't the one who had to figure out why a young woman would set herself and her boyfriend on fire in her car in a public place, risking the lives of the other moviegoers. If the car had blown up... Dr. Lee didn't like to think that way. Two burning deaths were already two too many. Let the cops worry about the rest.

He sat down at his desk like he usually did, getting ready to finish up his part of the work on the case and then maybe take a minute to eat. It had been hours since he had, not since morning, when he'd had breakfast with his wife. He was famished. It always made him feel just the slightest bit guilty feeling hunger, in that place, but that's how he felt, nonetheless.

His eyes fell on the clear plastic bag that held the victim's belongings.

There was nothing inside except a book. Nothing else survived the blaze. The car was consumed by flames; it took at least an hour to put out. The book shouldn't have made it out. It was old, nothing but brittle yellowed pages beneath a cover made of some kind of soft fabric. It should have gone up right away.

Someone said they saw her clutching the book to her chest while she burned...

Dr. Lee hadn't realized he had taken the book out of the plastic bag until he felt the cover beneath his hand. His bare hand. It was velvety soft.

Impossible.

He opened the cover and took in the smell, old and welcoming, nostalgic, though he couldn't figure out why. Not the smell of burn he had expected to catch, not the smell of flesh succumbing to flame.

He turned one page, and then another, seeing nothing but blankness, as though the fire had stripped away all of the ink, leaving barren pages in its wake. And then, the beginning of a story... the sound of voices singing, lifting above his head, carrying on the wind as they travelled up, up up.

"Dr. Lee," his assistant said, standing closer now. He had already gone out for lunch, the smell of onions floating heavily in the air before him, "you almost done? You should probably run out and grab something before... well, you know how it can get around here."

He did. One night they had four motorists come in right after a jumper and a stabbing victim. And contrary to what people might think, the dead won't wait.

"Right," Dr. Lee said distractedly. He put the book down reluctantly, wishing he could finish the story before he left, but knowing he would have no reason to give for even touching the book if someone asked. What could he possibly say... the story was so intriguing, he couldn't put it down? What reason could he supply for opening the book in the first place, or the bag besides? Fingerprints, residue, bodily secretions, whatever else the authorities might want to test the book for had been compromised because he couldn't control himself. But he had been drawn to it, hadn't he? Called to open the plastic, to stick his hand inside... to take a look.

Dr. Lee finished the last field on Megan Carlisle's autopsy report, signed his name, and pushed himself away from the table. The pen felt strange in his hands, heavy in a way that he found unpleasant, and he was happy to rid himself of the weight.

He wanted to hold something else.

Dr. Lee picked up the book gingerly. He traced his finger along the edge of the pages. So delicate; the pages were rosestted from wear, as though crimped with a scrapbooking tool. The ridges caught on the lines of his fingerprint, tracing, following, remembering. He felt electric, like the hair on his forearms stood on end to reach toward the book, like his skin, his very cells pressed toward the yellowed paper so that it might drink.

"...if you don't," his assistant was saying, but Dr. Lee didn't know what about. On he went, his tone gentle but urging, annoying then as it had been at others. The man meant well, but the mothering quality he took on got under Dr. Lee's skin sometimes. Especially now.

Prattling, on and on... about what? Ah, yes. Food. Right. Dr. Lee sighed as he looked at the book in his hands, the book beginning to be opened to the story he had started. He wanted to, felt like he needed to open it, but the space had been disturbed, the air disrupted by the assistant's urging. The mood wasn't right anymore. He chuckled under his breath at the choice of words his subconscious had floated him, wondering when he'd become so sentimental. He might think it was funny, but he'd listen to it, that internal voice. He wanted the reading to be special. He promised himself that he would read again, even if he had to steal the book to do it. That, too, earned a breathy laugh because no one would ever believe the book existed. How could they? How could it survive a blaze like that? No, they wouldn't think it survived, would never expect that it had been fused to her breastbone so completely he'd had to use the rib cutter to get it out.

Again, a laugh. More like a snicker that time. If the assistant heard, he didn't comment on it.

Dr. Lee held the book by the corners and thrust it into the bag, before sealing it again. He then walked away as if he hadn't been holding it in his hands not a minute before, as if he hadn't tainted evidence of the crime that occurred, but the assistant saw. He saw, but he didn't comment. The doctor's behavior struck him as curious, but he didn't ask.

With a sigh, Dr. Lee left the office, the building, the book, finding food and eating it mirthlessly, the fragments of the story he was reading flashing in his mind, showing him things.

A black dress.

The deep wrinkles of a hand that has served its owner for three-quarters of a century.

The wooden handle of a hand fan.

He began to wonder if he could hold it again, touch the pages of the book that had impossibly survived the blaze, touch the cover that was velvety smooth. Dr. Lee began to wonder if he could hold the book to his nose and smell the past and the future entwined, aromatic incense that would somehow soothe his soul.

Dr. Lee's hands trembled at the thought.

He heard singing off in the distance, loud and enraptured with a note of atonement and acquiescence lacing words he couldn't quite make out. *It's probably coming from the square, he thought*, as he listened. There was always something going on there at all times of the day, but even as he considered the possibility, he acknowledged that it was a bit late for such. It was loud. At once shrill and guttural. Voices twisted and turned, intermingled with each other as they lamented their dirge to caress his ears. If the cats that prowled the alleys at night had chosen that moment to add their voices to the caterwauling, Dr. Lee wouldn't have been surprised. He too felt like wailing in discordant harmony. He should go back to work. The dead were waiting. When he lifted his eyes to find himself standing before a flock of the incorporeal, pleats and pearls shifting upon diaphanous skin as their lips formed words to lull, words to appease, words that continued the story he had started and would die to hear the last of, Dr. Lee nodded. Indeed, they were. The sound followed him, voices twisting, turning, intermingling with each other as they lamented their dirge.

The assistant felt restless. He paced the space he shared with the doctor, puttering around, looking for something to tidy, to clean, to do. The office was quiet with the doctor gone, and that was ok. He didn't mind the silence, even in a room filled with the dead. Some people got used to the job and some never did. Him? He came into it being ok with death. And he had seen a lot now, enough to have made someone hoping to wake up desensitized to it one morning, quit and find a new career. Death was part of life, and he was there to help the process along as best he could.

Megan Carlisle's report was still lying on Dr. Lee's desk.

The man was brilliant but absentminded, and the assistant had taken to following behind him, dotting his i's and crossing his t's, and that was ok, too. He was fine being an assistant, didn't want his name to be the one on the report. They were a good team, and he wanted it to stay that way, even if it meant he had to clean up the doctor's messes every now and then.

Plastic shuffled as he picked up the report, pulling the corner from underneath what looked like a book. He picked it up, protected in the plastic bag, turning it over to inspect both sides.

"Where did this come from?" he said aloud to the empty room.

He didn't notice the air rushing out of the top of the bag, the seal breaking on its own as he held the book in his hands, or the turning of the pages to access the story that jumped out at him as it had Dr. Lee, the words glowing from the page to catch his attention. He only heard the words chanting in his mind and only then in the most distracted of ways, their hollow cadence more a curiosity than anything else. The words that echoed in his mind continued a story he had been directed to, but only after showing him a tale of his own. He hoped the promise in it was false, creative for the sake of art and not premonitory as he feared the words he recited in his head were, with their imagery of piety gone dark. He tried to forget them, to listen to himself as he read the terrible bedtime story that was on the page he could not pull his eyes away from, hoped that it would take over and obliterate the words meant for him without knowing why. But alas, he'd soon find out.

PART II

THE TALES OF TIME

PENNY CANDY

Penny candy loosely wrapped in dirty parchment paper. Lined up on a counter so caked with grime I could write my name in it. I did write my name in it after all, feeling like I had to, like it was the last thing I would ever do.

Stuckey wuz here.

I sighed as I looked at the parchment paper covering something that didn't look like candy at all. Too big. Too long. Too lumpy to be peanut brittle like the man said it was. The man who was sweating and breathing heavy as he looked at me. The man whose fingers twitched as I watched. The day's special, he said, when I came into the store looking for some sunflower seeds. Try it, you'll like it. Something about the way he looked at me, about the way the door clicked when it closed, like it was locking me in, something about the haze in the dingy old everything store made me think I'd better try it if I knew what was good for me.

Penny candy loosely wrapped in dirty parchment paper. Waiting for me. Mine to eat. As much as I wanted. But I knew as my dry tongue tried to retreat down my throat, I would only be able to stomach one.

$5.99

The movie went off and cycled back to the main screen, burning the stationary main page into the plasma TV more and more with every passing second. Carla had fallen asleep in front of the television again, as she had most nights since she got the DVD, unable to pull herself away from the screen to make it to bed. That really wasn't true though. She hadn't made it to bed because she didn't want to go to bed. She was right where she wanted to be.

Her sister thought she was crazy. Not literally, but she would have if she knew—if she *believed*. It wasn't like Carla hadn't tried to tell her, hadn't tried to share him with her... once... in the beginning. But Carla's sister didn't see it. He didn't speak to Tami the way he spoke to Carla. It was only right, really. He was Carla's, after all.

There wasn't anything special about the DVD, just a B-level movie with a cast that you think you might have seen before, but if so, you can't remember where. Carla got it out of one of those bins full of surplus movies discounted to $5.99.

But that wasn't all it was. Not to Carla.

The storyline was slow-paced and didn't really go anywhere, but Carla wasn't listening to the lines. The actors either never really "made it," were over-the-hill has-beens, or were newbies, but Carla recognized one of them. She should. She had seen him in her dreams for years.

Well, not him specifically, and not in the dreams like the ones you have when you're sleeping. But in her fantasies, in her daydreams, he was always there. He looked like a combination of her first love, a guy she knew from work, and the last guy she slept with. Such an odd mix, with unkempt hair, deep, penetrating eyes, the most sensuous lips. Carla could hardly tear her eyes away from the screen when he was in a scene and found herself reaching for the remote to fast-forward to his next one even if it meant she'd have no idea what was going on in the movie when she got there.

After her second time watching the movie all the way through, he started talking to her.

At first it was just a look. He would look at the screen, seemingly at her, when he should have been looking at the actor opposite him. The first look was just a peek, just a glance; Carla almost didn't notice it at all. His second look was so much more meaningful. There was a playful twist to his lips that was endearing. His third look was downright obscene, the way he licked those luscious lips of his and lowered his eyelids. It gave Carla chills. The good kind.

Twenty minutes into the movie he spoke to her.

"Carla."

She felt as though she was waking from a dream when she heard her name. He was looking at her again, full on, shoulders squared to the screen—watching her. He was smiling just enough for her to see a hint of white from his teeth. She felt herself respond though she knew she shouldn't. He didn't have many lines in the movie; he was nothing more than a glorified extra, really, yet he had spoken her name as clearly as if he were sitting in the room whispering it in her ear. Carla spun her head around, looking in all corners of the room to be sure that he—that someone—wasn't there making fun of her, laughing at her expense. But she was alone.

With him.

She watched the movie three more times that day and more that weekend, blowing off shopping with her sister, a date with a guy she had been interested in for months, sleeping in her bed, and eating. With every viewing he said more to her, sometimes telling her how beautiful she was, pouting his lips as he spoke, letting her see all the curves and contortions they went through as they formed words, other times asking her to remove garments so he could see more. She felt silly and excited at the same time. It was weird, strange; all of those things, but it was the best fantasy she'd ever had.

As Carla snored, catching her first reluctant winks in 30 hours, the screen flickered and blinked before finally catching again on the beginning of the movie. For a second, gone faster than Carla's eyes could have deciphered had she been awake, a roiling sea of red bubbled to the surface, washing Carla's face in blood as a tentacle reached out to stroke her cheek.

INHERITANCE

To Wilson's credit, his attempt had been a good one. Sharon was surprised he'd had the presence of mind and initiative to call Hattie into service before Sharon could find a suitable slave. The argument must have really burned him up, so much he went straight home that night and set to the business of concocting his potion. But Hattie had been easy to dissuade, at least thus far. Sharon didn't have to do much more than lock the door against her to keep her at bay. A quick sidestep and the old girl was lost. Wilson hadn't bothered to teach Hattie anything more than how to get up and walk again. He told her to go after Sharon and to kill her, but he hadn't told her how.

Sharon got used to the beating against her front door. Hattie could stay out there all night if she wanted to. It didn't bother Sharon any, and there wasn't a neighbor to complain about the noise for miles. She figured Wilson would wait until morning to see if Hattie had done the job. At least until after the funeral, just so it would look right. People would wonder why he wasn't in the family car, it being his brother-in-law's funeral and all. They would wonder why he would be anywhere except right by his wife's side.

Sharon had time.

Hattie hadn't figured out that she would do better to bust in the windows yet. Sharon doubted that she would. The woman hadn't been a brain surgeon in life. How could she be expected to do better in death?

Sharon sucked her teeth as she walked into the spare bathroom, the room where she brewed her potions and cast her spells. She thought back on how they had gotten to the place they were now—wanting to rip each other limb from limb as soon as look at one another.

Their mother had left the shop to both of them. She had been a respected woman in their village, a woman who was known to take care of people's problems. Half the time she didn't do anything except sell roots and dried fruit for one potion or the next; she told Sharon and Wilson herself that the whole thing was bogus. But it worked, and she never had to put in a hard day's labor in the hot sun in her life.

Wilson played around with it; 'Momma's mumbo-jumbo,' he called it. He was the oldest and the one who was supposed to inherit the business. He never caught on though, and was easily overshadowed by his younger sister, who seemed to have the real gift. When their mother died, she left everything to the both of them. And that's where the trouble started.

"You're making us look like fools," Sharon said from the back room of the shop that day. "No one will believe us if you keep gallivanting around the street like a commoner."

"They don't believe us as it is, Sharon," he said, tired of the argument. It was always the same thing over and over. "People are smarter now. They know this is a bunch of bullshit."

Sharon burst through the beads that hung from the ceiling to separate the rooms and growled, "Watch your tongue in momma's house."

Wilson chuckled. "Sharon, momma's been dead for ten years already. When are you gonna cut it out?" He turned his back to his sister and touched one of the dry herbs that hung from the ceiling.

"Her *ánimo* is still here, Wilson. She's angry that you speak of her that way."

"Right, sure," he said condescendingly. "Anyhow, I just came here to tell you that I'll be talking with a man about selling this dump. I'm gonna try and get whatever money we can out of this place and do something with it. Maybe I'll move to the mainland. Who knows?"

Sharon looked stricken. "You can't sell the place! This is momma's legacy!"

Wilson flicked the herb and sent it swinging on the string that held it. "It's not much of a legacy, now is it? We can barely live on what we make from it. I have to work a second job just to keep food on the table." He shook his head and stood to leave. "I'm selling it, Sharon. And there's nothing you can do about it."

Wilson walked toward the door, opened it, and turned to speak before leaving. "But you should have already known that, *bruha*."

Sharon cursed him then, vowing to stop him by any means necessary. She didn't utter a sound as she stood facing the closed door of her mother's shop, but Wilson heard every word.

～

The church was sticky, and the mosquitoes relentless. They couldn't resist the bounty they were getting: thirty people crammed in a small church with nothing but their hands to protect them. They feasted.

Wilson escorted his wife in and sat in front of the body of her brother. Clay had been a strong man, muscular and fit for most of his life, but that didn't save him. He worked out on the boats and was stung by a Portuguese Man of War during an afternoon pull. They didn't make it back to the dock in time to save him after he went into cardiac arrest.

As his wife sobbed, all Wilson could think about was Sharon. She wasn't at the funeral, so she must be dead. She wouldn't have missed Clay's service. She fancied him and was genuinely saddened by his death. Wilson tried to conceal his smile as he thought of Hattie taking Sharon by surprise. She must have been shocked to see her, considering she had attended Hattie's funeral a couple of days earlier. He would talk to the man after they put Clay in the ground, Wilson surmised. He would have his money in less than a month.

His wife's shaking grew intense, and a cry was stuck in her throat, choking her. Wilson turned to her and said, "Honey? Honey, are you ok?" He didn't see Clay fidgeting in his tight casket, didn't recognize the sounds of grunting from his chest and the ripping of the stitches in his lips to be what they were. His wife's eyes were wide open, unblinking, in shock. "Honey?" He shook her slightly, trying to get her attention and pull her out of day terror she was having. She wouldn't look at him.

Wilson turned his head in the direction of his wife's stare in time to see Clay sit up in the casket. An audible moan escaped his chest as the air escaped his lungs. Clay forced his mouth and eyes open, ripping the stitches apart. He lifted his right arm and then his left, inspecting them in disbelief. The whole thing was so much déjà vu to Wilson that he didn't move.

Then Clay climbed out of the casket.

Wilson didn't hear the shrieks and screams that emanated from the congregation as Clay planted his feet on the floor. He only saw Sharon standing at the back of the church smiling prettily, devilishly.

Clay moved quickly for one of the undead. He closed the space between himself and Wilson in three strides and pressed down on his shoulders, buckling his legs, making him submit. Wilson became aware of a pungent odor, the smell of meat that had been left out in the sun. Sharon had converted Hattie in the light of day and brought her along as backup.

With everything he could remember from Momma, with everything he had, he called Hattie inside. She came sluggishly, bewildered. She looked at Sharon who was too busy watching the show in front of her to notice. Then she looked at Wilson.

He intimated his command to her, deftly breaking Sharon's spell and reinforcing his own. Hattie was upon Sharon before she could turn around. He wished she had; Wilson would have loved to have seen the look of surprised terror on Sharon's face.

I'm better than you now, sister. I bloomed right under your nose.

The smell of fresh blood permeated the air as Hattie ripped away Sharon's scalp. Sharon's scream was nothing more than an afterthought as was her limp hand against Hattie's decaying cheek. She was dead as soon as her skull was exposed to the summer air. Hattie banged Sharon's head against the wall like a squirrel might a nut and pawed at the brain inside.

Clay smelled the blood just before Wilson did. He turned his head, loosening his grip just enough for Wilson to slip away. Clay lunged at Sharon, grabbing her leg and digging his nails into her skin, cutting through the flesh and muscle with determined swipes. He licked at the blood that spewed from the wounds before baring his teeth and biting into the supple flesh. Wilson slinked against the wall, trying to make a quiet exit while Hattie and Clay dined on Sharon. He noticed for the first time that the church was empty; everyone had fled, running for their lives, including his wife. He'd have to remember that she hadn't tried to help him at all, that she had just left him in there to deal with two zombies. Yes, that was useful information indeed.

Wilson stood in the doorway to watch as Clay sank his teeth into Sharon for another bite, sinews and fatty tissue draped over his working lips. He looked at Sharon's face one last time, at her ruined eyes and what was left of her exposed brain and smiled. As he closed the door to the church, his expression transformed from grim satisfaction to abject fear to please the waiting crowd. His wife ran up to him, tears streaming from her eyes, wetting her cheeks. He hugged her hurriedly, burying his face in her welcoming neck, deftly hiding the hatred in his eyes.

He'd meet the man later that day. He'd have his money in less than a month.

CEMETERY ROAD

I've never been afraid of the dark, but I'm damned scared now. Donnie said the trees looked like legs in the dark, and he was right. My flashlight ain't helpin' things either, just makes 'em look like they're moving.

I don't know why I'm here, but I am.

I know'd better than to come up here, but I dint use the sense God gave me. They was just talking so much shit about how I wasn't gonna do it and how I was a chicken shit, that I just had to. So I'm here, and I wish I wasn't.

I drove up to the corner, like they said to, and parked the car. They said they'd be watching to see if I would do it, so I followed every instruction. I dint want them to say I cheated. And I damned sure don't want to do it again. I started walking up the road and zipped up my jacket. It was cold as hell outside, no kind of weather to go playing around in a cemetery, but then again, when was? My footsteps sounded loud as I walked up the deserted road, not a car to be seen. I started to count the crunching of the rocks—made the time go by quicker. By the time I got to 150, I had made it up the hill and could see the headstones shining off my flashlight. The white ones seemed to glow.

Houses lined the street, every one of them with dark windows. Who the hell would want to live across the street from a cemetery anyway? Even if it doesn't spook you, it ain't nothing to look at. The only people ever outside are crying.

Six, maybe seven houses stood there and nobody in any of 'em. For some reason that don't set right with me.

I looked at the tombstones, trying to decide if I was going in or not. My granddaddy's stone was on the edge of the street, damned near paved over when they put up the new road back in '84. It leaned to the side, sunken in the ground, chunks taken out of it from the wind and rain. Just beat up. *That's what's gonna happen to me*, I thought as I stared at it sticking out of the ground like a broken tooth. Something about that made me want to run.

I looked back at the houses with their black eyes staring at me. I couldn't tell which one I felt safer having my back to. The cold made me decide quick.

I looked back to the cemetery and saw the same tombstones, the same trees, and decided to go in. Ain't no difference in a cemetery in the day or at night. Dead people there all the time, and they can't bother nobody. And anyway, Donnie and the guys're watchin'.

The first step inside was hard, but they got easier after that. I walked past granddaddy's grave and on down the Barlow line, ending up by my cousin who just got put in the ground a couple months back. I snickered at his grave and thought for a second about leaving that $5.00 I owed him on the grass, but nah. Why waste good money on someone who can't use it anymore? Poor sucker.

This shit is easy once you get the balls to do it. I walked around like I owned the place. Thought about what it might cost to buy a place like this. Make money off putting people in the ground? You could stack three or four coffins on top of each other and charge for a single plot! Do that over so many acres and you got a goldmine. Might need to look into it tomorrow when I get up.

I figured that was enough after I got to Sandy Laurelton's grave. Old biddy died back in 1837 at the age of, what was it, 96? I think that's what the cross said, but it was pretty splintered, so I could be wrong. Either way, old is old. I gave the back of Sandy's cross a slap like she'd probably never had on her ass when she was alive and started back the way I came, happy this shit is over. I dare them to talk shit about me now.

When I saw them coming I couldn't help but call out. And why did it matter anyway? Dead people don't care how loud you are.

"Hey Donnie!" I yelled, steam filling up the air like a white cloud. "I did it, dude! Smacked this little bitch on the ass too."

I thought Donnie would get a kick out of that. Hell, he's the one who likes to fuck 'em when they're damned near dead anyway. But he dint say anything. Well fuck him then, the jealous little bitch. I probably stayed in longer than him, and he was pissed. So who's the chicken shit now?

I stopped walking and let them get closer, the cloud in front of my face going in and out as I caught my breath. They dint have a cloud in front of theirs.

IDOL

"How can he be that beautiful?"

Millie stared in awe at the image on her smartphone, enlarging his lips, his eyes, even his undercut for a closer look. The sigh that escaped her lips was heavy with sweet admiration and laced with feels she hadn't been aware of before finding K-Pop. It didn't take long for her to become entrenched in the mania. She found her favorite group almost right away, their luxurious voices caressing lyrics she didn't understand, creating an exotic, taboo-like aura in her room when she put on their songs... which was every day, for most of the day. She bought all the stuff: the summer video packages, the CDs with special photo albums inside, the swag featuring her bias and the one showcasing her bias wrecker (then, guiltily, something with the faces of the other members too because how could she truly be a fan if she only supported a few of the members, right?). Millie had it all. They were going to be performing in the US later that year, and Millie had a great idea to pitch to her mom about travelling to LA to see them. LA is a lot closer than South Korea, she would say. I can work during the summer to help out on costs, she would add. Maybe her mom would understand. She'd had her own entertainer crush, right? I mean, what were all those tears about when Prince died if she didn't? Millie thought she probably shouldn't go there, not unless she really had to. Mom hadn't listened to Prince since he died – the mourning was real.

His oval eyes looked out at her from behind a fan of periwinkle-colored bangs (oh, how her bias loved to change his hair color!), giving all the fanservice he knew she and the millions of other screaming teenage girls around the world liked. He had just woken up in some other place on the other side of the world from where she sat and decided to go live on YouTube just because. Millie grinned from ear to ear when she got the notification and left the dinner table without warning. Her father said, "Don't forget about the movie," or something like that as she passed by him. Millie had shoved earbuds in her ears before taking her plate to the sink and had turned the volume up high so that she could hear every nuance of his voice before reaching the stairs.

She thought she grunted a response to her father but wasn't sure.

His face was filling her screen before she had gotten out of the room; his perfect pink lips parted suggestively as he worked to get the camera situated just right. She never saw her brother Chris smirking at her from the kitchen as she raced by, never saw her cat dodging her legs as they scissored wildly up the stairs. She only saw him, only heard his groggy voice speaking in his hypnotic foreign tongue.

He yawned.

Millie smiled.

He chuckled.

Millie blushed.

~

"Millie hasn't come down yet?" her mother asked of no one in particular. The kitchen was clean, and the leftovers put away. It was time for movie night, and three of the four of their little family were ready to get started.

Chris looked up, shrugged, and turned his attention back to the game he was playing on his smartphone. Millie's father sighed and said, "No, not yet."

Millie's mom looked up at the ceiling, a move she swore helped her to hear what was going on upstairs better, and listened intently. The muffled sound of a male voice speaking quickly could be heard. She didn't notice the staticky hiss that was deliberately, persistently there, but inconspicuously so. Like the assumption of crackling on the wind after an electric shock, the sound floated among the waves and pitch to mingle with his rich baritone. She strained, trying to understand something of what was being said, trying to determine whether the broadcast was almost over or not. She wanted to give her daughter a chance to join the family activity on her own. Choosing her battles these days, Millie's mom didn't relish the idea of pulling her away from something she wanted to do. On any given day, Millie might as easily bite her head off as give her a smile, and if the guy that was talking was the one from that K-Pop group she liked, and Millie tried to interrupt her…

"Go get your sister," their mom said to Chris reluctantly.

Chris' nose was stuck in the game. He was oblivious.

She looked at Chris and then over at her husband incredulously.

He cleared his throat first but got no reaction.

"Chris!" His voice boomed in the room.

Chris looked up, surprised.

"Your mother told you to go and get your sister."

The protest that rose in Chris' throat died on his lips when he saw the frustration in his father's eyes. He got up without a word, leaving his phone behind as he knew they wanted him to. Chris didn't want to fight. He wanted to watch the movie. This week had been his choice and he couldn't wait to rub it in Millie's face. He had chosen *Child's Play*, mostly because he knew Millie hated Chuckie. Crazy little demon doll, here we come.

Chris bounded up the stairs, talking all the way. "Time to say goodnight, sweetheart," he parodied, trying to sound lovey-dovey. "It's time for the movie." He stopped outside her door, hearing a male voice speaking in a language he didn't understand. "You don't even know what he's saying, Mil." Chris turned the knob and opened her door, still talking. "He could be telling you to take off your clothes in front of class and do the dance from his last video." This struck Chris as incredibly funny.

Chris' hearty laughter turned shrill, like the scream of a siren, when his sister turned toward him slowly. It wasn't the saliva that spilled from the corners of her mouth that frightened him most, nor the milky white veil that covered her chestnut brown irises. It was the way she spoke that sent chills down his spine; the monotone delivery of a question he could not understand,

"Eotteohge geuleohge aleumdab ji?"

NEW HOUSE

I can see them from my window.

Some glisten in the moonlight, others cast shadows along the dark-ened path—the one that leads to our place. The tallest of them all acts like a sentinel, watching over the rest as they reach toward the sky unabashedly. Do they call to the others to reach out too, the ones who hesitate, beckoning them to break free and stretch out their hands?

I can hear them.

Disturbing the ground, roots snapping, dead grass crunching, earth shifting to fall inside... earth smudging the satiny white pillow. I hear them.

I hear them grunt and wheeze and whistle with effort as the wind whips around them, courses through them, pushes, and pulls.

Silence floods my ears like a freshet; loud, empty, ripping, still.

Gargling, gnashing, grunting as my house creaks, groans, and burbles in the settling.

Warped shadows on the path limping to, fro, away, toward, as the moon sits high and the clouds pass low.

Tall trees, fern leaves, evergreen, limp hair.

Cloth centuries old ripped from bindings left to float in the wind, twisting, turning, writhing as they disintegrate into dust.

The dust from which they came.

Ashes to ashes.
New house trash littering the lawn.
Packing peanuts fill the new hole.

FAMILY DINNER

"You gotta be kidding me," Nick said as he turned onto the dark road... a road that looked just like the last one, and the one before. He had been driving for an hour into the deep woods and across state lines for a girl he had just met. *Come to dinner* she had whispered in his ear the week before. *Meet my family.*

Already?

They had only been out on a few dates, had only spent maybe 7 hours together, but who's counting? She talked about cavern hunting (who can resist stalactites and stalagmites?) and great skiing when he got there, but that wasn't the reason he said yes. It was her. She wore such a sweet smile when she asked him to come, looked so perfect in her tight jeans and loose sweater. She felt so warm when he hugged her close and felt her form underneath all that knit, so he said sure. It didn't matter that her family dinner was the same day that he was celebrating a win with his buddies, sending him in the other direction from her folks' house and adding 45 minutes to an already long drive.

Amy.

All that mattered was the smile she would greet him with when she opened the door and the warm hug that waited for him.

Assuming he could ever get there.

The drive from Fairfax was the easy part. He knew his old stomping grounds well enough to make it most of the way out of Northern Virginia and over to Warrenton, where the city lights were a distant memory, but that was as far as he could go without help. It didn't help that there was no interstate to get onto. The closest one would have put him a half hour out of his way, so he braved the side streets and back roads, relying on his GPS and, after a while, instinct. GPS, God love it. Such a great tool when it works. But like that early-adopt model he won at a casino in the late 90s, the one that had to be suction-cupped to his windshield and that sent him into the Baltimore harbor every time he made a turn off Pratt Street, the route his phone gave him was no use. It kept rerouting as if the mountains surrounding the sleepy hamlet grew up overnight, making a once-usable road impassable. Nick had gotten so sick of hearing that unaccented, mild-mannered female voice telling him to make a U-turn, he closed the app.

White's Taxidermy on his left. Margie's Good Eats on the right. Coincidence?

Nick would have laughed at his joke if he hadn't already told it before. He was sure he passed a similar combination a few towns back. Taxidermist Tull and Jake's Steak. Forever Pets Taxidermy and The Rib Shack. It was funny the first time, but not anymore.

Nick pulled into a gas station. He was happy to find one of those big chain stations like the ones he was used to at home. The drive itself was starting to look like one of those low-budget horror movies—he didn't need to add a broken down, one-pump station with the stereotypically grimy gas jockey to the mix. He and three other people filed into the brightly-lit convenience store at the station. He listened as the person in front of him asked for directions to the ski lodge near where Amy's family lived—the same one that had a hot chocolate with his name on it waiting by a warm fire. The route sounded like the one he had just come off, long and twisty and dark. When it was his turn, Nick told the attendant—young and clean, thank you very much—that he was looking for directions to the same place.

"But where's the highway," Nick asked after being given the same directions the woman before him got. "There's gotta be something that cuts through these mountains instead of sticking to the back roads." He picked up a candy bar and laid it on the counter. "I feel like I've been driving around forever."

The young man nodded imperceptibly, his eye twitching under the patch of highlighted hair visible beneath the rim of his red service cap. "I wish, but there's nothing like that," he said a little too eagerly. "This is the best way to get out to the ski lodge, especially since it's almost dark."

Nick smiled at him incredulously. That's why he wanted the highway! The afternoon light was fading fast, and he did not relish the idea of driving around the woods on winding roads in the dark. He did not want hitting a deer to be in his future.

"There's gotta be something. I mean, there's no way trucks take these narrow streets to deliver to you. What do they use?"

The attendant rang up his candy bar without looking at him.

Nick tried again. "I saw lights, but I couldn't get to them."

Giving Nick his change, the attendant said, "I don't know. But the directions I gave you will get you to the ski lodge in about 2 hours."

The attendant held out his bag with hands that looked like they could be shaking. Just a little, but it was there. Nick shook his head, thanked him, and got back in the car. Two hours? He'd been driving for an hour already, and the GPS said it was just about 2 hours away from where he started. Could he really be that far off course?

Nick looked in the direction that the attendant told him to go. Two of the three cars that came in with him headed that way. The other car, a guy in a button-down shirt open at the neck and dress slacks driving a nondescript black sedan that screamed company car, went the other way. Nick climbed into his own car and turned it on fast. He could feel the attendant's eyes on him, beseeching him to go the way he had been told, but Nick ignored the sensation as it crept up his back to caress his neck. He followed the company car even as the gas station attendant screamed, "No!"

Leafless trees.

Asphalt.

Dead grass.

Repeat.

There was nothing. Not even a boarded-up house to break up the monotony. Nothing at all. Nick had caught up with the other rebel and was right behind him. The man had even made a saluting gesture to him in his rearview mirror—just two compadres bucking the system. It was getting late. At 4:30, it was almost completely dark. There were no streetlights on the country road, but Nick could see some off in the distance. The road traversed a lazy hill. If he could just get down to those lights, Nick was sure he'd find a way that would cut through the spiderweb of back roads and take him where he needed to be. Amy's family lived in a college town—there were bound to be major routes leading to it. He just needed to find one.

Oh crap, Amy!

She had to be worried. Nick picked up his phone and noticed she had called twice already. When? He had the phone with him when he was in the gas station, and it had been sitting in the cupholder the whole time he was driving. It never rang.

"Technology," Nick said out loud, "Gotta love it."

Nick dialed Amy's number and heard nothing. No ringing, no beeping, no 'all circuits are busy' message—nothing.

He looked at his phone, taking his eyes away from the road for a second to see if he had missed a number somehow. He had just added her number to his favorites list, but now he wondered if he had put the number in wrong. Nick didn't see the front end of the company car disappear like it got sucked through an invisible portal. The man threw the car in reverse, and it lurched backwards. The doors seemed to stretch, pulling away from the side panels as if running from a magnet. The metal pulled like saltwater taffy, stretching in long lines of silver and black. The back tires spun against the asphalt, digging for purchase but finding none.

Nick didn't hear the tires screeching on the road, nor the muted screams left behind like an echo as the man travelled through the barrier. He didn't notice the country road rippling as it engulfed the non-descript sedan, the facade rising and falling like paper in the wind to reveal a glimpse of a black core that seemed to pulse with life. He never saw how flat the landscape was, how it mirrored itself every few yards, like cheap floor tiles keeping pattern. Instead, he heard the unaccented, mild-mannered female voice of his GPS telling him to turn around to start route guidance, only this time she was screaming.

THE EVER AFTER

CHAPTER ONE

Oh my God.

I couldn't stop myself from screaming. I had been screaming since it started. I breathed in and out, in and out, only vaguely registering the odd taste of the air, the sulfuric smell.

Dead.

I must be dead. Surely after a fall from so high, no one could have survived. I looked around at the bodies that littered the field, legs askance, arms bent at impossible angles, and I nodded. We're all dead.

My eyes watered as I looked up at the brilliant blue sky. I was up there. A shiver ran through me as I remembered. It was midday, maybe two or three o'clock—exactly the time when I always start to feel restless at my desk. I wanted the day to be over. I wanted to go out in the sunshine and play. Sometimes I wondered if I was really cut out to work in an office. The walls seemed to close in on me. I couldn't focus, didn't want to think. I hated my cube walls. I hated my officemates. I hated the work. So uninteresting. So unimportant. I wanted to do something real, something that mattered.

I was on the way outside for my normal break (I took five every day even though I don't smoke), and I was itching to get outside. I passed people I knew in the hall and mumbled hello, shared the elevator with someone and engaged in the obligatory chitchat, then barely stopped myself from running out of the front door.

"Enjoy your break."

That's what he said. Enjoy your break. Such a normal comment, a throwaway, something you really don't mean but you say just to be nice. It's like when people say, 'Have a good day!' or 'How are you?' They don't really want a response; they don't want to listen to some long, drawn out story. They just needed something to say. *Enjoy your break.* If he hadn't said it I would have escaped the image of what he would become.

"Enjoy your break," said the guard whose name I never knew. His smile was genuine enough, but he wasn't even looking at me when he said it. He had already moved on to the next person, addressing someone else from his cramped little room. I was just another faceless person to speak to as they passed in and out of the lobby. I smiled back anyway, a thin-lipped thing that could just as easily have been a grimace. And that's when it happened.

Gravity gave way.

First my hair lifted off my head and rose above me like a crown, then my feet lifted off the ground. What I felt was confirmed by what I saw: the guard, several inches taller than me, rose off the ground and struck the low ceiling of his security shack before he could even scream. Instead of stopping, he pressed through, breaking into the ceiling. There was a horrible sound—a wet, cracking, popping noise. Blood, bone, and matter rained down in a torrent from the hole he created.

Oh my God.

In one wild instant I caught a glimpse of the world below me. My purse had fallen off my shoulder and was lying on the ground. Papers and pencils littered the guard's desk to be splattered with his blood. None of those things were floating up to oblivion. This wasn't gravity giving way. This was something else.

I screamed for the guard as much as for myself. It was only after hearing my own voice that I realized I was moving toward the higher ceiling of the lobby and toward that poor man's same fate. I grabbed the doorframe and pulled myself outside, ducking through with barely enough time to clear the rest of my body before colliding with the door-frame. For the briefest of moments I tried to will my feet down to the ground, but there was no chance. It was as if I was on an invisible lift being raised up. My ascent was beyond my control.

People outside rose with me, some above me, some below me, some in sync with me. The ascent wasn't quick, and that was the torture of it; the ride was slow enough for me to take in what was happening, just long enough for me to become afraid. Smoke from car accidents below billowed up to us, giving chase. There was so much screaming and crying. Some cursing. Lots of praying. People tried to move toward each other craving touch, a hand to hold as we rose to our deaths. Surely that's what we were doing—rising to our deaths. Soon we wouldn't be able to breathe, or we'd freeze to death or…

I laughed through my tears. Leave it to me to forget which would happen first. Jenny the airhead forever. Never taking anything seriously. But this was serious all right. It was the end of the world.

Windows broke, and people rose through them, bloodied. Glass protruded out of open wounds, heads cut open to reveal the smooth sheen of bone. Severed heads and detached limbs rose from the crashes below, bobbing on the wind like grotesque Macy's parade float inflatables.

Babies cried. Perhaps that was the worst part.

The air started to get cold, and I began to understand with unwanted clarity that it wouldn't be long now. If gravity kicked in at this point, the drop would crush me. If I didn't stop rising, I would freeze to death. If I escaped that death somehow, I would not be able to breathe outside of Earth's atmosphere. That's the order, I realized after all. Crazily I wondered if a spaceship would pick me up. Would I stop on a cloud and see my grandmother waiting there? Delirium had already begun to set in.

My life had been aimless, a collection of unfulfilled dreams and wishful thinking. And now it was over. I cried for myself—for what I wanted to do but hadn't, for the pain I would surely feel when I met my end regardless of how. I shut my eyes to the terrifying world before me and opened them to this one with the strange blue sky above my head and rough grass beneath me. People lay scattered on the ground, lifeless, except the ones who sat ramrod straight looking up at the sun with unblinking, inky eyes.

When I sat up under that freakishly blue sky, they all turned to look at me.

CHAPTER TWO

I wasn't going to cut her.

The thought greeted me as I woke up in the comically green crabgrass. Even as it flitted away out of my grasp, I knew it was a lie. I meant to cut her and had wanted to from the moment I knew I was ready to leave. I just didn't have the guts to do it.

But I did it, didn't I?

I saw the knife in my hand, saw myself raising it above my head and thrusting it down fast. I heard Felicia yelling at me in that condescending way until she felt the blade pierce her skin. Then she screamed in pain. And fear.

I remember liking that part most of all.

I remember telling her that I couldn't take it anymore, that she needed to act like a woman and not a man. I already have a man, and he knew his role. She needed to learn hers. But she wouldn't. When I wanted her, it was because I craved soft, sexy, alluring—pretty, damn it. Not bossy, foul-mouthed, and rough.

She wasn't always that way. When we started seeing each other, she was sweet and loving. Her face lit up when she saw me. She used to call me Brandy when I hit it right. But when I met Paul and brought him home—when I kissed Paul before kissing her—she changed. She was waiting; I knew that. She was waiting for me to choose her over Paul. She pretended to like our three-way romance and probably did enjoy the sex

128

if she didn't think about it too much. But she wanted me for herself, and not having me made her mad and mean.

Cutting her meant I had chosen. Finally.

My apartment was covered in blood. The walls were splashed with it as I chased her around. Once I started cutting I had to finish, but she wouldn't stay still. I was on top of her when it happened, making sure she was dead. Her body was warm between my legs. Her little titties were pushed together in her bra, teasing me for the last time.

I should have fucked her one more time before I killed her.

I was thinking that when the sky fell.

It seemed like a cutaway for a TV show; my vision went all white for a second and then gradually came back, showing me this new, weird world. What I saw when I opened my eyes didn't make sense. People were staggering, leaning, falling over. I saw bodies on the ground—some were moving, but others were still. Most people were just staring up at that crazy sky. I looked too. I felt like I was being hypnotized. My body rocked, moving like a dandelion in the breeze. I imagined that my head was like the white fuzz on a dandelion with seeds blowing off in the wind. My hair, nose, and ears blew off too, twisting and turning in the wind and leaving droplets of blood on the ground.

That image is what snapped me out of it—whatever 'it' was.

I looked down, certain I would see Felicia beneath me, her chest destroyed by that piece of shit knife I used on her. I was covered in blood, had to be; I could almost feel it coating my arms. But there wasn't any blood at all. No knife either. And Felicia was nowhere to be found.

I was kneeling in grass with thick, curly lime-greenish blades that seemed to creep toward me in the wind, like they wanted to wrap around my ankles. I shook my head and laughed at myself as I stood up, only distantly wondering where these crazy thoughts were coming from. I felt a lot of things in that moment but the main thing was relief. And power.

I felt fucking awesome.

I killed my lady ('that bitch' seemed too harsh a name for her now) and got away with it. It was all cleaned up and left behind. It didn't matter that this new place didn't seem real. It didn't freak me out that the grass and the sky—the fucking sun—looked more like a kid's finger painting than something of this world. I didn't even give a shit that there was a guy on the other side of a tree that seemed like it came out of an animated Halloween special staring right at me with eyes that looked like black holes. I just figured it was part of the crazy-assed hallucinations I was having.

Fuck it—I'm free!

No blood—maybe it was all a dream. The thought made me laugh. It couldn't be true; I remembered how warm and slick her blood felt on my hands before waking up in this weird place too well for it to be my imagination, but go with it for a second. Maybe Felicia wasn't dead. Maybe I didn't even attack her—who gives a damn? All I care about right now is that she's gone, which means the shit is over.

Amidst all the screaming and whining, I laughed like I had never laughed before.

CHAPTER THREE

I knew that life the way I knew it had irreversibly changed the moment I saw a corpse driving a car. I also knew I was tripping but not so hard that I didn't know a dead man when I saw one. The man behind the wheel of a red Subaru that had seen better days was middle-aged, and his chin sported fresh stubble. His old-fashioned wire-rimmed glasses were perched on his nose. There wasn't anything discernibly wrong with him, not at first glance. He looked like a regular guy driving around town on a sunny day. Except this 'regular guy' couldn't be driving around today or ever again for that matter. I knew that because my mom went to his funeral just a couple of days ago.

Get your shit together, Carrie.

I sat up taller, took a deep breath, and put both hands on the wheel, trying to shake off what had to be the result of some bad Spice. I'll never buy shit from that asshole Tyler again.

Mr. Ridley nodded as I coasted next to him, coming dangerously close to hitting the Subaru and giving it (and him) the burial it deserved. Some of the lines that had etched themselves in his face when he was alive had smoothed out, and his hair, lackluster at best before he collapsed in front of the library clutching his chest, had regained some body and even some color. There wasn't any green decomposing skin, no withered lips and rotted gums, nothing like that. Is this what zombies really look like? Wait, are zombies real and this is what happens? I had convinced myself that I

131

was hallucinating somewhere along the way and was settling into the fantasy... and it was freaking me out fast. Do we just reanimate after we die and go on about our merry way? Shouldn't you move to a new town if you're going to do that? I mean, what if you bump into someone that knew you when you were alive—?

It was the wave that did me in.

Just a gentle flick of the wrist: an open-handed salute. It was so jovial, so natural. His hand seemed to glow. The sky behind him was the brightest, darkest blue I'd ever seen. It was like the night sky was backlit by a spotlight or something. It made the sky weird. Too blue. It was kind of like the color of the water you see when you're out in the middle of the ocean. That's how it looked on that cruise Mom and Dad took me on before I started high school. The water was so deep out there—it seemed like you would never find the bottom if you dropped anchor. I remember staring at it every day, getting more and more spooked. How could anyone survive out there? Who knows what lurks beneath the surface?

Blue, teal, turquoise, and midnight all rolled into one—that's what the color of the sky looked like. It was as wrong as Mr. Ridley was. His hand looked obscenely bright against it, but he didn't seem to notice. He just went on waving at me under the weirdest-looking sky I'd ever seen.

Please don't smile.

I don't think I can handle it if he smiles.

I didn't feel my car career off the road and hit the turnbuckle because I was too busy staring at Mr. Ridley and the sky. The sky and Mr. Ridley. I passed out before the impact praying that Mr. Ridley didn't smile and show me his pointy teeth.

CHAPTER FOUR

I didn't know I was looking for something new, but damn, he is gorgeous. Dirty blond, blue eyes, with abs that lead into the most perfect pelvic muscle I've ever seen up close. Australian accent on a velvety voice, barely legal, and eager. He's the polar opposite of any other man I've ever been with, but I'm not complaining. He takes his time and savors me like fine wine. I could listen to him moan all day long, and sometimes I do just that. He leaves me satisfied and crazy for more.

I'm so preoccupied with Dustin that I rarely even think of Jared anymore.

Dustin adores me. He says as much, but that's not how I know. It's when I catch him looking at me out of the corner of my eye that speaks volumes. His face goes through so many emotions at once, it's almost painful to watch. Love, admiration, obsession, lust. Fear. He wants this to last forever and doesn't know if it can.

He's beautiful and smart.

He loves the sun and lets it kiss his skin with zeal; watching him take off his shirt in its yellow glow is an exercise in restraint. He wants to marry me, but that will never be. Regardless of what happens between Jared and I, I would never go on record as being 21 years my husband's senior. Dustin just laughs when I say that. He says he'll push my wheel-chair out to see the surf every day if that's what I want. Ah, my pretty. I think he really believes he would.

He met me on the beach today. Just ran by me with his board under his arm; I sensed him more than saw him until he had run several paces away. He threw a kiss over his shoulder and dove into the tumultuous sea, ready to enjoy the waves for as long as the sunlight held. I was content to watch him move in the water, read my book, and feel the breeze.

This had become my typical day, and I loved every minute of it.

Sometimes I wondered what was going on between us. Is this just a fling? How did this happen? There are so many things that I don't remember. I feel like I'm drunk on whatever this is—passion, lust, love? I don't remember when I decided I was going to cheat on Jared. We weren't having any problems. Life was the comfortable normal that marriages slip into over time. I know Jared as well as I know myself—does he know what I've been up to?

As I watched Dustin come out of the surf I can understand what caught my eye. Any woman would be hard pressed to not do a double take. But I never thought I'd cheat.

As Dustin came closer those thoughts were invaded by others, ones that make me shift in my seat. It made the worries seem unimportant. For now.

I felt my cheeks get hot as he stood over me. His lopsided smile was my undoing. I felt flutters deep in my belly and had to look away. This is one hell of a forty-something-woman-going-through-a-midlife-crisis checklist item, that's for sure.

Dustin laid me down on the sand. He kissed my eyelids, my cheek-bones, my nose, my mouth. His touch, made rough by the white sand, still managed to raise goose bumps on my skin. He stretched my arms over-head, clasped one hand in his, palm to palm, fingers interlaced like first loves often do, and traced a line from my elbow to waist with the other, watching his fingers as they moved. I could see the desire in his eyes as he looked at my body, could sense the control he struggled to keep over himself. He bit his lip to keep it at bay, his desire threatening to quicken his pace. He wanted to go slowly because he knew I liked it when he did, even though he felt like he couldn't wait any longer. He wanted to savor me, though his mouth watered. That realization affected me in a way I didn't expect. The tears that stung the corners of my eyes were real. Exhilaratingly real, and so very scary.

He guided himself inside me without ever letting go of my hand.

The sky looked incredible. Such a brilliant blue. I was trying to come up with the name for it; the name was just on the tip of my tongue when

Dustin sent me over the edge. Then I started thinking about how I might never go home if this pretty young thing plans to fuck me like this every time.

And then I stopped thinking all together.

The last thing I saw before I woke up to the brilliant blue of that weird sky was the first thing I was looking for but couldn't find. Where is Dustin? I looked around taking in all the people scattered about in various stages of confusion but none of them kept my attention. But the sky did. It kept pulling my eyes away from task. Though the color was the same, it wasn't beautiful to me anymore. It was all encompassing and thick. Heavy. It seemed to bear down on me, as interested in crushing me as hovering above me. I felt its menace in every part of my body.

My clothes were the same, just a sundress and sandals, still hiked up over my hips the way Dustin had left me. My skin looked the same, and I felt the same. But everything had changed.

"Dustin?"

I whispered his name at first, not wanting to draw the attention of the others, though that might have been impossible anyway.

I was lying in a tree that was close to the ground. It was very much like the Divi Divi trees that grow in Aruba with their affected lean and gnarled roots. My toes scraped the ground from my perch, but the rest of my body was enclosed in the tree as though I was sitting in its mouth. And the leaves were so green. Breathtakingly green. The most intensely bright green I had ever seen before. The tree, the whole place, was alive in a way that nature wasn't intended to be. I felt like a cricket veering too close to a Venus Flytrap.

I pried myself out of the tree's grip and stood on grass that crunched underfoot. "Dustin?" I said again, panic invading my voice. He shouldn't be here—I know that now. More than anything I hoped he wasn't here. That sweet man who loved me right when I needed it shouldn't have to endure this. I didn't want to know what his face looked like in the light of the harsh crayon sun that hung overhead like a weight.

It dawned on me that this is exactly where I belonged. It felt like some kind of reverse Rapture. All the good people stayed on Earth and the bad ones—the ones who cheated and didn't think twice about their husbands —were sent to hell. Because this is hell, right?

It certainly feels like it.

I saw him approaching in the distance and wondered about his size. Jared was a big man, sure, but something about him seemed disproportionate somehow. And his gait—it was too deliberate. Almost like he was trying too hard to put one foot in front of the other. I shook my head in resignation. This is what I deserve, isn't it? Not Dustin but Jared—new and improved… and sure to be mad as hell. I bought it and paid for it, indeed.

"Corinne, baby! Oh, thank God!"

The words were his, but the voice wasn't. But that's all right. As Jared's arms encircled me, pulling me into his soft, fleshy chest, the name of that color blue popped into my mind. Cerulean. That's what it was. The color of the Caribbean Sea transposed in the sky. My eyes fell onto the faces of people I don't know. Some of them were paralyzed with fear, and others in blissful ignorance of what lies ahead. I'm too sad to be scared even though Jared's embrace felt more like a vise.

CHAPTER FIVE

Hazy.

That's what it seemed like but not what it was.

Maybe my vision was hazy—maybe my mind. I wanted to go back to sleep. But I hadn't been sleeping, had I?

Not really.

Wishing for it, maybe. Sleep was all I wanted to do these days. Being awake was a chore; the constant hemming and hawing about trivial things that most people my age engage in had started to grate on my nerves a long time ago. I wanted to shut all of that nonsense out. I did everything I could to make it go away, short of the final step.

Is that what this was? Had I finally gotten rid of that Catholic guilt and found the balls to do what needed to be done? Caroline would be disappointed to see me this way, if seeing the dead again is what really happens when all is said and done. She might say, in that exasperated tone she reserved just for me, 'Oh, Edward,' and give me a good smack to prove that point. But I would take it if it meant being with her again. I'd give anything to hear the sound of her voice again.

What took me so long to do it? When Caroline died all those years ago I thought I would go after her. I was sick. Hell, I had been sick first, so it made sense. But then my heart disease got under control (the doctors kept referring to my cluster of heart attacks as blips on my screen), and my health rebounded—not all the way, but enough to keep me kicking. The doctors patted each other on the back; the kids cheered and hugged, but I sulked. I pulled away, stayed home more because that's where it was quiet. I stopped seeing the doctor because I wanted whatever they did to be undone. I wanted to go with Caroline. Life without her wasn't much of a life at all.

But that was eight years ago. Eight years of living in the shadows, watching trash TV, crying over old pictures, only speaking to the kids when they pressed the issue: avoiding life. They knew what was going on —Robbie said he'd help me do it if I really wanted to. But I couldn't saddle him with that for the rest of his life. My good boy would suffer, too, and I didn't want that to happen.

I learned something over those eight years. You can't will death. It'll come when it's good and ready and not a moment before.

I remember going to bed with Caroline and the kids on my mind. I was thinking about an outing at the lake up in Greenbrier, Maryland, from 40 years ago. The sun was shining, and a cool breeze ruffled my hair. I could feel warmth on my cheeks even in the darkness of the one room I lived out of anymore. I couldn't make myself walk around the house much. Too many ghosts occupying the rooms.

I don't remember deciding to do it. I had contemplated the ways a million times—pills seemed the easiest. The thought of shooting myself and not dying made me sick to my stomach. I didn't think I could take a knife to myself, and I wasn't about to jump off anything. Pills I could do. I'd just take all the doses of Tambocor that I missed and let my heart literally skip a beat. It would be quick. Not painless, but that's not what I'm looking for.

But then this happened.

I looked around at the landscape I woke up to. It was beautiful, yet odd in a way that frightened me. My house was gone. In fact, I couldn't see any houses at all. There were too many people around, people who were paying attention to everyone else but trying to look like they weren't. And the sky. There was something wrong with the sky. It was like a kid's coloring page—the colors were too bright and unrealistic. And harsh.

Where the hell is Caroline?

If this is what I think it is, and I've checked out of life once and for all, why isn't she here to greet me? She can't still be mad that I put her in a home, not after all these years... could she?

Some people were crying quietly. Some cried out loud with such gut wrenching wails they made my hair stand on end. Some got angry, demanding an answer, a reason for being in this new place—they stood shouting into the open air. Others hugged themselves against the outside world. Me, I just sat and watched. I didn't think I had enough control over myself to do anything else.

CHAPTER SIX

The room was alive for the first time since the beginning, buzzing and beeping accompanied by loud, fast-talking nurses and doctors. There was a lot of reaching, running, and commotion. And then nothing. No movement, no people, no noise.

Dr. Mitchell stood in the middle of the room, his vantage point allowing a view of all of them. Jennifer, 28. Brandon, 33. Carrie, 19. Corinne, 41. Edward, 77. All wheeled into the large room that would end up being their death chamber within minutes of each other. All gone at virtually the same time.

The hallucinogen had been injected into each patient's IV in tandem. Brain scans for each of them showed hyperactivity spikes and relaxed rhythm at the same pace. They seemed to enter the new sphere, a place designed to comfort them as they awaited their deaths, at the same time also. Cerulean Fields was his life's work: a utopia for the dying. It was supposed to give them peace at the end instead of pain, a loss of dignity, and fear.

But it didn't. It couldn't have. In the end they were all writhing, fighting, clawing at the air. Something chased them to their death over there. Something unexpected.

He looked at the pictures of his patients that were posted on their bedside tables and felt a sadness well in him that he had dreaded from the beginning of the research. He had never met them; by the time they arrived at the facility their induced comas had already taken effect. He didn't want to know them, didn't want to see their eyes. That would have just complicated things.

The pictures showed each of his patients in the prime of their lives, their smiling faces a testament to their health in contrast to their present situation. Edward stood tall and confident, muscular in the way that men who enjoyed the outdoors were. His son Robert said that Edward had been an avid camper, taking the kids into the woods every summer. Robert couldn't bear to see his father like this, so frail and thin. It took everything he had to visit every week.

Jennifer's picture didn't look like her at all—the stroke paralyzed her entire left side and aged her overnight. Brandon's picture was of him out at a lake. You could only see his profile but that's the only image that his girlfriend would bring. She only came to visit once and didn't stay long. Carrie's picture was haunting. It showed a sweet little high school kid with her whole life ahead of her. It was Carrie before the drugs and the self-imposed isolation. It was Carrie before the accident.

Corinne was the true beauty in the bunch. Dr. Mitchell's affinity for her was evident from the start. He could see a beautiful woman beneath the graying skin. Looking at her grounded him, made him see the patients as people instead of research specimens. Every time he looked at the picture of her on the beach with her sarong flowing in the wind revealing slender, shapely legs, he grew more attached. Her caramel skin, sun-kissed in the picture, seemed to glow. She radiated confidence even before the vast sea in front of her.

He wished he knew her before the cancer ravaged her body, before chemotherapy stole her hair, before her eyes closed forever. If they had met in a coffee shop, would she have noticed him? Would she order a Chai tea latte and turn to see him staring at her? Would she smile the same way she did in the picture, joyful and provocative, and make his knees buckle? If they met on a crowded street would she be interested in him, or would his blue eyes not be her cup of tea? Sometimes he got angry because he would never have the chance to find out.

Sometimes he touched Corinne's hand when he thought of what could have been, wanting to feel her skin next to his own. He interlaced their fingers when the fantasy was particularly compelling, gingerly holding her paper-thin skin against his, gaining closer contact in the most appropriate way possible even though, in his mind, they moved from hugging to kissing to more. He imagined how he would caress her skin, run his hands through her hair, kiss her beautiful full lips—lips that had only been parted to brace a feeding tube since he had known her. Dr. Mitchell spoke to her about the places they would have gone if they had the chance, sharing a fantasy that could never come true with a woman he wasn't entirely sure could hear him. He felt like a kid talking about his hopes and dreams. Corinne made him giddy in a way that he hadn't been since he was 20 years old. He reveled in a past they never shared and mourned a future that would never be. Many times he wondered how life could be so cruel to show him true love in the touch of a dying woman.

Dr. Mitchell looked at Corrine, studied her. This would be the last time he saw her. Once he left the room she shared with the other patients their connection would be lost. He was not ready to say goodbye.

He puttered around the room a bit more, cleaning up, wasting time, trying to prepare himself for the inevitable. Soon the families would be notified, and the bodies would be claimed. They would be gone within hours. Corrine would be gone forever.

The thought was unbearable.

"Dr. Mitchell, we need your signature on the files."

The nurse's voice barely registered to him. The only sound he could hear was waves crashing on the shore.

"Dustin?"

The nurse had moved close enough to touch his arm. He had to restrain himself from shaking her hand off. She handed him the folders and left him alone. He saw the concern in her eyes as she did, but she was mercifully silent.

He touched Corinne's hand one last time. It was still warm. Perhaps that was the worst part.

ANSWERING MACHINE

I got a call from a friend today. She wanted to go out for breakfast to that place she likes. Wanted to eat pancakes with blueberry syrup and scrambled eggs with cheese. And grits. She always wants grits. That's what she said on my answering machine, the hulking dinosaur that still sits on my hall table next to the phone. She calls me old school for keeping it. Says I'm dating myself by even having it around. Maybe she's right. But there's nothing wrong with a little old school every now and then.

She sounded so perky, so excited. Something must be going right in her life. That's good. Maybe she finished the project she's been agonizing over for months, trying to get the right angle, form the right words. She was pumped up. Proud. And good for her. I listened to her voice with a wistfulness I didn't expect to feel. I'm happy for her, but more than happiness, I feel content. Like hearing that she is doing well today means she will do well forever. That's silly, I know. Part of me knows that, at least. But maybe forever is today. And that's not so silly after all.

My friend stopped talking before I stopped listening so I heard everything that came after: the wet sliding sound, the mucous-laden snorts that got louder and louder. I heard the wheezing—that was the worst for me, that sick, terrible sound emanating from the depths of the thing's lungs—the labored breathing. I thought I might be able to get away, thought I could borrow some of that "I am so awesome" vibe my friend just left on my answering machine, but I couldn't. Not now, when my leg, mangled to the bone, sits tied to the hall table leg. The table, God love it, is on its back now after my fruitless kicking, pulling, wrenching episode. Any energy I had was used up in trying to get away the first time.

Or was that the second?

I lost track.

The smell of pancakes with blueberry syrup was a figment of my imagination, I knew. Just a jab, a "you wish you could" zinger pushed up by my mind's evil eye. Or was it? Couldn't it be that the smell from my memory was given to me as a gift? One to occupy me while the thing slurping, shuffling, and, dear God, wheezing had its way? Maybe so. I don't know. In a different world I would think so. But as the wheezing thing stepped on the answering machine and played my friend's cheerful chirping again, I had my doubts.

OBSERVATIONS AT THE
SUPERMARKET

Cheddar cheese.

Swiss cheese.

Jack cheese.

Block.

Shredded.

She's standing next to me, staring at the cheese like she doesn't know which one to get.

Finely shredded.

Shredded—as in plain old.

The corner of her eye twitches—actually shudders, like wind causing the surface of standing water to ripple... like a shiver from a cold breeze.

Made with 2% or whole milk—come on, I urge silently from my perch next to her, in front of the canned pastry tubes, the ones you need only bang on the side of your counter to make the dough explode inside them... the ones that could put your eye out if you weren't careful... come on, I press with my eyes if not my voice, live a little.

Her eyes cascade down the packages of processed gunk—that weird canned stuff, those perfect American cheese squares wrapped in plastic. She tripped over the bleu cheese, the goat cheese, the queso fresco, seeing but not seeing, knowing but not caring. Oh yes, she knows I'm watching her. She sees me from the corner of her eye even as it twitch-twitch-twitches.

She licks her lips when I shift from the balls of my feet to the heel. Balls to heels. Back and forth. Back...

Cottage cheese.

Cream cheese.

How about goat cheese, hmm? Creamy and white. Soft like a cotton ball against a splintering table. Soft, unlike its overripe sister, brie. Soft like waiting skin in the warmth of the noonday sun.

Soft.

Supple.

Pliant.

Ricotta cheese.

Her lips part to reveal the bottoms of blackened teeth; ridged, the mamelons unsmoothed, unnaturally prominent.

Jagged enough to cut her skin.

In fact, I was sure she had cut her tongue, her finger, and anything else that had had come into contact with those teeth many a time. And just as I knew that, I knew she liked it too.

Colby cheese.

Monterey Jack.

Muenster.

She snickered.

She bit her bottom lip.

A trickle of blood blossomed against her flesh, rising like a fount, spreading, bubbling over.

Red.

Bright.

Dark.

Dead.

I knew it.

I need cheese.

Suddenly I need cheese more than I've ever needed anything before.

What do I want today? What's my fancy? Maybe a mix like Jalapeño Jack for my spicy burger or the gimmicky Mexican blend, which is just a mix of some regular old cheese bagged together with the illusory "quesadilla cheese" (yeah, I see you). Or maybe I need some old-fashioned mold in the form of Neufchâtel or maybe the saucy not cheese Velveeta for the nachos I didn't know I wanted.

My mouth is open and I don't know why.

She can hear me breathing.

A smile plays at the corner of her lips as she looks at me—looks right at me—without ever turning her head.

Just one beady little eye.

Parmesan.

Asiago.

I reach out to grab something, anything.

I beat her to it, her taloned hand jutting out a fraction of a second after mine to land on the thin skin that covered the bones on the back of my hand… metacarpal bones, fragile bones like those of a baby's, every detail exposed under the skin, protruding like a skeleton's—brittle, flimsy: weak.

A fraction of a second.

Long enough for me to wonder if I would ever get to taste the fresh mozzarella my hand had landed on, little balls of the stuff wet in the package, moving around like eyeballs in a sensory bowl—long enough for me to wish I hadn't—

Eggs.

Eyeballs in a sensory bowl are usually made of boiled eggs.

Eggs.

Brown.

Farm raised.

Quail-

UPPERVILLE

Upperville. The town where all the inhabitants are family. The town where nobody leaves because the world doesn't exist past the city limits. The town I'm from.

Getting out was always a priority for me. The streams that border the town, the well that stood in our backyard, all smelled stagnant to me. Like rot. Like death. I didn't want to be consumed, to be sucked into the very ground like it was quicksand or the hungry mouth of a Venus Flytrap. I didn't want to live and die only knowing Upperville's monotony, with its white picket fences and its picturesque winding roads. "Upperville, the sleepy hollow less than an hour from the city," it had been called in some magazine years ago. To me it was more like "Upperville, town of the damned." So I left. I jumped on 66 and made for the city. Washington, DC.

I even wrote an article about it, one of my first features at the paper before I got moved up. "The Decline of Rural America," I called it, proudly typing Susan McCoy in the byline. I had to rewrite it so it didn't smack of Upperville bashing, not because I cared what the people back home thought—I didn't think they would get the paper anyway, and if they did, they wouldn't read it—but because I wanted to make a good impression at my new job. When the paper came out there were grumblings, Mother said in her usual, I-just-happened-to-hear-it way. But there were always grumblings, at least, as far as I was concerned. People never seemed to like me or the things I did. Mother said it had more to do with her than it did with me, but she would never explain it. And she would never leave, no matter how much I begged. She said she was bound to the land just like my soul was bound to be free. I never listened when she started talking that way. Instead it strengthened my determination to get out. If that's what Upperville did to you, I didn't want any part of it. Sometimes Mother acted as kooky as the rest of them did. I wasn't going to let that happen to me.

I hate Upperville with a passion.

And now I'm going back.

Even my mother's death hadn't brought me back to Suckerville. I had her body shipped to DC and forced anyone who wanted to pay their respects to leave their comfort zones and come to me. No one did. I found out later they held an informal service over my mother's body at the morgue. The coroner had lived in Upperville all his life, so even though it was against the rules, he lit a candle in front of mother's body on the slab along with the rest of them.

But now Bobby Zucker was dead. I had to go back.

The drive was over before I knew it. Memories of Bobby and me stealing kisses behind the school and copping feels in the cab of his father's pickup flooded my mind, wiping away the road and replacing it with his face. He was my first kiss, my first lover, my first love. I lived and breathed him until I left for college. He stayed behind to work at his father's hardware store. I begged him to come with me, to leave Upperville and start a life with me in the city. But he didn't. As the years passed and Mother told me about Bobby's life—sending me the invitation Bobby gave her for his wedding to Mary Lou Kramer (a cowgirl if there ever was one), giving me baby pictures when his children were born—I couldn't believe I had been so wrong about him. He wasn't the person I thought he was, wasn't the free spirit who thought for himself and did what he wanted to do in life. He was just like the rest of them in Upperville: a drone.

But I never forgot about him.

Even with all the dating I did, all the near misses, I never forgot about Bobby. I always wondered what it would have been like had he left Upperville and come with me. He might have been a lawyer, like he wanted to be. He might have had a successful practice in Northwest DC, might have been a real player. We might have been happy.

But now he's dead.

Carlene, my mother's best friend and the only other person in

Upperville who knew how to reach me, said that he fell from a ladder and hit his head. She said he never regained consciousness, using a sympathetic tone that made it seem like that was for the best. But it wasn't. The Bobby I knew would have wanted to wake up and say goodbye to his family and friends, would have wanted one last moment to see the sun from his window. But I kept that to myself. There was no sense in upsetting Carlene's "Uppervillian" logic, her untested, all-knowing sensibility.

Damn him for making me come back.

Damn him for not coming with me.

The main road—aptly named Main Street—looked the same as it had when I took it out of town twenty-one years ago. Same old stores, looking the worse for wear in the diminishing light, the same old church at the end of the badly pocked street. People went about their normal routine as I drove by, talking with each other in the entrance to the post office while scratching at their oversized, dirty overalls and plaid shirts, tipping their hat to the old woman who strolled past. Doing nothing. I've seen it all before. It hurt to think that Bobby had become one of them.

The funeral home was off a side street with even more cars lined up than on Main. People had come to pay their respects. Bobby must have been well-liked, and why wouldn't he be? He was one of the most handsome kids in school, one of the most grounded people I had ever met. I bet he was a magnet, someone who the cowpokes wanted to be around. It made them feel better about themselves. And now that beacon was gone.

That's what he was, wasn't he? A beacon that had called me back to a place I swore I'd never step foot in again.

With a deep breath, I walked into the funeral home. It was suitably muted, as were most places like that—no sense in turning up the lights so you can see the death mask in plain view.

I didn't recognize Carlene when she approached me. "Susan? Is that you? My God, you look so different!" she cackled louder than she should have in a funeral home.

"Carlene. It's great to see you!" I lied. I didn't care if I ever saw her again. Bobby was the only person I cared about in that godforsaken town. And now he was gone.

Two other people milled behind her, openly listening to our exchange. "Well, you remember Karen Whitetower and Vern Glover, don't you?"

I nodded my greeting, desperately wanting to get away from them.

"I bet you're anxious to see Bobby, then," she said, her face twisting in a sly smile. "I know how close you two were."

Something about her troubled me.

"He's right in there," she said, turning my shoulders and nudging me toward the room where Bobby's body lay. "Go on," she urged, flashing her too-sweet smile.

The whole drive there all I wanted to do was see him, see that Bobby was dead with my own eyes, but now that I was there, in the place where he was laid out, I was afraid. Seeing him would mean that it was really over. Everything we had ever shared was done, gone, finished. Even when he got married, I thought there might be a little something left, something we might grab onto later in life. But now that he was dead, there would be no chance of that. I was terrified.

"Go on, Susan," Carlene said, her voice more urgent this time. "Go in and see Bobby."

I started walking before I allowed my thoughts to register. Carlene's behavior, her expressions, everything about her bothered me. Why did she care if I went in to see Bobby? Why did it have to be so rushed? I brushed the concern away, chalking it up to my nervousness. I was, after all, at my first love's funeral. Maybe I was a little sensitive.

I heard the whispering among the people who ringed the corridor—

"That's Lizzie's girl, isn't it?"

"She ain't been back here for twenty years!"

"Not even for her mother's funeral."

I turned to see who made that comment, but no one met me eye to eye. Funeral? I had mother's funeral in DC. If they were talking about their cultish sendoff in the morgue, fine. But they said funeral. Had they held a service that I missed? Anger welled within me, swirling inside my stomach. How dare they not let me know about something like that? *I'll have to ask Carlene about that before I leave*, I thought as I turned their whispers around in my head. I approached Bobby's casket at a snail's pace.

It was open, with a yellowish light shining on the place where Bobby's head should have rested. But he wasn't there. I didn't see what I expected to see, Bobby with his eyes closed and the lids pulled a little too tightly over the eyes to look natural, Bobby with makeup dusting his temples to cover the greenish gray tint his flesh had taken in death, Bobby whose glued lips looked nothing like the soft ones I had kissed so long ago. I picked up my pace, ignoring the voice in my mind that insisted that Bob's body laid lower than usual, that his wife must have sprung for the deluxe model casket, high walls, plush satin and all.

No casket is that deep, a stronger, more resilient version of my own voice admonished.

He wasn't there.

The casket was empty, its silk bedding untouched. As I turned to ask the nearest Upperville moron what was going on, I caught sight of a stocky man, about six feet tall with dusty brown hair and twinkling brown eyes. Bobby. He was older, but I'd know his face anywhere.

"Bobby, what—?" I started to ask him. His smile spread into a wild grin as I shrank against the casket. I never saw who hit me in the back of the head, never even felt the blow. The blood running down my neck felt warm, calming as I rested my head on the pillow and looked at Bobby. I didn't feel them hoist my legs over the side of the casket, didn't hear them laugh and jeer, condemning me for leaving as I bled out. Only the touch of Bobby's lips on mine registered. When he parted my lips and put his tongue in my mouth I closed my eyes like I did when we were kids.

GOLDENROD SUN

So beautiful, that time just before twilight, when the sun sits low in the sky. Its rays cascade a brilliant hue for a time; like looking through yellow lenses. Her eyes absorbed the light illuminating everything around her, sucking it into the blackness that was creeping in, suffocating it as a drowning swimmer overtakes his rescuer. But beautiful was she in that goldenrod sun, if only for a time.

CHURCH

The windows are blacked out, but there is still the faintest glimmer of light coming from inside.

I'm waiting on the steps, unsure if something has changed and the meeting is off. Yvette told me to come on time, so I did. Going to church after hours (or at all, if I'm being honest) had never been my thing, but I did it for her. I love her. I want her to be my wife, and if coming to church to meet her Bible study group was what she wanted, I would do it. What could it hurt? Lord knows I have enough to make up for, so maybe this is a start.

If I can ever get inside.

There's no wind out here. Nothing at all—not even the little something that barely flips your hair. It's still and quiet. And I am standing here alone.

My watch says it's already 10 minutes after. People should be parked here and ready to receive the Word—that's what Yvette would call it. I say they're ready to get their daily fix. Maybe that's the wrong way to think about it. Maybe that's why I haven't had the guts to stay away from Nicole yet, or to ask Yvette for that matter. Maybe I am thinking about this thing all wrong. Maybe when I get inside I can—

The glimmer in the window, the one that was way back in the recesses of the room a second ago, is now right in the front window, hovering next to the chipped white paint frame. I can't tell if it's inside or outside, but it doesn't matter. Not really. There are more of them now, more than just the one hovering in the corner. There are so many I can almost see...

DESTINY

"If we were meant to be together, you'll find me."

That's what she said, though she never thought it would be *this* way... or did she? Maybe she did, and this was the culmination of her plan laid carefully down throughout the years, hidden in the shadows of truth or some such bullshit. Maybe she had wanted me to come here like this, stumbling and thirsty, wanting. She always liked to keep me wanting, didn't she? Hoping she would see me, desire me, crave me the way I craved her. As I sit her, dying to look upon her face once more, it is more of the same. Me wanting. Her laughing. The story of my life.

It had always been her and me, even when there were others around, others involved, others between us. To say that wasn't true would be to lie, and she knew that as much as I did. She cut herself, and I bled, it was as simple as that, except now... most markedly now, hmm? Her grand plans come to bear in the most amazing of ways.

"If we were meant to be together, you'll find me," she said as she backed out of the door, walking away with just the clothes on her back, saying goodbye to me forever. After I loved her, after I cherished her, after I drove myself mad trying to please her. Still she left without so much as a backward glance once the words had come out of her mouth, leaving me to stare at the open door as if waiting for her to return.

That was ten years ago.

Ten years ago to the day.

Could I have lasted longer? Maybe. Should I have? No. There is no should, would, could when it comes to her, at least not for me... except this—that I *should* do what I desire when it comes to her because she *would* have no other way.

Will she watch me come to her? Wait for me to shut my eyes in bliss before she graces my mouth with a kiss, her hot breath tantalizing me to slip deeper and deeper into her? I wonder as my call swirls bitterly on my tongue. I close my eyes, giving in to the very thing my body wants least to do but is compelled to because we are so very tired. But in that acquiescence comes familiarity, the sweet sound of laughter given to raspy ruin.

It rubs.

It burns.

"My darling," I whisper, the shuddering breath pulled from me relentlessly, lovingly: definitively. "I found you."

ONCE A MONTH

Gasping awake… it's a thing.

Damien found himself sitting bolt upright with the remnants of said gasp in his ears, chest heaving, a thin sheen of sweat coating his brow. It was still dark, and the house was relatively quiet. He could make out the muffled sound of music from his older brother's room—even through the closed door, he was still able to hear the hook of Lil Watts' latest track, the one that bit off Juice WRLD's last album so much Damien couldn't stand to listen to it. It was loud—too loud—and if their mother woke up, Jared would have a problem, but Damien was thankful for it. It was normal. It was expected. It was the only thing that let Damien know he was really real.

Come on, man.

Chill.

Damien focused on controlling his breath. He picked up his phone.

3:38 a.m.

He sucked his teeth.

When was the last time he had been up at that time? Why was he even up now? Damien wracked his brain, trying to remember the dream he was having before he woke up, trying to figure out what had bothered him so much that he found himself looking around his room in search of something familiar just to be sure he had resurfaced in the right place.

Had he been running? He was sweaty, so maybe. Had he been afraid? It seemed like he might have been. But of what?

Vampires and werewolves and voodoo priestesses making zombies. It had been Chris's turn to pick the movie for their Netflix Party that night, and he always chose horror. Even with *Hobbs & Shaw* or restarting the Marvel Universe—who doesn't like a little *Iron Man?*—on the table, he still went with some creepy foreign flick with demons that none of them could pronounce. Damien had watched. He wasn't going to wuss out, not with 10 of his friends active in the chat. He watched without interruption, even as it got later and later because his parents had become a little more lenient during the pandemic and staying up longer wasn't an issue. Normally he would have had to go to bed right about when the ghost in the movie showed its face the first time. Damien would have had to get off the laptop long before that, the 'no technology after 9:30 p.m.' rule he had been so irritated about alive and well before the days of social distancing and wearing masks everywhere you went had become the norm. Now his mom didn't freak out if he was online late with his friends. Now his dad didn't make a big deal about him posting videos all the time, even if the rest of them were in the background. Because now everything was different. Now online life was real life.

So, Damien watched the movie, and now the images were burned in his head. Creepy ones filled with darkness and strange sounds coming from deep inside someone's throat. He had been thinking about how the sound that the pantry door made was just like that if it was opened really slow when he fell asleep… and then he found himself sitting straight up in bed with a scream threatening to spill from his lips to chase the gasp.

He listened.

Had anyone heard him?

Was his mother rolling over, swinging her feet to the floor to pad into his room and check on him? It had been a long time since that had happened, and if he had anything to do with it, it would never happen again. He was 13 now; they had celebrated his birthday crowded in front of the laptop for half the day, a virtual party with friends and family keeping him rooted in place at the kitchen table so his parents and brother could drop by and say hi to whoever was on screen. It was cool and really weird, and he hoped he didn't have to celebrate another birthday like that ever again. But still and all, he was 13, and he didn't need his mother coming to check on him to see if he had a nightmare like the one when he couldn't find his way out of his closet or the one where the ice cream truck driver had no face. Those dreams might have seemed silly to his teenaged self but they were legitimate nightmares, ones that had wrenched him from his sleep, ones that had caused him to scream his mother's name. Terribly dark nightmares. And that was what he'd had just then... wasn't it?

He listened closer. Holding his breath.

Nothing but Lil Watt's voice, muffled and low.

Good.

He ran a hand over his face and sighed. It was too early to just stay up and wait until morning like his irrational mind wanted to—it would just as soon not meet the thing that had woken him up again. Besides, school-work still had to be done—virtual school or not. It was the one thing his mom made a stink about, but if he got it done early in the day, she let him do what he wanted afterward. He didn't want to give her a reason to change that.

Damien sighed and laid back down, the covers sticking to him more now than before. He wriggled into his go-to sleep position and, taking a deep breath, slammed his eyes shut. He was going back to sleep. He was. It was going to happen.

...

His eyes opened without him wanting them to, moving on their own, his vision changing from the nothingness of the back of his eyelids to his bedroom even as he tried keep them closed.

Damien sighed, said something he would never admit to, and tried again, but he couldn't keep his eyes closed for longer than a few seconds. He looked at the clock, but what he saw didn't make much sense.

3:62 a.m.

Yeah, ok.

He rubbed his eyes, trying to clear them, was about to look at the clock again, when he heard laughter coming from his brother's room. Laughter over a beat. Loud laughter over a loud beat.

He sucked his teeth. It was too loud. His mom would definitely hear it if he kept it up, and she would crack down on music overnight, using earbuds, whatever she was in the mood for at the moment. That would trickle down to him too—he had suffered enough restrictions that his brother had earned to know it would, it definitely, absolutely would—and Damien didn't want that. He liked his life right now. Sure, not being able to go out and do the stuff he liked to do stank, and the Xbox was getting old, but for the most part, his parents were being cool about a lot more than they would have been pre-crazy world. But Jared might mess that up. Damien couldn't have that.

Damien got up from bed and raced to Jared's room almost as if floating on air. He was trying to be quiet, stealthy, and quick. He was all of those things and more, he noticed, as he opened the door and found himself standing somewhere entirely different than expected instead of his brother's messy room. Instead of clothes strewn all over the floor, Damien saw a game cabinet, one of those old-time stand-up machines from the 80s where you shot a centipede and dodged spiders and hid under mushrooms while wasps dive-bombed you. Instead of colored LED lights rimming the ceiling—Jared's pandemic project—he saw a black-lit miniature golf course with colorful neon paintings on the walls.

"Wha-?" Damien started, speaking out loud in wonder as he took it all in. The arcade was busy; clumps of kids stood in the simulator line, others waited for the indoor bumper cars. His brother was standing with his friends laughing at something, and Damien was suddenly sure it was him. He looked down at himself, confident that he was standing in the arcade with his pajamas on or worse, naked, some sleepwalking gene awakening in him at the worst possible time. But no. He had on one of his favorite outfits, too, so that wasn't it. He touched his hair, remembering the COVID-cut his mother had tried to give him before just letting it grow, but no, his fade felt tight under his hand. It wasn't him. He couldn't stop himself from sighing in relief.

Damien turned his head to see who the poor, unfortunate soul was and saw the back of a girl with a huge mallet in her hand. She was standing in front of a tall pillar that had lights on both sides of it and a digital gauge in the center. It reminded Damien of the high striker that he saw at the travelling carnivals that used to set up camp in the far corner of the old mall's parking lot, only that one wasn't digital. It had a little piece of metal that, once you hit the pad with the mallet, would shoot up through the channel toward the bell waiting at the top. He used to beg his dad to hit it, to show everyone how strong he was, and once he even made the bell ring. He walked around the rest of the day with a smile on his face. He could feel a similar smile breaking out there now.

Because this girl... she was... wow.

She was dressed like everyone else was—jeans, a hoodie, Vans, but the jeans had lace patches on them and the hoodie was some kind tie-dye pattern in orange and yellow and red... maybe a sunburst or something... and the Vans were orange-on-orange checkerboard. Her hair was braided or twisted or whatever, cascading down her back before a hair tie caught it. She wasn't wearing anything that made her stand out, and he couldn't even see her face, but Damien knew somehow that she was amazing. She was fantastic. She was important.

"Hey," Damien heard from somewhere behind him, next to him, all around him, but he knew it wasn't directed at him. He knew that he wasn't supposed to answer; he wondered if he had said it himself, even. He looked at the girl and knew he wasn't supposed to look away—that if he did it would be the worst mistake of his life.

Time slowed down as she turned, the way the shopping carts in the supermarket slowed and sometimes stuck when they encountered a rock in their path. It took forever, this turning around, and he thought he might scream if she didn't get it over with already, if she didn't turn around all the way so he could see her face.

Then he realized he was still looking... still looking at a girl he didn't know—who didn't even know he was standing there. And he wanted to avert his eyes, he wanted to look somewhere else... anywhere else. Because if she turned around and caught him staring at her she might... she might...what *would* she do?

She turned...

Her eyes were oval-shaped and chocolate brown with long eyelashes that curled at the ends and looked like she was wearing makeup on them but she wasn't, and he didn't understand because he had never noticed anything like that about anyone before, and he wondered if she noticed that he was still staring because he was and –

"...and?" Chris said, cramming chips into his mouth, one hand on the Xbox controller, Damien's voice a little louder in his ear than he wanted it to be but, his headset was spotty to begin with, so whatever. The tournament was coming up, and Damien had just started talking about real stuff in the practice room. Chris hoped they didn't have to postpone.

"That's it, man. Then I woke up." Damien still sounded tired but at 1:00 p.m., he had been up for an hour already.

"You only saw her eyes, though? How could you only see one part of her face?" Chris asked incredulously. The way Damien was describing it, it was if her face had scrolled down like an unravelling roll of paper and then gotten stuck right under the eyes.

"It was like her nose and mouth were like, fuzzed out? I don't know how else to explain it. It was like they weren't there."

"That's creepy."

Damien's response was noncommittal, nothing more than a grunt, really. Because while he understood why Chris might think it sounded creepy, he remembered how he felt when he saw her, how he knew he was supposed to be standing there right there, right then. Nothing about it had been creepy at all.

"... right? Like that lucid dream thing we learned about in class. But you went to the *arcade*? I mean, if I could pick where I went in my dreams I'd go to a Ferrari dealership and test drive one," Chris said and Damien could see him weaving the Ferrari he was going to use in the tournament onscreen as he spoke. "Or maybe Wakanda."

"Please tell me you're joking," Damien groaned, wondering how much of what his best friend had been saying he'd missed as memories of some dude who had tattooed the word 'Wakanda' in glowing ink on the inside of his lip flooded his head.

"What?" Chris asked, his car zigzagging on the track, virtually warming up the tires for the race.

"It's not real, my guy."

"Yeah, but none of it is. It's a dream. So, why not do something you can't do in real life?"

Chris snickered under his breath, but it was still loud and clear in Damien's headset.

"This dude went to the *arcade*."

"Whatever, man," he said, ready to stop talking about last night's dream or the girl or the weirdness that surrounded her. But he didn't forget. Even as they entered the tournament and summarily whipped two teams back to back, he didn't forget.

An article out of some online magazine out of the UK said he should go to sleep on a schedule, so he did. A medical reference said he could tell himself he was going to have a lucid dream and that suggestion might work after a while. A guy he met in an online gaming meet-up asked him how he didn't know *this* wasn't the actual dream and while that was weird, continued conversation revealed some ways to check, and that constantly practicing those would help him if he was ever able to get back into that state. This garnered a fair amount of laughter from Jared, though, so Damien kept his practicing down to a minimum. He even gave up electronics right before bed because a doctor in Australia said it could help induce lucid dreams.

He tried.

And tried.

And tried.
Almost gave up.
But then he remembered her eyes.
And tried again.

~

"No, that's water. You can live like 11 days without sleep."

"But what actually kills you? How do you die from not sleeping? I don't understand."

Damien was raising his voice but he didn't mean to. It was just that everything was so quiet in the house. His mother and father were in bed, and Jared had actually come to his room to talk. Even in his fatigue-induced haze, or perhaps because of it, he realized that it had been a long time since he and his brother had just talked without it being orchestrated by their parents.

Jared didn't pull any punches. He told Damien he looked like he hadn't slept in days, told him that he knew he had taken some of his Red Bull stash, and could smell the coffee on his breath. Damien didn't have the energy to argue.

"I don't know, man," Jared answered, rubbing the back of his neck. *He* was tired, so he knew his brother was... in fact, he felt like if they were quiet for a few minutes he would fall asleep right there. Why wouldn't Damien? He could see that he wanted to—he was almost asleep on his feet. What was stopping him?

"There's a word for it," Jared continued, looking at Damien through red, scratchy eyes. "Something that means you stop being able to figure out what is real and what isn't."

"Yeah, derealization, I know," Damien said irritably. He pressed his finger into his opposite palm, driving his nail into the skin, watching what happened intently. If his finger stayed on the outside it was ok, everything was ok because he knew that world, knew what should happen in it. If his finger went through...

That guy in the meet-up told him this would help... said it was a sure-fire way to know...

A crescent moon-shaped indent formed on the inside of his hand.

He sighed.

"Still awake... I hope."

Jared stared at his little brother, unable to find words to help, unable to ask anything except why.

"I-I can't go back," Damien said, asking the unanswered question in Jared's eyes. "I can't see her again because... because she might..."

Damien's shoulders slumped, and he covered his eyes with his hand. Jared sat up in his chair, leaning toward his brother who had never acted like this before, had never frightened him so badly before.

He was quiet.

Jared waited until he could wait no longer.

"She..? She who? She might what? Come on, D. Tell me."

"I saw her again, a couple times after that day," Damien started. "At first we just played games. We would go away from the others—you were there—and we would play the old games, you know the ones Mom and Dad like. She was good at Frogger. Really good. She could get on those logs faster than I could. Then we would shoot hoops, and I would beat her, but not all the time. She was good at that too. In the beginning it was just like that. We would play games and laugh and then I would wake up and try to get back in but I couldn't. But then I *could* get in, and it was all good. She was always right there waiting for me to come back in. But then she wasn't her anymore."

"What do you mean?" Jared wasn't tired anymore. He was somewhere between confused and scared to death.

"She was different. Older. But she still smiled at me. And once I could see her whole face I realized she was the most beautiful woman I had ever seen. And she would take my hand and run with me and look up to me because I wasn't really me anymore either, and then we were watching a sunset and then we were holding hands on the beach. Then she was smiling with a baby in her arms and then she was crying in some kind of auditorium. And she was older every time and still beautiful to me. I could feel myself smiling back at her and laughing with her and crying too. I tried to go in all the time but could only get in every once in a while. I guess that article was true—they said once a month if you're lucky. But I don't know if this is luck or what because she..."

Damien took a deep breath and shook his head, unable to meet his brother's eyes.

"She... the last time I saw her she was old. Really old. And she was looking at me differently. She was looking *down* at me, man..."

Damien didn't say anything else because from somewhere behind him, next to him, all around him, he heard someone speaking... just one word... but as clear as a bell.

"Hey."

The girl in front of him, dressed in a bright colored hoodie sporting bantu knots was standing in front of Space Invaders Frenzy. He could hear the rapid-fire shooting coming from The Walking Dead arcade game next to them, could hear people laughing and talking all over the place, and it all felt so normal. People were getting back to normal and that was good. It had been a long time since people had been able to go out and do something as simple as playing games in an arcade. Damien was suddenly happy to be there, happier than he had ever been to be anywhere in his whole life.

Except for the ringing in his ears, everything was fine.

The girl turned around, head haloed by flashing game lights. Her face mask, a homemade tie-dye job in yellow and orange and red, had one word written in the center in fancy script:

Forever

MINE

Five-ten, golden skin, longish black hair, brown eyes, thin nose, high cheekbones, plump lips, medium build, rounded shoulders, hairless chest, tan nipples. Inny. Above average-sized member. Muscular thighs. Muscular calves. Average-sized feet.

Pretty.

She took a deep breath; this had to be done right the first time.

She opened his sleeve, watched as his hair fell out of place to cover one eye.

Very pretty.

"You don't want to look some more? You've only seen the one," he said from the back of the store, but she ignored him. She didn't need to see any others. This was the one.

"What kind of voice box does this one have?" Her voice sounded breathy, even to herself.

"Whatever you want," he said, still calling to her from somewhere else, some unseen perch she imagined was littered with food wrappers and smeared with lithium grease. "Tenor, bass, high-pitched, squeaky—whatever you like."

He sounded like he was chewing a particularly tough piece of meat; she could hear the saliva sloshing around in his mouth.

"What's there now?"

Impatient.

"A74?"

Keys clicking.

Spit sloshing.

She ran a hand along his thigh, just at the knee, where the muscle was taut. Good to touch.

"That one's a baritone."

Smooth, silky, warm.

Yes.

"I'll take it."

She looked up at him, his lips slightly pouty, straight face slightly stern. Resting bitch face.

Perfect.

Paid.

Prepped.

Alone in the back room. The staging room. Could try him out here if she wanted, he said. Private, private except for the peep holes he had likely drilled in every wall.

She looked at her phone one more time to make sure she knew what to say. The rules said she couldn't read it from the screen: it had to be recited from memory. The rules said she could only say it once and that if she made any mistakes, it wouldn't work, not on this one. And she wanted this one, with the tiniest mole on his neck and the long, slender piano playing fingers. She only wanted this one.

She looked at him once more, this time imagining him dressed in all black – slacks, a button-up open at the neck, jacket. He would look like the clothes had been made with him in mind, cut to fit the curves of his body exclusively. The thought of how the shirt would allow glimpses of his collarbones, how it would anchor the column of his neck made her turn away in embarrassment more than his nakedness did. She wanted to see him that way, wanted to touch his neck, run her hands along those collarbones and down his back, letting her fingers dip into the gentle V that his shoulder blades created.

She needed to.

She cleared her throat.

She started.

"Spells and bells, coattails and entrails, speak ye my name in thy soul once became…"

She closed her eyes to finish the magic they had promised would work, afraid to watch, afraid to see if they had been wrong. She spoke the words she remembered and then waited. And then there was silence. Quiet—not even the sound of her breath broke through. Until...

"Your name, my elixir and for you, no more pain."

Rich.

Full-bodied.

His voice was as melodic as she had hoped it would be.

She opened her eyes to look into his attentive grays, to view his lopsided smile, lips parted to reveal perfect teeth, and said simply,

"Mine."

THE GARAGE DOOR

There's something to be said about the stamina of a 4-year-old.

People are always saying, 'I wish I could bottle some of that energy,' or some other annoying little comment that always strikes me as hollow. Those cute little one-offs always made people sound like they were just trying to find something nice to say to draw attention from the fact that the kid in question is acting like he's hopped up on something. The 'I've been where you are' comment that older ladies say to young mothers when their children run wild in the aisles of department stores, or when they eat all of the grapes before they are paid for, or, and this is priceless, when Junior decides it's time for America Idol tryouts at the deli counter, is really judgment thinly veiled as commiseration. *Tsk tsk* that seemingly understanding smile really says. *Get your shit together, Miss.* But of all the offhanded comments made by spectators of the parental variety show, that one rings true. Now, as the mother of three, shall we say, spirited children, I do want to bottle that energy. I'd sell it to folks in their fifties who are just starting to realize that the flexibility from their youth is never coming back. I'd sell it to people trying to lose weight; jumping around like the energizer bunny from sunup to sundown will surely do the trick. I'd sell it to anyone who wanted it and make a mint. Even at $1 a bottle, I'd be a millionaire within days. But one of life's cruel jokes is that you can't bottle it. You can't put it in the freezer to defrost when you really need it. All you can do it use it when you have it.

My 4-year-old understands that concept really well.

I thought maybe we could watch a little TV after music class and a play date at the park. Thought just maybe we could relax a little before naptime when I would, inevitably, fall asleep too, missing my chance to get something done. There's only a short window between having one wild thing in the house and three—just about an hour and a half. I try to vacuum, do some laundry, clean up, start dinner, and sit down for 10 minutes in that time. Sometimes I can get one or two things on the list done, but on days like today, when Mr. Baby is excited about everything he sees, I don't do anything but sleep. So I sigh, as my eyes get heavy, and settle in to a nice recline on the couch, watching Nick wind down like a top losing its juice. I didn't realize I was lying down until he climbed on top of me and got comfortable, his head on my chest, his soft hair tickling my nose. Maybe we'll just stay here on the couch for our nap instead of trudging upstairs to the bedroom. The TV's on, but that's ok. It's on a kiddie channel, so there's no chance of us waking up to a mob movie or something like that. As Nick put his arms around me, his clammy skin sticking to mine, feeling good in a way that only moms know, I decided that yeah, a nap on the sofa with my little guy would be perfect.

The sound of the garage door opening should have woken me up, but it didn't.

Oh, I heard it (its low hum is unmistakable through our paper-thin walls), but I didn't wake up. I should have—the door opening in the middle of the day is unusual to say the least. My other two kids don't get out of school for hours, and Chris isn't due home from work until after six. More disturbing is the fact that knowing these things, I still didn't get up. Someone could be breaking in. Or what if we overslept and the kids were opening the door with the keypad? What if someone was *making* them open the door with the keypad? For some reason, in that place between deep sleep and awake, I didn't think either of those things was happening. I just figured it was Chris. He was home early, and that was all it was. Some part of my subconscious wondered why he was home early —slow day at work; playing hooky; laid off?—but didn't care enough to wake my body up to find out.

At first.

Chris took a long time getting into the house. In fact, I never heard him come inside, but I heard him moving around. That was weird because I could hear Nick's rhythmic breathing, could feel his hair under my nose if I reached for the sensation like a swimmer coasting to the surface for a breath of fresh air. But the door didn't unlock, and the alarm didn't announce his arrival with a beep. He was just there all of a sudden, puttering around in the room. I heard him drop a bag, then unzip it and rummage around inside. I heard the volume on the television turn up— one of those incessant cartoon jingles blaring suddenly, ramming the sugary-sweet lyrics about being four and, each day, growing some more down my ear canal, as if I couldn't already recite them in my sleep. I heard footsteps, Chris' socked feet approaching Nick and me on the sofa to kiss our heads like he always does when he finds us asleep on lazy weekends. I could feel myself straining towards his lips, expectantly reaching for his touch. But none came. Instead I heard raspy breathing overlaying a sickening whine—barely audible, but there, persistently there. It was so primal it affected my soul. I felt the heat from his skin as he stood over me, leaning in to peer into my face. I heard him lick his lips, his tongue flicking out like a snake's over dry lips.

That was enough to get my attention.

It wasn't that I hadn't heard ragged breath from Chris before. It had been a while, but not that long. Something about this sound, the base desperation in it, made me feel different. The usual butterflies in my stomach followed closely by warmth cascading down past my navel didn't happen. Instead I felt a sensation that I couldn't really put a finger on. Edginess? Maybe. Fear? I didn't want to admit that.

I tried to open my eyes; ready to tell him about the weirdness that started the moment he came home. He would appreciate it for what it was —an overactive imagination going full tilt. I chastised myself. It was obviously because of Nick's clammy skin and the drool that had slipped out of his mouth and onto my skin. That's why I was thinking about a wolf or a dog that we don't have, or some other panting, heavy breathing thing. He would laugh and hug me the way I like, and everything would be fine. If I'm lucky, maybe I can slip out from under Nick without waking him and have a little play date of my own. But I couldn't get my eyes to obey me. They were stuck together so well, it was as if they had been glued. I couldn't stop my mind from going to a place I had hoped I would forget. When in the dim room blanketed by humidity so stifling it was tangible and surrounded by the sickeningly sweet-smelling combination of fresh flowers and cheap perfume, I must have been the only one to see the glue giving way on Uncle Wally's eyes, the whites (well, grays considering his state of repose) winking out at me. But this time my memory of that day distorted into something far worse. Uncle Wally's right eye opened all the way, blinked, and then he turned his head toward me, his neck popping and cracking as he did it.

I tried to scream. I knew I would scare Nick and ruin any chance of having a little afternoon happy, but I needed to wake up and in a hurry. Before Uncle Wally decided to get out of the coffin and come see me. But I couldn't. I felt like my mouth was open, but there was no sound coming from my stretched vocal cords. I tried to sit up, to shake myself out of this crazy vision (oh God, why is Uncle Wally smiling?), but I couldn't move. I started to panic. I could still hear that feral breathing over me, like an animal waiting for the right time to pounce. I could see Uncle Wally lifting his head out of the coffin, his body slow to react, but moving, nonetheless. I imagined that Nick, my sweet little boy, was staring at me as I struggled, his face unreadable, impassive... cold.

I screamed.

I screamed long and loud. But that's not what I heard. The smallest, weakest crescendo emitted from my lips, building to a faint whimper, before all my limbs jumped to attention at one time. The jerk snapped me out of whatever spell I was under. It also woke Nick, my beautiful, still asleep and not staring at his mom like she was an experiment boy, up.

"Mommy! No!" He protested groggily. I kissed him on his head, the action making me acutely aware of the fact that we were alone in the room, and laid him down on the sofa. Children have an uncanny ability to fall back to sleep right away as though nothing happened. I was grateful for that today.

The room was still. I don't know why, but that made me uneasy. I mean, it should have been still if there was really only Nick and me at home, but just seconds before, I knew someone was in the room with me. Knew, not felt. And now there was no one here.

Was this a game? I almost let myself buy into that as I stood tentatively and peered into the kitchen. Hide and seek maybe? Come find me, and quick so we can steal a couple of minutes to ourselves? I wanted to believe that. But as I saw the red Virginia clay on the floor leading from the family room—from the very sofa Nick and I were on—to the garage I knew it wasn't true.

I thought I had shut my eyes. I imagined I was standing in the family room, facing the dining room, imagined I was still waiting for Chris to pop out and whisk me to the bedroom. It was safer than where I ended up. But the door handle beneath my outstretched hand couldn't be ignored. Neither could the hot air that hit me in the face like a blast from an oven when I opened the door. I tried to shut my eyes then, tried to will away the sight of it all. But I couldn't. Partly because it didn't make sense. Chris' car would have been in the place where his shoe lay on its side. It would have filled the space where his leg bent obscenely under his body if he had come home. But he didn't come home, did he? He was still at work.

Chris' eyes were cloudy, his beautiful brown covered in a white film. That doesn't happen right away, the part of my mind that was fighting off the paralysis fear was trying to impose, rationalized. It takes at least a couple of hours for that to happen, right?

I stood there trying to figure out what I was looking at, my mind flitting back and forth between thinking it was an elaborate dream or if I was standing on some alternative plane, where reality was just a little different than the one I am from. I was in the zone; sweat coating my brow as I tried to make sense of the scene playing out in my garage, when the shuffling of feet brought me back to reality. And Chris was still there.

"Mommy, I don't wanna be 'wake," Nick said rubbing his eyes, the beginnings of a major pout sprouting on his lips. I looked at him, his hair all over his head, his eyes squinted against the light, and then back into the garage at the man I planned to spend the rest of my life with, and bit my lip. I wanted to keep biting and biting until I drew blood. Maybe that would snap me out of it. Maybe the dead Chris would disappear.

I didn't want Nick to see anything, so I closed the garage door. With any luck I could keep him away from the garage until everything was said and done and Chris had been moved.

Uncle Wally's joyless smile nagged at me.

I bit my lip a little harder than usual (just in case) and let the sob that was rushing from my throat turn into a yawn.

"Me either, baby. Me either."

HOME PARTY

You gotta be kidding me.

The front of the trailer was barely visible beneath the overgrown bushes, if they could even be called bushes. They looked like the stuff that grows at the base of trees, wispy and vine-like, with pathetic little leaves that were more brown than green. Camo green. They covered the front of the trailer in clumps, like someone tried to fashion them into bushes years ago but gave up the effort and let them grow wild. Where there weren't switch-type bushes, there were bins of empty beer cans. Four of them on the splintered porch and at least three in the tall grass that made up the yard. The place stank of beer, piss, and sweat.

Carrie looked at the place, noting that two of the windows facing the front of the house were boarded up, and that the window in what might be the kitchen was so tiny, it was hard to see into. But was someone looking out? She looked around the yard. Given the state of the house, she expected there to be a bunch of discarded, rusted out cars littering the lawn, but that cliché didn't fit. There was an older model Ford, but aside from faded paint and an ancient dent on the passenger side, it had been kept up. There was a sticker in the back window from the local college. There was also a brand new pickup truck. All this was odd, but not *that* odd. They could have needed a pickup for work and maybe it isn't really new... just new to them. The Ford made total sense—a college student paying for something herself. You get what you need. That explained the

175

beer cans too, and maybe even the boarded-up windows. One party with college kids could produce half the amount of bottles in those bins. And what's a good college party without a broken window?

But as she sat in the car, trying to rationalize everything she was seeing, she didn't believe it. The trailer didn't feel like a college hangout or a hauler's dive to crash in when he wasn't working long hours. It felt... wrong. It felt empty, but not because no one lived there. It felt lost.

Carrie swallowed, her mouth going dry while thoughts of crazy hill people of the Texas Chainsaw Massacre variety ran through her head. She forced a self-deprecating smile and got out of the car. *It's no mansion, but it's someone's house,* she told herself, and allowed for a hint of reproach to show in her inner voice. She had never been one to judge a book by its cover, as the saying goes, and she wasn't going to allow herself to start now. She straightened her smart blazer, red for the season and a perfect accompaniment to the new product line she toted with her to this afternoon's soirée. She has been excited about showing the new bags to this group of people. The lottery she posted in the local nail salon gave her entrants who wanted to have a home party and look at the new catalog items. Michele Davenport, resident at this trailer, was the lucky winner. After weeks of excited conversations, party day was here. And alone in the gravel driveway of a broken down trailer stood Carrie.

It was quiet for mid afternoon.

Carrie got back in the car, suddenly spooked. She looked at her watch. 1:30. She was supposed to get there a half an hour early, and she was late. She got stuck behind Sunday drivers on the two-lane road leading to the place and got there with only ten minutes to set up. And she ate half of that time up staring at the trailer.

Maybe there was no one there. If there was, surely they would have heard her car idling, would have seen her sitting there. As annoying as that would be (driving 45 minutes to get stood up was not her idea of a fun afternoon), Carrie didn't really want to go in the trailer. In fact, she thought, *come hell or high water, I'm not getting in the trailer.* There was something in the trailer that she didn't want to see. Something that was watching her, waiting for her to knock on the door, to look too closely at that little window in what might have been the kitchen. She could almost hear it breathing; a wet, phlegm sound that made her skin crawl. And it was watching her. It had been watching her the whole time.

Carrie turned the car on and put it in gear without looking back at that window. She didn't see the front door open, didn't see the college student's odd, slow gait toward the car. She didn't see what trailed behind her, coloring the high grass. Carrie threw her arm over the passenger seat to back out of the driveway, but a car parked her in. Laughing ladies in the front seat smiled at her, excited about the party, the games, the goodies. She didn't see the larger of the two lick her fingers as she pulled herself out of the car.

CAUGHT

Its bulbous eye rolled its way back over to me, staring at me appraisingly, almost lasciviously. It could smell me, that much I knew; the scent of my fear was attacking my own nostrils, so I was sure it could smell me too from where it stood.

Right on the other side of the glass.

Locked between the entrance and exit—caught just like I was… almost close enough to touch.

Could they see it? The ones trying to trip the sensor, to bypass the lock and release the doors? No, they couldn't possibly. If they did, they wouldn't work so hard to get me out even if that meant they'd have to watch me die in here, the glass giving them a front row seat to my suffocation or starvation, whichever came first. No one would let something like that loose in the night, not when they couldn't be sure it wouldn't turn around and train its murderous stare on them.

Would my eyes bulge when it wrenched the life from me, wrapping its huge hands, hands as big as potato sacks—hands bigger than anything I could ever imagine—around my throat to squeeze? Would my tongue protrude? Would it stay there, distended in death to turn purple then black? Would my bowels give way, leaving a mess for the cleaning crew to deal with… my final *fuck you*?

Probably.

And wouldn't that serve them right for letting me die in here, making me pay the ultimate price for the stupidest of mistakes ever recorded? Because it was recorded, sure it was—there are cameras everywhere these days. And the guys watching the display—the two-man security faction in place during the light foot traffic hours sitting in a room the size of a closet and watching shitty black and white monitors rippling with inter-ference every few seconds—probably laughed their asses off while I, lost in thought, walked in a circle, following the door as it crawled, spinning slowly enough to go gray waiting for it to come back around. I ignored the exit not once or twice, but four times only to find myself locked in the revolving door of an aging hotel, one that had sprung for motion sensors but had neglected to actually put one *inside* the contraption. What was on my mind that was so important escapes me now as I listen to the obscene licking of lips, spitty and wet, and hear the hiss and sizzle as saliva falls to the floor, burning it like acid—something about changing my clothes before the night's festivities, or—no, it wasn't just that. That's not enough to make you walk around in a circle, passing go but saying screw your rightfully earned $200...

I know full well what I was thinking about and maybe, just maybe, I deserve this shit because of it.

The men outside the revolving door had brought out the power tools now.

Someone had the company that manufactured the deathtrap on the phone, but at this hour—pre-witching hour, but dead of night still the same—they were likely talking to the poor sap saddled with overnights... the one who hadn't needed to handle a trouble call in years.

That bulbous eye is looking at me again, sending the visual to its brain to devour.

I stare back, unable to look away though my mind begs me to, trying to chant it out of existence even as its saliva burns through the metal at the bottom of the door.

SENSORY BOWL

"Eggs," Darryl said matter-of-factly, like he knew everything about everything. "They use eggs for the eyeballs."

"No, they don't," Sherry said, coming back just as confidently and with a hint of irritation that would grow sharper when she moved into her teenage years, morphing into a kind of condescension that could bring a man to his knees. "They use mozzarella for that. The fresh kind. You know, the stuff that comes packed in water?"

Darryl *didn't* know—that much was clear by just looking at his face—but he wasn't willing to admit it out loud. I didn't know either, couldn't even call the memory of seeing cheese in water before, let alone how they could use it for eyeballs. I mean, what? Did they take the slices and roll them into balls or something?

"No, they don't," Darryl said, but when he said it, he sounded like every bit the twelve-year-old he was, obstinate and adolescent. Not like Sherry, who sounded mature and smart. Not like Sherry, who was twelve just like they were, even a few months younger than they were, but seemed three years older, seemed like she was already a teenager, looked like she was already a teenager.

"Are you serious?" Sherry said, a laugh playing on her lips, lips with sparkly lip gloss on them, the one she always put on after she left the house and rounded the corner out of her mother's sight, like now. I didn't get why she hid it—it wasn't like it was lipstick or anything. It wasn't even

180

red. But then I remembered that one day when her mom saw her with it on, called her back to the house, and made her wipe it off. I remember that I looked at Darryl to see if he was hearing what I was hearing. Sherry's mom was yelling at her about it, saying she wasn't allowed to wear it, said she *knew* she wasn't, and how disappointed she was that Sherry had put it on. When she came out, Sherry was embarrassed, but we didn't say anything.

I guess whatever happened between her and her mother didn't matter, though, because her lips were glistening again, catching the light and reflecting it back to me like the stars in the night sky.

"—right, Chef? I mean, I know *you* know."

Know... what?

Know *what*!?

I don't know what she's talking about, wasn't listening to them, not really—at least not right then. I had been looking at them, sure, at least... ok, I had been looking at her, watching her glossy lips as they formed the words, as they formed my name—well, not really my name, but what they called me all the time. Chef. It's stupid, really—the reason they call me Chef. One day after school, they came over to my house because both of their parents had to work late. My mom got pulled into a conference call right before we walked in the door so she hadn't made the snack she had planned to, so I made something instead. It was nothing—just cinnamon sugar chips. Literally four ingredients—cinnamon, sugar, butter, and flour tortillas—but because I knew how to cut them into perfect wedges and how long to cook them in the oven, I would forever be known as Chef. And maybe it stuck because me and my dad watch *MasterChef* every week, and I mean, ok, maybe I have been not-so-secretly hoping for a revival of *Turn Up the Heat* with G. Garvin.

Chef.

Whatever.

"Chef knows, he's just trying not to make you feel stupid out here in these streets," Sherry continued in my silence, mercifully filling the space with her words like she knew I needed her to take the spotlight off me, like she knew I needed her help. She never says my name anymore, I realized. Neither one of them did. They were my best friends in the whole world, and neither of them called me by the name my parents chose for me, the name that I actually really like. Kyle. I don't know any other Kyles, so I feel unique, special.

Kyle Spencer.

An entertainer's name. Maybe an actor's name. Not a football or basketball player—that'll never be me—but it's still a name that might be up in lights one day.

Maybe I'll be on TV.

Maybe I'll have my own *cooking show* on TV...

"-—have to fold you—"

"What?!?"

I spoke before I realized I had planned to, said it louder than I had ever intended to. But if Darryl had been stupid enough to threaten Sherry, well, I wasn't just going to stand by and let that happen. We were best friends. She was, I mean she was *Sherry*. Silly, opinionated, pretty—

Wait, wh—

Darryl was laughing.

Sherry was laughing.

Darryl and Sherry were laughing.

Together.

Hands on shoulders, hands over mouths, hands covering stomachs, and resting on top of knees as they bowled over, laughter shaking their bodies.

"You—you should see your face," Darryl said between breaths snatched before laughter took over again.

"It was like you woke up from one of those dreams, the ones where you can't move and you're all freaked out and you start yelling—"

"Sleep paralysis," Sherry supplied, tears coming to her eyes as she tried to quell her laughter. "Only you were awake. It was crazy."

Laughing. Not fighting. Darryl hadn't been stupid enough to try to hit Sherry. Come to think of it, the voice talking about folding was too high to have been Darryl's in the first place. Too high and too melodic, sweet, lyrical. And totally facetious. Threats of folding people came out of their mouths all the time. The reason why didn't really matter—it was almost like a way to end a disagreement—a closing sentence in a conclusion paragraph. None of them had ever hit the other, unless you called fouls on the court hits. And they never would. They were friends. Friends who had grown up together, respected each other, loved each—

Wait...

"You good, bro?" Darryl said, finally straightening up, his laughter trickling down to a chuckle at the back of his throat.

"Yeah, you ok?" Sherri said, only I heard something different. They weren't words, really, at least not ones that I could pick out. But she sang them, and they danced in the air between us. She sang them, and the breath she used to form them tickled my nose.

No, I'm not ok.

No, I'm not good.

"Yeah," I said instead, getting hold of myself just before my mind betrayed me and professed my undying love to the girl I had known since I was in diapers. Because it *is* love. I know that now. And I am so very screwed.

"W—what are you gonna be?" I said, tearing my eyes away from hers, addressing no one in particular but really, really, really anxious to hear what she was going to say.

"I don't even know," Darryl said, speaking first. He said he didn't know, but he did. He had been planning his costume for longer than he would willingly admit.

"Last one," Sherry said, and a kind of melancholy descended on us, slumping our shoulders a bit, slowing our steps. It hung in the air in front of us, that comment, what it meant. Last one. Last Halloween before we might be too old to show that we cared about Halloween. The last Halloween where we could trick or treat without feeling silly, like little kids. Last one before we became TEENAGERS and started driving and having sex and smoking pot and going to college and getting real jobs.

It was the last one.

"I'm going as The Joker. The new one from the movie," I said, my voice sounding far away in my head.

"You didn't even see the movie," Sherry said, her voice dripping with incredulousness that I might come to hate at some point but right now I loved every bit of it. And yeah, she was right. I hadn't seen the movie. My mom said it was dark, said it was complex and more adult than it should be considering it was about a comic book character. Sherry knew I hadn't seen it because her mom and my mom were besties. Same with Darryl's mom. The three of them met in a Moms club when we were just about a year old—just starting to crawl and knock things over at the playdates they had twice a week. We've done it all together—started school, gone to camp, watched our first scary movie, gone on vacation. And it was good—always good, except we had no secrets. If one of us didn't tell the other about something, our parents told each other and somehow the information got to us. I knew Darryl was afraid of Ben Grimm before he told me because his mother and mine were looking him up in our kitchen one day, trying to figure out what the big deal was. My mom got mad at me when I turned on the Fantastic Four when Darryl was over later that week and even though I tried to play it off like I didn't remember, she knew. Whatever. Darryl kept blocking my shot on the court at recess—had been doing it for a whole month before I decided to make him squirm. Basketball star I am not, but I didn't need my boy showing me up like that. He deserved to piss his pants a little.

"You didn't see *Hellraiser*, but that doesn't stop you from being a pinhead," Darryl said, and I laughed in spite of myself. Because it was right on time. And funny as hell.

Sherry screwed up her face at him and then at me when my laughter broke free from my throat and shot into the air. She hit me then, like she always did when a burn was actually funny but she didn't want to admit it. She hit Darryl too, but I didn't see it. I was too busy feeling the place on my arm where she had struck me tingle, grow warm like it was under a laser. I rubbed it, then covered it with the palm of my hand as if to protect it from the elements. If I didn't think they would notice and call me as sus for it, I would have brought my hand to my lips and kissed it.

"Your mom's going all out for this one," Sherry said, moving on gracefully.

"Yeah, 'cause it really is the last one. The last Halloween party—at least the last one she's gonna throw. She said that when I turn 13, I'm gonna want to go to somebody else's party, do things outside the house."

"She's kinda right," Darryl said, but there was a hint of sadness to it. The Halloween party had been an event we had looked forward to for years. Our house had been the place to be on Halloween since we were babies. We would party together, go trick or treating together, and then come back and watch a scary movie. We graduated from Scooby-Doo to *Goosebumps* in my living room wearing sweaty costumes and stuffing our mouths with candy.

We fell silent, walking at the same pace that we always did, first me, then Sherry, then Darryl in a row. I know what they were thinking, just like they knew what was in my head: everything was about to change. You could almost smell it in the air—there was just no escaping it. And even if we railed against our parents when they didn't let us have take-out when we want or caught attitudes when they asked us if we had homework even though we did, some part of us wasn't ready to let go of candy apples, not-so-scary movies, and freeze dance competitions to "Monster Mash". It was embarrassing, all the decorations and the activity stations our parents set up for face painting, pin the tail on the donkey, and find the creepy crawlies. Sometimes I cringe when I think about what my friends—the ones from school—will think when my dad wins the annual "Thriller" dance competition again, like he does every year because he grew up mimicking Michael Jackson, and he is all too eager to pull out those dance moves even if he has to do so in a ghoul costume. The corny maze in the backyard, the pumpkin stab, the candy sort—it was all kid stuff, but what we weren't saying out loud, what was taking over our minds as we walked to Ms. Elianna's house was that we *wanted* to sit in the middle of the floor sorting our candy while *Goosebumps* played in the background and my dad caught his breath on the sofa. We wanted that because it was as much a part of us as anything else and not having it made us wonder who we were.

"Why'd she make us come all the way over here to get a cauldron? You can get one of those from the store," Sherry asked as we approached the house.

"She said something about art too, something else we're supposed to pick up." We slowed to a stop as if in lockstep, finding ourselves in front of Ms. Elianna's house before we realized it. I didn't know who Ms. Elianna was—none of us did—but we were in front of her house anyway, picking up stuff Mom bought for the Halloween party on the online community garage sale. Stuff for the *last* party.

Ugh.

"Art? How are we gonna get that home?" Darryl asked a little too loudly.

"It can't be that big. She wouldn't have sent us if it was. And it's not like we have to walk a mile—we're like two streets away from the house."

My house, Sherry's house, Darryl's house—all of them were 'the house' because each of them felt just like home.

"Man…"

"Shut up, dude. It's for the party."

Darryl and I cut across the grass but Sherry used the path, making me feel both childish and disrespectful instantly. I wouldn't meet Sherry's eyes, but I could feel them on my face, just knew she was making a face that screamed her disapproval, lips screwed up into some kind of half grimace/ half smile that I didn't fully understand but didn't like the look of anyway.

"That's what's up," I said because I felt like I needed to say something. I pointed my chin in the direction of Ms. Elianna's door and the wreath that hung on it. It reminded me of something I saw on a bumper sticker that said COEXIST in all these symbols I didn't recognize, well, except the peace sign, the yin and yang, and the cross for the 'T'. Mom said it was supposed to show that there's space for everyone. I just liked the way it looked.

The wreath on Ms. Elianna's door kind of looked like the one the sticker used for the 'X' but with more peaks and loops. I found myself trying to follow the loops as they wove around the straight lines that formed points and would have kept doing it even though the sounds of the streets—the birds chirping, gears shifting as cars started up the hill ahead—were fading away, if Sherry hadn't snapped me out of my reverie.

"What?"

"That wreath."

She didn't respond. I was surprised how irritated I was to have to look away from the wreath to see why.

Her face as screwed up again. I was noticing a pattern.

"Hmph."

Lips curled into a side pucker. Hand on her hip.

"What?"

Same face, some posture. I felt the back of my neck getting hot.

"No cap. I like it," I said, and I meant every word.

Sherry rolled her eyes and looked away from me, turning her attention to the wreath. I wanted to tell her not to look at it with that smirk on her face, wanted to warn her that it might not like it.

"I bet your mom is gonna use the cherry pie filling for the blood this time," Darryl said as he mounted the steps toward the front door, oblivious of the exchange between Sherry and me. "It'll be thick and nasty, like congealing blood."

"Ooh, and gummy worms and licorice laces for muscles and tendons," Sherry chimed in, a light switch shutting off whatever unpleasantness existed before.

"Maybe rock candy for brittle bones. She'll mix it all up in the bowl." Darryl actually sounded excited.

It was contagious.

"And don't forget gummy tarant—-," I started but then the door opened without us knocking, and a woman who looked like she was 200 years old stood in the doorway. We had to look down to see her; the bend in her back was that deep. When she spoke, it was no louder than a whisper and Darryl leaned toward her to hear, using his polite voice to ask her to repeat herself, and I wish he hadn't. I wish Darryl hadn't stepped inside to see whatever she was gesturing towards. I wish Sherry hadn't followed, smiling at the old woman and saying she would help Darryl. I wish we were kids again and the last Halloween party was a long way off, so far off that my mom hadn't thought about a way to make this party the best one ever, hadn't tried to give it a big sendoff. I wish I could have passed out before thinking about

Eggs.

Darryl had said they used eggs for the eyeballs in the sensory bowl, but he had been wrong. So had Sherry when she said they used fresh mozzarella. They'd never guess what was really in the bowl... never.

GOODBYE

He heard their footsteps more clearly now; they were right above of him, racing around the top floor in search of the scent that tantalized their nostrils and fueled the pit of desire sitting heavy in their stomachs. They were in search of food, in search of blood. He gathered his papers, documents that would mean nothing if he didn't get out of his sister's renovated home, perpetually under construction. It was a place she had put so much time and work into—a place she would never see finished. He tossed the papers into the tattered duffle bag that sat by the front door and forced the zipper over them and what clothing he could gather before they broke the upstairs window and came inside. They would find enough to occupy themselves upstairs, at least for a few minutes; his niece, his precious Julia, wasn't quite in the throes of death when he'd left her in her bed, knowing it would be the last time he laid eyes on her. Surely, she hadn't died yet. If she had, there would be no hope for escape.

With a fleeting glimpse around the house, his eyes falling on antiques his sister had combed Paris for, their grandmother's rocking chair, his sister's lifeless eyes staring at him from the sofa where she had succumbed, he said goodbye to everyone he held dear. Staying to pick up something—anything—to remember them by would mean certain death. He knew that, logically, but still he eyed the picture of his family on the table next to the sofa. It had fallen over onto its side, knocked there when his sister had stumbled into the room, taking her last steps. He wanted to take the picture with him, to walk the five steps between the foyer and living room and snatch it from the side table, but he couldn't. Walking into the living room would leave him vulnerable to spying eyes on the top floor. As it was, they might be able to see his shadow along the wall from where he stood.

They could be looking at him right now.

Either way, it wouldn't be long before they would know there was someone else in the house. They would smell his blood like they smelled Julia's.

He had to go.

His life depended on it.

The closing door almost spared him the muted shriek escaping Julia's dying lips.

NEXT

Loud.

So loud when he left, the door slamming behind him, echoing throughout the room, bouncing from one side to the other of my head, my brain, my soul.

Gone.

Gone because his job is done.

It is over for him, and he can leave, can run, can distance himself from this forever if he chooses to, really.

But for me, it has just begun.

She looks so pretty there, with her hair haloing her head, brown and thick, curly, glossy.

Healthy.

Liar.

He left without saying anything, nothing at all, actually, not even as she spoke her frustrations, choosing then, then, even then to tell him how she felt. How he failed her. How beneath her he was.

How base.

Fine.

That was her choice.

But didn't he know that I was here? Sure, he did—he saw me at her hem, small there where I had never been small before. He saw me, yet he still left and that, well, that is fine. It has to be. What else can it be now?

The door boomed when he left. Could she hear it where she was?

Where is she?

What is she now that all of this is said and her armor has been laid down, battlement left unguarded?

What am I?

White and gold.

And red.

Her velvet, saturated through, dark red against the wine.

Makes brown.

Like a stain.

Gold bangles to accent skin that won't be the same tomorrow, today, ever again.

He left me there to watch still set and gray color with the hope that osmosis, proximity, divine clarity showed itself between these gilded walls.

Coward.

Bring forth the bejeweled cup and drinketh yourself, you bastard.

Perhaps she had been right about him all along.

Her hair is splayed so beautifully on the floor. Gold and purple hair tinsel thin as filament threaded through, spiraling delicately among the strands: the identity of the royal. So like my own but more in every way... more prevalent, more vibrant, more deserved. I touch my own strands, find the tinsel and pull but it doesn't come, honey's paste secure and the practitioner talented as they are expected to be considering the coif upon which they work.

My ringed fingers twitch, unsure what to touch next.

The eyes of the seer to see.

The tongue of the speaker to speak.

Pray tell which first? Which not at all?

Legs cramped beneath my frock but still I sit as I am destined to do. My place here is written, and I shall not move unless struck down.

But for how long?

How long am I to sit here as I fell, not moving a muscle, feeling my limbs turn to stone, grow cold as the floor, cold as rock, cold as she?

How long?

The books were never read, my lady, the rules never navigated. When does the sexton mark the death knell?

Cold.

Chill in the air from the window open to the world. Cold outside as it is within. Even Mother Nature bends to her will.

Silent.

Quiet as death.

Death outside.

Death inside.

Blood on the ground.

Blood on the floor.

Seeping, pooling, sinking, congealing, permeating, invading, red, red, red death the final and I see, I see I see it from here I see it, I tell you, I see it all.

Sight to blind me.

Sight to school me.

Predator, you fiend, I know you well.

Spare one or none, I no longer care because the tinsel in her hair stays firm even when they would rot out before long, rot out by the heat of the sun. Rot out because rot it must as she no longer is.

But then who is next?

He left because he was supposed to. Prince that he was, from family outside of the province. Never given proper title and oh, did it anger him. 'Twas girl that was born and only one such that he could not kill to take the throne. Ah yes, he left because he cannot stay. And that is fine as well.

I shed my rings. They are of no use to me now.

Imperial Topaz cut in the shape of her mother's tears sitting in the finest Indian gold. Too big for my finger, but I feel it grip me as it slides easily down, slick with blood.

And I sit.

The hills beyond are green in the spring when life buds new all over the land. I see them now, and though they should be covered with grass and flowers that I might pick and bring home for her to smell, to see, to love, they are brown to my veiled eyes. Though life abounds there, I see death, can feel the soil littered with bodies and choking on the blood that waters it relentlessly, forcing it to drink, to fill to the brim, to die along with the one that cultivated it. Go on, then. Die as you might, fickle grass. I shall never see your beauty again, not even the innocence of a tulip will sway my eye. Should I ever get up to see you clearly again, that is. Therefore, it matters not if you die or do not.

Mouth open.

My mouth is open.

Her mouth is open.

Breath tickles my nose.

What comes from the open mouth when the speaker has lost their voice?

Over that hill is the town named for her father's father, or so the story goes. He was beloved there, was a soldier that had saved the town from conquer. In his honor they named it so to remember him by, painted his likeness, and put it on the map.

People care about us, she said.

Then where are they?

I sit.

I wait.

The sun dips behind the hill that marks my territory, and I wait.

Where are these people that care for us so much? Where is the one who should be here to decide what comes next but cannot?

The queen is silenced, I want to yell but know that I should not, because it isn't true, is it?

No, the queen is not silenced, is she? Because she...

The people of old made it so that people could eat, she used to say. Right over that hill stood tall buildings, bridges, and motorized cars. They went to work every day, buying and selling, creating and testing, giving and taking. They had more money than they knew what to do with and spent it all, letting it flow from their hands, their pockets, their bank accounts, like water running from a tap, greed the font. They laughed gaily throughout the night and woke up ill but did it all over again at every week's end. There was theater, and there was shopping, and there were sporting events to rival our own. The rich were so very rich and the poor, in some places, still had enough to fund an existence for the down-trodden our rule were accustomed to. But then he died, and the world stopped.

It froze.

It waited.

It waited for someone to say something, do something. Take over. Take charge. Take initiative.

But the ones who would do so were dead, and the town sank to its knees.

Money burned.

Towers burned.

People burned.

My family left.

Came over the hill and fortified the land to protect them from anyone else who would do so after them.

They waited.

They watched.

The shots in the night used to be numerous, Mother said. And this is what her mother had told her when she was a child. But by the time my mother was old enough to listen for them herself, they were gone. The sounds of the night, the low, wailing hum that accompanied every moment of every day in their beautiful valley, the only sound that was ever heard. And you never heard it, not really. Because it was always there, it was part of the background as much as the zebras that graze in the fields were.

Until it was gone.

Then all you could hear was the absence of it.

Nothingness.

What's over the hill now, Mama?

What do you see, Mama?

Nothing.

Corset too tight.

Mine or hers to loosen first?

Ankle twisted beneath her as she fell, broken bone pressing against skin.

Black and blue.

Bruised when blood flowed.

My ankle aches, bent awkwardly beneath heavy, motionless girth.

Must I mirror or can I move to prevent the ruin, Mama?

Must I be...

... Mama?!?

Flies buzzing overhead.

Flies with little legs that land on anything, everything. Legs with spiked hairs on them, barbed hairs that catch bits and pieces of whatever they landed on and take it with them. Pollen, dander, feces. Carried to and fro, clinging to them as the flies buzzed overhead looking for something new to land on.

I hate flies.

I hate bugs.

I hate their very nature to invade personal space, claiming everything in the world for their own if only for a second, a moment in time. Nasty, dirty, despicable things that carry disease, germs, the blood of enemies, the blood of...

Buzz.

Buzz.

Buzz.

Lands.

Lands on her face.

Rubs its legs together while sitting on her cheek.

Walks into her eye.

I want to swat it way.

Shouldn't I swat it away?

Did she swat away the flies that landed in her mother's eyes? Her father's?

Laying eggs.

I am sure the fly is laying eggs in her eye, and they will fester there, safe, warm, and protected until they hatch. And they'll hatch before the pyre, won't they? Hatch just before she is placed upon it so that all can see the movement beneath the sheet, so that all can imagine them crawling , wriggling free, stretching their newfound wings, rubbing their feet together to rid them of her viscosity.

Twelve hours... maybe 24.

Soon.

She told me of the day her mother was stung by a bee. How she passed out when they took out the stinger and didn't wake up for days, months, years. I was six then and had just swatted a bee when my mother told me that, and I cried and cried, afraid the bee and his whole bee family would come after me for all my days, never letting me rest until they had all stung me to sleep.

Twelve bees... maybe 24.

Life.

Death.

She doesn't blink when the fly dances on her eye, so I blink for her.

She told me I would one day wear the finest silks and lace. I would trot out a handsome man to take as my partner while I sat on the throne. She said I would be ready for love but not ready to lead when my time came, but that it wouldn't matter. I answered no, that time would never come because men were all bores, especially the pretty ones. And as for leading, well on that account she was right. I would bid her goodnight if only to play along with her rhyme. But she always *tsked tsked* me as I spoke and told me she knew more than I did.

Indeed.

I am not ready.

Not ready for love nor ready to lead.

There is no handsome man to stand by the side of my throne. My intended has no interest in the trivialities of the throne. He would rather hunt and gather, go over the hill and make money to bring back to his garden to bury at night. My intended does not know he is my intended at all. He does not know how I watch him as he goes in his travels, reading his commentary of the world so close but yet so far.

Parasocial.

Paranormal.

Parasomnia.

I talk to him while I'm asleep.

He looks like he hears because he smiles and laughs, and oh, when he smiles I can't help but smile too because she had it right on that score, she knew what she was talking about when she said he'd be that, for sure.

Pretty.

So very pretty.

And when he smiles he lights up the room, and his eyes squint, and his face glows.

Eye candy.

And when he laughs he can't breathe, and his body leans to the side, and you hold your breath because all you want to do is laugh too, but you don't know if you should because he doesn't know you, doesn't see you, doesn't hear you, doesn't get you, but oh, he is laughing again, and I can't stop watching.

He likes blue, and I like him so I watch him laugh and chuckle along quietly alongside him from across the kingdom, wondering if he notices. Lots of girls choose him, but he will choose me because I am perfect for him because he is perfect to me.

He is so pretty when he smiles.

My giggle is so loud it is deafening but so quiet I wonder if he can hear.

He will stand beside me as I sit on the throne that is mine, mine, rightfully mine. And he will smile so pretty, and the kingdom will adore him because he looks like he should be adored, and they will throw flowers at his feet, and he will give them all to me because it is me that he serves and will serve forever.

Can you see him, Mama?

Can you see me and him?

I will leave the castle and live by the beach because I love the water and that is where I want to be. The kingdom will be there, and they will throw rose petals at my feet as I walk along the sand. I will kick at the water, and it will tickle my toes in retribution because it loves me and I love it and it is mine and mine alone. And that is how I will spend my days, kicking at the water and watching movies in the sky.

Tell me, Mama, tell me what I am to do now that a skin has formed on your blood as it grows cold there on the white, staining the white, marring it forever and always?

Do I cast out those who would not fight for me?

Do I make my first decree, say something pertinent, something important, something you would never say but that you have already said long ago when you were young and it didn't matter?

Do I call for my love to be by my side because he is mine and not hers, mine and always has been, mine forever?

Perhaps.

But after.

Once my legs no longer feel attached to my body and they are as cold as ice.

Once the sun dips down past the hill and the lights turn on on the other side to glow in the sky.

Once the fly is done playing in your eye and leaves to light on something else.

I once impaled a moth on a toothpick.

I watched it as it wriggled, the throes of death short and sweet.

I showed the toothpick to my mother as she was the only one I thought would look at it and truly see the beauty. She said I should not make it suffer so unless the other moths saw and understood.

Did the moths see and understand? Should I open the chamber and let them pass, giving the queen a wide berth as they looked on, the message hanging before them like a neon sign.

What was the message?

For whom was it written?

I will trail my finger in her blood later and scribe along the white to make matters clear.

I will write it on my body so that I remember too.

War paint.

Tribal markings engraved deep in the skin, deep in the soul.

Contouring.

Mask donned, removable not removed.

She told me once about a tattoo she had that no one knew about. A small thing that looked like a blemish to anyone who might get close enough to see it.

I want to see it.

I want to see it now.

The queen is dead, and I want to see it.

I am the queen, and I want to see it.

I think I shall get one of my own once I know who I am.

I think I shall hide it in the manner of a queen.

My decree: all queens shall get a tattoo that they hide for the rest of their days.

Is that good enough, Mama?

He is back, but I want him to leave.

He is here to light the torches, but I want the darkness.

The white glows against it like a fluorescent. The red is as black as tar.

"Go," I tell him, "for I have not learned all yet. There is more she can give me."

I can feel his concern from here, but I do not move. I do not turn my head. I do not shift.

He does not come closer.

The blood has long ago been cut off from my leg.

Numb feels like something.

Numb feels like nothing.

Nothing hurts.

She told me once to stop doing something if it hurt, but I didn't listen. I did it anyway. I flapped my hand back and forth until my wrist felt it might break; I forced my legs into a split when they didn't want to go.

I stared at the sun even though she told me not to.

It showed me black dots.

It showed me death.

Her blood on white, black as midnight.

My blood.

"Do you see?" I asked the unfortunate who was volunteered to stick her head in and look upon us. "She lies so peacefully."

The woman wants to say something but knows she shouldn't. I could have her tongue if she spoke words I found distasteful. Mother would not have liked that. Mother would not have done that, but I am not mother, cannot be mother, will never be mama. And so she is silent because she knows what is good for her.

Be kind and rewind.

Her mother played hopscotch with mine as children. She thinks that matters to me.

And it does.

If you do the crime, you do the time.

They played hand clapping games on park benches, thick paint, soft from so many coats, covering splintered wood.

Miss Mary Mack Mack Mack
all dressed in black black black
with silver buttons buttons buttons
all down her back back back

She thinks that matters to me.

And it does.

Mama smiled when I missed.

I smiled too.

Maybe we will go over the hill together, my pretty thing and me. Maybe he will put me on his back and carry me over it, and we'll never come back.

Maybe she was the last queen.

Maybe the queen has decided to call it done.

But then where would they get their grain? Their hay? Their wood?

Where would they sing their songs or drink ale as they pleased after a long day in the fields?

What would they do?

What if everyone over here followed me over there, crowding in, dimming the beautiful lights that light up the sky with their numbers?

What would she think when the kingdom was chewed up and spit out?

My hair would be long and straight, pink and purple and turquoise and blue.

I would have lost the gold, it wouldn't have mattered anymore.

And what of it?

What could she do?

She couldn't reprimand me, send me to my room, banish me to the badlands, make me live with the crows. She couldn't ground me, take my access, forbid me to watch my pretty as he goes to the restaurants, the movies, the park making everyone turn their heads, smile at him and hope he deigns to return it. I'd still see him because he'd be on the other side of the hill in my hand, rubbing shoulders with those who walk the sidewalks and wear sundresses and shorts. He'd be there with lights illuminating his face while glasses clanked and silverware clinked against plates. I could speak to him while he ate, his bite my bite because he made it so, showing me everything because he knows I would love it as much as he does. She couldn't stop me even if she could try.

But she can't.

Try.

She couldn't do any of that because the red is on the white, and it is black like the night.

She can't even swat the fly away from her eyes.

One hundred billion stars and she sees every one of them.

Tell me, do they gleam? Do they shimmer, mama? Or are they muted and cold, burnt out?

Do I want to know?

Shadows crawl across the floor, and I hear my breath retreat into my mouth. A new day is dawning outside, and the people over the hill are waking, stretching, yawning.

The house is awake because the queen is awake.

I sit looking at the ring... her ring... my ring and know that my leg will work when I move it from under my body, heavy with responsibility. I know that she has told me everything I needed to know and that I have heard it all.

I know that she is dead.

He comes to the room tentatively again, footsteps outside the door pacing, waiting, milling until I bid him enter. He looks tired, and I know that he will step back. I know that he wants to step back. Leading had never been the thing that he wanted. He had been her handsome man standing next to her while she sat on her throne. And now that she was dead, he would be happy to let the next man come in to perform the duty that was no longer his. And that was fine.

"I rise, father," I say but he doesn't hear me. I move to stand but my legs don't obey. I look at the sky and notice the clouds forming. The pyre will be pretty on this gray day.

"What you want you already have, child," he says without saying it, eyes cascading over me again as they had yesterday.

He does not look at her.

He does not see what I saw move under my gaze.

He does not see…

He leaves again, a heavy sigh causing him to shiver as he walks away from her, away from me… away.

Perhaps, dear father, you were right after all.

Daylight comes, and I can no longer bear to look at her.

She told me this moment would come and here it is. But I cry anyway because I can feel the door closing, the page turning. I can feel my growing pains as she told me I used to as a child, can feel myself growing larger even as she grows smaller, her light extinguished and body changed. And it hurts, and it is real, and I cry. I cry for myself. I cry for her. I cry for the queen.

I hope it pleases her that I now know the steps are my own, just as it was for hers. Her journey was unique as mine will be, and my beginning was epic and noteworthy in its silence, in its bloody residue. As I come out on the other side of the night that was to be the last as I knew it with the common eyes I was so desperate to keep, clarity has been granted. She could no more have helped me than I will help mine when the time comes.

She told me once that I was formidable, and I believe that now. She said I could withstand anything, even the horror of night, and she was right. The red on white is proof of that.

I draw my sword and don't hesitate to make the cut that is required, the cut that is expected. My palm bleeds freely, and that is fine, coating her hand and drenching the floor, my blood mingling with hers spilled so many hours before.

Rusty, oxidized topped with the fresh red of life.

Out with the old and in with the new.

I stand, and it hurts but that is fine. I look at the ring that is now mine, the one that fits me perfectly the way no other has before and know what needs to be done. Movement catches the corner of my eye as it had a moment ago, as it had an hour before.

White.

Small.

Like a grain of rice.
A nothing.
But it is everything in a wink.
The pyre will cleanse it all.
The fire will get them before they get her.
Long live the queen.

COMING

They came in the dark.

Like a mob, they gathered together in motion, moving as one, advancing, coming, coming.

The streetlamp illuminated the face of a neighbor who drank his beer on his front steps and exchanged pleasantries the other day.

A wayward flashlight beam revealed the face of the cashier at the supermarket around the corner.

With guns and bats and chains and knives they came, sure and steady, enjoying the press, the terror, the fear.

Silence from one direction, loud music from the other, rhythmic bass thumping and electric guitar squealing cutting through the silence, warring with each other outside in the dark... deep down beneath the skin.

Voices rising, wrestling for control, out of sync in the din but the message so very clear.

Bang!

The cross was hammered home in the soft grass, on the sterile wall, on the casket lid.

Bang!

The door shook on its hinges, sound erupting in the dead of night.

Bang!

The blood, deafening as it rushed to the head, pressing, beating, pleading.

Bang!

White looks gray against an overcast sky.

Bang!

Branches snap beneath weight they were never meant to hold.

Bang!

Cellphones flash, snapping pictures that will shape history but be too late for security.

Is the lamb's blood painted above the door?

Are the papers in order?

Bang...

ICE CREAM

How does it feel?

She had watched as it happened, saw the color drain from his eyes as his capillaries burst and his skin seemed to rip apart, to disintegrate, the destruction brought by something inside... something that wanted, demanded, required center stage.

Did it hurt, that usurping, that overtaking?

Did it... hurt?

She had watched him go through the stages like she was watching a movie on the silver screen. It was method acting at its finest—a real display of talent if ever there was one, 'Man Afraid to Die' the prompt. He got angry, thrashed as he felt the teeth rip into him, pulling at his flesh to take some away. He screamed in anger as he cut down the one that cost him his life, releasing all that welled up from his stomach to his chest, up his throat to spill out of his mouth in loud, foul torrents. The anger gave way to sobs which brought on tears that hadn't stopped until he breathed his last. He was sad that he was dying, sorry he had hesitated, had turned the wrong corner, had ever moved to the state, wished he'd never bought her an ice cream by the lake... never told her he loved her. He regretted every perceived misstep—wished he'd never laid eyes on her at all, but he had... he had, and his only solace, as his mind fractured under the weight of true understanding of his fate and the poison actively taking root, was that he had exacted revenge. He mourned every decision that he had ever made that brought him to that place, the ones that condemned him, damned him in those final moments.

And then he felt the pain.

But what was it like? The pain… was it searing, like a fire burning the layers of skin one by one, making its way down to the nerves, driving him mad with the relentless heat? Was it cold like winter, numbing and sharp like the tip of an icicle as it pierced the flesh? Did he want to rub at it—the place where he had been bitten—did he want to pull at it, squeeze it the way one might a pimple, rip out the bad?

Did he feel the powder on the back of his tongue, residue from his grinding teeth protesting the loss, the fast-approaching rot? Was it bitter?

Did he feel hot?

Was he sweating? Or was he parched and dry?

Did he smell something sweet?

Did his feet and hands tingle with anticipation? Could he feel his blood slowing in his veins? Could he smell himself, the fecal matter he had prematurely released, the pungent muskiness that was nearly intolerable to breath in?

What was it *like*?

She had asked him. Over and over as she watched the cone—double chocolate and peanut butter fudge—melt on the sidewalk, discarded, forgotten. She had begged him at the end, seeing his eyes cloud over, knowing she was losing her chance to find out.

Drip.

Drip.

Drip.

But he never spoke. The bastard. He never said a thing… at least not when she could hear him over her own screams.

DISC GOLF

It wasn't the red that distracted them, though that would easily have been enough.

Growing there, one small tuft with seeds on the tips, wispy like wheat, waiting for the wind to carry them away so they could take root somewhere else, plant themselves, infest the ground... it looked out of place. It *was* out of place. The place is its now. And even the animals knew it.

Alone.

Left alone to flourish.

To multiply.

But no. It remained small, compact, red blades against the most brilliant green Lori had ever seen. Emerald and basil and pear infected by some poison, some other, some parasitic more.

Red.

Lori opened her mouth to call Kelsey over to see it, but then closed it without making a sound. Because she was already seeing it. They all had to be—the red was almost glowing in the shaded wood, the canopy of leaves above them trapping the light and muting everything else.

Millie had found the car, some rusted out 1950s vintage model that Lori's boyfriend Steve would have flipped over had he come along. But he hadn't come along, and maybe that was good, she found herself thinking. Maybe that was better.

Steve wouldn't have known what it was either. But he would have texted

Matt, and he would have looked it up. He would have tried to find out. He would have gotten help. He would have—

Steve would have touched it.

What would have happened if Steve had touched it?

A gasp.

Billie?

Millie?

Kelsey?

It was loud enough to snap Lori out of her head. Brought her back to the present just in time to pull her outstretched hand away from the red.

Kelsey was looking at a pick-up truck nearby. It looked like it was part of the hill, dirt and moss, grass and roots pulling it in to something that could only be described as a gaping maw compressing, chewing it to digest somewhere deep in its belly, deep underground... below their very feet.

Sarah stared at the net wondering how long the disc had been inside. She could make out the corner of it, thin and yellow underneath the moss and dirt, buried beneath the skeleton of something tiny, something indecipherable on quick glance, but obviously mammal if you dared to stare. It was the disc you used for long distances, the one that could land you within dunking range if you could throw it straight. It had the number 17 scratched on the bottom.

Grace found herself on a bridge staring at the wreckage beneath it: an engine, a rudder, a refrigerator door.

Vials... full, empty, pretty, red.

There were holes in the bridge.

There were holes.

Red, red, everything red.

Pulsing.

Swaying.

Writhing in the wind, dancing to an unheard melody.

Lori started to say something to them all but didn't. She didn't need to. It reached up from the car, out of the cab of the truck, though the netting, up between the slats to caress their faces as red seeds somersaulted in the wind.

IN SERVICE OF HER

It hurts more than she says it will. Especially when she needs.

She's not gentle when she is blinded by want. Nothing she does can trick me into thinking it will be ok, that I'll enjoy it too, even though she tries.

It's the pulling that hurts the worst.

The piercing, the skin giving way to the intruder, the digging for purchase—none of that is as bad as the first pull, the first suck, that coax to get the blood flowing. My muscles fight against it. My very veins draw away, shrinking from it in fear even as my mind bids me stay still. Fighting it is futile. Fighting it only makes it worse.

She doesn't mean to hurt me, but the syringe was a bother. And anyway there was something about the sinking of the teeth into my skin that sent a tingle down her spine, made her sigh. No, she didn't mean to hurt me. Doing so would only hurt her more in the long run. Who would pay the bills, keep the house, keep up appearances? Who would hunt for her, lure the pretty, make them feel like they were important, smart, needed all so that she could have them when she wanted them? Sure, she could find another, someone else to play the familiar and do whatever she wants, but would she find one so willing to bare their neck when she wanted it, to mount on demand and be mounted if commanded? Would she find someone to endure the pain, the vice-like grip that everything that looked beautiful on her offered, the cruel duality of her essence threatening to rip him to shreds? Many would die under such weight. Many would rather kill themselves than endure it more than once. But I am trained. I know when to bark and when to heel.

There's never much to clean up when all is said and done.

And that was good.

And sometimes she smiles on me when she's done, sapphires in pinky rings and thick links of gold mine for the keeping, like the leash around my neck.

I SEE

I see blue skies with cotton ball clouds hanging over my head ready to dump the rain they carry onto me.
    I see pineapples on the vine
    Pumpkins roots crawling, spreading,
    invading
    permeating
    dominating
    waiting.
    Blood oranges pinpricked, crying thick, sappy tears for me to see.
    And
    I
    see flowers with hair for petals,
    eyes that roll in sockets too weak to hold them still.
    Flies land on the lidless things, bite at the flesh, dip their feet in the carnage, let it soak in deep, and then rub them together.
    I see want on her lips,
    blood red and foul,
    smelling of waste and false promises.
    Wipe it away
    Smear it like so much lipstick drawing on pale cheeks.
    A crayon on canvas.

L. MARIE WOOD

Lick the juice from the pocked skin, bitter and sweet to trick the senses
Bittersweet like wool on a summer's day
to trick the mob
to fool the fool.
I see orange light under a black sky and bite my lip
make it bleed
to pay for passage.

THE NEIGHBORS

The sun was hot.

She spiraled her wrist, jostling the ice in her drink, ice that was melting rapidly, watering down what was left of her Arnold Palmer. The ice clinked against the side of the glass, and it was rhythmic; it was mesmerizing, and she wondered about the things that lived between the spaces of each chime.

Clink

Why was her drink called an Arnold Palmer? Just because some golf guy liked a little sweet with his sour didn't mean he should get a drink named after him-

Clink

Why was it so damned hot? It felt like the sun had moved closer to the world, closer to her town, settling right over her house to heat the air, warm her skin, melt her ice—

Clink

What time was it? It was already past noon—she knew that much—so why was it as hot as hell itself in the middle of the afternoon? No, it wasn't even afternoon anymore—it was evening... right? She had finished making tuna pasta salad, had put it in the fridge right before coming out to read. That was at least an hour ago—

Clink

When does evening start? Like, technically? 5 pm... 6? Doesn't the sun have to be setting for it to really be evening? Can you even call it evening if it isn't actually getting dark? What if the sun never rises to be able to set later in the day, like in some part of Alaska during winter?

Clink

Is it Alaska? Where the sun doesn't rise... Alaska, right? Wait maybe that's where the *midnight* sun happens—where it never *sets*—not the other way around. Either way, God! How do they live like that? How can they stand it being light all the time?

Clink

'The midnight sun will never set... it shines forever in my heart...' Who sang that? Billie Holiday? No, her voice wasn't as introspective as Billie's. Dinah Washington? Carmen McRae? No—deeper, haunting. How could I forget! The Divine One. Sarah Vaughan-

Clink

Condensation wet her fingers as her mind twisted and turned, whiling the day away.

The trees whispered answers to her unspoken questions, helping her piece together the puzzles her mind occupied itself with.

Shhhhh

Clink

Shhhhh

Clink

The hair at her temples was damp, sticking to her skin in dark swaths. Dark *yellow* swaths. She knew what they looked like without having to check; she had already caught a glimpse of how wrong the color was in the shower that morning. Near perfect when dry, golden with chestnut highlights and glossy—so very glossy—but when it was wet it was the most ridiculous shade ever. Artificial. Deliberate. Fake. She felt like everyone could see the partitioning, could see where the highlight foil added visual interest. When it was wet the whole damned thing looked like it came out of a box. And even though it did, that was beside the point. It was a damned expensive box, if that's what it came down to, and if Everett wanted her to continue paying for it, he'd better fix this—

Slam

A new sound.

Broke up the ice and tree duet.

Made her jump.

Her Arnold Palmer shot up like a geyser, almost came out of the glass onto her hand.

It was loud—louder than it should have been.

Her neighbor.

Thirty feet between the houses yet the sound was loud enough to rip her away from her thoughts. Now she felt like she could hear everything, every creak of the wood planks on the deck, the whine the chairs made as whoever had come outside laid something upon them. Who was it—Jeff? Or was his name John?

Or… Jack?

Jerry?

Wait… was it Pat?

Mike?

Rick?

Shit.

She had never taken the time to learn their names, commit them to memory. How long had it been—three years since they moved in? They had bought the place after Jason and Kim moved to New York, some new opportunity opening up for her that, for some reason, couldn't be done remotely. She didn't know if she believed that—*everything* was online now. You could have doctor consultations online, order groceries.. You could even do house walk-thrus online now, which is exactly what Jason and Kim had done. There might have been a job opportunity, but it was more likely that they were sick of it all. Tired of the grass, tired of the HOA, tired of having to drive 20 minutes to go shopping, no access to anything but the family movie theater and mom and pop restaurants.

Sick of the sticks.

She sniffed, remembered a conversation in their kitchen a few years back. Jason had said that they were living in suburban hell without the benefits. And yeah, it was true—sometimes she could feel the cows closing in on their little development, the cement sidewalks, identical mailboxes, and paved trails encircling the complex not enough to keep rurality at bay. But for her, the sound of the wind working its way through the leaves beat police sirens and elevated voices any day.

They left, and those people came, and she hadn't been in the house since. Not that she had been over there a lot when Jason and Kim lived there—Jason worked from home and was always on one call or another and Kim… well, she was Kim. But still they had gone over a few times and had the couple over to their house a time or two also, but now Jessica or Jennifer or whatever her name was wasn't letting them in.

Her eyebrow arched reflexively.

Maybe that was a stretch.

Whatever.

The bottom line was that there had been no invitation for drinks or game night. No afternoon chats or sharing a grocery run.

Jeff/Jack/Pat/Mike raised a hand and smiled, all teeth and charm above his tie dye t-shirt.

And that was that.

Who didn't call over to their neighbor and comment on the weather?

Who didn't ask how they've been, offer them a drink, chitchat about garbage pickup or the mailman leaving the mailbox door open or people letting their dogs defecate on their lawn and not picking it up?

All of the other people on the street did... at least the ones on their street. They greeted each other as they walked by, talked while standing on their respective driveways, kids and dogs running circles around their legs. They stopped mowing their lawns to talk about gas prices or the new recycling pick up schedule. They were fucking neighborly.

She was neighborly.

But maybe they weren't like that where they were from.

He was sorting things out on the grill station—from where she sat it looked like seasonings and sauce, maybe some bread or buns. Maybe it was a rub for ribs? She couldn't really tell. She peered closer, dropping her foot from the chair it was propped up on so that she could lean forward lower, closer, nearer.

Not ribs.

Some kind of meat, but not ribs.

She could only see the pink flesh through the new fancy black aluminum balusters they installed. Damned thing looked like a gate. What had been so wrong with the deck railings that were there before? Jason and Kim had had the deck inspected before they put it up for sale, and they were just fine. But no, Jeff/Jack/Pat/Mike and Jessica/Jennifer needed something *different*... something *special*. Just had to waste money on a fancy cedar deck with black rails on the back of their house where nobody would ever see. A fancy deck that looked like a gate. Like bars at a jail. What were they trying to keep in? What were they trying to hide?

"Almost too hot to grill," he said, and she almost didn't hear him. She was fully leaned over by then; the angle of her body was so severe, she was nearly coming out of her seat. Could he see her? Maybe. But maybe not. She had heard he didn't see well from a distance.

She sat up gradually anyway, hoping her movement wouldn't be noticed.

"Y-yes," she stammered as she fought the urge to pat at her hair and smooth her skirt. That was something her mother would have done, her hands always fluttering in an effort to tidy when she got nervous. When had she become like her, patting, fidgeting, fiddling under the weight of a man's stare? She didn't know, and she wouldn't let herself wonder about it too long because to do so would turn her attention to the real question hanging in the air.

He smiled and turned back to his hunk of meat, big and marbled with fat.

Did he smile... or did he smirk?

She was afraid to keep looking and find out.

He was fiddling with the meat—she could almost hear the squelching of the juices as he massaged it smugly, so smugly like he owned the place, could almost smell the seasonings he rubbed into the flesh, the arrogant bastard, could almost smell the blood...

The wife or girlfriend—she didn't even know if they were married—told her that they were from just outside Washington, DC, when they were moving in. The movers had had to work hard that day—there were so many boxes to unload, such many heavy wood pieces to bring in. But there were a few boxes that they wouldn't let anyone touch. A few that only Jessica/Jennifer and Jeff/Jack/Pat/Mike touched. What was in there?

Unmentionables?

She couldn't help but laugh at herself. Unmentionables... what even *was* that? And how old was she all of a sudden? Had sitting out in the sun cooked her brain? There had to be a better word for girly magazines and toys than that, even if it had been a while since she had thought about those kinds of things...

No, that's not the point. What she and William did or didn't do in the bedroom was not the point at all, although some nights, when she was awake and the snoring beside her drove her mad, forced her up and out of the bed, out of the room... sometimes she wondered what the sounds she heard carried on the wind were, sounds that could have been born of pleasure as easily as of agony, sounds that seemed like they were right next to her.

They had a dog.

The day they moved in there was a dog on a leash being led by a little boy. He looked like he might have only been nine years old—the girl, presumably his sister, was a little bit older. The dog was just a baby, a pup of around 4 months by the looks of it. A mutt. A shaggy little thing who would grow into his paws before they knew it and then eat them out of house and home. Like the boy would.

The boy and the puppy would start eating, and eating, and eating, consuming everything they could get their hands on. And it would be so much, too much to keep up with, everything Jessica/Jennifer and Jeff/Jack/Pat/Mike bought would be eaten, sucked in, swallowed whole.

She hadn't seen the dog in a long time.

The boy was two inches taller now than he had been that day.

Was Jeff/Jack/Pat/Mike smiling or was he smirking as he finished massaging the meat and opened the grill lid, effectively blocking her view of him, his house, and everything he wanted to keep secret? Because that's what it was, wasn't it? He was keeping secrets. People like that, ones that keep to themselves, don't invite their neighbors inside, and set their grills up so that they block the world out when they cook – those people are always keeping secrets… aren't they? Hiding behind something like they hide behind the grill lid. But hiding from what? Keeping secrets about what, she wondered? And why? The prospect gave her chills. Were they running from something they did back wherever they came from? They moved in fast after the sale—was that why? Did they take something with them when they left, bring it here, hide it somewhere in the house? Is that why they never invited her over—because she might see—

"I can't believe you're still out here, Mom."

She hadn't noticed the door opening and closing nor her daughter coming out onto the deck, but there she was, dressed in a white sundress that showed off her curves. She remembered when she used to look like that in a dress, remembered when she would let the sun kiss the tops of her shoulders, smiled when it left tan lines there to remember it by. It wasn't that she couldn't wear a sundress now—she could… she exercised four times a week, didn't smoke, didn't drink… much. But it was different now—gravity had had its way, and what a bitch she had been about things.

"What time is it?" she said, sounding as if she were coming out of a fog.

"Almost dinnertime."

She nodded. William had talked about shish kebob. She wondered if he needed help.

"I brought you another drink. I figured yours had to be watered down by now," Krista said cheerfully.

She loved the sound of her daughter's voice. So melodic, so lyrical. She was cavalier, worry-free, stressless, and you could tell. Her voice was airy and light, confident and nonplussed. Like a bird chirping in the sky. She marveled at the thought of her pretty girl with her pretty boyfriend and her pretty life.

She looked into her glass and smiled. She rubbed her hand over her daughter's cheek in thanks.

"Oh look, it's like yours!"

Another Arnold Palmer. Her favorite. A few ice cubes and a wedge of lemon to top it off. And this time William had frozen the cubes fast enough. The iris was still hazel.

BLIP

"What the hell?"

Laurie couldn't stop herself from saying it, even though she'd been trying not to curse as much since life had changed and the kids were now at home during the day. But it was hard, harder than it should have been —harder than she would ever admit out loud that it was. Oh, who was she fooling? Everybody in the house knew she was having a hard time keeping her language PC. Some days she gave up trying before lunch. But this time she had been in the middle of a report, and yes, she had saved it, but not in the past five minutes, and she had been on a roll typing, cutting and pasting, damnit, she was almost finished. So, yeah, she cursed out loud. 'Hell' wasn't as bad as what she almost let slip.

"Nooooooo!" was the call from downstairs from a voice that sounded a lot deeper now than it had when the pandemic started, a voice that was attached to a kid who was also taller than he had been before the world went to hell in handbasket—a kid who was taller than her now. That wasn't saying much with her being all of 5'4", but still. Seven months ago she was looking him in the eye, and now she most definitely was not.

The other one didn't say anything—probably didn't even notice anything because she was on her phone. It seemed like overnight the phone had fused with her hand like an appendage, and even though she couldn't make calls on it yet, she could do everything else: learn makeup tips from people who painted their faces to look like cheetahs and then somehow made it all come together into something beautiful, listen to songs that teetered on the edge of questionable, the lyrics clipped just before parents' ears would perk up and pay attention, fawn over some boy band from another country and learn words that nobody else in the house understood. Thank you, COVID-19, for the premature teenaging.

The hum of the house kicked back on not even three seconds after it turned off, adding insult to injury because she knew it was too damned late to salvage anything. Because Laurie wasn't using her laptop, not right then—she was signed into a meeting on her laptop, but the report she was writing was being created on her desktop. Why? Because she was a dinosaur, that's why, and she was kicking herself for it now. The laptop hummed along during the power surge, only offering a slight hesitation when the power cut off—just enough to miss a word or two from the fast-talking New Yorker who didn't know the answer to the question he had been asked but was trying to talk himself toward some kind of solution anyway. The laptop, thanks to its nifty battery pack, stayed on while her desktop summarily cut off, no fade to black for good ole' Betsy, no, just now you see it, now you don't. When the power came back Betsy waited for Laurie to boot her back up, the old bitch, and Laurie obliged, knowing what she would find—the saved copy of the work she had completed before her coffee break, all formatted and spellchecked to boot—ooh, she could be so anal about things sometimes—but the work she had completed in the past few minutes were gone with the wind.

Laurie remembered when she and Rob had talked about home-schooling—remembered how she was dead set against it. And there were so many reasons to be against it, she thought as she listened to the CPU booting up again, hoping the power stayed on long enough for her to email the document she had been working on to her work email so she could finish it on her laptop, but she had her doubts. There were at least seven other households filled to the gills on her street alone thanks to the pandemic, and that was nothing compared to what it would look like when everybody had to give up the ghost and stay home. They had to vie for connectivity and power all day, things that were usually in abundant supply. When the world was normal, there were only maybe 35 people working from home in their 400-house community. But now, with just about half of her community (which ended up being more representative of her county and even her state than she ever expected) having their kids go to school online at home, there were more people than she could iden- tify by face toiling around in their houses. Sometimes she looked out of her window and saw people taking walks, which was normal under any circumstances, but these were people she had never laid eyes on before. People she had never seen in the supermarket, in the restaurants on what they called restaurant row, the cleaners. Not even in Target, and it seemed like everybody she knew or knew of in her little town ended up in Target at least once a week. When the pandemic hit and people started to work from home or lost their jobs or whatever happened to them, there were people milling about that she hadn't even known existed.

The Punjabi family.

The couple speaking what she thought might have been Dutch and walking at a fast clip no doubt racking up steps on their Fitbits.

The Nigerian grandmother who taught her how to say 'I love you' in Yoruba after Laurie heard her yelling, "Mo ni ife re!" to her children as they drove away (that was before things got too bad. Laurie couldn't help but wonder if she has seen them since, thinks she should maybe check in on the woman to see if she needed anything).

Laurie was also getting used to people's habits—like the guy who drank coffee on his front porch in his bathrobe, come rain or shine, and the kid who rode his bike down the middle of the road, always popping a wheelie where it curved.

Every. Single. Day.

She had even stopped being startled by the family—all five of them... mom, dad, daughter, and two sons, each under the age of 10—who took their daily walk at 2:30 in the morning. Laurie had to believe there was a reason for it being so late—maybe the dad worked the nightshift or the mom worked overnight in one of the big box stores. It couldn't be that they were a bunch of vampires, looking for somebody's blood to suck... right...?

They weren't... hunting for meat yet, were they?

It couldn't have come down to that already... right?

No, of course not. The bigger question, and she had to remind herself about this often enough, was why she was up to see them on their daily jaunt in the first place?

Dogs barked.

Cars passed by.

All seemingly on cue.

Sometimes she felt like whipping her head around fast to try and catch the camera crew recording her life like she was the new Truman in The Truman Show: Pandemic Style. That would be strange, but so was staying six feet away from everybody and wearing masks every time you stepped outside. So was looking up recipes to make hand sanitizer because you can't find any in the stores.

Blip.

Careful Miss, your slip is showing.

Booting up slowly, but booting up.

The boy still yelling downstairs, so close to dropping a curse of his own, she thinks she almost hears it, wonders distantly if she'll say anything about it if it does fall out of his mouth, or if she'll let it slide this time. Rob was lucky he missed all of this stuff, if you could call that lucky. He was usually stuck at work, the firefighters sleeping in on the job bunking together like they were in dorms. When she was feeling sentimental she thought he might actually miss them, miss their little family and all the noise that came with it. But then she imagined booze, and ashtrays overflowing with butts, tables filled with take-out wrappers, videogames, and porn playing on the big screen, and she realized how silly she had been.

Kid stomping up the stairs.

The man-child coming.

Taller, taller. Laurie had time to think that if her daughter, curiously silent but almost looking her right in the eye at age 11, kept growing at the rate she currently was, she'd be taller than Laurie in a year or so before her son started in.

"It's so messed up!" he said, pacing in front of her, the sound he made against the floor too loud for what she envisioned coming from his six-year-old feet. "I was in the middle of a match!"

"It was a power surg-"

"I know, Mom, but I was in the middle of a match! We couldn't get on all day—somebody always had something else to do—and now, when we *finally* get in, this happens."

Oh, God, what will we do if we miss the match?!

It's been ALL DAY LONG, even though all day amounts to maybe two hours now, at noon.

My life will be over if I can't get into this match, you don't understand, for real, no cap, honest, on the real, yo, you just don't get it, man.

A smile crept onto Laurie's lips as she considered the back and forth that could happen if she responded the wrong way. It was comical, really, how worked up he could get over matches and arsenals and power packs and whatever else went on in the world of the game he and his friends connected in. And she supposed that was ok. Because stuck in the house like they were, that world was his world, at least for right now. And in that world he could run around outside and jump off stuff and break down doors and dance over people when he did it. Just like in her daughter's world she could learn dances and post them and get likes and thank people for them and then do it all over again.

"Jes—" Laurie started, but the man-child cut her off again with more of his ranting.

"—Dave is like never on—"

Probably because his parents find other things for him to do. They are better parents than me, I guess.

She shook her head and knew he didn't understand why, and that was ok.

It was still quiet upstairs.

But not where Laurie was. No, not at all.

"—planned since yesterday," Bobby continued, "and now it's all messed u—."

"Jessie?" Laurie yelled up the stairs like she did so often, letting her voice carry rather than climbing them.

Her son kept talking, undeterred. He was flapping his arms, nearly flinging himself around the foyer.

Laurie thought the stench that every parent stuck in the house with kids aged 10 and over knew all too well might knock her out.

No answer.

"Jess—Bobby, hang on a second, ok?"

Teeth sucking.

Sighing.

Laurie almost laughed.

"Jessie, honey?"

… what? Are you ok? That's what Laurie wanted to ask for some reason, but why? What could be wrong? Jessie was upstairs looking at her phone like usual and from where she was, likely on her bed propped up on that furry armchair pillow thing on her bed that's on its last legs, nothing had even happened. If she had her earbuds in, Jessie hadn't even heard Laurie call her name.

Technology… gotta love it.

"Mom!" Bobby groaned, and for some reason Laurie was accosted with the memory of his father catching his toe on something as they waded into the water in, where was that, Aruba? Barbados? She couldn't remember. She had been waiting for him to get in the water—he took his sweet time putting on sunscreen and putting his hat and sunglasses somewhere safe so they wouldn't fly away, get up and walk away—whatever it was he was afraid of. Everything he was doing was so slow and methodical. Laurie thought she was going to jump out of her skin. She wanted to get in the water, to feel the sand between her toes, to taste the saltiness of it on her lips. And when they finally waded in, when the vacation finally started to feel real, Laurie heard Rob scream. Laurie didn't remember if it sounded exactly the same as Bobby did as he called out to her in complete and total frustration, but it might as well have. And from underwater on some sunny day in her past, how was she to know that she would hear that sound again, somewhere down the line from the kid who calls the screamer 'dad', his namesake, as melodramatic as he was. She dove underwater that day, acting like she didn't hear him, buying herself maybe a minute more of bliss. She wished there were something to duck under right then.

"What if I can't get back in—?"

"Go check," Laurie said, before looking at her computer to make sure they had connectivity and that he could actually log in. She just wanted him out of there, wanted to stop the onslaught of his yelling and the funk of not washing in days because nobody was going anywhere, wanted to silence the grating pitch his voice was taking on. And that was ok. She wasn't up for the Mother of the Year award anyway, not this year, "but go check on Jessie first," she heard herself saying.

Laurie hadn't looked away from the door, hadn't realized she was planning to send her first up to see about her second, but she had done it, and now it was out there. Bobby sighed again and mumbled something under his breath but started toward the stairs anyway, calling Jessie's name once more, hoping she'd save him the trip. When he settled down enough to notice, Bobby could see that there was something about the way Laurie was staring up at the stairs from behind her desk, hardly moving a muscle, that didn't allow any room for questions.

If Laurie had ever had the chance to tell the story, she would have said that Bobby, her sweet boy who looked like her uncle more and more every day with his hair growing long in the quarantine, but not unpleasantly so, only made it up one stair before it happened. She would have said that they were both taken aback because he had been in the basement and she had been on the main floor and Jessie most certainly had not been on either of those. She would have had to have been to be where she was right then but she hadn't been—they were sure of it. But there she was, outside, looking at them through the window, the blinds open just enough to let in some light but closed enough to keep out some of the heat that sometimes came on fall afternoons, those days when Laurie found herself dressing and redressing, trying to keep up with weather that was inherently schizophrenic during that time of year. There she was, outside the house with no way of getting there, unless she had climbed out of her window and jumped down. But she couldn't have done that either, not and just walked away from it. And besides, the alarm hadn't gone off when Jessie opened the window... *if* she had opened the window... which she couldn't have... Laurie was sure about that too.

Jessie was smiling.

A dog was walking.

The powerwalking elderly couple were pumping their arms, their neon orange weights glowing as they went about their normal routine.

Bobby was on the stairs.

Jessie was smiling, but there were too many teeth. Too many in her preteen mouth, too many for an adult's.

Something wet was dripping, pooling somewhere on a carpet; the wet, plopping sound was deafening.

There was a whine, something faint, almost not there. Like a sound caught in the back of someone's throat when the thing they were most afraid of looked like it might really be coming for them, like a dog who knew it was trapped and begs for mercy because it ought to, but knows it won't get it.

Like the sound of the electricity going out everywhere, for the last time.

Lips working, undulating, pulling back to reveal bloody gums, puckering out in a grotesque kiss and through it all, she was smiling, her lips splitting, gore spilling out, all mucus and puss tinged with red.

The lights flickered.

The power turned off again.

One

Two

Three

"Ghaawwwwdddd, *what?*" Jessie yelled and flung open her bedroom door to find her brother standing in a pool of urine and her mother's mouth open so wide it was if her jaw had distended, unhinged, broken.

They were staring at the window, staring so intensely that they hadn't heard her... until they weren't.

Laurie and Bobby whipped their heads toward Jessie so fast, Bobby lost his balance and fell against the wall. She would have laughed were it not for the looks on their faces. Surprise—like really, she scared the hell out of Bobby and deep down, she was happy about that. At least he actually *saw* her for once—ever since they had been locked away in their house, Bobby had only noticed her if she was standing in front of the TV. But it was more than just surprise. There was also confusion on their faces, like they didn't understand what they were looking at. And something else, though it took her brain a few cycles to get to it—fear.

They were afraid.

Black lines in front of her eyes, encasing Bobby and her mother too. Black lines like borders on a picture, like bars on a jail cell. Shimmering, waving, moving, like hot meeting cold on an abandoned blacktop

Four

and it was getting darker around them, darker around her mother, blurring her face behind it, creeping into her open mouth. Jessie called to them, but they didn't hear her. She reached out, but her hand met the black bars instead, and they felt solid even as her hand dove into them as if they were water, sank in there and tingled in the unseen space.

The cellphone in her other hand was warm, so warm, too warm.

Her hand was in the bars, disappeared at the wrist and prickling like it had fallen asleep... like a thousand needles were bouncing off of it—not penetrating, but bouncing, bouncing, bouncing like her hand was a trampoline and the needles were who had been stuck inside the house for too long.

Jessie yanked her hand back, and it wouldn't come, it wouldn't come, and she screamed for her momma and her brother and they didn't hea—

Blip.

PART III

IMITATION OF LIFE

Black Dress

The closet is full of her things
from baby clothes
to teenage dreams.

Always some new trend
changing every week
up 'till the very end.

Searching rapidly,
haphazardly,
for the black dress.
Plain-Jane,
fashionless
black dress.

Tears fall like rain drops
on her cheeks
as she pulls,
pushes,
prods,
and peeks.

All the way in the back
just beyond her reach
hangs the black dress
she desperately seeks.

Unchanging,
timeless,
eternal
black dress
for to 'dorn her daughter
at rest.

Four Crosses

Four crosses on the side of the road
white with floral wreaths around their tops,
colors of blue and red and purple and yellow there
waving goodbye.
White so white it glows against the backdrop of brown
soon green
was green
always green but brown now as the soil heals.
Driven and churned
puddles form in the imprints
grass spouts to trace it
pattern it
remember it.
I don't remember it.
Not there when I passed by this morning.
Or any morning before
Before
Never there
Never blue nor red
Never purple nor yellow.
Never.
Never seen against the emerald green
Illuminated in the noonday sun
spotlighted
highlighted
There.
Never glimpsed in the dark on a rainy night.
Trimmed neat and low, grass never overgrows
Until the bridge is knocked down and the road detours.
Town proper no longer the destination for those lanes.
Just emptiness and regret beyond.
Trimmer gone and reasons forgotten.
Rust and rot with no tie to bind.
Still I don't remember them there,
those four crosses.
Stark white with black letters,
letters that spell names.

Names lovingly picked
lovingly spoken
loving mourned.
Lovingly.
Grass whole and lush just before the bridge
Always there
Always there
Now pocked,
marred
Adorned with whites and blues and reds and purple
and yellow, just like the sun.

Pink Nails

Beautiful looking
deeper rotten shell of lies
conniving sweetly

Repeat

Hot
Sour
passion pink
lover's kink
but blind eye turned so I can't see
can't feel
can't think.
They stand on the edge
blurred and dark
shadowy and staid
even as the cries come
the bargains and barters
the offers bathed in blood.
Sink ye into the dark, they whisper
and succumb most do, sedate and resolute
but claw to bring welts and tissue under the skin go others
as I
as I
borne of blood yet be
until drained and gray
to force them to kiss the mottled flesh.

Catch 22

Magic clouds
circle the earth
protecting us from
impurities.
As progress abounds
we break down
our semi-porous
immunity.

Façade

Dark.
Light.

Shades.

Never the same
but
always so.
Different sizes,
shapes,
rhymes,

reasons...

yet typed.

A budding rose in a dark hand.

Beautiful?

Yes...

BUT NO.

Sleeping Light

I saw you last night
over by my closet
where you always came to me
when I was young and had no inhibitions.

I saw your brilliant blue
sparkling brightly but subtly,
almost airily.

Your face was faint.
I saw grain and texture
within your chest.
You smiled at me.

Last we talked
I told you my news.
The new happenings and
excitement I told of a life watched.
To cold, frost-covered grass
I spoke my happiness
with no response.
I came to you.
Do I look the same?

Last I remember we sat
and talked my kid talk.
Gibberish that amounted
to not much more than
elation over a cartoon
episode.
Snuggled in your warmth,
I remember that you
talked the talk with me,
laughing jovially at my innocence.

Last I saw was you
half-sized

in brilliant sparkling
blue-
but not you.

I thought I saw you
last night.
Smiling that smile
that used to warm me
when nothing else could.
That warms me now from
within.
You were wearing your
brilliant, sparkling
blue.

The Silence of Morning

I awoke today
in search of my love
no warmth did I feel
from the arm that held me.
No love did I see
in the eyes that used to caress me.

I'll search the heavens
and this cold earth
for my one love.
To make him warm
within my soul is my desire.
To keep him whole and safe
I crave deep within my loins.

Where are you, my love?
I fear you've gone
beyond my reach.
I cry at your feet.

Storm Warning

I see a storm in the distance.
I can feel its rumble beneath the surface.
The clouds are darkening over the land in patches.
The air is thin.

I see a storm in the distance.
Rains that will wash away the constant stream of blood
that runs rampant from our mother's womb
as she hangs her worn head.

I see a storm in the distance.
One that will manifest a fire so hot
it will disintegrate all in its path...
...in an instant...
...with no forgiveness.

I see a storm in the distance.
And it will encompass the earth
beating heavy upon our beings and,
in its wake, will reveal a utopia
unparalleled...
for some.

Bad News

I saw him standing there
poise slightly mistook.
Stay away, my head tells me
but my heart beckons me look.

Temptation and Consequence

It's there
looming overhead
discretely
but blatantly

It does not move
rather mills atop
prepared
with its hind-legs
smooth and long
humming a sweet,
treacherous song

To Hesitate

Brick.
Reddish brown, like burnt umber
Red like fall leaves
red
dead
on the ground
trampled underfoot.

Brick.
Brick that speaks of blood
That speaks of pain
That tells of Fortunato's folly.

Mortar
White, not gray
White
bright
blinding
glowing as the day turns,
as the wind shifts,
as the
sun hides behind the clouds
afraid to show,
afraid to see.

White, not gray
gray as it should be
gray as pallid skin
gray as ashes that blow in the wind
to mingle with the leaves.

Under the Blue Moon

Night falls, orange burning from the center to fry the moon
too soon
too soon.
All tuned is my scythe, my sickle quite nice
oiled and ready to cut
to prune.
But mind's eye can see
me
me
not ready.

As the moon turns blue, I wonder after eyes that no longer see
skin turned gray in the haze
after the flay.
Taygeta bites at Maia
dead upon the dead
strange cannibalism in the sky
so bright
too bright
blinding in its brutality
as particles, like so much flesh, fly.
Work to do
blades to lick clean of the blood they let
still I stand watching the flame turn to black
engulfing the sky in ash
blue moon turning skin blue black.

Scattered brain
scattered me.
Come ge' we?
Don't you agree?
It's scary...
Talons, bloody and dirty, all up in my tea.

Si.

Because I do.

I see and know and understand and confirm.
Sasquatch and prophets
Samson holding his hair in his tattooed hand
bloody scalp be damned.

And the cabal says, "Amen!"

I see.
They're in need.
Dying
living
the blade they seek.
Cold metal thrums in response
Hot with want
Orange me.

So, oui.

I come
para ti.

Do This

When the days are long
Speak spells to keep the beasts back
Eyes closed, fingers bent
Bloody hands, scrapped knees give true
All to sate the fickle's mood.

What Voice Does Speak

It calls to me
The dark
From the shadows of cast by rotted eaves
Or with the voice of the wind.

It calls to me
Beckons me forth
To greet it with open arms
Cracked and chafed from nightly encounters of
Its hateful whims.

It calls to me
Softly at times
Like a mother might a child.
Like a lover would another,
Of which it is mine.
Then loudly
Mockingly
Painfully divine.

It calls every night
Its only desire that I not see the evil beauty of my love,
the beast controlling me.

Food for Thought

Trees.
Sky.
Sun.
Moon.
Land.
Water.
Air.
Food.

End soon?

Hell

Darkness thick as tar
unyielding
surrounding me with fear.

Lost memories float above
Teasing me with the remnants
of times past
when I was happy
when I was whole.

Those times seem long gone and distant
even though I can taste your lips
like jasmine.
My mind cries out in pain
as I touch your blackness
and curve you in my dark

and turn my head in shame.

My Darkest Hour

My darkest hour
shone brightly in the sun
to me, 'twas gray,
overcast and solemn
as I felt my lowest
and stood at my blackest.

The warm day and pleasant breeze
beat my skin mercilessly
as the glare blinded my sight.
Black and White for me
yellows and oranges for the world
as White hands on Black arms
did drag.

My darkest hour descended on me
like death
like departure
like sin
while laughter and joy filled the air
deafening me with shame.

The beginning of summer they relished
and mistook my open-mouthed cries for glee
as I watched the play
unravel before me.

In The Distance

Through the glare of the sun
I saw you standing
alone
waiting.

How clearly I saw your face
in my mind
for you have left me
and all
behind.

Through the haze of the sweltering sun
I saw you
smiling
in the distance
at me.

How brilliant and full your smile
was
then
when you smiled at me
from eternity.

Night Visitor

By the light of the moon
It comes to me
Traipsing lightly on air
just above the ground
invisible to all
but to me, I see

Over outstretched lands
he travels to me
in the dead of night
to light my dreams
or my reality

Differently it loves
from times past
he brings happiness
that today will never see

Hot Summer Day

Long summer
come to an end
'tis when my sorrow
do begin

I seen 'im out
in the street
ain't e'en tryin'
to be discrete

Hot summer musta caught 'im
when he saw her sexy brown
always up on her
when she come to town
but now he cain't catch her
'cause she won't never come 'round

Cool an' still
her body do lay
after I met her in the park
yesterday

She gone now, for good
but in this new day
I's gone too
'cause they takin' me away

My Place

The water envelops me
circling me in its warmth,
teasing me with its wave
imagined.

I listen to the silence
and see the crayon sun
shining above my head.
Casting a brilliant light
on all it touches
in my porcelain shell.

Life

I passed the dregs of down
quickly
running through the
adversities that held some
by the legs as they
lunged
toward my existence.

I turned to help
but they were stone,
as Lot's wife a
pillar of salt.

Through down
quickly I ran
chin to chest
hand outstretched
warding off pain
and suffering
fall at my feet.

Full Circle

I look down upon the hunter green fields of night
and see
Towards fields of sorrow
my love runs
Away, said he,
my journey calls
I bid thee farewell

Evermore, I asked
needing to know
why

My darling, what speak you,
a voice
his voice
yet not
asked thunderously,
for I have not gone

I look out my window,
suddenly compelled by
the hot summer streets below
and all there is to see

Full of life
yet dead with loss
(away your being)
cops chasing
glass breaking
sweaty bodies form a
barrier of eager,
interested
exploitative eyes
quest not flesh, but poison get
at the lifeless form
at one with the earth

L. MARIE WOOD

Evermore, said he.

The Wall

Hard as stone
cold and dark.
Its ominous structure
talks to me harshly,
barking incongruent
insults, confidently
excoriating me for
imagined wrong doings
as if I were meant
to understand.

Rough
jagged edges jut out
at me
piercing my skin
but they leave no scar.

Invisible hands grab me
and pull me into its
redoubtable darkness.
I shrink underneath
its strength
mentally rebelling but
unable to verbally protest.

Stark, dim fissures
like eyes stare stoically
through me seeing my soul
and being disgusted
with it.

I pound my fists
relentlessly against
its austere surface
until they are bloody,
as bloody as my face
from the blow of the wind.

The Dark

Peering into the darkness
I have a sense of one
with me
searching also
for themselves
but finding me.

Voices in the Wind

Sometimes when I walk
I hear voices.

I turn my head but I am alone.
Just me and the wind.

Are you there?
I can feel your touch on my skin.
It burns under the warmth.
It stings.

Dust and grit flying in the wind as it whirls around me
at top speed.
Are you there?

I can hear you.
The sound is faint, but ever so clear.
You call my name.

No.

The wind howls in despair.

Suffocating.
I can't catch my breath.
Life in movement surrounding me
as I watch mine float away.

I fall.
I stand.

I shake.
I am still...here.

Are you there?

Still

Still
Skin toughened by the elements, the sentiments, the precedence to form
armor that protects

Still
Impenetrable, imagined so, but the air finds its weakness and pushes its
poison slow

Still
In the room, in the womb, bespoke doom even though painted smiles bid
hello and goodbye unseen

What the Water Brings

I close my eyes to sink
to fall
to succumb
mouth filling
metallic brine
as I transform.
From the shore they watch but don't see
can't see
because it isn't me they look for
call for
shriek for as their knees weaken
and give way to the weight on their shoulders from the bodies they bore
the bodies they paid nevermind.
It isn't me who will emerge to lift them
hold them
encircle their throats with an icy hand
leaving a trail of weed in its wake.
Not me
the me they want
the me they expect
but me evermore.
Through bloodshot eyes and gaping mouth I change
I see
I be
who I am
naturally
and they cower
they scream
when they see.
The water lifts me above their heads
my feet at their chests hoisted by the foam
majestically
eternally
unmistakably
and they stare reverently
at
Me.

Society

That sound traveled fast.
His agony on display.
We stood and watched death.

PART IV

THE LOST STORIES

THE CLEANSING

The flames licked, danced, engulfed the wood eagerly like a hungry beast. She watched it flicker then build, climbing the walls like vines on the side of a house, undulating against the wall like lovers.

Wanting closure; wanting release. The orange glow, tinged with the faintest hint of blue, she knew, would give her peace.

BEYOND THE CHAIN

I used to want more.

I used to want to hear dogs barking, hear the laughter of children, get hit with the sprinkler every evening at dusk, and hope that baseballs didn't do any lasting damage. I wanted that, but what I got was a patch of grass hardly long enough for a grown man to lie down in heel —to — head, and trees so tall you could only see me in in the dead of winter, and then only if you squinted.

No dogs bark, no children play, not after they chained up the gate and took him away, not after what they found inside.

Gerald.

They never listened to him, not even when he swore he didn't know they were there, playing house in his shed, sitting around the table waiting for him to get home.

I knew they were there but I couldn't tell.

I wouldn't tell.

They couldn't make me. Nothing could.

I knew they were there, but they shouldn't have been. They were trespassing. They weren't invited. They didn't belong.

He said he didn't know, but that was a lie. He had to have known. I secretly think he put them there. For me. I fancied that for years, imagining that he had brought them there for me to see, for me to play with. I thought of what his voice might sound like when he told me to do what I wanted with them, that they were mine to do with what I would. He would sound strong and confident, nothing like the whimpering imbecile they dragged away that day, wide-eyed and pointing at me. I fantasized that he lied to them to make them stay, and oh, what a good liar he turned out to be! Maybe he told them that everything he did was for them, and that they had nothing to worry about because he cared for them and always would. Maybe he told them that my soul spoke to him and that I loved them too and that I wanted them there as much as he did. Their stench still sits in the wallpaper they had lined the walls of the shed with, trying to make the place look like a proper home.

He lied to himself about them, about me, about it all. Even as he set fire to the weeping willow that had been my friend, the massive thing that had sheltered cardinals and bluebirds over its 250-year life—even as he tried to use to it to burn away everything he ever knew, he couldn't murder the truth, couldn't clean away the stain. Even as he sits in his cell, far away from me now, still he knows, he remembers, he feels.

The table is still set for dinner, modestly, for three servings instead of five. The pitcher upon the table, with the painted rooster on the side and the chipped spout, is empty now, but that can be easily remedied. All one need do is ask.

No one comes past the chain or ventures into the woods to peek anymore—that time has long gone. Now they pass by without a second glance at the overgrown driveway, the cracked asphalt barely visible beneath layer upon layer of dead leaves and weedy undergrowth. Someone left candy once, had thrown it past the chain and into the gaping maw that yawned behind it. I imagine a child being teased on Halloween when I think of it, their candy bucket snatched and ransacked by older kids. Perhaps they threw the candy inside and dared him to go after it. But it was only one piece of candy, hardly enough to dare with or risk repercussion for. No one ever came to get it. Had they come they might have seen me, might have said hello, might have dug into their eye sockets to pluck out the things that had betrayed them and shown them such a sight.

I would have shared the candy with them if they had.

SOMEBODY WAS CLAIRVOYANT

"What does this one go to?"

She could feel the cool stream of sweat run from the base of her neck down her spine as his hand hovered over the yellow ethernet cable.

It should have been red.

Red meant stop, alarm, don't.

Yellow said come play with me in the sunshine.

It should have been red... like she said.

But they had all said no, no, let's keep it uniform, hide in plain sight, this is the way it should be.

And finally, the one that made her inner self laugh so hard her voice was nothing but a rasp at the end of it all, 'No one's ever gonna touch it anyway.'

Should she say something?

Saying something might make him want to touch it all the more. If she told him that this was the only cable in the place that mattered, the only one that could make everything go boom if he even jiggled it. That it would be back to card catalogs, back to typewriters, to chalkboards and rail travel, beyond jump drives to floppy disks and back before that. Vinyl and talk radio. Kerosene lamps and carrier pigeons—he would set it all back, back, back, further than he could ever imagine if he just unplugged it. If he just...

No, she couldn't tell him that.

But if she said nothing...

"I said, what the hell does this one do?" he asked again, anger furrowing his brow and seeping into his voice. She forgot what she was up against while she daydreamed, forgot about the taser positioned under her jaw.

Fine.

Fuck it.

The cloud can disintegrate; data can be lost; DMs never answered, stories never be told. Vacation pics will be gone forever and contacts lost. Dick pics wiped from the face of the earth.

No more likes.

No more following.

No more friends.

It was her job to keep it all going, to protect the world... to protect the cable from water, heat, some asshole bumping into the rack and shaking loose a power cord. It was her job to make sure updates were applied and that the fans kept blowing. And there were others, others who were supposed to guard her, protect her from the outside, make sure her area wasn't breached, but they fell down on the job. Taking the water break she never had. Bullshitting about the game she'd never see or the weather she'd never feel because she was always in there, always there with the cable. They were screwing around while the cable was being threatened.

Fine.

Pull the damned thing.

"You got three seconds to tell me what the hell this goes to or —"

"Everywhere."

His eyes squinted in confusion.

"It goes everywhere. It does everything. It *is* everything."

He laughed incredulously, not knowing what else to do. His face twitched as he tried to put a response together, and she had to hold back a smile. She couldn't stop the words of a spiritual the old people used to hum from creeping into her head, almost sang them out loud. Maybe if she had it would have helped reset him. Maybe he would have just used the taser and this would all be over... for her, anyway.

"No shit?" he said and she couldn't help but think about how brilliant a response that actually was.

He looked at his hand still hovering just above the cord but trembling now.

She looked at him looking at his hand, thought of the war on the other side of the world actively transmitting locale coordinates over the dark web, and willed him to do it.

SHE

The smell was luxurious.

It turned my stomach.

That from within the cabin I could still smell the eclectic perfume, a mix of fried chicken, wet pennies, and Eau De Toilette that only she could make sweet, made me weak-kneed. The scent, long cleared by earth and element, filled my nostrils as my mind first commands, then pleads, "You don't recognize, you don't recognize, you don't, you can't…."

But still, I do.

JUNK MAIL

He sighed as he took out his keys and juggled the mail crammed in his hand. *Nothing but junk mail,* he thought. There never seemed to be anything important in the mail anymore. Unless…

Rick stopped in his tracks, one foot on the steps leading to the door of the brownstone, one still on the sidewalk. Maybe, just maybe…

He sifted through each circular announcing weekend deals, each request for help from local shelters, each bill, but there was nothing. Nasim had promised to send him a card with her new address on it. She had insisted on sending the note via snail mail—she liked the simple things. Sending a card instead of a text was right up her alley.

Just the thought of her choosing a card carefully, addressing the envelope in her steady hand, and dropping it in the mailbox made Rick smile. Then he felt that familiar tickle in his nose, the one that had been making an appearance every week or so since she announced she was moving to Boston. He never let her see, never let on that there was anything other than a friend missing a friend going on. There was so much more going on in his head though, especially since the dream job in Boston had become a reality. Happiness, frustration, sadness—all those emotions mingled inside him, bouncing off the walls, jostling as they vied for center stage. He felt angry with himself for never telling Nasim how he felt. They had been working together for years; their cubes were side by side. He saw her walk in and out every day, until she literally walked out of his life. They went to lunch together, jogged in the park on the weekends. She lived near his mother, which meant they bumped into each other at the supermarket, the coffee shop, the movies—everywhere. It was like they were supposed to be together. All he had to do was say something. But he never did. And then she left. Admiring someone from afar has its perks, but sometimes it just sucked.

Rick sorted through his keys, grabbing the battle-scarred gold one that fit his mother's door and thought about Nasim's smile. Not her mouth and the way it pinched at the corners to hint of dimples, as much as her eyes. They were so expressive; he couldn't bear to look at them for long. Recently her eyes held a sadness that was almost palpable. Could it be that she dreaded the thought of losing him as much as he did her?

Rick whipped his head toward Nasim's door. Maybe she would send him the picture they took in the office the day before she left. Rick wished it was of them alone, but Beth, the nosiest colleague in the office, jumped into the frame as if it was her rightful place. He'd have to deal with it—at least he got the chance to hold Nasim in his arms for a fleeting moment.

Rick almost dropped the keys when he saw the man looking in Nasim's window as his mother's door swung shut.

Maybe it was a potential new tenant coming to view the apartment. That would make sense since Nasim had just moved out, but that didn't make him feel any better. It was akin to a man marrying another woman as soon as his divorce is finalized. The ink on the paper wasn't even dry.

Rick watched as the man took a selfie with the apartment and then stepped into the vestibule to take a closer look. He choked back a sob and, instead, let out an audible sigh. Nasim was gone, had moved on and was starting the next chapter of her life somewhere else. Without him. If ever he needed a reality check, there it was.

Rick took the stairs to his mother's front door like a man with the weight of the world on his shoulders. He wanted to look over at Nasim's door again, but what was the use? He wouldn't see her smiling face looking back at him; her dancing eyes wouldn't sparkle with excitement because she wasn't there. She was never there. Her apartment was nearby —just a few blocks, really—but not across the hall where he could knock on the door with a pint of her favorite ice cream and an invitation to watch a late-night movie. Rick didn't even know if he was really seeing someone look through the window and into the apartment across the hall at all; that he could was implausible, if he was being honest. He'd have to look at just the right time to catch someone standing on the stairs outside the building, would have needed to time the door swings of both his mother's and the brownstone's front doors to allow him a second of unobstructed view of the street to notice someone looking into the unit that didn't belong to Nasim, that didn't belong to anyone he knew at all. It could all just be his imagination; the way things had been going since Nasim died, Rick couldn't tell anymore.

Rick squeezed his eyes shut, cutting fat tears in half to wet his eyelashes. The tickle in his nose was becoming unbearable, and his skin felt so hot, so very hot. And there was something else too, something Rick wasn't sure he truly understood… wasn't sure he really wanted to.

Rick breathed deeply, felt perspiration dot his brow, as he registered the smell clinging to the air in his mother's apartment.

RED NAIL POLISH

Dainty. It's not a word I use often, but that's what her toes were. Small, delicate. They looked like they were handcrafted and never used, like the toes on a porcelain doll. Red nail polish on alabaster skin. Like a speck of blood on new fallen snow.

I smile when I think of it. I can be so poetic in moments like these, when it's quiet and dark. So witty in my mind, yet it never comes to my lips. My lips, pink and full of life, as usual are closed, my voice as silent as my captive audience's when people are near. And how could you blame me? What, with their sneering and snickering, their leering and salivating. The frozen smiles I set never sneer. To a poet, they listen. To an artist, they sit in awe. They are rapt. As they should be.

Red nail polish on unblemished skin. Dainty, like a girl rebelling for cotillion, a little spice beneath the frill. No one to see it except me. But to last for eternity.

HYPNOPOMPIA

The numbers spun—they spun!—right before my eyes, and I know I'm groggy, I know I'm having trouble waking up this morning, but I know that's not right. When I woke and looked at my alarm clock, bastard that it is, beeping incessantly like a truck backing up, high-pitched and monotone at the same time... when I woke up and looked at the time, it was steady. 6:33—I might have tried to ignore it for a few minutes and that's why it was 6:33 and not 6:30... sue me. It was overcast, but the sun was trying to peek through the blinds. I know that because I saw it. Everything was the way it usually was. Me not being able to haul my ass out of bed was normal too. Nothing to see here, folks, just your average Monday morning.

But I *did* get up. I didn't hit snooze this time. I trudged across the room like the walking dead, my eyes mere slits as I made my way to the bathroom, the commode, the sink, and then back into the bedroom. I sat down on the edge of the bed and put on the TV. A little news was what I needed, I thought, other voices in the room to coax me along. The distant thought I'd had last night about working out this morning was like a joke that some comedian had tried that fell flat. I had a moment to consider that I could dial my wake-up time back an hour if I was just going to let that fantasy go, felt the corners of my lips twitch in the beginnings of a smile at the thought before all was blank again. I fell asleep sitting up, remote in hand, and mouth wide open. I know that because I woke up that way too.

It couldn't have been long—*couldn't* have been. I would have fallen over or dropped the remote if it had been, right? Neither of those things had happened so I figured it had only been a few seconds, one of those moments where you doze off, are out of it so completely that you're disoriented when you wake up. I rolled onto my side, deciding to just give in, get another hour of sleep. I have a meeting in a few hours that I need to be sharp for and I was anything but that then. I laid down. Got into position to shut my eyes. That's when I saw it.

The guy on camera was talking about the weather—some storm system coming from the north that will cool temperatures and make it feel like Christmas in July. His back was turned, so I couldn't see his face, but what I did see made me sit bolt upright. His suit jacket was slit up the back and so was his shirt. There was raw, pink flesh peeking out beneath all of it. I could see a huge blister between his shoulder blades.

The temperatures showed on the map. At first it was just local, but then the map expanded to the United States, and then to the world.

"It's 90 °F in Calgary, but we're working on that. Parts of the US are hitting 175 °F and temps in Nigeria topped 325 °F last night. The Seine in Paris as well as the Canale Grande in Venice began to boil in the early morning hours. The Nile has boiled off completely, leaving lungfish and bolti to cook in the sun."

My mind couldn't process the words he was saying. I was distracted by the other data that was posted in the corners and running along the bottom of the screen:

Birds take flight in Florida only to burst into flames in the sky.

Woman fused to her car in Leeds.

Fissure opens in the ground to reveal lost ancient civilization beneath.

My mouth is open. I can hear myself panting.

The time on the screen, the one that I usually look at to confirm that I need to get up off my butt, get in the shower, and get going, was broken. The digital numbers were rolling, spinning, flying by. It was 6:45, then it was 7:22, then it was 3:14, then it was 5:58. It changed every second, and it was driving me crazy. Every time I tried to look at it, pin it down, see it clearly, it was something different.

And the world boiled.

"Do you want to go back to sleep? It might be best to stay in bed, sleep it off and wake up dead."

I looked at the weatherman, and he was looking back at me through eyes that had pushed out of their sockets to perch themselves outside of the skin, skin that was falling away in big, wet clumps. They moved independently of each other like bug antennae, and I couldn't stop looking at them.

They tipped toward me, almost like a man wearing a fedora might do his hat in greeting.

I smiled.

One of them winked at me.

I nodded.

BIDING TIME

The chair spins slowly, teasing me, taunting me. I wait, bound by anticipation; raw and savage like the belt that cuts into my skin. Red streams into the wind like hair flowing in the breeze; spittle carried by the wind. Drops that stain the carpet fall in slow motion, reflecting what waits.

AFTERCARE

The polaroid was grainy, but that's how she liked it. Dim and from a bad angle, the picture captured everything she needed to see to spark the pleasant contraction in her lower half, the one that made her legs weak. She had hoped for this, wanted to feel the fresh excitement she was feeling at that moment, and she caressed the picture to express her thanks. Such a good boy. She would make sure the flowers she'd have delivered matched his suit.

MODEL HOME

The light turned on in the darkness, a faint red glow indistinguishable in the unnatural greenish haze of night vision. Cabinets look creepy in the dark. So does the stillness of a sleeping house. Watching for too long can be terrifying—the feeling that something will show itself in the shadows is enough to drive someone mad.

Still, the camera came on for a reason...

Something floats before the lens. One would dismiss it as backscatter —indeed, most did that very thing—there is always dust in the air so the camera catching glimpses of it wouldn't surprise anyone except that shouldn't set off a motion-sensored security camera. If a camera can be calibrated to ignore a 25-pound cat, then surely it should be able to discount a speck of dust. If they watched long enough they would see the orb take a decided turn and cross in front of the camera once more before travelling deeper in the room and disappearing into the shadows. Another speck of dust? Not likely.

But they wouldn't look that long—most people didn't. Because that's not what they would be looking for if they turned on this feed. There were countless other feeds of this very room when the demons came out to play, their forms sometimes translucent when wandering specters entered lost or angry; sometimes solid flesh and blood as looters lifted and squatters broke, but none of those recordings would be important if anyone found out about this one.

If they noticed.

It's there, just a little bit of heel, but still there, in view if you looked hard enough. But would they? Was anyone ever really looking anyway? It's late—past 3:30 a.m. Who would be looking at this hour anyway?

They wouldn't see in time, wouldn't be able to save him, this man whose heel is the only thing in the recording. A dark, solid colored sock— Black? Blue?—still covered the toes, but the heel was bare… brown skin against a backdrop of shadows in a darkened house in the middle of the night. Infrared will pick up something, make the heel more visible if nothing else, but what good would that do? From such a distance and without the benefit of the toes it won't look like much of anything—it could be a Styrofoam cup just as easily as the only thing visible of a dying man. And no one would think a Styrofoam cup suspicious, not with as many people that come in and out of this place every day. People were always in and out, picking up things, stealing things, chatting up the agent but never intending to buy. Sometimes the realtor invited her boyfriend over to have sex. Sometimes she hooked up with one of those people who had entered the house that day wandering, wandering, just like those wayward spirits. But the camera was never on then, so nobody ever knew. But it's on now—does it make a difference?

They brought him here to dump him, did away with the alarm before any notification could be sent, but not the camera sitting inconspicuously on the hutch, the one that had the broadest arc of the room. Different system—one of the really good ideas that the team designing the newer model homes came up with, because petty thieves wouldn't think outside of the box about a thing like that. As far as they were concerned, the place was empty at night which made it prime pickings. Snip, snip on the wires, use some computer geekery to screw up the Wi-Fi and you're in.

But these weren't thieves.

They brought him there to dump him, but he wasn't dead yet. They carried him in, left him there on the floor, and walked out, never realizing that he would squirm a little before he died, moving just enough to bring his heel into view, never realizing that he would add his low moans to the sounds of the house settling.

If the design team had thought about manning the camera, periodically watching live, they would have seen it. But they never would have saved him.

An orb shot out of the room followed by another, heading right for the camera, on the heels of the first. They were racing each other, like children in a park, flying so quickly they almost looked like a streak. An old friend coming to pick him up, showing him it was all right and now they would be together forever? Perhaps. Backscatter to those who might look after the body was found, just dust floating in the air, if they saw it at all.

IMPURE

He sat in the shadows watching her as she moved, savoring the way the light caught the red in her hair, the way her chin dipped slightly to the left as she thought. He was tempted—that went without saying. But it went beyond the innate desire to satisfy the burning in his lap. Indeed, his hand resting there, absently stroking, was far removed from his thoughts. Instead he spoke to her, told her exactly what he wanted to do to her. He caressed the words, leaving them silky and smooth. He reached for her and felt her rise to meet his waiting hand.

The silence served to mask his passion, and he was happy for it.

No distractions. Nothing but him.

From the recesses of her mind she felt him pressing, his heat permeating her mind, exploring her with an eagerness that made her moan. She looked around the room to find herself alone, as she knew she was… as she wished she wasn't.

LEVEL-UP

The room was dark, but not completely; the waning light seemed to glow on the other side of the blinds. When they started the movie it was still light outside, but as the hours went on and the movie started getting good, no one had gotten up to close the blinds all the way.

The TV screen was dark—only the outline of a woman, her hair sweated out into long, stringy strands that stuck to her face, the only thing they could see. Her breath pushed the strands in the front away from her face every time she exhaled.

In.

Out.

In.

Out.

Faster with every second.

She was going to make herself pass out soon, hyperventilate or something. It was too much too soon.

"Overacting," Gabe said, and Wally nodded in agreement. It was ridiculous. Indie films either had really amazing acting or such shitty performances that it seemed like the actors were somebody's cousin or sister. This one was the latter, down to the smeared convenience store mascara that had managed to run all the way down her cheeks and dip under her chin before diluting.

She fumbled and found her phone, told the audience she was having trouble finding the flashlight function on it by hemming and hawing and 'Oh no!'-ing and 'Damnit!'-ing. When she finally found it, she had the nerve to say,

'Ok, found it!' before turning it on, as if they wouldn't have known she had when she illuminated the room. Gabe and Wally expected there to be something behind her, something grotesque and freakish, but only as far as a doctored Halloween mask could go. They hadn't seen the thing chasing her yet—the whole thing had been very *Cloverfield*-esque so far— but the free soundtrack they'd downloaded off the internet was building, crescendoing in a way that was supposed to make viewers' backs arch, make them sit up taller in their seats. They'd oblige—the movie was working hard enough for it, so why not?

But there was nothing.

Good on them.

Wally let out the breath he hadn't realized he was holding, and Gabe chuckled, probably because he had done the same thing too. As corny as the movies they always ended up watching were, he loved them—the jump scares, the stupid decisions, the predictability. He loved all of that shit.

The girl onscreen inched forward, moving painstakingly slow.

All of a sudden there was no soundtrack anymore, and Wally couldn't put his finger on when it had stopped.

Ingenious.

It was quiet.

So very quiet.

And then three things happened all at the same time, though Wally would never admit one of them out loud.

The lights went out on the screen right when his brother came into the room asking what they were watching. And Wally, well, he almost jumped out of his skin.

"Never heard of it before," Eddie had said when Gabe told him the name of the movie. "Sounds cool! Can I watch?"

"No!" they'd yelled in unison. Wally knew he had shouted because Eddie had scared the hell out of him. He wondered if he had done the same to Gabe.

"Come on!" Eddie whined like clockwork. It was always the same.

'Can I watch?'

'No!'

'Why?'

'Because.'

'Because why?'

'Because I said, now go before I tell mom.'

Wally didn't really feel like going through it again, but there they were.

"Because—" Wally started but Eddie stopped him.

"Because you said," he said, defeated.

"Why'd you even ask, then? You could have just kept on walking instead of messing up the movie."

"Yeah," Gabe said, turning back to the TV where the woman was now backing up wide-eyed and comically terrified. It would take her at least 30 seconds to get on her mark so that the guy in the gorilla suit could jump out and scare her. She was probably going over and over how she'd execute her big horror movie scream in her head as they watched.

"You scared the shit out of Gabe," Wally said, fighting to keep a serious look on his face as he looked over at his friend. He failed.

"Me? You're the one who almost got air. *You* surprised me more than Eddie did."

"Oh, so you admit that you were surprised, which is just code for scared?"

They laughed.

The girl screamed on cue.

Gabe and Wally turned to watch.

So did Eddie.

It took Wally and Gabe longer than it should have to realize that Eddie was watching the movie, committing *Mutant Antennae* to memory as much as he could. All three of their heads were turned toward the screen, lured in by the feelers that left a viscous residue on the girl's skin after swiping at it, stretching across it, poking at it. And she screamed and screamed and swung her head around, more hair sticking to her face with every turn.

But then Gabe saw Eddie, mouth open, jaw slacked, eyes wide. He nudged Wally. Wally looked and had time to wonder how much trouble he would be in when Eddie woke up with nightmares for the next few weeks.

"Yo!" Wally yelled and stood up, blocking the TV from view. Eddie's eyes cleared, his vision no longer of the carnage onscreen but of his brother who didn't look happy at all. He wanted to bite it back, but he couldn't, the response more knee-jerk than anything.

"Hey! Get out of the way!" Eddie whined.

Always whining.

"Get out of here, man. You've seen enough already."

Wally walked around the sofa to where his brother stood trying to make his body heavy, hard to move. Gabe had sprung into action and paused the movie already so no more damage could be done, and Eddie hated him for it.

"I'll tell mom you let me watch," Eddie tried, but immediately wished he hadn't. He looked up to his brother too much to get him in trouble over something like that, and Wally knew it.

"You do that and I'll tell her what really happened," Wally said in response, playing along, and Eddie knew they were good. "Just go to your room—do some homework or something. It's almost over anyway."

Eddie left reluctantly, and Wally waited for him to go, listened for the door to the basement to open and close again signaling he was really gone. He didn't know how he missed it the first time, didn't understand how he missed the sound of Eddie's footsteps coming down the stairs, but he had. But not this time. Wally even leaned over to see if the kid had tried to trick him, had only opened and closed the door without going through it. He hadn't. Eddie was gone.

"It's like some kind of bug or something," Gabe said when Wally came back and sat down. The image on screen was that of the girl, her mouth open in a scream, looking behind her at the antennae reaching for her again.

"Duh," Wally said and pointed to the movie title displayed on the paused scream. "I kinda figured it would be."

Gabe laughed good-naturedly and continued, "No, I mean it's like some kind of ant. I would have thought it would be like a fly or something like that."

"What, like Mothra or some shit?"

"Something like that, yeah. Something that could lift people off the ground and drop them. Who's gonna be afraid of an ant?"

"Ants are beasts, though," Wally said, reaching for the bag of chips on the table between them. "Battle strategies have been formed around ant behavior."

"Yeah, but other bugs eat ants. Even butterflies eat ants, bro."

Wally laughed—there was no comeback that made more sense.

"They could have made it be a spider or something scary looking," Gabe continued, thinking.

Wally shook his head no.

"Been done way too many times. It's like with any horror movie set in Egypt—you know there's gonna be a mummy. Or if you see an Asian girl with her hair covering her face, you know it's one of those ghosts like the girl from *The Ring*. Enough with that shit."

"I mean, they try to change it up," Gabe said, settling into the conversation. "Zombies run now."

"True, but they aren't any stronger than they were before. You may not be able to outrun them now but you might be able to beat them. They're weak. The weakest link," Wally laughed, proud of the connection he made.

"What the hell are you talking about 'the weakest link'? Zombies are tough as hell. Remember the first episode of *The Walking Dead*? That woman was cut in half on the ground still trying to get at Rick."

"Yeah, and all anybody would have to do is side-step her. You don't even need to waste a bullet." They laughed because it was true, both of them remembering that scene in the show and nodding in agreement. "If a human can beat it, anything can."

"A mummy can't beat a zombie," Gabe said.

"A mummy *is* a zombie," Wally retorted. "And so is Frankenstein, so let's take them both out of the equation."

"Some people say Frankenstein isn't a zombie 'cuz he's a bunch of body parts put together. The new thing was never alive like that before."

"Yeah, and some people would go back and forth with us about how Frankenstein isn't the monster at all—that he was the doctor—even though they know damn well which one we're talking about right now."

"True. But he could be a golem."

Wally looked Gabe like he had grown two heads and kept going.

"Ok, so how about this. A werewolf can beat a zombie for sure because its gonna tear it up, rip its body to shreds."

Nodding, Gabe said, "Yeah a zombie wouldn't have a chance against a werewolf. And a vampire would completely kick a zombie's ass."

"Absolutely. A zombie wouldn't be able to catch it if it tried. A vamp could shapeshift into mist or a bat or whatever. Plus it could look into its eyes and Bella Lugosi it, tell it to go away."

"If its eyes weren't already rotted out," Gabe corrected. "But yeah, even if a zombie could catch a vampire, it couldn't do anything with it. Its body would be too hard to destroy."

Wally nodded and then thought of something.

"Come to think of it, a werewolf wouldn't be able to kill a vampire either. It would break its teeth on it.

Gabe nodded slowly.

"A ghost," Gabe started, rifling through his memory banks to find the information he wanted. "Dude... a ghost may be the baddest of them all."

"How do you figure?" Wally asked, his mind filling with images of long black hair and pale faces.

"Because it chooses how it manifests, right? So if it stays all see-through and shit, nothing can get a hand on it. You'd have to go destroy the body or get someone one to clear the house and get it out, exorcise someone, what have you. By the time that happens, the ghost could have already fucked shit up and taken off. A ghost wouldn't even waste time trying to beat a zombie—it wouldn't have to. It could just stay invisible. And then what? The zombie wouldn't even see what was dismembering it, picking up poles and shoving them through its skull. Boom. Over. Next."

A smile crept onto Gabe's face that spoke of a new understanding of everything important. "It's the Ultimo."

Wally smiled too now, the name bouncing around in his head and coming out good. When he spoke it, his voice was nothing short of reverent.

"Ultimo."

Eddie shook his head from his perch on the stairs as he listened to them talk about things they did not understand. They didn't understand who Ultimo was, what power he wielded. The fact that they spoke his name so randomly upset him, but he had to remember that they were ignorant. Yes, there was an Ultimo, but it wasn't any of those characters his brother and friend had been talking about. No. Ultimo was so much more than that.

Fast.

Strong.

Skin like armor.

Eyes like lasers.

Respawn capabilities.

He could shapeshift into any animal and any person—could speak whatever language the people around him were familiar with... in fact, they heard their language in their ears when he spoke, regardless of how many people were in the room.

He was fearless.

Ageless.

Didn't require oxygen to breathe nor food to eat. He definitely did not drink blood, could walk in the daylight if he wanted to and stay up all night if that was the plan. He was impervious to zombies and werewolves —his being was like metal to them, so they never tried to attack. He was deaf to sirens and poison to insects. He showed himself as Slender Man, Candyman, Freddy Kruger, Kayako, The Babadook to keep people at bay. Because if they knew about him—about who he really was—he would have to correct the situation.

He could use all weapons but he didn't need them—he *was* the weapon.

Nobody controlled him and all feared him.

He was Ultimo.

And Eddie knew just where to find him.

I HAVE NOTHING TO WEAR

How does this go?

What do you wear to something like this?

Choker, accentuating the neck? V-neck to show more skin? Tight dress, short dress, loose dress, long dress, no dress, maybe pants instead?

Do you wear a jacket, a vest, ruffles, lace?

My hand lands on a crushed velvet top with buttons and strappy things, none of which I remember. When did I buy this?

Sequins?

No.

Burnout? That paper-thin material that always seems like it will rip and show off the things it barely concealed in the first place?

Maybe that. Yes, maybe so.

Do we dance or is this one of those drinking and smoking parties? I wouldn't mind feeling a body next to mine, pressed up close, hot breath on my neck—

Yeah, I'd better make sure my neck is out instead of in so I can feel all the sensations I am supposed to feel.

So...

Flower or stripes? Polka dots? Midriff shirt and leather shorts?

Damn, it's been a long time since I went out.

But he called and he's hungry and I want.

Black lace with a matching bra beneath and those same leather shorts I was thinking about before because he likes the way I look and them.

Maybe the others will too.

Maybe she'll tell me so and lick her lips, anticipating what my neck will taste like, wishing she was at the fount, lapping sucking, coaxing out more with every heartbeat.

Maybe he would grab her, spirit her away to sink his teeth in the other side, the unblemished side, claiming it for his own.

Lace scoop with the prettiest scalloped neckline for my coven divine.

THE SCIENCE OF IT

The pot on the stove wobbles because it's too big for the burner, the middle warping and rising up into an arc as the heat turns the core red hot.

The pot on the stove wobbles because there's moisture beneath the metal and it's changing into something new, into something different, before it dissipates, dissolves, disappears.

The pot on the stove wobbles because he isn't quite dead yet, the nerves causing eyes to flutter and cheeks to rise in a smile, a grimace as flesh too fresh to know it's dead singes against the side.

GLASSES

I went back for them.

I went back because I knew he dropped them and someone would see.

I saw them fly off his face and land in the mulch, one frame obliterated by the blast and the other cracked and splintered—ruined beyond repair. They wouldn't need to be repaired, though; his blood smeared on the rim, on the lens, all over his face and hair, doubling back to mingle with what pooled in the gash at the top of his head told me so.

I went back for them.

I went back for them because I knew he'd want me to. I knew he'd like to have them with him wherever his body ended up, likely at the bottom of the quarry past the old farm because it was abandoned and the water was murky, filled with old shit that had sunk there decades ago—not even the sex-crazed idiots over at the high school used that spot for a romp because it was… there was just something off about it.

He'd like that.

If he had to die, he'd like to make a difference, and so I would put his body there. There he could be part of the lore, be one of the ghosts that haunted that old, shut down place.

Plus, nobody would think to look there because nobody would have the guts to.

I went back for them, and they were there, right where he left them, right where they landed when they fell off after his eye was ruined and his

298

face collapsed, little bones poking through the skin, piercing, cutting, flaying.

Except they were different.

They were bloodless.

The temples—arms, I called them, but he knew what the real word was... of course he did—were folded as though he had taken them off on purpose and laid them down.

But he hadn't.

He hadn't had the chance to do anything, least of all set his glasses up nice.

I went to pick them up but didn't because somebody must have done this and the realization washed over me like a cold breeze. Ok, an animal could have come and licked the blood clean, got a little appetizer before its main course. That made sense. But no animal could fold those arms—temples, shit—that way. Not a single one.

I went back for the glasses alone, in the dark. Nobody knew I was coming because if they did, they would know I had a body in my trunk and maybe even how that body got there.

I was alone out there and now it seemed darker than it was before, darker when I let loose the shot that lit up the sky and blew up his head, darker than I've ever seen it before.

Was he still there... watching me?

Why did we always think it was a 'he', anyway? It could be a 'she' just as easily because there's some sick bitches out there too—just as sick as some of the dudes I know. It's ridiculous to just think men—

What the fuck? I hate when I got off on a tangent, thinking about something stupid instead of paying attention to the shit happening in front of me. Because somebody fucked with his glasses and they could be—

I went back for them because I knew he'd want them but maybe I should have let them go. The leaves crunching under some bastard's foot told me so.

SAY CHEESE

Blood on the viewfinder draws fangs from smiles and opens wounds that bake in the noonday sun.

SUNDAY MORNING

1

_____

He stood on the steps, listening to the choir lift their voices, a last-minute practice before the morning's service. He wished he could plug his ears, blot out the sound with his screams, something. He didn't want to hear them thanking God for their lot in life, for the streets that stank like piss and vomit, for the bread and milk the government let them have for free. He didn't want to open those heavy doors and feel the oppressive heat greet him. It was cooler outside. He didn't want to smell the foyer, its odd mixture of incense, sweat, and sulfur ever present. He couldn't bring himself to bow his head in supplication again. He didn't feel anything when he did anyway—just the hot, sticky sweat that coated his neck cooling in the air that had been whipped up by the dirty fan propped in the window.

But he had to.

Just as sure as he knew his own name, he knew he had to enter that place, hear those sounds, and smell those smells again. The thick, glossy tenement paint that caked the walls had his name etched in it. The hymns that the choir wailed incessantly spoke to him this time... every time. At least that's what it felt like. He was afraid of what would happen if he didn't respond to their deafening call.

He opened the doors to the church—big hulking things made of dark wood with antique gold trim—and slipped inside. He didn't want to make a sound, didn't want to draw attention to himself. He just wanted to do what he had to do and leave. He might never come back if he could get away clean.

"Where you been, Caleb? You know he been looking for you."

The sound of the old woman's voice startled him. She was there, sitting on her perch like she always was, her Sunday outfit covered by a thick black shroud with her head bowed as if in prayer. A stack of fans advertising Bedman's Funerary Services sat on her lap, waiting to be handed to the parishioners that would fill the sanctuary soon. Everything was the same as it always was inside the church where he had begged for forgiveness all those years ago, his knees bruised and bleeding. This Sunday morning was the same as every Sunday morning, yet the scene frightened Caleb to the core.

The old woman didn't look up when she spoke.

He passed by her without responding. There was nothing to say anyway.

He had been gone for too long.

2

The cognac cap toe lace ups had been polished to a perfect shine. The gray slacks he wore touched the tops of the shoes, fitting the pastor the way only tailor-made clothing could. His robe, pressed crisply, fell mid-shin. He was smoothing it when Caleb entered the room. As the pastor took off the onyx ring that sat majestically on his right pinky, Caleb spoke.

"Hello, Pastor."

"There you are," the pastor said in a rich baritone. There wasn't happiness in his voice, but not anger either—frustration, perhaps. Caleb had been gone for longer than anticipated. He had almost caused a delay in the festivities.

Caleb closed the door behind him, knowing that was what was expected of him. He tried to remain quiet and still, wanting to say nothing under his gaze, but his will was weak. It would take a much longer absence for Caleb to escape the pastor's control.

The pastor waited in silence; his will was far stronger than Caleb's could ever hope to be. An explanation was expected, and Caleb knew he had better give one or suffer the consequences.

"They've taken to the streets again," Caleb started, trying to buy time. He glanced out of the window and saw the first of the congregation making their way to the weathered doors of the church. Sister Clara and her niece Magnolia were early, and Caleb had an idea why. He didn't have much time.

"St. Augustine Baptist is out there with their pastor sitting on a throne hoisted up on their shoulders," Caleb continued, trying to act normal even as he spied more people heading to the church doors, snatching glances at the upstairs window as they did. Brother Charles made eye contact with Caleb and nodded. Caleb wasn't sure if he nodded in kind or not. "They're carrying him around and singing hymns up and down 5th."

"Is that so?" The pastor groomed his mustache in the mirror, pulling his lips into a frown as the little comb tugged at the coarse hair.

"People are paying attention." Caleb didn't know why he said it. He shouldn't have, if he wanted to get out of there unscathed. But it was out, and Pastor heard it. He turned around with eyes ablaze.

"They can look all they want, can't they? Stick their heads out the window and watch the parade go by. But we know what we have here. We know where the true message of salvation lies, don't we Caleb?"

Caleb could already feel the pastor's cold, clammy hand on his arm, and he shivered. He didn't think he could bear the man touching him, not another time, but he had to. If he wanted to make it out of that room, he had to.

The pastor's hand stopped in mid-air, his eyes trained on Caleb's face. He studied the younger man, letting his gaze course over Caleb's nervous, darting eyes and sallow skin animated by trembling muscles. After what seemed like five minutes, he dropped his hand, busying it with something else; dusting his robe, slicking his hair back—Caleb didn't know. What the pastor did with his hands after the fact didn't matter. The smile that played at the corners of the pastor's mouth did.

Caleb began to pant—open-mouthed and shamefully.

The pastor walked away from Caleb and toward a desk that took up most of the small room. In an amused voice that belied a secret Caleb would never know, he asked, "Why you been gone so long, boy?"

Caleb's mouth felt dry. He couldn't peel his tongue from the roof of it.

"I—I had to go uptown to get what you needed."

"Is that so?" the pastor asked, his back turned to Caleb now as he fingered the hymnal on his desk. "And did you get what I need? Because you know I need it for today—right now, in fact."

"I didn't, Pastor. See, that's the thing," Caleb started. He knew the fidgeting and fast-talking he had started up was going to make everything worse, but he couldn't stop himself. "They didn't want to give it to me," he continued. "They told me you would have to get it yourself this time, or they can't help us no more."

Caleb inched toward the door as he spoke, focusing on it, thinking he might have to make a break for it before long. The pastor did not like to be disappointed.

"Didn't give it to you, you say?"

The pastor's voice seemed like it was coming from all around him. Caleb turned his head toward the desk where he had been standing but didn't see him there. He turned left and right but did not see him in either place. An involuntary gasp escaped his lips as the realization that the pastor was nowhere to be seen hit home. He decided that if he ever had a chance of getting away, it was then. Right then.

Caleb turned to the door and grabbed the handle. It was hot to the touch. Hissing in pain, he threw the door open and ran down the hall, barreling past the old woman so quickly he didn't notice that she was slumped over on her side at an unnatural angle, the fans that sat in her lap pooling around her feet like water.

Caleb ripped open the church doors, pulling them with such strength he almost ripped them off their hinges. He was almost out. He could feel the fresh air on his face, could smell the fragrance of the city: hot dogs, motor oil, and cigarettes all rolled up into one. He could be free if he could just take one more step.

Caleb put one foot onto the church steps that led to the door in triumph and cast a glance over his shoulder. The pastor stood before the amassing congregation, smiling with teeth that were unnaturally white. He carried on conversations and shook hands, all the while his eyes focused on Caleb.

His smile turned Caleb's blood cold.

3

Caleb left the church feeling numb. He stumbled down the stairs, bumping into people on their way up, grabbing onto them for balance.

"What's the matter with you, boy?"

"You're going the wrong way!"

People pulled at him from all directions, trying to redirect his steps.

"No," Caleb exclaimed weakly, fighting to move away from the church steps and out into the world, the free world, where no one knew his name.

Where no one wanted anything from him.

"You know what I need, Caleb."

The pastor's voiced sounded inside his head. Caleb slapped his hands over his ears and howled in the morning light. He felt his legs give way, the concrete biting into the scars on his knees, splitting open skin that had long since healed from the last time he acquiesced under the weight of the pastor's gaze. His chest heaved with exertion as he screamed over and over and over again.

When his breath gave out and he lay gasping on the ground, he lifted his head and looked toward the church doors knowing he had to see, but afraid of what he might find. The splintered wood seemed to jut out at him like daggers. The antique gold that had once outlined a latticework of symbols adorning the door had melted into a ruddy stream, donning an ancient patina the color of dried blood.

The congregation stared at him in expectation.

DARKNESS AND LIGHT

It was dark, but I could see as if the sun were shining, as if the blackness that engulfed the night was nothing more than shade from a tree. It writhed there, its body moving in waves, the vibration unconcealed by its paper-thin skin. It could smell me. I knew that. It could taste the salty-sweet scent of my fear on the air in a way that a true sommelier understands the composition of fine wine. But its anticipation had a scent also; one so enticing it woke me from my sleep. It salivates there in the woods, waiting for me to turn away, to unwittingly expose my neck to its teeth. I knew that too and would happily oblige, for a meal is a meal. And as the door locks behind me and the pulsating in my hands begins to ache, I wait to be sated as well.

THE CONVERSATION

"I don't want to go."

"What? Come on… you have to."

"Maybe I—"

"Maybe nothing. You already said you would—you can't just—"

"I said that years ago. I was a kid. He shouldn't have taken it so seriously. How could I say I would—"

"Wouldn't you?"

"Wouldn't I what?"

"Wouldn't you take it seriously? If you were getting everything you ever wanted, wouldn't you take it seriously?"

"How can he hold me to that, though? I was too young. It's—it's not…"

"Fair? Stop being ridiculous. There's no —"

"What are you talking about 'ridiculous'? How is it ridiculous? This is bullshit! I was too young to agree to something like that! No one in their right mind would hold me to —."

"—stupid."

"What? Why…"

"Are you kidding me right now?"

"I'm fucking serious. I'm not go —"

"And that's why I said you're stupid. He'll never go for it."

"Wha —"

"I mean, you know that, right? You can whine about how unfair it is and how you were too young, wah wah, but it's not gonna matter."

"You don't know —"

" —not now. Not ever, probably. It's gonna happen."

"I —I can't… I can't do it. I just can't."

"You will. You will and then you'll wish you'd never opened your mouth, never looked his way… never called him in the first place."

"No… I —I can't —"

"Hun, you don't have a choice."

ANOTHER DAY

It rained the day I took them, trapped them, kept them inside—clear, where I can see. I took them all, let them settle, mingle, comfort each other as they rippled, moved, fought against the confines, their pretty little place, until they stilled.

No, not all of them.

Some I sampled. I couldn't make myself wait, not knowing when the day would come when I could visit with them again. So, I tried them—I tasted them. And I loved them.

I looked at them, those from that first day, that rainy day under a sky that seemed to hate me for what I was doing, sought to stop me by growling and clapping its hands. I looked at them every time I added another, even if I never looked at the other so often, never so intensely. I looked at them, and they saw me too. They called my name and it made me smile. Sometime the rain came again when I was looking at them, but it was less effectual each time, pouting instead of raging, punished, put in its place.

It rained today, and I took them out in spite of it, because of it. And tasted again. Tasted nearly each of them, leaving myself with almost none. Because it is another day, and I've saved for this… just like you told me to.

OUT OF TIME

Running.

Blind, aimless movement, like a wave crashing onto the shore, rolling over and flattening the sand, removing all distinguishing marks: the hearts carved by fallen branches, the initials inside.

K. T.
+
L. M.
4 eva

Or at least until the tide came in and wiped it all away.

Wiped away.

Obliterated.

Razed.

Like Gomorrah and the Ark.

Starting over.

Starting again.

Hands pushed and grabbed. Legs pedaled, propelling men, women, and children toward the back of the store. The sweater she had been looking at seemed to disappear into thin air as if part of a magic trick—now you see it, now you don't—the garden variety activity provided for the very old and the very young at resorts when the parents go off to play.

It had been ripped out of her hands by someone running by, face a blur. The tag came off in her hand, one of its corners puncturing her skin to draw blood. She thought to put the wound to her mouth and lick at it in that vampiric way that people did when they saw their own blood in the open air, selfishly recalling it into their own bodies before anyone else could partake. She thought to do so, to taste the metallic notes, but as the next person to barrel through the racked space nearly bowled her over, taking that route instead of the tiled path that was mobbed with runners from the café at the front of the store, the customer service section, and the bathrooms, she thought better of it. If her hand was in her mouth and she took another hit she might knock her own teeth out. She might bite so deeply into her flesh that the soft lapping of her tongue wouldn't be enough to assuage the pain.

Running.

Everyone was running. Yet their feet made no sound.

Because of the siren.

The siren started up, crescendoing to its highest point within seconds, its tone even and persistent. It sounded like an old-time ambulance, deep and full, not shrill even though the hair on her arms and the back of her neck stood up, responding to it the same way it did to high-pitched noises. She had always thought the gooseflesh came because of the shrieking nature of it all: babies crying, nails scratching on a chalkboard, the undertone of a fire alarm—that shrill beeping that seems to ring in the room even after the alarm has been turned off: all of it was enough to set her teeth on edge.

But that wasn't it.

That wasn't all.

The siren was going off.

The one that most people living there had never heard before, including her.

The siren that meant it was over.

Everything they knew was unequivocally, irreconcilably over.

Because They were there.

She watched an old man fall to his knees a few rows over from her. He had been in the toddler clothing section, perhaps shopping for his grandson, the one he would never see again because he would never get out of that store. She saw him drop to his knees because the racks that had separated his body from view just seconds before had been pushed aside, toppled, fallen upon. And there were bodies. Arms and limbs tangled, twisted, bent under the weight of their own bodies. Still. She felt her mouth open, felt her jaw unhinge as her eyes fell upon some of the bodies stacked on top of each other: big, small, tiny.

Tiny.

And there was blood.

THEY were there.

She tried to take a step, to run with the rest of them, to succumb to the understanding, the stark reality the older man had already allowed, to *move*, but she could do nothing, nothing, nothing at all as she thought of her parents probably trying to get into the basement, to get into the tub, to hole up like it was a tornado. She could do nothing as she thought of her dogs running around her house, ears flattened to their heads to block out the sound, whimpers escaping their throats—could imagine them bouncing nervously as they peered through the sliding glass door into their familiar yard, though that space likely didn't look so familiar anymore. She thought of her colleagues running into the storage closet like she would have if she hadn't gone out to lunch, pressing their bodies into a space filled with things that could kill them if turned into projectiles, but having nowhere else to go. And it wouldn't matter. Because this wasn't a hurricane; this wasn't a tornado, or a tsunami, or dust storm, or any other kind of storm. It was Them.

It was THEM.

And it was time.

She stood there, looking out of the store window, marveling at how much she could see now that there were no racks or display stands in the way. She could see the whole parking lot, the kaleidoscope of colors that the cars made. She could see the neon signs atop the storefront doors, noticed their names as they blinked out one by one, a backwards stadium wave, a wink, a caps off goodbye as the ground opened and then the clouds parted, asphalt, concrete, wind, and earth shifting to support the tether.

AWAKENING

Night when I thought it was day.

Cold, but unnaturally so, or so said the daffodils that had pushed through the ground already, showing their brilliant yellow. Unlike the pinks and reds and yellows of the azaleas that bloomed in my neighbor's yard, the ones she fussed over and pruned, the ones I vomited into over the fence before I fell... fell while we were talking about summer vacation and watching each other's dogs: fell and never got up again.

Days?

Weeks?

Years since that day, the world cycling on without a care while I lay in my grave, cold and dank, trying to get out.

To get out.

Because I shouldn't be there... I shouldn't be in the ground.

Locked away.

Forgotten.

Because I am here and I can remember the way the sun kissed his hair while we sat on the deck, how the night sky looked when it was full of stars.

Because I can remember what it was like to laugh and walk and run, yes run, so I did run because I could and my legs could still carry me. They carried me right back to where I should be. Right back home.

Cold.

Unseasonably cold for April or May or whatever month it was. Killing my daffodils. Killing my follower that would come up even if I wasn't there to see them.

So yellow. I want to touch one but I am afraid to ruin it. When I see my fingers in the moonlight, gnarled and discolored, bloody because I had been clawing, clawing, clawing at the lid of the grave, beating against the cement enclosure, kicking my way up through the dirt, dirt that fell into my eyes to blind me... dirt that slipped into my mouth and down my throat to choke. I was afraid to touch the daffodils, not because I didn't want to make them like me because they were already like me—dead and revived, awakened, denied rest. No, I didn't want to touch the daffodils because I would soil them with the dirt from my grave and the dirt was my own.

Happy.

Laughing.

Music in the night.

They were probably dancing, maybe watching a TV show, the kids might be playing a game and maybe cooking together in the kitchen, maybe...

A new car in the driveway.

A new car where mine used to be.

They were probably loving anew.

The wind guided my steps and for that I was thankful because it meant I didn't have to think about it anymore, didn't have to find my way back to a place I didn't want to return.

But here I am.

The ground welcomed me back, kissed my skin as it peeled and left memories behind, let me pull its blanket over myself like an old friend.

POTENTIAL

Anger boiled down to complacency and it was quiet about it.

He didn't know what to do with that.

Like wine reduced to a concentrated flavor, what had set his teeth on edge, made him feel like he was going crazy, the clattering and banging of what she had become he feared would drive him over the edge and out of the door, became a smaller thing, a manageable annoyance once he spied what she hid behind her back. Down home squeeze brought to knees before the thing he'd hoped would hold them, and it didn't take much imagination for him to see how she'd played with his insides, torn free what she wanted to taste right away and wasted the rest.

Impulsive.

Greedy.

He'd have to teach her how to dress them properly so she didn't spill.

Oh, but her knifework was divine.

Time.

Give it time.

She might be ready for the ball after all.

ILL-GOTTEN

It was hot and musty in the club even before the show got started. The air was thick, almost like you could see it hanging in front of you like wool, and Will had to stop himself from reaching out to touch it. He was surprised they would even let that many people in the place—it had to be some kind of violation to have wall-to-wall standing room only events in the old, single-stage bar, but it happened every week, and nobody said anything. They would when the floor caved in. There'd be a whole lot of shit to say when that happened.

Will didn't intend to be there for that, even if Mack indulged him a little, let him have more time before they had to run.

If... but that was a pipedream.

Will knew better.

Michelle, Renee, and Tip were nearby; Will had told them to stay close, kept reminding them about it like they were little kids on a playdate and he was the weary parent acquiescing to a detour in the park. That's kind of how he felt, truth be told. He liked them all right; there wasn't anything wrong with them, unless you wanted to call Tip out on his wigger shit, pull his hat off and let the lights hit that blond crown. There was money in his low hanging jeans, trust fund money that he didn't want the others to know about, but Will did. Will knew everything about him and the girls—he had known everything about every single one of them. Mack made sure he did in case he needed to make something happen.

Keep that in your back pocket, he'd said. Old gangster shit. Will's back pocket was full of all kinds of things now.

Did they even say 'wigger' anymore or was that from another life, another jump, some other blood stuck between him and Mack, or beyond, one that left behind remnants of shit that wouldn't mean anything to anyone who came after? Will didn't know and didn't have time to figure it out. Something big was coming if he could make the cards bump. The last run was a set up for him. Will had to make it count.

The beat was manufactured, muffled bass and what sounded like whispering, nothing like the music with live instruments that his grandfather used to play around the house. Will thought the 80s were bad... watered down, Jheri-curled whining that it was, and the 90s with passable slow music poisoned by sex-fueled lyrics, but this? This was on another level. He wished Mack hadn't come to him in his dreams, hadn't demanded his service, hadn't bothered with him at all. He didn't even know how to use the wormhole he had reached through to fuck with Will —Mack only knew that he *could* do it, so he did. Mack would keep on doing it until he got what he wanted and though Will tried his best not to think about how many people would get tapped for the job if he couldn't deliver—how many had already tried and failed—he couldn't stop his mind from going there, drawn to the thought like a beacon. Their eyes. Something inside him wanted to count the eyes of the ones who came and went, but Will shook the thought away. No more. Will was determined to make it stop... that night.

Michelle and Tip were dancing close, sparks flying between them, and Will wondered why they didn't just fuck already—leave the dancefloor and do the deed. They might not have the chance to after this—none of the others who had taken the ride with him ever got the chance to do anything but spill their blood on the asphalt and die. Will didn't have any reason to believe it would be any different for them either, and in the end, that didn't really matter. He only hoped that Mack knew why it had to be done and that he was right about it. After seeing what happened to the ones who had tried before, Will knew he only had one more shot—there would be no time to even take a breath after meeting the breach this time.

He was in his head.

Will was stuck in his head, and he knew he shouldn't be. Worrying about what had happened or not happened was a mistake. It would make him slow, sluggish, nostalgic for something that was never his to mourn. But still, he had seen all of their faces, ignorance and youthful optimism coloring their expressions the way it should color his but would not... not ever again.

Will had seen their faces as flesh separated from muscle, skulls gleaming in the cold, fluorescent light under an inky sky.

He had seen them in his dreams. He had watched as their mouths gaped, wishing them away, their swift passage his only desire. And even though Will didn't want to, he remembered.

He remembered them all.

When the man bumped into him near the bar, bodies packed so tight he couldn't help but do so, Will didn't hear what he said in response, and that was good. The words the man would have uttered might have helped Will figure out what decade he was in—at the very least, maybe even the actual year, but knowing how to respond might be a challenge. A misstep would make him stand out. Overthinking would bring on that misstep, so he didn't. He didn't look at the man either, for fear that he might stare. Will couldn't afford that, didn't have time for the problem that might come from it. Instead, he reminded himself that he belonged in that time and place. It was his, regardless of what Mack had shown him. He was himself and he was right where he was supposed to be.

Except that he couldn't be sure anymore, not when he could find an onyx pinky ring next to a pick with a fist for a handle on the nightstand where his cell phone charged. No, he couldn't be sure of anything anymore.

Biggie Smalls was asking for one more chance but that didn't mean anything; the greats play forever. KRS-One had just been booming through the speakers with a track from a decade before Biggie's hit; yeah, some shit is immortal. But Biggie coming through the speakers gave Will a starting point, one that made him feel even more confident that this time he could pull it off.

Because no one else had been able to do that yet.

If they had, what would he be doing now? Will knew it was foolish to think about that, to worry about what might have been, but he couldn't help it. Would he be across the country like he had planned when he thought he had some say about what came next? Would he have been travelling the world, maybe have gotten married and seen the sights with his wife? Would his mother still be alive if the dreams hadn't come... if Mack or one of the others had done what they set out to do and left him out of it? This was the question he hated most, because he knew the answer. Part of him wanted to kill Mack, even though he knew that was as ridiculous as threatening a corpse in a casket. But still, it's what he would do if it were possible. And who knows? None of what was going on—what had *been* going on since Mack had shown him everything—should be possible. So maybe, just maybe, there was a way to kill that motherfucker before Will sliced his own throat. Because that was what the other part of him wanted to do: kill himself, remove himself from the gameboard: lights out. It was only right that he do so after what he was planning to let happen to Michelle and Renee and Tip. He would think of his mother when he did it too, would make sure he conjured up her dying eyes to stare at him while he breathed his last breath. He'd hope she knew it was for her, even though she would never have wanted it to happen. But it was the right thing to do, and he was a good boy, after all. If there was anyone watching, anyone who cared about penance in any real way, Will would be able to do that for her.

Like a fly on the wall, Will had been disturbed from a dreamless sleep and brought into a room that existed in a time long before his own. He was made to listen as Mack and his partner talked about things Will didn't understand. Will recognized Mack from an old photo album—a cousin; his mother's granduncle's son or something like that. He had been wearing what could only be described as a zoot suit in the picture Will saw, pinstriped and replete with a chain dangling from hip to knee. The picture showed him standing with three other people—two women, one man—whose names Will's mother did not know. They weren't written on the back in his grandmother's neat cursive either. Only the year—1955, no month, no day—and 'Friends', as she had labeled them, was scrawled there. 'Friends', and that is how they would stay in perpetuity, at least in his family's records. Will hadn't seen the picture a lot; it wasn't one that sat on their mantle, so he wasn't sure if the man in the room with Mack was one of the two in the picture as well, but that wasn't what was fore-front in his mind when he came to grips with who he was seeing.

He knew immediately that it wasn't a dream. He also understood, with all clarity, that this was the fork in the road.

"I mean, the first Negro talkie was shot here," the other man said.

"The what?"

"The first Negro movie with sound… it was shot right here."

"What?"

Will's long-lost cousin looked irritated, and instantly Will knew that sometimes the other man got on Mack's nerves talking about random shit. Mack sent the other man every signal he could to hurry things up.

He looked at his watch, frowned over the time, pulled his eyes away to stare daggers at the other, then checked his watch again for good measure. When Mack spoke again, he was exasperated… beyond frustrated.

"What are you talking about, Carl?"

"Yeah," Carl said, stuffing his mouth with corn nuts, crunching them with his back teeth so loudly it could have made the bum in the corner stir, "Oscar Micheaux did it. Shot it right downtown."

Carl pointed toward the entrance they had used to get into the alley, and Will knew they had entered that way many times over many years. The entrance was in the direction of the George Washington Bridge that connected New Jersey and New York through Fort Lee and Manhattan. Will peered through the entrance to look at the sliver of sky he could see, but then Carl switched angles abruptly to point in the other direction.

"Or, no… I think it was that way. Wait… I'm screwed up," he said as he shifted his attention to the original direction he had pointed in again, a question on his lips.

"None of this shit would have been here then, so I'm all turned around, Mack, but it was here, that's for sure. Right here in Fort —"

"Nobody gives a shit about some old movie that was shot here!"

Will knew Mack didn't mean to yell as loud as he did—he could sense his cousin's thoughts. The idea of that telepathic connection was so disconcerting, it made Will dizzy. But it was real. Will knew that Mack hadn't meant to yell like that not because he didn't want to hurt Carl's feelings, but because of the bum in the room. Mack didn't want to have to deal with another surprise. Will had the distinct impression that there had been many surprises along the way already.

"It's history, Mack. It's important."

"Not to me, and it shouldn't be important to you… not if you know what's good for you."

He'd done it.

He'd threatened his best friend.

Will could feel the man's consternation, understanding context that he shouldn't. It had taken 20 years to get to that point and both men knew nothing good would come of it.

"It *better* mean something to *you*," Carl said as he stood to his full six feet, "if you know what's good for *you*."

Carl was imposing and he knew it. Mack tried to glower back but his heart wasn't in it. Carl knew that too.

"Carl...?" Mack said, unpuffing his chest, hoping that would be enough to cool things down, "what are you going on about? We need to get a move on—we don't have time to fool around with —"

The Exile—that was the name of it," Carl continued as if he hadn't heard Mack talking and while that made Mack angry, he knew there wasn't anything he could do about it. He already made the mistake of trying to use his weight to force Carl into doing something once and it was like running up against a brick wall. He wasn't interested in being repositioned like a child again, so he waited him out.

When Carl sat back down on an upended milk crate, Mack was relieved. Will knew all of this like he knew his own name.

"Made it back in 1931," Carl continued, the southern drawl of his people taking root in his pace, if not his pronunciation. "It's about a cowpoke who falls in love with a city girl, something like that. She's rich and wants to open a club or whatever they used to call it... a speakeasy, yeah. Anyway, they—"

"Carl!" Will saw Mack tense as if he expected the interruption to earn him one on the chin, but it was a chance he thought he had to take.

"History is *important*, Mack," Carl said, his eyes trained on his friend in a way that made him look soulless.

Mack's jaw worked, his teeth were grinding into powder as they sawed their way down to the gum. But Carl kept on.

"It's the ignorant who can't see that, and they will always be in the dark. As much as you come and go, you should care what goes on in between."

Mack's skin felt hot and Will felt flush too, especially when Carl looked away from him, ignoring the mounting anger on Mack's face to gaze thoughtfully at the high-rises peeking out from the mouth of the alley.

"She ain't mean us no harm," Carl said mournfully, looking at his calloused hands lying limp in his lap, "not at first. But we couldn't let well enough alone, could we? We just had to go, had to see. Once we caught a whiff of what smelled good, we had to have it. But it was hers and we shoulda left well enough alone."

"Carl," Mack started, but Carl kept talking.

"Ain't supposed to do folks like that. I knowed it and you did too. But it called to us like a bitch in heat, ain't it? I couldn'ta said no even if I tried. Be careful, pap. Be careful what you ask for, 'cause them roots'll get you."

"Carl," Mack tried again and this time the man looked at him with solemn eyes, "You's just tired, that's all. Just tell me where you put it and I'll get it back for us. We'll be livin' high on the hog uptown. Get us some dancin' girls to warm our beds. Come on, man, just tell me."

Carl's laugh came from deep in his chest and started slowly, bubbling up, building on itself as it rose to the surface. Mack didn't much like that —it made the hairs on his neck stand on end. Will could feel Mack's resolve cracking.

"What's so damn funny, man? Look," Mack said, shooting a glance around the room before lowering his voice, "we gotta get that shit before somebody else does, ok? It's *ours*. *We* did the work for it, not some, some bum whose gonna find it and run off."

Mack pointed at the man on the floor but Carl did not look at him.

"It's ours, man. Let's get what's coming to us."

Carl's laughter roared in the dilapidated room and a mix of emotions danced across Mack's face. Will could see that Mack was contemplating striking him; the tension in his body was as readable as words written on a page. But Carl didn't notice. He wheezed, and even though his chest ached, he took a deep breath, trying to take in enough air to speak. It was harder to do than before; Carl's breath grew labored and shallow as he deteriorated before Mack's eyes.

"Oh, we'll get what's coming to us... no matter how long it takes, we'll get it." It hurt... Will could see that everything hurt the man now, even though he had appeared strong moments before.

"Yes!" Carl said animatedly, his furrowed brow releasing as Carl spoke the words, misreading the message and thinking his friend was coming around. "That's right, my man. We will get what's coming for us, that's for damn sure. Just tell me where you put it and I'll get it *for* us."

Carl nodded, still laughing. Mack was almost jumping up in down, his excitement was so complete.

"It's time."

"It is, man. It's long overdue, I'd say. But you know what, you're always right on time."

Carl stopped laughing abruptly and looked at the man he had called friend once upon a time. Disdain colored his features. His lips curled into a snarl before he spoke again.

"It's time to pay the piper, Mack."

Carl coughed and it sounded like the effort split his lungs apart.

Mack deflated as Will stared on incredulously. Mack didn't notice what was happening in front of him, didn't see what Carl was going through. Instead, he punched at the air in frustration, expending the anger and pent-up energy that had gathered in his joints as he coaxed Carl out. Mack wondered if his friend had grown senile waiting in that place. Was there really a screw loose like his own mama had thought there had been? Mack had never wondered before, but the prospect was too hard to ignore now.

"... can't just go on like we don't have to. We owe, and they gonna collect."

Carl had been talking but Mack hadn't been listening. He wasn't listening when he cut in either, not really. All he knew was that this—all of it—was bullshit.

"Are you calling me stupid, Carl? Huh?"

Mack's voice was loud but he didn't care. Not even his mama called him stupid, and he wasn't going to stand there and take that kind of guff from someone who hadn't even finished the 6th grade.

"I may not know whether I'm coming or going most of the time, but that don't mean I'm stupid. Are you saying I don't have no sense —"

And then it hit him—Will could see understanding dawning on Mack's face. It was a terrifying sight.

"Christ, I *have* been stupid," Mack said, in awe. "Dumber than a door-nail, in fact. 1931, you say," he whispered, and Will felt like he could see lights dancing in his eyes. "The year the bridge went up."

Carl nodded and Will could tell that he was pleased with Mack for the first time in he didn't know how long. "I put it where the first Negro sound movie was made by the biggest Negro movie maker there had ever been, at least at that time. I'm sure you've seen bigger now. Me? I'll never get up from here, won't be here when you get back neither, and that's ok. Something that hard to have ain't for me no way, I guess."

Carl looked beyond Mack at the bum on the floor and Will followed his gaze. He almost screamed out loud when he saw the man's countenance in two place—animated in one and stone dead in the other. Will looked back at Carl quickly, feeling seen.

"That movie... the bridge... man, it's brilliant," Mack gushed, oblivious to all else. "How did you even *think* of that?"

Carl ignored Mack as he marveled over how intricate the plan had been, all the while trying not to let the admission that he would never have figured it out on his own leave his lips. Instead, Carl mused like an old man sitting in a rocking chair on a porch before a setting sun. He nodded in the direction of the George Washington Bridge.

"That's the world's very first two-level suspension bridge right there, did you know that? Went up the same year Micheaux did his thing. To me, can't be one without the other." Carl kept talking, his eyes landing on the bum's body reverently, his own bag of bones on the floor where it fell. "Why'd I do that? Because history is important, Mack. It's everything."

Carl leaned in and for a second Will wondered if he was about to slug Mack after all. But instead he said, low so nobody could hear,

"Find Metropolitan Studios and you finds the money."

When Will had woken up in bed the next morning, he had questions. When did the dream take place? It couldn't have been 1931, because they were talking about that year as though it had been in the past. Not in 1955 like the date on the back of the picture either—the man in the picture with Mack had been sporting a pompadour and there was not even the suggestion of one on Carl's head, though he might not have been in the picture at all—that was a possibility Will couldn't afford to forget. But something about Carl seemed more modern than that. Somehow, he seemed more wizened than Mack, more aware. He spoke of history and how important it was and Mack didn't seem interested in that at all. They were two different people, sure, but Will couldn't help but wonder if it was more than just different interests that stood out. Will wondered if the difference was deeper, more experienced, more grounded…generational.

He didn't have long to think about it.

Every night after the first one, a different dream came to Will. His vantage point was always somewhere in the room where they couldn't see him, but he was still part of the action. Will may have called them dreams but that was only because he didn't have another word to describe them, but he knew they were more than that. He knew that right away and didn't have time to let it frighten him. There was an urgency to them, a buildup he could feel in his very bones. Will needed to pay attention to what was happening in that weird state because not doing so might be the mistake he couldn't take back.

Tired man in checkered pants with cuffs that rode high off his shoes, his white sweater vest tight against his flat stomach walking across in the pedestrian path, crossing the bridge with the city lights of Manhattan's upper west side illuminating the sky behind him.

Afroed girl in a yellow tube top and brown and gold striped bell-bottoms riding in the back of a car, eyes wide in the dark of night.

Teenager in stone-washed jeans cuffed at the ankles but otherwise ballooned around his skinny lower half, skulking, trying to stick to the shadows once the

cliff presented itself, almost like he would rather scale the rockface than pay the toll.

Man with a hightop fade and a gold herringbone chain that caught the light driving a black Ford Escort that had seen better days at top speed over the last joint that connected the bridge to asphalt, where it swapped suspension for firm, hard ground... a man who looked suspiciously like Will himself.

All of them, their friends, every last one compressed against the air before crossing properly into New Jersey, their bones broken, crushed, ground against something unseen in that nowhere land between states, dying without a home. *If* they had truly died. Will couldn't tell because before he could make himself look at the gore, the utter mutilation, they were gone, wiped away, like they never existed. No blood, no entrails, no bone. Just nothing. And then he would wake up in a bed soaked through with sweat and a promise on the air that he too would suffer the same fate if he didn't figure out a way.

"Hey man, we gotta go," Will heard himself say to Tip, his lips close enough to touch the man's ear. He didn't remember crossing the room and going out onto the dance floor to break up the love fest but there he was. He could see the disappointment on Tip's face but didn't stay long enough for the man to think he could ask for more time. They all knew they had to go, that being at the show was just to have an alibi if they needed one. Will hadn't told them everything, hadn't mentioned the dreams to anyone at all because they seemed so off the wall, but they knew there was something big at the end of the bridge, over there in Fort Lee, if they could just find it. But they had to go that night—not during the day, not some other time... *that night.* The prospect of a big haul kept their mouths closed, which Will had counted on. He hated himself for what he had done and what he was about to do, but there was no time to wallow in that either.

It was time.

The dancers came out hot, bouncing so energetically the makeshift platform buckled and threatened to break. Will wondered if the idea he'd had about the floor caving in had been some kind of premonition. There was yelling in his ears too. It had been coming to him here and there since the last dream two nights before. But Will assumed it was just his conscious trying to get hold of him for once, to make him change course and do something else. But his mother was dead because of the dreams and what Mack wanted him to find. She'd tried to stop him and he'd steamrolled over her a few jumps ago, and he owed. He couldn't remember how long it had been and that drove Will crazy, so he focused on finishing since that was the only thing he could do. There was no turning back, even if Carl's voice, deep and rich, boomed, "No!" in concert with every other step Will took.

He needed the dreams to stop.

He needed to finish this for his mother.

He needed to find what Mack wanted him to find.

"But where *exactly* are we headed?" Tip asked from the back seat. They were speeding across the George Washington Bridge and Tip's arm was curled around Michelle. Will was happy for him. She was into him—Tip didn't know that yet—he only hoped it was true—but she was. They probably wouldn't ever be able to do anything other than this—hug in the back seat of a cramped car—but at least they'd have that. Michelle's friend Renee had been quiet all night. She was supposed to be there to hang out with Will while Michelle and Tip figured out what they were going to get into, but she and Will had barely spoken two words to each other all night and that was ok, because it didn't matter if they spoke or not—she was supposed to be there because she was always there, her or someone like her. They all were. And that was ok too. In the end, everything would be.

Will answered the question, thought it was only right. After all, he could already feel the fillings in his teeth wrenching away from the enamel, struggling to get out, stretching, drawing, reaching toward something outside the car as if summoned by a magnet. Soon he'd see the flesh from Renee's face pull away from her skull, he'd watch Tip's eyes pop from their sockets as they followed the same yearning his fillings had. He'd hear the audible slaps their flesh would make as it hit the glass that would be pulsing by then, in and out, in and out, like a heartbeat, before it became liquid and overtook Tip's ruined eyes, submerging what was left in an impossible pool of metallic gray and sickly yellow.

Soon.

For now, only his teeth knew what was to come. And they began to ache.

Michelle was oddly quiet, her eyes reflecting the lights that illuminated the bridge like mirrors.

Will started, his voice gravelly, "We're going into Jersey to—"

"I can see that, man," Tip laughed and something inside Will didn't appreciate being the butt of the joke, just like his dear old cousin. "What I *don't* get is why we'd leave a bumpin' party right when it was startin' to get hot."

Tip let his hand dip lower than Michelle's shoulder to pet the flesh just above her breast. He thought he was really doing something, but she kept staring at Will with her dead eyes.

"To go to shitty-assed New Jersey."

Tip laughed, but nobody else did. It didn't stop him, though.

"What are we going to *do* in Jersey, pray tell?"

Pray tell? Will thought and fought the urge to shake his head. You could take the rich boy out of the country club, but you couldn't take the country club outta the rich boy.

"There's some money waiting for me there. At Metropolitan Studios."

Will told them that much because it didn't matter. They would never be able to stop him. They would never be able to tell anyone else either, not if his dreams were right.

"Money? *Just* money? Man…" Tip said, as if it were the most ridiculous reason to mess up an otherwise perfect night. "You shoulda just said something. We didn't need to drive all the way out here for some *money*. You know I got you. Somebody owe you or something?"

Will stayed silent, listening. He tasted blood in his mouth.

"Man, we coulda taken care of this some other time."

Tip looked over at Michelle, noting where his hand was and let the corner of his mouth raise in an anticipatory smile he probably thought was charming. He let his gaze linger as he continued,

"I coulda fronted you whatever it was if you needed it like that."

Tip was genuinely upset and Will could appreciate that. He thought about saying something to placate him but dug the tip of his tongue into the gaping hole one of his fillings had left instead.

"We're all gonna die," Michelle said, her monotone voice filling the cabin as Tip ranted about how he thought there was jewelry or gold or other shit waiting for them out there in Jersey. He said a whole lot of things that didn't make a lot of sense but it was all background noise to Will. Will was entranced by Michelle's words and the faraway look in her eyes.

But he seemed to be the only one who heard her.

When he looked at Michelle, turning in his seat to face her, he noticed that one of her irises had detached and was crumpled over itself in a heap of brown.

Will turned back to the road and smiled. Blood stained his teeth.

"Wait. Will… man, did you say Metropolitan Studios?"

Will didn't trust his voice so he nodded.

"There *is* no Metropolitan Studios, dude." Tip laughed incredulously as he pulled Michelle closer. All Will heard was, 'Stupid idiot. Stupid nigger. Stupid ass.'

"What?" Will managed and spat blood onto the steering wheel. "What the fuck did you just say?"

"Yo, are you all right?" Tip asked, leaning forward to peer closer at Will and the bloody spit dripping down the center pad of the steering wheel. "Is your nose bleeding or something? I used to get nosebleeds all the ti —"

"What. The. Fuck. Did. You. Say?" Will's voice wasn't much more than a growl.

Tip sat back carefully, keeping his surprised eyes on the back of Will's head.

"I said the studios are gone," Tip hedged cautiously, all humor gone from his voice. "That place burned down a long time ago. Decades ago, man. Before our time. Been gone since the 50s, I think."

The lights on the bridge illuminated the cabin of the car like the searchlight of a helicopter and Michelle's eyes reflected it, shooting it at Will like laser beams.

All white.

All white.

No red.

No cars on this bridge because we're all dead, the voice in Will's head trilled.

Movie magic.

Dead magic.

He should have known...

...would have, but Mack would never believe.

And Michelle was laughing.

"Whoever told you they left money at the studio for you was pulling your leg. There's nothing left of the place."

Will didn't hear Tip tell him that he thought it was a park now, didn't notice when Michelle's voice cracked and broke, nor when she started hitting her head on the glass, thud thud thudding against it until it broke. He heard only Renee because she had started screaming, screaming like she had seen Hell through the split that was opening at the mouth of the bridge, screaming like doing so would save her from the jagged, gnashing teeth that waited inside. And then he heard Mack's voice, and he was screaming too.

I KNOW

When the board creaks I know.

Shadows playing with the moon, making finger puppets on the wall and yes, I know that it's him and not me, that it's him come for me because he loves to play even if he has no hands to do it with anymore.

Cold.

Cold as the ice that encased him, trapped him, blanketed him below, down under, deep in the frigid blue. It's like that outside when the board creaks, and I feel it. I feel it and I cover up, shield myself, tell the air, the clouds—whatever will listen—that I can creak too.

!

The light. The light came on. The light came on and I am alone. The light came on and I am alone in the house, alone on the street, alone in this world. The light came on and I am alone in the house. Alone in the house.

Alone.

In.

The.

House.

Downstairs. The light came on downstairs. The light came on downstairs and that is my only way out. My only way out of the house is down the stairs, downstairs, where the light came on... where someone turned the light on.

Was the timer on?

When I go to visit my cousin and we sit on the lake for hours at a time, I sometimes set the timer to turn the lights on so people think I'm still home, still here, puttering around and watching TV. If they watched close enough they'd know that the timer comes on too late. Later than I would normally watch. Later than I would normally walk the house. It was too late, and they'd know that if they paid attention.

Was someone watching?

Had someone noticed me, my patterns, and what I do? Did they know I don't do anything, nothing at all, and I would be here if they wanted to come in, if they wanted to scare me, if they wanted to hurt me?

The light came on downstairs and I know the timer was off. I turned it off a few weeks back, after my last trip. I didn't catch anything. After all day, I didn't catch anything and I was tired, so I turned if off and went up to bed. Right?

Sure. Because if I hadn't, I'd have seen the light every night since then.

Unless I fell asleep before it came on.

Had I?

It came on late, too late, so I might have fallen asleep, been in Lalaland by the time it came on, still asleep when it went off. Could be. But I turned it off when I came home that day. I turned it off... I'm positive I did...

The light came on downstairs and I looked for the clock upstairs. I looked toward the darkened guest room because that was the only room I could see into from where I was standing near the top of the stairs. I couldn't move, couldn't walk to my bedroom to look at my cellphone, or check the time there because my feet were frozen. So I squinted as I searched the darkness of that room, trying to see the alarm clock with the red digital numbers. Is that a 6 or an 8? The numbers merged together beneath my meshing eyelashes, blurring, obscured. I squinted again. I raised a hand to shield my eyes, but in the end what did it matter? It didn't matter if it was either a 6 or an 8. Neither of those would be right. It would be early. Too early for the timer to turn on... the one that comes on late.

Too early.

The light came on downstairs and I back away from the stairs terrified of what comes next, terrified of making noise... terrified because I know I turned the timer off, just like I know it isn't 10 or 11 o'clock at night and, therefore, late. I know it is. I'm up too high and would break a leg if I tried to jump out of a window. I know that too. Someone was there, down there, in the kitchen or in the living room waiting for me to come down and say hello. I knew that much too. And if I said hello, I'd never be able to say goodbye again.

TRADITION

"Zettaidesu."

The sweat that had formed when he realized what they expected him to do, leaching from his skin to form pools that turned cold in the evening air, had spilled over his sparse eyebrows to drip into his eyes, stinging them. It was not a joke. In this day and time, in the midst of the 21st century when practices like these seemed antiquated and backwards —when the threat of such consequences seemed the stuff of legend, the reality of another time and place—they were really going to do it. He had laughed at first, wanting to be ahead of the joke, ready to take the slap on the wrist he would surely get for what they considered an indiscretion— something that he thought was less than what that son of a bitch had deserved —and walk out of the door. But his oyabun was there, and he was never out in the open. Kaito hadn't even seen the man more than twice in the six years he had been Yakuza. But he was there, waiting. It had been him who had handed Kaito the tanto that had apparently been passed down for four generations, an ancient looking thing with a wooden grip and tempered blade.

Kaito tried to stop himself from wondering how many times it had been put into service.

The sweat dripped onto the table, falling from his hair as if wet from a shower. He was shaking. He could see the hair moving above his eyes, his usually straight high-top fade weighed down by the heat of panic, strands dipping into view at the edges of his peripheral vision. He was trembling, wiggling free fat droplets of sweat. *His* sweat. His *fear*.

A grunt sounded from somewhere in the room; a noise that spoke of impatience, bordered on disgust. If the penalty for beating up their enemy's son, a man who had ogled his sister and had been a stranger to Kaito before war was waged, bore the knife, he feared what the disrespect of making his oyabun wait might be.

Fingers littered the floor. Kaito imagined he could see fingers all around him, mounds of them like so much dirt, as one returned to the soil in rot another lay atop it anew.

Fingers on the floor next to his shoe, expensive imported sneakers he wished he hadn't spent his money on.

Fingers on the chair behind him, cauterized by an unseen flame held by a phantom, nerves still twitching, writhing, responding to the pain.

Fingers on the table next to his sweaty palm wearing the ring he had taken from the man whose blood he spilled.

Ninkyō dantai they liked to call themselves—so-called chivalrous organizations. His snicker sounded loud in the room.

Kaito looked at the knife.

He looked at his finger, the scales he'd had tattooed there years ago seeming to glow under the strain.

Sweat dripped from his head to pool with the rest on the table.

"Dekimasen," Kaito whispered desperately, hating the tears that sprang from his eyes to join the sweat.

Akio was standing close enough to hear Kaito say he couldn't do it, close enough to see that he was crying. He wanted to help him, wanted to come to the aid of the junior leader who showed him kindness more often than not, but he was low man on the totem pole, a shatei, even lower than Kaito was. If he kept his head, Akio might be pulled up in rank after this, might even take Kaito's spot as wakashu and get trained to lead. He hated that he would be advancing on the back of his friend's misery but he knew all too well what the alternative was: if they saw him showing Kaito any sympathy, he might see the business side of the tanto as well.

"Dekim —" Kaito started again but heard the sharp voice of the man he had taken under his wing. Akio. Nothing more than a kid, really, but stepping up to be a man... now.

"Meiyo," Akio hissed and Kaito thought he might kill him one day for spouting off about honor when he was on his knees. That is if he didn't get an infection from the rusty blade or bleed out right there surrounded by underlings and overlords.

"Yubitsume," Akio said firmly, earning an appreciative nod from his oyabun.

Yes, Kaito decided. If he got out of that situation alive, he might relish pulling the blade across Akio's neck.

Kaito picked up the tanto, deciding it was better not to look at Akio lest he see the fear in his eyes. He raised the knife over his left hand, the blade catching the light as it waited to connect. It was sharp and that was good. Maybe he could avoid gangrene.

"Moushiwake gozaimasen. Kanben shite kudasai," Kaito said, begging for mercy when he knew none would be given, but doing it anyway because it was expected. He bowed again for the same reason, all the while repeating a manta in his head, one that was supposed to reassure him but that failed,

"Just the pinky… it's just the tip… just the pinky… it's just the tip…"

A white cloth lay on the table waiting to receive his finger. He would then wrap it up and present it to his oyabun in an act of contrition.

The white would be soiled, ruined forever.

The red of his blood would be so bright it would appear to glow.

Kaito thought he might be sick.

He raised the knife higher and thought of an old mystery he had once watched on television as he drove the blade down, his thoughts passing in slow motion as it cut through the air. It was a black and white affair, something from the '50s that his grandfather had turned on and promptly fallen asleep in front of. Ten fingers sat in a pile on the floor behind a closed door. There were no bodies and the door had not been locked but when the maid came into the room she found the digits there, ends still wet with blood. There had been no other way out of the room than that door and the maid swore no one had gone in or come out since the original ten had gathered there to drink, talk, do whatever it was they did in movies like that. The window was closed. There was a fire burning in the fireplace. The police had no idea where to look. Kaito wondered what kind of clue his finger might have given them if they found it, tattooed with the scales of a dragon, nail manicured and neat.

IT KILLED THE CAT

"I heard they do it twice a year, sometimes three. Whenever their schedules line up," Charlie had said, chewing absently on what Jun Bae didn't know. What Charlie said so casually would resonate in Jun Bae's mind, would echo there later as he realized he had overstepped, when he knew it was too late to save himself, but Charlie would never know it. When he heard the news Charlie still might not think of him, make the connection. The name would mean nothing to him or anyone else in their world. Jun Bae had effectively become 'JB' to everyone in the business, and by "the business" he meant the sleazy, picture-taking bastards he had cast his lot with; the ruiners of reputations; the demons who held the keys to happiness and sadness and would gladly give them up... for a price. Jun Bae adopted the moniker 'JB' instead of letting himself get saddled with June Bug. It had been eight years since he had started introducing himself that way and he still thought the former was a better look.

Mok Jun Bae, son to a professor and a dance instructor, brother to a seamstress.

Junie, friend to few but loyal to the ones who stuck around.

Jun Bae, boyfriend to none, lover only ever to one and that distinction he truly regretted.

JB, trespasser, rule breaker, son of a bitch.

Dead man, he reminded himself. *Don't forget that one.*

He didn't need to feel the barrel of a gun on the back of his neck to know he was a goner—the story was laid out before him in vivid color, full color bleed, centerfold.

He had seen too much.

He had seen it all.

He wouldn't be allowed to tell.

Charlie told him everything he wanted to know—it was like a love story, poetry, dew on rose petals—all that shit. It was exactly what someone like Jun Bae wanted to hear—exactly the type of thing he'd love to destroy, burn to the ground so that the ones who enjoyed it couldn't have it anymore. He was the *sasaeng* who went into the bathroom stall after a K-Pop star left to collect any urine they could find. He was the paparazzo who stood outside of schools hoping to catch a picture of a celebrity picking up their kids. Jun Bae was the combination of the most obsessed fans and the most unscrupulous photographers times 10. Free-lancer, he liked to call himself, but the people he stalked had more colorful words to describe what he did for a living.

No one understood why he did what he did. He didn't have to—he had prospects. Mok Jun Bae had graduated magna cum laude from a top-ranked college, had companies reaching out to *him* to join their ranks, which was all but unheard of anymore. But he didn't want any of that—at least not yet. Junie's friends figured he'd join them in the mind-numbing grind of office work one day—figured he'd be their boss as soon as he got there, his foray into whatever he called what he was doing being considered self-exploration rather than fucking around. They assumed that Jun Bae, as the girl who'd let him make love to her knew him, would mature from the shy, inexperienced sophomore into the confident man he should be considering how broad his shoulders were, how gorgeous his eyes. And now he'd never get a chance.

Because JB liked this shit. All of it. He'd had a supermodel from London offer to blow him if he'd burn the pictures of her shooting up between her toes. An action star from Mumbai first threated to kick JB's ass then offered to set him up with a castmate if he would forget about the conversation he'd overheard between him and his cosmetologist about skin lightening. A K-Pop star tried to seduce him, offering him exclusive access to what was between his legs if he'd just delete the pictures of him at dinner with a male prostitute from Busan. And then there was the American actor's transgender fiasco... Jun Bae hadn't taken any of them up on their offers and not because he wasn't tempted. Truth was, he was tempted by many of them. But the money tempted him more than a one-night stand ever could, even with one of the most attractive people in the world.

Infinitely more.

Charlie told Jun Bae that they were meeting that night and it was bound to be good because they hadn't gotten the chance to get together in almost a year. He said he was sure that it would be hot, so many pictures to be taken, so many angles. Charlie said he wished he could go with him —actually looked like it pained him not to, and that should have made the alarms go off in Jun Bae's head, but it didn't. After all, this wasn't the first time he had heard of such a story; celebrities had whole networks in place so they could live normal lives. They took over Podunk towns, had supermarkets and movie theaters, post offices and gas stations—the same stuff every place has, only these towns weren't on the map. They could walk the streets and not worry about someone catching them looking less than runway ready. At least that was the rumor. Jun Bae, JB —hell, he didn't know who he was anymore—had never seen one of these created towns, but he could believe they existed. It made sense to him in the same way that whole neighborhoods could be formed around one ethnicity, a place where people could buy what they wanted, go where they wanted, be who they wanted because everyone else was just like them. Without places like that, JB was sure he'd have more work because the celebrities would lose their shit on a regular basis. He'd be rolling in it if that happened because behaving badly sold just as much as blurry sex pictures did.

Jun Bae had never been to one of these gatherings he'd heard rumors about, but he was game—of course he was… he was counting the money he'd make before he even snuck in, visions of the Brazilian underwear model doing a split for the Canadian rapper while the German director watched with his bottom lip clenched between his teeth, dancing in his head. It had been a while, Charlie said. They might be horny as hell, Jun Bae's mind supplied. He checked the battery life on his camera again, just to be sure.

The room was dark—dark leather furniture, huge oak bookshelves, dark green, dark brown, dark everywhere.

The light was dim.

The music was low—some kind of Egyptian trap music slowed down and reverbed in a way that wasn't unpleasant. He liked it; it drew him in.

In fact, he was listening too closely, closer than he should have been, at the expense of everything else as he walked into the room, wondering who might have chosen this music to set the mood. The new Japanese heartthrob who split his time between his home country and Morocco? The American singer rumored to be engaged to the Malaysian model who was so sought after that even veteran outfits couldn't seem to book him?

Somewhere deep down inside Mok Jun Bae was disgusted with himself.

JB salivated.

The door closed behind him and Jun Bae jumped because he had closed that door himself ever so quietly only moments before. He had taken a few steps into the room, lured like a snake in a charmer's basket by the music, so rhythmic, enticed by the orgy he expected to find... the combination a promise of the perfect photo lingering in the air like incense. And yes, there was skin on skin and hands moving and bodies writhing in unison, but he didn't get to see it for long. It was just a distraction, one designed perfectly for him. While the hand that held the camera twitched, as his arm began its ascent toward his face to position the lens for the perfect shot, he had not noticed that someone had opened the door after him, had slipped into the room behind him, not until it was too late and the cold steel against his neck was cutting into his throat. They came for him then, money in hand, mouths open to kiss, leaving dollar bills in their wake—his pockets filled as they bit his skin to drink what flowed. Naked some, but that didn't matter anymore, not when someone kept cutting his neck, cutting and laughing, cutting and drinking. The sounds filled his ears as did the voices that followed, disembodied and fleeting as they paid to play.

Money in his pockets.

Money in his eyes.

Snap.

Snap.

Someone taking their own pictures from a perch unseen.

A glass filled from the fount of his neck and handed to the Brit wearing the blue paisley ascot.

The Nigerian actress laughed heartily at a joke that the Scottish DJ was telling her, licking a finger that had been dipped in JB's blood.

Snap.

Mok Jun Bae wondered if they would accept his sincere apologies for his indiscretion.

Junie cried silent tears.

Jun Bae tried to scream but his vocal cords had already been destroyed.

JB smiled for his close-up.

BLIND

They didn't see her when she listened to the reading, her eyes closing in rapture as the author spoke their words, revealed their truth... spoke of things that sat in her soul. They didn't see her then and they wouldn't see her later, when she listened to the call to action, leaned into her destiny, exactly the way she was encouraged to. They didn't see her—never saw her—but they would, and then they would know, then they would understand. They would see judgement on her face, years of it after enduring unnoticed. They would see, and never forget.

DOPPELGANGER

He would never let it happen again.

The man had slipped him the last time, disappeared in a sea of faces, another body among the throng. But not this time. Jace had followed him across three states, had stuck the shadows while he stood in the light. Jace had been everywhere he had gone for months, watching opportunities come and go, but he was determined to finish it this time. No more running. No more hunting.

Jace couldn't afford the alternative.

The man, the one who wore his face, had taken things that Jace knew he could never get back. The people in his life who would have believed him were gone. Many had died before the imposter had shown his face, but some were taken in, exploited, and killed by the man and his lies. They believed that he was who he said he was—who he looked to be, and really, who could blame them? The man looked like he did. Jace didn't have a twin brother, so when he said he was Jace himself, why wouldn't they believe him? And they paid for it. With their dying breaths, they paid handsomely.

His coach.

A colleague.

Jace was there to settle the score.

Jace was there to kill him.

He'd been following him ever since finding blood on the floor in his kitchen, blood he tracked around the house after stepping into it. How he'd gotten in, Jace didn't know but none of that mattered anymore. He saw the police pull up to his house ready to arrest him for the crimes the imposter had committed. He didn't stick around to see what happened next.

The man mingled with people day in and day out as if he hadn't left bodies in his wake. And Jace followed. Closely, but not close enough. Not close enough to wrap his hands around his throat. Until tonight.

And Jace was ready to settle the score.

The city lights were beautiful, red and amber hues backlighting tall buildings, but Jace didn't have time to appreciate it. The knife he'd held in his waistband, the one that nearly sheared off a sliver of skin from his hip when he sat down without adjusting, had been brandished as he began moving in anticipation, moving without forethought—moving outside of himself, in spite of himself. Everything was heightened now, the chase was over and it was time for the showdown—the moment he had been looking for since the man, the fucking bastard had ruined his life. And he was ready, god, so fucking ready to do this thing, the cut out the cancer, then pluck out the eye and cut off the hand and whatever other biblical punishments he could think up. Because he deserved it.

The knife felt heavy in his sweaty palm.

The echo of his screams bounced off the walls of the alley in a cacophonous fury as he noted, with as much anger as there was confusion, that he was indeed alone.

AGREE TO DISAGREE

Out of a mouth that promised gifts so sweet, with garlic and wine, the notes were a delicacy, flesh supple, luscious: exquisite.

FAMILY PLOT

Jonah came to the cemetery with his family. He dropped flowers around like he was spreading birdseed, said no prayers, and dawdled when it was time to go. Something always caught his eye—a funny name (Penelope sometimes, but Gertrude at others), or a date that seemed older than time itself. His parents would call him along, hurry him, admonish him for lagging behind. Hands reached out unseen, pressing him forward, helping him on his way with a pat on the bottom or two for good measure. It made him giggle when someone ruffled his hair or another lifted him off his feet, made him feel like he was walking on air. At least, it did when he was young. But they'd known enough to stop when he no longer threw the flowers, to visit from afar when he stayed near his mother, his father long gone.

They bid silent luck to him and his intended when he brought her by to meet the family.

They mourned with him and wrapped their arms around his mother when they said their final goodbyes.

He brought flowers and placed them on every stone with care.

He had a bench installed near his mother so he could visit with her.

There were picnics and happy times when he shared stories of what was happening on their street, their neighborhood, their lives. But then his back rounded and his legs failed and he only came once, twice, three more times, hair thinning more with each autumn.

The child who came to tell them where he was stood tall. She was 35 and had children of her own, she said. Their grands and great-grands— faces they had never seen. He was gone, she said, and wouldn't be back there. Neither would she, not to sit before their graves, not to visit as she had at his knee... at least not for a long time. He and her mother were elsewhere, laid to rest in some town none of them knew, and she thought that meant they couldn't find him, that they had lost him forever. She was sad for them, grieved their loss of company for them as she sat on that bench, her father's bench, for the last time. But when she spoke, there was music in her voice—his favorite song he said, as he gazed upon his daughter's face. Jonah smoothed her hair even though they told him not to, and when she felt the unexpected warmth on the crisp autumn air, she smiled.

THE ROOM

"It was coming from over there," the maid said, though she didn't really need to. Anyone standing in the hallway could have figured that out—maybe even anyone who happened to be in their rooms. If they were smart, and some of them were, they would have stayed inside, keeping the drywall and insulation between them and whatever was making that godawful noise. Some had done exactly that—had maybe even slept through all the commotion, though there was little chance of that. But others, a small few but still some, had cracked their doors and peered out to see what they could see. There was nothing *to* see, as it turned out, but what they heard would play in their dreams over and over, for the rest of their lives.

The hotel manager blew past the maid, hardly even seeing her. He had wondered why she hadn't opened the door herself with the passkey she used to get access to clean, wondered how much this was going to cost him in noise complaint allocations and online reviews, wondered how many people it would take to clean up whatever the hell was going on in there—thought about all of this while he was in the elevator heading up to the 5th floor where, apparently, all hell had broken loose, but when the doors opened and he stepped into the hallway lucid thought was replaced by all-encompassing noise. His body moved toward it of its own volition even though some small part of his mind tried its best to make him stop walking, back up, retreat into the safety of the elevator and let it take him away from there. But he kept moving, moving toward the maid, rounding the corner where she stood looking as if she might urinate on herself, and heading toward the room.

Room 515.

It was loud.

It was so very loud, like someone was being killed inside. And not just killed—gutted, eviscerated, innards pulled out through the tiniest hole in the stomach, skewered with something... maybe the free pen they left on the desks, the ones with the hotel logo on it... small, small so it could hurt that much more. His mind, never particularly creative before, provided him images of a rounded ballpoint protruding from something pink and tubular and bloody, black ink spilling out over it, mixing with the red of the blood, shining in the fluorescent light of the room.

Those bright, daylight bulbs that he hated so much.

He had told the board not to invest in those, said they were unnatural, accosting to the eye, made the place feel more like a hospital. An uncharitable laugh coughed out of his mouth, and he wished he could have bitten back, could have swallowed it down before it fell all the way out into the air and into the memory of anyone listening, anyone who might recount the story of what happened at the Mandrake Hotel that day—anyone who might remember the callous manager laughing dismissively about what might be happening in Room 515. But that's not what he was doing—it wasn't what he was doing at all. He was laughing, true, he couldn't deny that, but not because anything struck him as funny. No, he was laughing because the fluorescent lights he had cautioned them against, the ones that were probably incredibly bright against what had to be a massacre, were perfectly utilitarian now, just as they would be in a morgue.

The manager held his passkey, pulling it from his hip, unravelling the reel as far as it would go, watching the cord grow taut, but it wasn't far enough. Self-preservation had made him stand back from the door, further back than would allow the sensor to read the card. He cursed as he watched his fingers tremble. He had pushed for this too, but the board decided to put upgrading their access system on the backburner and refurbished the restaurant instead. That meant instead of holding the card up and watching the pretty red light turn green, he couldn't get into the room without swiping his card in the card reader and that meant he had to get close—much closer than he was now, much closer than he was comfortable with. At least the people in the restaurant could enjoy their shitty food in button-tufted chairs.

He hesitated.

Why wasn't security trying the door? Isn't that what they were supposed to do in situations like this? Unlock the door and go in first? Break the damned thing down if they couldn't get in any other way? Surely they were supposed to do something more than breathe down his neck... right?

Everyone was looking at him.

He was too far from the door.

The hand holding the badge shook. The arm of the hand holding badge did too. Everything on him shook—he felt sure he looked like a kid's cartoon, knees knocking as he stood there in front of Room 515 doing absolutely nothing to help the woman inside, and she was screaming, screaming so loud, dear God she was screaming like she was being mutilated.

The hotel manager took a deep breath, cursing himself for not leaving the company like he had thought about doing the year before, signing on with one of the larger conglomerates in the city—the ones who didn't know your name but gave you a bonus every year just the same. He took a step forward, hoping that would be enough to reach, wishing he hadn't come in that day, that he had rolled over and hit snooze, that his car had broken down.

No.

Not far enough.

He took another step and hoped no one heard him gulp.

He swiped the card.

The light turned green.

Security did their job, pushing into the room before he had the chance to take another step, and he was more relieved than he cared to admit. As they moved past him armed with nothing more than their size, the hotel manager realized how much of a farce the whole thing was. There were no weapons, no handcuffs, one of them wasn't even taller than he was. They just had muscle. And that wouldn't be enough to protect them against someone who could make a woman scream like that.

And they hadn't called the police yet.

Not yet because the description he had been given at first only said that someone was yelling. That could have been anything—a party that moved from the bar to the bedroom, wild sex, the television. He had seen it all. But as the first guard dispatched made his way toward the elevator, another call came in about the noise, and then another. The hotel manager hadn't decided to come along as much as he had been ushered along, recruited, disturbed from his coffee and pleasant conversation with the bellhop. So he hadn't had the chance to make the call, not yet.

He should have called when they were in the elevator.

He should have called when they stepped onto the floor.

He should have called..

The room was empty.

He would have called out to the guards if his feet hadn't propelled him backwards first, his body acting on instinct. It would have been futile anyway—he knew they hadn't disappeared into another room and out of view. They couldn't have—not that quickly. Besides, he saw. He would never get the chance to tell anyone that, but he did. One of them walked into a nightclub where all the women looked like Juanita Boisseau and Cab's swing was keen. The other one took the hand of a goddess in blue whose feet didn't touch the floor.

Everyone was looking at him.

The maid.

The nosy guests.

Waiting...

for him to do...

something.

The white rug was too bright when the fluorescent daylight bulbs were on full bore: he was right about that. The blood pooling at the top of his thin mustache, that stupid little thing he had insisted upon keeping even though it made him look ridiculous, seemed entirely too red as it shined in the light. What did they think he should do about that?

IT'S THE LITTLE THINGS

He had time to wonder if the switch downstairs was stuck in that halfway position, neither on nor off—stuck right in the middle just waiting for the right jostling to move it. He had done that before—not turned the switch off all the way and it popping back into place and he didn't know why. It could have been the house settling or someone walking heavily on the floor above: anything could have created enough of a thump to make the switch pick a side. Only there wasn't anyone else in the house this time— no one to jump around on the floor above and bang the ceiling to shake the switch into action.

It was just him.

He had enough time to think about that, the fact that he was home alone. It was a rare occurrence these days—with school being out and his wife working from home, there was always someone else around, beating him to the room he had planned to claim to watch TV or using the last of the cheese and forgetting to write it on the grocery list. When the kids went to their friends' houses for sleepovers and his wife and her girl-friends decided that their girls time was long overdue, he couldn't believe his luck. His wife had asked him if he was going to be lonely at home all by himself and for a moment he thought she might change her plans to have a date night with him instead. And that would have been fine too, but he was going to stay up and wait for her to come home anyway, add a part two to the evening. He wanted her to have a part one doing whatever she wanted to do and he wanted one too—one that was just him and an action movie playing as loud as he wanted it; him with a cold one and some explosions, popcorn and bad acting. He wanted to be alone in the house for the first time in what seemed like years.

His wife of 15 years, love of his life, and mother of their kids, understood.

So, out she went with her friends and out he went to drop off the kids. He expected the kids to stay up half the night doing the same thing he was doing—watching loud movies and loving every minute of them. One would be watching horror movies and the other action. None of them would get any sleep. But he'd deal with the sleep deprivation tomorrow. Tonight was his.

He had time to remember that the microwave would beep soon to remind him that his butter was ready: melted perfection just waiting to kiss the popcorn he had already made. He also wondered if the fan on the stove would come on again while he was standing there, stuck, glued in place. That's what it had done when he came into the house after dropping the kids off—just turned on for no reason. He thought it too was in that weird middle position—the knob precariously there in limbo. He wondered who had cooked last and left it like that. Probably his daughter. She was good for that, was always cooking, always filling the sink with dirty dishes. It was probably her. His son rarely turned the fan on at all, even when the room was filling with smoke.

He checked, but no. The knob was in the off position, pointing straight up, just like it was supposed to be. Yet it was on.

Electrical problem. It had to be that. First the stove and now the light switch. He would definitely have to call someone out to fix it—he had time to remember thinking he might not be able to fix the stove on his own when he saw it earlier, had time to wonder how much that little visit would cost. One burner had been running hot recently, burning up all the food, even when it was set to 2 or 3. And now the fan was having problems.

He had time to remind himself to send an email to his account so that he didn't forget. Had time to wonder if he'd really get the chance to do that or if this was just his brain trying to save itself because time… time was for someone else to worry about, for someone else to spend, because his was up.

It was dark outside; night had fallen while he was prepping for his time alone: renting the movie, grabbing the beer, popping the popcorn.

He had turned the light on as he made his way up the steps because the stairwell was darker than it had been when he had left it and he didn't want to run the risk of tripping over something the kids had left out—the hoodie he saw balled into a wad on the floor near at the bottom of the stairs was chief in his mind, but there could be more stuff left around that he didn't remember. It was smart, he thought—turning on the light like that. His father had once fallen off the last step because his foot twisted on the face of some toy. He could remember the way his father's glasses had slid across the floor, how mad he was to find himself on his knees. It probably hurt too, but his father had never said anything about that.

He didn't feel like taking a detour to that pain if he could help it.

He had time to wish he hadn't set himself up in the basement, the place that had ceased to be his as soon as the kids got old enough to commandeer it, the place he hardly even went into anymore except to check that the sump pump was working and that the furnace wasn't blocked by anything.

He had time to wish he had brought the butter down with everything else even though he knew he would have dropped something if he had tried.

Stuck in the middle… the switch. Curious.

He had time to consider reaching for it, time to think about taking steps toward it to change its position… time to realize he'd never make it, not with legs that no longer seemed under his control or a mind that knew, was absolutely certain, he couldn't change it—would never be allowed to. It was finished and as much as he wanted it to, time would never deign to wait for him.

Quiet.

So very quiet.

He had time to wish he wasn't alone in the house, so very alone, but was grateful that it was him who was standing in the stairway, halfway between floors, in the sudden darkness, because he didn't want his family to see what he saw when the light went off.

A WARM FALL DAY

"You know you shouldn't just stare at people's houses like that."

Brendan's voice pulled Jim back into the world, jolted him out of whatever reverie he had been in. He jumped unconsciously as though Brendan had shouted in his ear.

"What?" Jim asked and was surprised to find his voice hoarse. He cleared his throat, fought the urge to bring his hand up to rub at his neck.

"I said what if someone did that to you—stared at our house like that —and you caught them? You'd be more than a little pissed, don't you think? Especially with the face you had on just now."

Jim looked at Brendan with confusion dancing in his eyes. He let himself be led away from the front of the modified bungalow and over to the decidedly less conspicuous side of the house where the odd sloping roof met the edge of the porch railing. There were fewer windows there and that was probably good because Jim was still staring at the house, his lips slightly parted in that weird way he affected when he was surprised, taken aback, knocked off-kilter. He let Brendan move him where he wanted because Jim wasn't sure if he could do it himself. His legs felt like they were pinned in place, heavy like the soles of his shoes were lined with cement that had begun to harden as he stood in front of the house, the brown house that looked like a man tilting his head to the side, dipping his fedora, the window not hidden beneath the would-be brim threatening to wink at Jim while he looked. He thought that if it winked, if someone went into that room and rolled down the shade at that precise moment, he might faint dead away. As curious as that idea was, as unbidden and fantastical as that train of thought seemed, what bothered Jim most was the cold terror that snaked up his neck at the thought of what would happen to Brendan then.

"Come on," Brendan said good-naturedly, but Jim knew that tone and it was anything but. Brendan's happy go lucky, 'what—are—you—doing—silly' lilt really meant, 'Get your shit together, Jim. You're embarrassing me,' and Jim supposed he was. Or would. If not today, then one day when he didn't walk quite as fast as his decades younger partner or when the break he ended up taking on a park bench ended up being where he wanted to stay rather than hiking or playing frisbee or doing some other random athletic thing that would get his heart rate up where he didn't want it to be anymore. There would be embarrassment then, when he was breathing heavy and squatting like the old man that he was, staring at his too pale legs and rolled over socks. "What are you doing, babe?"

"I...," Jim started, but didn't know how to finish, so he didn't. Instead he turned back to look at the house, to look into the hazy windows, at the shadows on the ceiling.

"Jim..." Brendan said, taking long strides toward him, covering the ground between them quickly.

Jim could feel Brendan's eyes on the side of his face, felt how hotly they bored into him. He couldn't turn to face him; he didn't want to. There would be frustration in those eyes, maybe even confusion, but those weren't the things that would bother Jim long after they'd left that sidewalk in front of the creepy old house. It would be the hint of disdain in them, hidden behind his beautiful hazel irises, that unnatural glint that would show as if it had been caught in the noonday light. That's what would poke at Jim, nag at him, eat away at him in the middle of the night.

"It's nothing," Jim said, letting his eyes linger on the house a beat longer before turning and smiling at Brendan, looking at him but not looking, not closely at least... giving himself time to recover the way he knew he had to if they were going to move on, have the fun they had intended to when they started out of the house that day. Antiquing Brendan had called it, but Jim recognized it for what it was immediately: shopping. They'd find themselves in an overly expensive shop in some old West Virginia town turned tourist trap by the historic railroad that cut through the hills. They'd buy stuff they wouldn't know what to do with when they got it home, and Jim would shake his head when the credit card statement hit his inbox. But the weather was crisp and clear and the sun was catching all the gold highlights in Brendan's hair.

Jim let himself look at Brendan real that time, make eye contact.

Brendan's eyes were concerned but at least the other things Jim had imagined seeing in them had receded if they were ever there at all.

Jim smiled reassuringly.

Brendan patted Jim on the shoulder then rubbed at it a little rougher than Jim would have liked but beggars couldn't be choosers while standing on a sidewalk in the middle of a chilly morning.

A pause.

Quiet.

Too quiet.

Brendan broke the silence as he nudged Jim, urge him to walk away from the house that had seemed to catch him in its web and hold him there.

And Jim let him.

"Come on. The map says there's a gourmet muffin shop at the end of this street."

"Gourmet muffin shop," Jim said amicably, hoping his voice sounded as skeptical as it normally would have. "Sounds like an oxymoron to me."

And off they went the way they would have before because there really wasn't anything keeping them there, no murk to be mired in, no cement on the bottom of his shoes keeping his feet in place, nothing there, nothing to see, nothing in the window, no shadow moving along the ceiling, nothing—

"Hold on," Brendan said in that way he spoke when something unexpected but fabulously intriguing caught his eye. Jim had learned to both love and fear that tone. "The map didn't say *anything* about this."

"About what?"

Jim looked around for the shiny thing that had caught Brendan's eye but could see nothing but a single level self-storage eyesore that was completely out of place in that little idyllic town, and a cemetery.

No.

"What do you mean 'what'? Do you not see that amazingness in front of you?"

Jim had to fight the urge to cringe at the word choice. There were a lot of things that were amazing in the world: seeing a parrotfish on a dive; sitting on the Lincoln steps at night; the first bite of a warm chocolate croissant among them, but a cemetery? No, not amazing... not in Jim's book.

But Brendan had always loved cemeteries.

"Can you imagine the history?" Brendan said, already walking ahead of Jim toward the open gate. It didn't matter that he had walked ahead— Jim didn't even need to hear him. He could have recited the lines himself. He had already spent countless hours peering at the gravestones of people he didn't know, that no one who was related to him had likely ever known, because Brendan could *feel* the history, was enthralled by the stories of the people who lay beneath their feet. Somewhere along the line Brendan had started looking for the oldest birth year—he had to beat 1754 now—and they had spent what felt like a thousand weekends trying to find it. Time he could never get back. He was not in the mood to do it again, not then, so close to that house with its chipped paint and buckling paneling... paneling that looked like it might be expanding and contracting, as if the house were taking slow, lazy breaths.

"Brendan..." Jim heard himself saying as some part of him wrangled itself out of that weird hazy space he had been in. Brendan was far ahead of him now, almost to the entryway of the cemetery, its weathered stone pillars standing just a little taller than he did at 6'2". If there had been a gate blocking entry before, it was gone now and what would have been the point? The walls that bordered the furthest-most headstones were shorter than waist height. Even if there had been a gate, that wouldn't have stopped Brendan, Jim knew. The lure of "history" would have been too much to ignore and over the wall he would have gone with Jim soon to follow. Keeping him young, Jim rationalized, but that argument left him cold at that moment.

"Bren? Come on, this isn't what we came out here for—" Jim started as he stepped off the sidewalk heading toward the cemetery. He thought he had finished what he intended to say, had maybe added a little bit of an indignant flair at the end to see how that would play, but when he found himself on his ass in the middle of the street looking at a mature tortoise-shell cat with bright green eyes, he knew better. It stood near his feet looking accusatorily at him over its shoulder and Jim instantly knew he had stepped on it, might have even hurt it.

"Hey," he said, his voice taking on a consoling tone he seldom used, "are you ok, buddy?"

Jim leaned toward the cat, marveling at how still it was standing, how beautiful its coat was, how it never hissed at him. He had almost touched it before memories of seeing cats dig their claws into people, climb up their bodies, and find a soft spot to bite stilled his hand in mid-air.

"You're not gonna hurt me, are you buddy? I didn't mean to hurt you."

Jim didn't move his hand.

The cat stayed where it was, fixing him with those gorgeous green eyes.

Jim had time to think that the cat's eyes should be added to the list of amazing things in the world before he felt Brendan drop to his knees beside him.

"Jim! What happened? Are you all right?"

Brendan's hands and eyes were everywhere at once.

"I'm ok, I'm ok," Jim tried but Brendan still checked for blood, checked the ground for something that could have tripped him, checked for anything and everything. "It was just this silly cat. It ran right out in front of me."

Jim turned back to the cat with laughter on his lips that died when he found the space by his foot empty.

"What cat?" Brendan asked.

Jim looked past his toes in the direction the cat might have run but didn't see any place it could have ducked out of view as quickly as it had.

"There was... it was right there."

Jim disliked how uncertain he sounded but could do nothing to change it.

"It probably just ran off. Had enough excitement for the day," Brendan said as he stood up. He reached down to help Jim, but he wouldn't let him... just couldn't.

"Yeah..." Jim mumbled as he stood, eyes still scanning for the cat, trying to avoid getting a good look at the house with the hazy glass and the shadows on the ceiling as he did.

"Or maybe it's a ghost cat," Brendan said, trying to coax Jim out of whatever was setting him on edge.

Jim responded belatedly. "Y—yeah. A ghost cat. Would make sense around here."

"What?"

The chuckle in Brendan's voice wasn't derisive but something inside Jim wanted to take it that way. It took everything he had not to scowl at the smiling face facing him.

Brendan's eyes searched Jim's face as he spoke words that were code for something else, words that tried to mask the real concern brewing behind them but fell short.

"I was kidding," Brendan said flatly, holding onto the smile even though there was nothing incredulous or even remotely funny about what could be going on in front of him... the thing his family had warned him about when they realized he was serious about Jim... the thing that had already started to haunt his dreams.

Jim blinked and then looked away from Brendan, his eyes searching for the cat even though he knew it was futile. But there was something there. At the edge of his line of sight where things distorted and blurred, merged together, there was *something*.

By the house.

Brendan issued a sound that was meant to be endearing, maybe a bit indulgent as well, but didn't quite work.

"I can think of a hundred other ways you could have told me you didn't want to go into that cemetery," Brendan joked as he smoothed Jim's clothes, fussing over him unconsciously.

"No, it's not that," Jim said without thinking and he immediately wanted to kick himself. Because no, he didn't want to go into the cemetery and look at headstones, stare at the graves of people he didn't know... not again... not ever again if he could help it. But that was less important than the weird tint the world was taking as they stood there on a street they didn't know, in a town they had never been to before. It was like a veil over a camera lens.

"Really, babe, you didn't see it?"

"No," Brendan deadpanned even as a new smile crept onto his face, one designed to lighten the mood, to lighten *Jim*, "I did not see your ghost cat, and I doubt you did either, though this is a bit elaborate to get me to change course."

Jim struggled to keep his expression even, or at least the way it was.

Brendan paused. It told Jim everything he needed to know.

"You really don't like doing these things with me, do you?"

There it was. Jim had two choices: fix it or ruin a perfectly good day.

"Of course I do," he started, but knew he had to change tack to make it stick. "Well, I mean, you know I could never go inside another cemetery and that would be fine by me, but I love doing things with you. You're so... I don't know..."

Brendan's eyes were on him.

"So interested in things. It's refreshing. I love that you let me tag along on your adventures."

Jim hugged Brendan, gave him a real one—none of that hand shaking, shoulder bumping bullshit they usually did outside of the house. He needed to drive the point home, make Brendan see that he was sincere. A bro hug wouldn't cut it.

"So, come on. Let's go in and see if we can beat our year."

Brendan's eyes smiled first and that was good. Jim let him lead the way through the entryway, trying not to let himself see it as an open mouth waiting to swallow them whole. He listened as Brendan first asked Jim if he remembered what the year to beat was then recalled it himself. He nodded and "mm hmmed" when Brendan talked about how much information used to go on tombstones—some of them were as lengthy as obituaries—and how beautiful that was and how everything seemed to be about cold efficiency these days. Jim smiled after Brendan as he moved briskly between tombstones always careful not to step where he thought their bodies were because that, to him, was disrespectful. Jim looked at the stones too, playing along, pulling up the rear as Brendan moved ahead among the weathered, discolored tombstones. Jim had to squint at some of them, the writing worn away. And that was ok. It gave him something to do while Brendan was on his mission. He was used to being left to his own devices in cemeteries: it was par for the course. Brendan was the resident historian in his family. He researched his family's genealogy, figured out that they had been free in America long before the end of slavery, and was still actively trying to trace his lineage back to Africa. He found his Caucasian family first because there were clear records for them. In doing so, he became intrigued by the history that lived on that side of his bloodline—founding father, Native American, change the trajectory of the country type of history. And he was hooked. Jim understood that. He was just thankful Brendan didn't have any charcoal or rice paper in his pockets to rub tombstones.

Jim found the emotions he was supposed to respond with when Brendan talked about the grave with the lamb and the ones that had rocks sitting on top of them. He heard Brendan when he wondered out loud about what was in the overgrown patch, might have grunted a response when Brendan guessed at the birth years of the people to whom the stones buried in the brush belonged, but Jim wasn't entirely sure if he had... not after what he saw. What Brendan would remember about that moment, what he would never speak about but would stay in his head for the rest of his life, was how limp Jim's body had looked as he stood in front of that grave, leaned in close, standing on what Brendan assumed was the deceased's chest. And he never did that, never trampled the bodies that way; he maintained the invisible coffin-shaped boundary if for no other reason than breaking it always gave Brendan the willies. That was one of the things that Brendan appreciated about Jim—he would just go along with all of Brendan's hairbrained ideas. So when he turned away from the overgrown spot at the back corner of the cemetery having chickened out of going in because of the possums, rats, and zombies he was suddenly convinced were in there, Brendan was surprised to see Jim standing so close to the headstone, standing over the dead person like a night hag.

Brendan wanted to call out to him but something stopped him. Something told him it was too late, that he would never hear him... that Jim would never be able to hear him again. His mouth felt dry, as though it had been hanging open for a long time, and he supposed, in retrospect, it had.

Jim had first been drawn to the tombstone because it was tall, so tall he could almost read the name without lowering his eyes, and for him, at just under 6 feet tall, that was unusual. But the curiosity he felt about that was usurped quickly enough, rendered unimportant and totally forgotten within the span of a second because the name...

Jim would have told Brendan about the weeping willow above the name, how deep set it was... how purposeful. He would have spoken of the way the name looked as if it had been stamped but the rest of the words were done in a cursive that could have easily been etched into the stone by someone's careful hand. His mother's careful hand. She'd had beautiful handwriting, her loops graceful and sure. She had tried to teach Jim how to write in cursive before he went to school and then again when his teacher's lessons failed but Jim had never quite mastered her artful control. That he hadn't been allowed to write with a pen in school until the 4th grade and not until he was 12 years old at home was something they joked about. He heard her laughter in his ears as he looked upon the stone bearing his name, the one that only his family called him, the one he wished he had heard out loud just one more time. His mother used to sing his name to him, made a song up about him the way she did so many things. She could hardly cook a meal without singing a song of her own creation. There were precious few that she could repeat, as random as her lyrics were, but the one about him was a constant. More poem than song, the melody changed often but not the words.

> *"Jameson Reeves*
> *Born in times of peace*
> *in the year 1961.*
> *Been lots of fun*
> *since his life begun*
> *And will be so until he's done."*

Jim would have told Brendan he wasn't done yet, that he had more to do, more places to go, more things to see, more graves to visit if that's what he wanted. Jim would have asked him what day it was because didn't they have that thing in the city to go to if it was the Saturday he was thinking it was? Didn't they need to head back home and get ready for it? He would have remarked at how creepy it was to see Jim's name and birthday on such an old headstone and Brendan would have wanted to take a picture of it—a picture he would never look at because it was, indeed, extremely creepy to see his uncommon name with his exact birthday on a tombstone that looked centuries old. And the other part... well, that just couldn't be right, not if he had the right Saturday in mind and they had that event in the city that night. Jim would have shown Brendan that curious date, asked him if he ever heard of someone memorializing such a bad joke. They'd seen a few doozies together—it was as if, at some point in time, people went out of their way to write unique epitaphs. He remembered the tombstone that read "Shit Happens" and Porky Pig's famous sign off. They had found one that talked about someone owing another person money on their last outing. But had someone ever carved a future date of death into a tombstone? Were they even allowed to do that? Wouldn't somebody be afraid that some bastard might try to make it come true?

A splash of color caught his eye. Sunflowers on the ground, the golden yellow stark against the paling green grass. Jim's favorite.

Jim opened his mouth to tell Brendan about the tombstone with its weird date, today's date if he had the right Saturday in mind, about how weird it was to be seeing it there under the name he apparently shared with this poor sap whose family or friends or somebody thought it would be a great gag to pay for a headstone with a future death date on it, to mention how beautiful—yes, amazing—the sunflowers were, but he couldn't find his voice. The sun was different now; its heat no longer muted by the cool air that had tousled Jim's hair as they walked, as he stood looking at the house with its shadows on the ceiling. Jim could see the sun, how bright it was, but its warmth didn't make it to his skin and he wanted to comment about that to the man standing before him, wanted to move out of the way of the grave he had come to visit, the grave he had thrown the sunflowers onto

onto his chest. The flowers are on his chest

and let him visit in peace, but not before that bit of small talk, that affirmation that he felt the lack of heat too. But as he looked into the man's watery, eyes, the greenish brown irises going hazy with cataracts, as the sunlight seemed to get smothered by his dull gray hair, Jim realized he already knew.

NIGHT VISION

If you watch the road at night, when the world's asleep and the air is still, you can see them. A bubble, nothing more than a flex, so slight you don't know if you really saw it. Subtle, like a corpse exhaling. Summer heat shifts the asphalt to crack, to open, to let, and they come in droves under the light of the moon. Iridescent translucence with a red-hot core, like blood coursing through veins in a clear husk as they survey the terrain. Plotting, scheming, planning, they move through manmade boundaries as if they weren't there. They stand at the foot of the bed, hide in the webbing of dust in the corners, measuring effort, sizing us up. They smile when they see us, like lights shining through windows and reflecting on the wall.

If you watch the road at night you'll see them when they retreat, their bellies full of dead skin and hair, nail clippings and earwax, satiated by the taste, the touch, the smell. You'll see them hesitate, unsure if they should leave or stay, conquer or acquiesce... again. Don't let them see you hiding as they dip beneath the surface. Don't let them sense your fear because they are waiting, always waiting for the right moment, the right reason— any reason—to stay.

WHAT NATURE KEEPS

Trees sway in the wind, their leaves moving like wet hair shaken joyfully, clean and fresh. They whisper secrets to each other; the wind carries the tales from one to the other down the line, threading through the wood like fingers combing, massaging, adoring. Leaves undulate, take flight like children clasping hands, making airplane wings to fly, fly fly. They steal the moments to enrich the soil, to feed the bark, and nurture the beasts that call it home. *Don't tell them*, they whisper as the branches reach out to prick skin, draw blood... to feed, *never let them see.*

THE MAKING OF A LOVE STORY

Monday, April 24

6:44 AM I taste your skin in my dreams.
I can feel the curves of your chest and arms against my own

6:46 AM sry. Up early

7:02 AM u up?

7:35 AM yt?

8:11 AM Thinking…

8:37 AM Take me

8:53 AM Take me

9:28 AM Take me

? 9:28 AM

9:29 AM 'Take me,' I whispered as your tongue searched

369

for my treasures and caressed them.

9:30 AM I sat quietly in the moonlight that streak your hair
with majestic silver.
'Touch me', my heart begged but you laughed
low and sultry.

9:32 AM I blushed under the navy sky.

wym 10:05 AM
the fuck? 10:09 AM
when dis?

10:09 AM I beg you
Touch me.
With your strong hands, hold me.

Yo… 11:10 AM
I can't come thru til l8r

11:10 AM Hum lightly the melody of the
twilight dance so I might meet you
among the stars.

… 11:11 AM
mkay 11:15 AM

11:15 AM Call me stupid
call me dumb
call me anything

no diss r u ok? 11:37 AM

11:38 AM Feeling insane

Word 11:39 AM
yeah, got that gud gud

11:39 AM Possession and jealousy

all in the game

tmi rn fr fr 11:40 AM

11:40 AM You are the only one alive
who can make me feel inside
that I want to be your bride

wtf 11:41 AM

11:45 AM Screaming silence that shatters eardrums

11: 48 AM Kill me softly as sweet sounds escape my lips

11:51 AM yt?

11:57 AM yt??

12:02 PM rly?

12:05 PM u gud?

12:06 PM sry

12:07 PM jk

12:08 PM fr jk

12:10 PM srsly

12:11 PM ok ttyl jk ok?

12:12 PM k?

1:10 PM yt?

1: 11 PM we gud?

2:05 PM ily

Jk

2:10 PM jk fr

2:25 PM xxxxxxx

3:28 PM srsly

3:48 PM omfg

4:06 PM sos

4:07 PM wtf

4:58 PM cul
k?

5:41 PM fr?

8:11 PM come thru soon?

8:12 PM babe?

8:15 PM babe??

8:59 PM …

10:31 PM The rustling of the leaves
The warmth of a breeze
They bring me to my knees since...

10:33 PM My pleasure has dissipated.
Life seems so complicated.

10:34 PM No sensation has penetrated since...

10:35 PM I feel your skin in my hands.

10:36 PM I shut my eyes and trace your face

10:37 PM hoping to keep its contours fixed in my mind

10:39 PM Ooh, to feel your warmth

10:40 PM Your skin, so close, almost my own
Warming

10:41 PM sheltering
consuming
my being

10:46 PM Against me, stay
protect me always

10:47 PM warm me ever

THE DEAD MAN'S COUCH

Willie heard the older folks talking about it; his parents and the neighbors had used hushed tones to gossip about what happened as they watched the family pull into the driveway, go into the house, and begin the process of dismantling a man's life. They asked each other if the other had ever seen those people before—this *family* that caravanned from parts unknown with a moving truck in tow, ready to take what they wanted from the man's life and discard the rest. They spoke with anger in their voices... anger and disgust... and something else too. Something sharp that he couldn't identify because it was buried beneath emotions that his nine-year-old mind *could* figure out, and those were more than enough. His mother shook her head and the neighbor who fed all the stray cats, cats that left surprises on everyone's lawn and yowled late at night, sighed because 'He' was dead. Had died somewhere in the house.

Alone.

Willie listened as they talked about 'Him', about how meticulous he was about his lawn, about how he painted his mailbox stand every year, about how no one ever saw him at the store or in town, like he didn't exist outside of his driveway. They guessed at how long he had lived there, houses away for some but in Willie's and his parent's cases, right next door. Ten years? Fifteen? To Willie, he had always been there, had always been part of the fabric of the neighborhood, as much backdrop as the street signs and the houses themselves were. But no one seemed to know his name. Willie didn't, and he was sure none of his friends did either. He thought for sure his mother would, living next to him for however long she had, but she wasn't saying it. He knew from experience that when his mother knew someone's name she would use it, would say it more than she needed to, almost as if she were trying to remember it. But she wasn't doing that then as she spoke with Ms. Lenore from three doors down. No one was.

That bothered Willie.

He didn't say much, the man who he'd lived next to all of his life. He never said much of anything to the kids who cut through his yard en route to the bus stop, nor to the people who let their dogs urinate on his lawn. He was invisible unless you looked hard enough and caught the brim of the sun hat that was as much a part of his persona as everything else was. He was always just *there* but not anymore. Now he was gone.

Dead.

Alone in his house.

The man's family was making short work of clearing out the space. They had brought out dressers and boxes full of whatever old men kept in their closets, tucked in the back in the dark. They had brought out a dining room table that looked like it had never been used and a bike that most surely hadn't been ridden in decades. All those things sat in the driveway waiting to be put into the truck and taken back to wherever his "family" came from to be divvyed up and sold, showcased, whatever. Maybe they'd tell a story about who had owned it first, but maybe not. Willie would never know. He figured he shouldn't care, thought that was an odd thing to think about anyway, but still, he did.

They were bringing out a couch now. Two guys who looked like they were old, but not as old as his mother... definitely not as old as 'The Man' who had lived there with his perfectly trimmed bushes and emerald green grass, carried it out grunting and groaning every step of the way. Their foreheads glistened with sweat. One of them cursed when they put it down on the driveway in line behind the other things waiting to be hoisted into the moving truck, hissing something about catching his finger between the asphalt and the wooden base. He shook his hand and cursed again before noticing that Willie was watching him. He jammed his finger into his mouth and softened his eyes, smiled around the digit, which had started to bleed, and waved hello with his uninjured hand. Willie smiled back, let him believe that it was all good, that his Jedi mind trick designed to disarm the nosy kid had worked. The man went inside, finger still in his mouth, a curse still on his lips. Willie watched him go back into the house, wondering what else he might drag out with him the next time he emerged, but as soon as the door slammed shut, his eyes shifted back to the couch. It was white, but not really—more like a grayish pearl. It had a striped pattern: bluish purple flowers in the middle of two thin lines of the same color blue repeated on the surface opposite a swath of solid gray/pearl with some kind of embroidery in the sick-looking solid. The arms had metal balls that looked like studs running up from the base to spiral in the center. And it was worn. The cushions were weathered and stained in some places. It was old timey but not in an antique kind of way—more like it had been in that house since the 1980s, had worn a groove into the rug all its own. Willie knew it would have stayed there forever if those guys hadn't yanked it out of its cave.

He looked back at the house to see if anyone was coming and saw no one. There wasn't anybody out on the street either, not walking or driving, which was odd for that time of day but Willie didn't think about that. It was just him and the couch. Alone.

Willie cleared the few steps between himself and the couch tentatively, curious but apprehensive. His hand led the way, reaching toward the sickly gray upholstery with a finger that was both eager to touch the couch and afraid to, but before he knew it, without even feeling himself move toward it, sink into it, lay the bare flesh of his thigh where his shorts rode up to revel pale skin against it, Willie was sitting on it, his weight depressing the cushions. A faint, stale smell of cologne wafted up to his nose, encircled his head, made him dizzy. It was hot. The heat from his body was making the cushions warm, so warm that his leg began to sweat, that *he* began to sweat and wet the couch, to *soak* the thing, there was so much. His palms lay flat on the cushion next to his sides, his skin tingling against it, alive with electricity, but that did not scare him... neither did the sound of voices around him, disembodied and rapid-fire, shouting things at him, spitting them, beseeching him the way his 5th grade teacher had the year before when she asked the class to focus because the topic she was covering was important, so very important. One of those voices was his mother's and even though she sounded strange, he could tell it was her. Even through the distortion that kept her voice from his ears, like she was under the water that lay beneath the fog at the other end of a tunnel, Willie could still make out her meaning. Any kid would, if they'd been a kid like him, one who forgot to check in from time to time and came in ten minutes after he was supposed to on hot summer nights. She wanted him to—

Willie smiled when 'He' laughed, wondering if he had always sounded like that... like he had tossed a handful of rocks into his mouth and gargled them with what... water? His own blood? Willie didn't know. He didn't ask 'The Man', who sat next to him on the couch in his driveway, posted up on the rotting thing in the broad daylight, rays of light shooting through him like the sun does a cloud on an otherwise beautiful day, what happened. He didn't ask because he could keep a secret too.

THROUGH THE LOOKING GLASS

Air.

She needed air and even the stale bathroom in the back of the two-room funeral home would do.

There were still a few minutes before the service would start, and she intended to use all of them there in that tiny little space. Besides, they'd wait for her, wouldn't they? Even though she wasn't the belle of the ball, she *was* paying for this shindig after all. It would be in poor taste to start the service when the wife of the deceased was holed up in the bathroom.

Emma looked at herself in the mirror, going through the motions to keep up the ruse. She was freshening up, tending to the smeared mascara and the makeup withering under the weight of the day. But that's not why she was in there, not really. She hated things like this. Funerals. All the crying. All the 'I'm sorrys' and the platitudes that dripped from people's lips as they streamed by. Hated it. She would have rather had Dominic cremated and taken his ashes out to the woods to spread. But no. No one else wanted that, not his siblings, not his children, not their friends. No one but her. So here she was.

Emma sighed as she looked at herself, at the 'she' that she was now, post-Dominic. Post her end of college hook-up-turned-boyfriend-turned-husband. Post her friend-turned-lover. She looked at herself, at the hair that looked different than it had the morning Dominic died because she was at the hair salon when he died at his desk, was under the dryer when the EMTs tried but failed to revive him. Did he recognize her with the short hair? Emma hadn't mentioned what she was going to do, thought she'd surprise him with it, but he never got to see. Was he looking for her now, looking for an anchor and finding someone who looked like her but with short red hair that he didn't recognize?

Emma looked at herself, searching her eyes for the woman who showed up when she was feeling vulnerable, the girl she had once been before the years had passed and age had added weight and bitterness to her carefree frame... the girl she was beneath the years. And she was there, right there, staring back with a smirk on her face. The sun was kissing her skin, highlighting her hair with gold. And she beckoned older Emma to look closer, to go to her, to become her again. Emma could see the street where she stood, knew that the movie theater stood opposite her, just out of view, and that her favorite bookstore stood next to it and had a cat winding through the display in the window. She knew that younger Emma was going into the bookstore, and she wanted to go with her. The movie would come later, when she and her friends would go out on the town, such as it was. Home from college but living in a two-light village: the movies and dinner was as good as it got. Emma would see more friends from high school there, friends who didn't know what she did when she was away at school, didn't know about the boys she'd met and the things she'd done. They'd do their own things too when they separated again after a few days, when break was over and it was time to get back to the books, and she wouldn't know what they did either. But none of that mattered because they knew each other better than any of those college friends could. The insecurities, the good, the bad, and no one could take that from them... not then or ever.

Max was there.

He wouldn't be on the Harley that he'd die on in 15 years, but he'd be there. And Emma wanted to go there too, to that street at that moment when the cat's tail threated to knock over John Saul's precariously perched new release. She wanted to go there and hug him and never let go. She didn't love him anymore, hadn't for years before he would meet his end on a lonely road between Winchester and Roanoke, but Emma wanted to hold him there, keep him safe, keep him alive. On that day, when the cat treated the books like dominos and the sun would set with one of the most beautiful displays of color she would ever see, Max was alive and happy. He hadn't started working at the radio station yet, hadn't realized his "On Air" voice yet. Emma hadn't taken Russian Lit yet and wouldn't have met Dominic on the quad after running back to class to pick up the companion book she'd need, the one that took her forever to find in the first place... the one she would fail without. She wouldn't have met Dominic yet and maybe she never would, not if Emma hugged Max tight, tight enough to make him remember how much he liked it when she did that. Maybe they would have gotten back together, bought a little house, had a few kids. Maybe Max wouldn't be dead.

Maybe Dominic wouldn't either.

Max smiled at her from that place way back when and Emma cried in response because he was dead, he was dead, and so was Dominic, the love of her life, the man she had planned to grow old with. And now she was old and he was gone.

Emma sucked her teeth at the young version of her who had started waving at her to get her attention, to make her look closer and climb in. She sucked her teeth and adjusted the wayward red strands that danced along her forehead. She swiped at her eyes and blotted the mascara she had foolishly put on before taking the deep breath that wiped young Emma and Max out of existence for now... maybe even forever. She didn't have time for them, not anymore.

She had a funeral to attend.

SPOILED

I didn't ask for this, the cold disinterest, the impassive grunts of response and affirmation, sentiment unheard.

I didn't ask for this, the pregnant pauses and pus-filled boils bursting on blemished skin that burnished scars of red with high sheen.

I didn't ask for this but he did, and he always gets what he wants, especially when he screams.

NO REST

"Anyway, they dared him to stay there overnight, so he went to the cemetery and sat by one of those big tombstones—the wide ones that look like they're for two graves or something. He sat with his back against it and read the name engraved in the weathered stone out loud. 'Matilda Carter' it said, and when he read her date of death, he realized it was that same date!"

Amanda paused for effect, and Tim and Anna started laughing, the sound bursting from them as if breaking through a taped-up box. Ray didn't want to laugh, was trying his best not to even crack a smile at the girl he was planning to ask to marry him in a few months, the one he had bought a ring for already and building up the nerve to give her, but he did. It was just so cheesy, so predictable that he couldn't help it. He didn't know what he was expecting from her or any of them, really—none of them did. This was the first time they had decided to tell stories at a cemetery at night; it was their first time hanging out at a cemetery at all, regardless of the time, so it wasn't like any of them knew the etiquette. But, Amanda drew the short stick, so she set the bar. Ray would have to try hard not to blow it out of the water.

"What?" Amanda said indignantly. He knew that sound, understood what it meant. He forced his laughter to die in his throat.

"It's just so obvious," Anna said, flicking hair dismissively. "It's not scary when there's no, I don't know, *soul*."

Anna was pontificating again, talking like she knew everything about everything, like she was so enlightened about the world. Amanda hated when Anna got like that, acting like just because she would be going off to an Ivy League school after summer was over and Amanda was heading to the community college a mile away she was somehow better than her. Amanda looked like she might push Anna if she kept talking like that, like she definitely would bang her head on one of those headstones 'by mistake'—just enough to make her feel it—if she didn't shut up.

"Yeah, and how could he read the name on the tombstone if his back was against it? He wouldn't be able to see it. And don't say it's the tombstone in front of him because they don't put names on the back of tombstones," Tim said, and true or not, Ray didn't like the way he sounded. He was siding with Anna just because that's what he always did—everything Anna ever said was magically so amazing and accurate and totally profound and no one else could say or do or think anything better. Tim was being condescending and he was pandering to a girl who still didn't give him the time of day. But he still thought he had a shot and because of that, Tim talked like she did —you could see up his nostrils as high as he tilted his head most of the time just so he could look down his nose at people. Or at least he and Amanda. Ray didn't like the way the conversation was changing, turning into something serious, something mean, a challenge that went unstated but was as much an 'us versus them' as it could be. He didn't like it one bit.

"Do you have a better one?" Ray asked, cutting Amanda off right when she started talking. By the look on her face, he had saved Tim... he had saved them all. "You're busy laughing but I don't hear you scaring anybody."

"Yet," Tim added and straightened up to start telling his story.

Tim began, talking in a hushed tone that was as uncertain as it was pretentious, especially once he realized that everyone was looking at him, including Anna, and that it was otherwise quiet in the cemetery. It was dark, and the place was closed, so of course it was quiet, but there was something about the cemetery in the dark that didn't sit right with Ray—wouldn't sit right with anyone if they had half a mind.

Ray looked at Tim whose eyes had grown wide in response to the chill in the air, the darkened sky, the realization that they really were out there in the middle of the night. He kept talking but his eyes said something different than his mouth did.

Fuck, what were they doing there?

"Not yet, chile, not yet!"

They heard the voice at the same time. Tim's words stopped, cut off like a switch, the echo waving in the air for the shortest of seconds after it was gone. They whipped their heads in the direction of the sound, all the while telling themselves that it was nothing, a bird, a wolf, damn it, but nothing else, not what they were afraid of, not what their nightmares were made of.

They saw her. She was three rows over and she was lurching, her gait interrupted by whatever she was pulling along behind herself. It was slowing her down, was awkward and making her stumble but she was determined to bring it along anyway. They crouched behind the tombstone they were in front of, trying to make themselves small, willing themselves not to run to their car. But she didn't look in their direction; her eyes remained trained on the grave she was heading towards. When she got to it, she threw the sack on the ground in front of it and slapped the marble face with an open hand.

"There you go, you bitch, there you go," she said, her voice slurring though they didn't see a bottle. "Drink up."

The woman was clad in a business suit and heels. Her pantyhose had a run in them, noticeably beyond the salvation of clear nail polish. Her hair was in a not-so-neat bun. Her makeup was streaked, her mouth painted a too—dark plum.

They couldn't tear their eyes away from her.

"Make it last," she growled, her voice thick with emotion. She kicked the tombstone, the heel of her shoe breaking against it, almost falling backward from the force, "'cuz I'm not ready yet."

Anna gasped as the woman plucked off one nail and then another, taking them off at the cuticle, ripping them from the nailbed like they were press-ons but they weren't, they weren't, because the blood spurted up from them, up like a fountain, like one of those stone frogs spitting on flowers in a garden. Anna gasped, and it was so loud, so obnoxious, so utterly damning, and the woman looked.

She looked right at them.

Ray wondered if Anna knew what she had done, if she realized that she had bought the woman the extra time she wanted—four times more than the thing in the sack would have gotten her. He wondered if Tim knew what his ignorant crush had done with her college-bound, smart-aleck mouth. He wondered if Amanda would push Anna out front before Ray could do it himself.

THE PITCH

"Ok, so imagine you're sitting on the train taking selfies or maybe doing a live or something like that and then someone starts acting crazy. At first it looks like a prank, just some dumb shit—oh, sorry—but you know, the same stupid stuff you see on the train every day, but then they start, like, killing people," the guy said animatedly, his hands bracketing the space in front of him as if he was holding a box that was jiggling around of its own volition. He was in his mid-40s, judging by the wrinkles popping up on his forehead, but trying not to look like it; his clothes screamed 20-something, but not just any 20-something... a 20-something who was a fashion influencer, finger on the pulse of pop culture but in a casual way type of guy. He was selling his idea hard; his eyes almost bugged out of his head with excitement. It made Julie tired.

"Think *28 Days* meets a New York City subway station, right? Totally enclosed—there's no way out."

"Running zombies," Julie supplied.

"Running zombies, yes!" He banged the table. "See, you get exactly what I'm saying, right? And they're falling down the stairs, falling onto the tracks, getting crushed by the train coming into the station. The girl— well, *I* see it as a girl, but it can be whatever you want it to be, right?— she's doing her Live and—"

He started gesticulating wildly. Julie didn't know if she was excited for or afraid of the jazz hands that were likely to start up soon.

"—she catches all of this in her video but she doesn't notice—she's too busy looking at herself, right? So the people watching are like, 'Girl! Watch out!' and she doesn't know what they mean and she's all smiling for the camera and her followers or whatever and then, you know…"

Julie waited, holding her tongue. She'd have to leave him in a moment, she knew that, but for a few seconds more, she wanted to wait to see what he would say.

Five seconds.

Ten.

Twenty.

Uncomfortable now.

Twenty-five.

"What?" Julie asked, knowing the answer, but hoping against hope that there was more to it than there seemed.

He squirmed in his seat. His hands drew in, more of a parenthesis than a bracket.

"You know… she dies. They all… die."

Even he knew that wasn't enough.

"The zombies get them?" Julie asked, just to be sure he understood that she understood that there was nothing else to the story.

"Yeah," he started, searching for something else to add but finding nothing. "The zombies get them, but maybe not all of them."

Epiphany!

"Maybe they only get some of them and the others fight them off."

"And then what?" Julie prompted, knowing what would be next so well she could recite it with him.

"Well, then they would escape the subway and keep going, keep running, right? Head for the suburbs where there are less people —"

"Like every other zombie movie," Julie finished, putting him out of his misery. He didn't stop talking, but she had stopped listening. She thought about turning her camera off to see if he would get the point, but decided she wasn't that person… not yet.

" —and it could be whatever you want, you know? You could go survivor view or zombie view. Yeah! It could be a whole different kind of party then, right? There's so much you could do —"

" —with an old horror antagonist that owes its resurgence to a comic book."

He looked at her in confusion.

It took everything she had not to snort.

"Thanks so much for telling me about your idea. I will give it some thought."

"Yeah, cool. And remember, right, it can be whatever you guys want to do. I'm totally flexible, right? I mean, you guys know best, and—"

"Thanks, sure," she cut in, looking at her wrist at the nonexistent watch telling her she was late for her nightly series binge.

"Right? And it would be super cool if—"

"Ok, yeah, goodnight."

She left the meeting.

She left the meeting while he was mid-sentence.

She left the meeting after talking over him and he was mid-sentence.

Damn.

She was turning into a bitch.

But he wasn't going to stop, she told herself as she prepared for her next round. He was going to keep going even though he knew the idea sounded like everything else—maybe a different setting, but maybe not; Julie thought she might have seen a zombie apocalypse in a subway done before, maybe before streaming, maybe even coming out of another country. He was never going to stop, even though he knew it was a lost cause so she had to save herself. Maybe she could have done it differently. Ok, she'd admit that much, but in the end what was done was done.

She opened a new video call. The woman waiting for her was visibly nervous. The lighting didn't do anything to help the situation at all—it threw blue on their shared screen making her skin appear almost translucent. This made Julie feel like she could see the woman's veins, the one in the center of her forehead specifically. And that vein was pulsating.

"Ok..." Julie paused to confirm the name, causing the woman to shift in her seat.

"... Val. Whatcha got for me today?"

Val took a deep breath and then began.

"Singer in a band that was popular like 20 years ago meets his current wife, the one who is ready to leave him now, at a signing after a show... only the show was way back when—like way back before the band even had a deal."

Julie nodded.

Val nodded, eyes widened and chin dipped conspiratorially.

Julie waited.

Waited some more.

"Go on," Julie said, more than a little anxious to hurry it all up.

"Yeah, so, he wakes up, and the day is normal. He does a show unconsciously looking for this estranged wife in the crowd even though she shouldn't be there—she lives on the other side of the country—but doesn't find her at first but then, when they are about to leave the stage he sees her and she's young. He asks his bandmates if they saw her but," she shakes her head and sits back from the camera, relaxing into the story, "they didn't."

Another pause that Julie dutifully waited through, but this time it didn't seem like Val was going to say anything else. She waited a beat longer before speaking again.

"And...?"

Val looked at Julie like she had spoken in another language. Then she offered,

"The woman... she wasn't there...?"

Julie was talking before she meant to be. Had she had a chance to slow herself down, she might not have added so much edge to her voice.

"What is the big deal about this, Val? It's cool, sure, maybe even a little creepy, but where are you going with it? Is this going to be a life on different planes/alternate reality kind of thing? Is it horror? If so, how? Is it romance? If so, it needs a little edge. What do you want people to get out of it? What will they talk about after the last scene?"

Val looked nervous again, and this time Julie didn't care as much.

"I don't know... I mean, I guess it could be a romance," Val started. "Maybe they find each other again after all that time. Maybe he was tripping or something and he just keeps imagining her."

It was Julie's turn to shake her head this time.

"You haven't written this yet, have you?"

"Well, no, I thought I was here to talk about my —"

"Your *script*. You're here to talk about your script, not pitch an idea so you can go write a script and then think I'm going to do something with it. You're not there yet."

"But they said —"

"Put some bite into your idea and get it on paper. Come back next year."

Julie left the meeting, this time totally ok with doing so. She looked at the time. Ten minutes until this chore was over. She'd have to take one more person. Julie sighed, closed her eyes. She was irritated that she was there: manning pitch sessions wasn't exactly the highlight of a film festival and online made it even worse. You were truly a captive audience then, each person looking at you, your backdrop, your personal space and assessing it, whether for meaning, relevance to the discussion, or just to be nosy. It was exhausting, but somebody had to do it and she had drawn the short straw that year. The good thing was that she wouldn't have to do it again the next year—she'd get to have drinks or screen a film or just sleep if she wanted to instead. She could do whatever she wanted, which was anything but this.

Ten more minutes.

One more pitch.

She took a deep breath and opened the call.

… And there was silence. Silence and blackness. It seemed like no one was on the call, yet her window had adjusted to accommodate two videos. Whoever was on the other side didn't have their camera turned off or their sound muted. It was just… blank.

"Hello?" Julie said the same way she would answer a call from a phone number she didn't recognize, the lilt of her voice as it rose to form the questions loud in her ear.

Nothing.

There was no silhouette—it wasn't like someone had dialed in from a dark place and didn't have the right lighting to illuminate themselves properly. It was as if the camera were shooting a black wall.

"If you're there, I can't see you. Can you turn your camera on?"

That had been one of the rules. You had to have your camera on to pitch your screenplay. As festivals tried to pivot and figure out how to make the online experience worth the price of admission, several changes had been made to the process. There were online movie screenings and forums for feedback, panel discussions you could watch live and pre-recorded material as well. There would be an awards ceremony that no one would attend in person. And then there was this virtual pitch thing she had been doing for the last hour. Several houses were doing it, including some indie outfits. The rules stated that both parties had to have their cameras on and have adequate microphones. They also stated that there shouldn't be a whole lot of distractions either—dogs barking and your kid playing his drum kit in the basement were not welcome. It was ten minutes of time—if you couldn't spare that, don't sign up.

Easy peasy. Yet here she sat with a blank screen.

Julie sighed and fingered the edge of a bradded screenplay sitting on the desk. She hadn't planned to read it; it had a pink cardstock cover, for God's sakes, so she had planned to throw it in the trash, but she opened it instead. It would give her something to do while the person on the other end sorted out their problem. She read, smirking expectantly.

INT. POST OFFICE—MR. LEVY'S OFFICE—EVENING
MR. LEVY, a mid —forties, overweight, balding man paces the floor in his office. He walks to the door and LOOKS at the empty lobby. He walks back to the mailroom and SEES Cal smoking a cigarette and talking to POSTAL WORKER #2.

MR. LEVY
Cal.

Cal looks up.

MR. LEVY
(continuing; sternly)
Come into my office, Cal.

Mr. Levy retreats back into the office.

CAL
(mumbling)
I wonder what the hell he wants now.

POSTAL WORKER #2
Sounds like you're in deep shit.

CAL
He's always bustin' my ass for somethin'.

POSTAL WORKER #2
Same shit, different day.

CAL
Yeah, you ain't kiddin'.

POSTAL WORKER #2
I'll see you later, Cal.

CAL
Yeah.
Cal walks trepidatiously into Mr. Levy's office.

CAL
(continuing)
You wanted to see me?

MR. LEVY
Yes, I did.
Mr. Levy sits down with effort.

CAL
What's this about?

MR. LEVY
It's about your behavior.

Cal looks closely at Mr. Levy.
MR. LEVY

(continuing)
I've been watching the way you handle customers, and I have to tell you,
Cal, I don't like what I see.

Mr. Levy's sweat is forming a ring around his underarms. Cal is getting MAD.
MR. LEVY

(continuing)
Now, I've told you about this kind of thing before, and it hasn't gotten any
better since then. As a matter of fact, it's gotten worse!

CAL
I don't think I understand what you mean, Mr. Levy.

Julie exhaled incredulously and made a show of depositing the screenplay
in the trashcan next to the desk as she mumbled under her breath,

"Going postal... I mean... do people even go to the post office anymore?"

The screen was still blank.

"Hello?" she said, irritated.

She could just hang up and Julie really thought about doing just that because the event was pretty much over anyway and who would care. But then she thought about whether or not they were logging time somehow, could see that she kicked off early. If they could and that bought her another year of manning the pitch booth she'd gnaw at her own wrists.

"Hello? Are you there?"

Nothing.

"Look, you're supposed to have your camera on, so..."

Nothing.

Maybe they had a bad connection? Had gotten kicked out somehow? How long was she expected to stay if no one responded?

The recording light, the inconspicuous little dot, showed itself in the corner of the screen. Yeah, they were watching.

Julie sighed, looked at the clock.

Seven minutes.

Seven minutes, seven minutes. She could do anything for seven minutes.

She tapped her desk, looked around her room. Took out a screenplay they had bought and got back to marking it up.

She waited.

Four minutes.

Julie shook her head after checking the time and went back to work. But then she lifted her head to stare at the screen. What if they thought she should have logged out, should have picked up another call instead of goofing off in the room doing nothing? The festival folks—they really take pride in their programming and if she wasn't pulling her weight, her boss might hear about it.

Julie's eyes flicked over to the recording button. It was still on.

"H —hey... is someone there?" she tried but got no response. She tried clicking around on the screen just in case it had gone to sleep and somehow kept the call visible, even though that didn't make a ton of sense to her. She was grasping at straws.

Julie leaned closer, trying to decipher movement in the other video, so when it happened she was too close to see it for what it was. It was only when she leaned back in her seat, resigned to the fact that she was either going to catch hell for wasting 10 minutes editing a screenplay that was already bought and paid for or slip under the radar that she saw something in the other video screen. It was an outline of her head—black on black, so it was difficult to see , but it was surely there. Julie could see her hairstyle, pulled up in a ponytail, windswept bang over her forehead. She could see her large hoop earring and the absence of one in the other ear. She could see her features, engraved on the black like ink, her teeth an outlined block.

Her eyebrows furrowed.

The action was mirrored onscreen.

She leaned closer and the reflection did the same, some weird doppelganger dance with her computer twin. When she was young, she'd had an idea about something like this happening, but it was in a mirror. She had pulled her medicine cabinet mirror open one day and held it against the big rectangular one in the bathroom she and her sister shared, creating at least 10 reflections—little Julies standing in the mirror wearing a parochial school outfit. She remembered thinking that it would be creepy if somewhere way back in the line of reflections, one of them changed; if that Julie turned her head or changed her expression or something like that. She remembered thinking that would be an excellent movie.

She didn't see the hand come through the screen to caress her face until it was too late: she was too busy staring at her eyes reflected in the pitch, the emptiness and recognition inside battling each other for first dibs. It was the mouth that won, the mouth, dripping with something black and viscous... something she felt roll down her chin—the mouth that made the first cut, and that was the way it should be, after all.

In her head as much as with her ears, Julie heard a voice that sounded like it was speaking from underwater ask the question that had frightened her into a corner before she had jumped the desk, taken ownership of it, and fashioned it into a weapon more times than she cared to admit. That it would be the last thing she would ever hear never dawned on her—she was too busy taking in the shape of her eyes reflected in ink, like a coin stamped with a stencil that was too wide for it—but if it had, she wouldn't have been surprised.

She almost let the hand that came from the screen cradle her head, the hand that wouldn't show up on the recording when staff looked back to try and figure out what happened to Julie Stafford from Media Mix and why she stood up her last appointment. Indeed, the video wouldn't show much of anything—mostly the top of her head as she read something on her desk and the occasional glance at the screen. The tech tasked with reviewing that meeting was about to turn off the feed when he noticed Julie leaning forward, her head cocked to the side in an unnatural way. It gave him the chills—he would never say it that way, but it was the truth. Her chin seemed to reach toward the screen, tilting her head to the side and distending her neck. When she spoke the last word she ever would, he didn't jump—that wasn't the thing that made him call his manager in and tell him to check it out. That she had said, 'And...?' seemingly unprovoked was weird, but what made him stand up and back away from his desk was when she looked at the camera dead on, seemed to look right at him and, with her neck too long and her chin thinned into a point as if someone were squeezing the flesh there, she smiled.

9-1-1

"9-1-1. What's your emergency?"

"Oh my god… oh no!"

"Ma'am, tell me what your emergency is."

"There's… there's… I think…"

"Ma'am, I need you to calm down and —"

" —there's a m-man… I think it's Charlie…"

"Do you know the man? What is he doing?"

"It's Charlie… I mean, I *think* it's him. But he-he's been in some kind of accident, I guess. Some kind of—"

"There's been an accident? Did it happen where you are now—579 Sycamore Lane?"

"No, no… I mean yes, that's where we—oh my God!"

"I'm sorry, ma'am. I just need you to tell me what you see. I'm sending help right now, just tell me what is going on."

"He's-he's… Mitchell… he's heading for Mitchell."

"Mitchell?"

"My neighbor. Charlie… he's trying to—"

"Ma'am, please calm down. I assure you, help is on the way."

'Mitchell! Over here! Hurry!'

"Ma'am —"

'No… no! NOOOOO!'

"Ma'am?"

"Oh my God."

"Ma'am?"

"Mitchell…"

"What happened to Mitchell? Is he with you now? Mitchell… he's your neighbor?"

"Oh, dear God."

"Ma'am, wha—."

"His neck… I can't believe what happened to his neck, oh God."

"What happened to *whose* neck, ma'am?"

"…neck, it's…"

"Was he in the accident also? Are you saying there's damage to Mitchell's neck?"

"He… he… he…"

"… ma'am?"

"Charlie…"

"Help is coming for Charlie, ma'am. But is there another injured party? Where is Mitchell?"

"Mitchell is outside. With Charlie. They're both outside."

"Ok, help is on the way. They will take care of Charlie and Mitchell, if he needs help too."

"No. No! Don't let them get close —"

"Ma'am, everything will be ok. You just stay here on the line with me. Help will be there very soon."

"No… they can't help Charlie. He… oh my God… nononono!"

"What's happening ma'am? What's the matter?"

"Mitchell is back. He's back. It's impossible."

"Mitchell from before? Your neighbor?"

"Yes. He's back. He shouldn't be here. Shouldn't be—not after… Charlie… they —."

"It's ok, ma'am. We've got enough room for them both in the rig. They'll get the help they need. Do you know what hap —"

"*He* did it. Charlie… he—they're trying to get in."

"Try to keep them still until the ambulance comes. They shouldn't be moving around too mu—"

'*Get away! Get away, you son of a bitch! Noooooooo!*'

"Ma'am?"

'*…Na… no…*'

"Ma'am? Are you in danger?"

"Mmmmhmph…:"

"Ma'am, is someone there with you?"

"Oh… god…"

"Ma'am…? Are you alo-… Can you get somewhere safe?"

"Stay on the line with me and hide, ok? Stay on the line so I can direct the police to you. OK, ma'am?"

'Unit 517, there's a possible 240 in progress at 579 Sycamore Lane. Bus dispatched. Proceed with caution, that's a 10-31.'

"Ma'am?"

'Sto…'

"Ma'am, the police are on their way, ok? Just stay hidden and keep me on the line."

"Ma'am, are you there?"

"Ma'am?"

EN MEDIAS RES

I see them jump as if I was watching a movie. They cut the air, hair flying, eyes trained on the spot they would inevitably land. As they descend, something snaps inside me and tells me I'd better get going. No sense making it easy for them.

I crouch and run, digging in, hauling ass.

I hear them behind me, the sound of their grunts and growls ringing in my ear.

I could feel the heat of their breath on my neck.

I broke the door—damn it, I broke it and it can't help me now, can't slow them down, can't create a barrier between us. Thinking about the destruction my ill-placed hit caused slows my feet and the one called Hawkish is upon me, tackling me to the floor in the middle of the orange room: an oasis amidst the chaos. The orange room. This is where they bring the happy people, the ones who get to leave after a short visit and smell the flowers, feel the air on their skin. This is where I will breathe my last breath.

I turn to face my captor; my killer. He hoists me up; slams me against the wall; throws me around like a rag doll, but it doesn't matter. Hawkish hurts me. He always has.

He's saying something threatening as per usual, challenging my audacity to attack the one who somehow makes being a halfling sound like committing a sin, leaning close to intimidate me into acquiescence, but it doesn't matter. Not this time. I can't help the faint smile that plays at the corner of my lips at the sight of the blood that trickled from his hairline.

I can hurt too.

A CHRISTMAS TALE

She could feel it before she opened the door; something dropped in her stomach as she reached for the doorknob, protesting, begging her to turn away... to leave. *I hate that tree*, Marley thought as soon as she walked into her house, the blinking lights accosting her before she could close the door. Green. Red. Orange. Blue. White. Blinking fast then slow, then fast again because her mother hadn't set the speed, just left the lights to cycle through whatever the factory setting was. Marley knew they were Christmas lights, but they felt like eyes when she came in the room and saw them there, changing color while she watched...

...almost like they were winking at her.

Winking at her from behind gaudy Christmas ornaments clustered in front; ornaments that almost drowned out the incessant blinking.

Almost.

Marley groaned as she walked in, unable to pull her eyes away from the monstrosity.

The *monster.*

She eyed it and from somewhere beneath the lights and ornaments, and tinsel, it stared back at her.

Marley walked toward the tree, walking deeper into the living room scattered with the storage bins that held those offensive ornaments and other collected tree trash for most of the year, her shoulders instinctively raising higher and higher with every step. She didn't feel it happening but knew what was going on. Marley was preparing herself to fight, preparing herself for battle.

Because it was in there. And this year she was going to get it out.

The wind whipped outside the open front door, pushing in the cold air and letting out the warm, but Marley didn't feel the chill on the air. She threw her backpack to the floor; she needed her hands free for what was to come.

Marley's chest heaved as the tree vibrated and thrummed.

The tree reached out to Marley, surprising her.. She craned her neck, cringing, spine arching, desperate not to feel the coarse bristles against her skin as the branches elongated, stretched their plastic tips toward Marley's face. Her feet tangled beneath her and she shrieked in surprise as she fell, a sound she wished she hadn't made because now her mother would come to see what was wrong; her mother would come and ask why the door was open… her mother would see what lived in the tree and it would go after her too.

Its bloody mouth spread into a smile as if it could read Marley's thoughts.

Marley could see its eyes now, set deep in the thick of the fake tree that was older than she was. Marley knew her mother had played Christmas songs by Johnny Mathis and drank wine as she trimmed the tree just like she did every year, and just like every year before that one, the beast in the tree woke up, blinked its hateful eyes, and waited. For what, Marley didn't know. Maybe for Marley to get too close so it could stick its metal fasteners in one of her eyes or scratch her face as she reached for presents?

Her mother never seemed to notice.

Maybe, Marley had time to wonder, *it was just waiting for* me.

Marley's hair pulled from her scalp as a branch she hadn't noticed wound itself around a few braids… enough to hurt… enough to trap her. Marley wanted to scream, wanted to call for help, but the branches pressed into her mouth, ripping her tongue from her jaw and diving through the tunnel of her throat to strangle her breath.

Some of the tinsel on the lower branches was knocked loose and tangled itself in Marley's hair as she was dragged under it… into it; it was the perfect wrapping for the perfect gift. Joanne came up from the basement with another bin full of ornaments and put them on the floor in front of the tree. She stood straight and placed her hands on her hips, tired from walking up the stairs mostly but also because there really wasn't any more room for more ornaments.

She plumped the limbs, marveling at how such an old tree could still look brand new, full and flush like she felt after a satisfying meal. Then she spotted it.

Maybe there is *room for a few more,* Joanne thought as she smiled, *right there, where Marley dropped her bag.*

THE COLOR OF BLOOD

"What do you make of it, Detective?" he finally asked after staring at the side of Richardson's face long enough to be uncomfortable. He knew the question was coming but didn't have an answer; the officer, fresh on the street by the looks of it, could have watched him for hours and Richardson still wouldn't have known what to say.

"Hard to tell," he started and let his words linger, deciding that was enough. He had poked the bloody shirt with the end of his pen and knelt next to the conspicuous dark spot on the porch long enough to have more than that, but nothing was coming to him, none of the ideas he was known for around the office. The detective he shadowed during his first few months in plain clothes used to say it was like he had committed the murders himself, gave him the side eye every once in a while like he really believed it might be true. Back in the precinct they settled on him having second sight, being clairvoyant, seeing things; the words changed depending upon who was saying them, but not the sentiment. He told them they'd better be careful talking like that; the brass might take their badges and require psych eval before they could get them back. They'd laugh and so would he, but they still wondered how Richardson was able to figure out the most obscure cases —the woman whose skin looked like she had been in the water for days but had just been pronounced dead 30 minutes before; the mummified digit lying in the middle of a busy street. He always figured it out—that's probably why they'd called him for this one. He wasn't up next. Hell, he had been thinking about taking a few days off in Syosset.

Richardson looked over at the front door of the place. It was weathered and old, warped from years of swelling in the sun and settling against bitter winter winds. It needed a coat of paint and so did the porch he was standing on, both more like the weathered wood of an old barn than the cookie-cutter facades of suburbia. Curious. More than that. Downright odd. Because there was an HOA in place and homeowner's associations didn't take too kindly to people not keeping up their homes. Property value was a thing, and it seemed the HOA's sole purpose was to complain about lawns not being trimmed or flowerbeds in disarray. If painting the shutters bright pink could get an owner fined, leaving the front to wither in the elements had to be cause for concern. Richardson looked on his phone to make sure he'd gotten it right. It felt funny doing it even though it's all he'd ever known. When he was growing up and the people around him called him by his first name rather than his last, he watched all the police shows on TV. Columbo, Kojak, Magnum P.I., T.J. Hooker. He wanted to be like all of them. And he was, at least an amalgamation of them, though he doubted any of them would have appreciated the device he spoke into in his hand to take notes... except maybe Inspector Gadget.

It was the second note he had taken and yep, he'd heard the beat cop correctly: Someone at the HOA called the police after walking around the grounds and smelling something foul.

Richardson smelled it too, and it was strong.

What the busybody from the HOA didn't know—what the stench didn't allow him to trespass further to figure out—was that all the windows were closed too so the source of the smell must be fresh and there was likely more than one. That bothered Richardson, of course, but what made his hair stand on end was how they had gotten to that state, the two people inside whose blood had seeped into the floorboards of different rooms, rooms that had seen gatherings and celebrations and happy times before their deaths. Because the door had been nailed shut from the inside.

The door to the front, the doors to the bedroom where the father lay dead. The note they found made it sound like she had killed him, slit his throat because she was angry, she was tired, she was finished. Her friends said they didn't see it coming, said they had been out that night and she was happy, so happy, too happy to have done this... killed him and then herself... and then her son? What about her son? Where was he when this happened? Why was his door free of nails? Had he not tried to protect himself from his mother? Had she gotten him as he fled? The bloody shirt Richardson kept worrying with his pen said maybe. But then where was his body?

Nailed shut. Nailed inside. If slit from ear to ear, he wouldn't have had the strength to try to keep her out that way, find boards and nails and a hammer and bang. He would lose too much blood if the energy was exerted like that; there would be a pool of it by the door. But there wasn't. Indeed, there wasn't a drop spilled.

And the mother... would she have gouged out her eyes the way she had if she had done what the letter said she did? She meant to do it, it said. She knew what she was doing and she meant it all. But Oedipus gouged his eyes out because he couldn't bear to see his life laid bare the way it was anymore. Had she? She bled through the sockets, bled through the holes she made in her head, bled until she had nothing left. Her last few words damned her, condemned her, sent her straight to hell for spilling her child and husband's blood, and then she bled on the floor where she sat. On the floor across from her son's room.

Richardson poked at the shirt again then called someone over to tag it. Generic brand cotton pullover—nothing that couldn't be bought at any store anywhere. It would be tested, analyzed, the blood staining it compared to the parents and it would be a DNA match—Richardson knew that. But none of that would tell him what he needed to know.

Where was he?

Neighbors said they hadn't seen him in a while, that they hadn't seen the parents either, but that was no big surprise. Work, school, the things that keep the wheels turning—those are the things that force people into their houses in the evening, deposit them on the sofa until 2 a.m. when they wake up to find the TV watching them. Nobody saw anything. Nobody ever did.

The shirt didn't have to be his, Richardson tried to tell himself but he knew better. The shirt didn't have to be his—it could be someone else's, a bum off the street who decided to roam the suburban neighborhood he found himself in and ditch what was likely one of his only garments because it had a little blood on it, all this in the chill of early spring. And the mother didn't have to be covering for someone—her words, the ones she had written with such a heavy hand that she broke through the paper in a few places before scrawling her name, they could have been the god's honest truth when they said she hated her family and hated herself and wanted them all to die. Her, she had said emphatically—she was the one who hated them all and had done this. The father had tried to say something, more of the same Richardson thought, but they would never know. His writing was unfinished, 'It's m —' as far as he got, the letters jagged and oddly spaced, written in blood. Everything could be as it looked. It wouldn't take much to connect dots that shouldn't be connected, make up a story that was just plausible enough to be believed. If he went to one of the cops standing around looking at him, busying themselves, waiting for a cue from him about what to do next—if he went to one of them and said that one or the other of them did it, mounted a decent enough argument for why he thought so, they would call it a murder suicide and it would be over. The DNA match on the shirt wouldn't point a finger at the son—it would just prove that the blood on the shirt was a match for the dead people in the house. And of course it was—one of them used it, after all.

Easy paperwork.

Wrapped up crime scene.

Pat… because no one could nail up a door behind them, not from the inside.

Murder suicide, sure. That's what it looked like and that's what it would be. Except the woman in the window looking toward the sun and crying black tears told him otherwise.

STRANGERS: A REIMAGINING

The waitress watched them from behind the beaded curtain, the American and his lady. They were upset with each other, but trying to look serene, as if any drunk stumbling out of the bar couldn't see what was going on. They looked out at the hills, gazing off in the distance at some unknown thing, hoping to defer their problem, to give it over to the hills as a form of offering. But it didn't work. It never works, no matter how many people stand in that very spot trying to do the very same thing.

The heat was oppressive inside the kitchen where the waitress stood, one ear to the conversation in front of her and one listening to the cook who was humming while he chopped, but it didn't deter her. She could have ducked into the walk-in and felt the cool air on her skin—only a second would have been needed in respite—but she didn't want to miss anything. He was trying to convince the lady to do something, something she didn't really want to do. He didn't want to make it seem like he was, but there was desperation on his face. The waitress felt sorry for the woman; she looked like she was losing her very soul as the conversation trod on. She thought maybe she would interrupt them, offer more water, tell them of the man that lives on the other side of the very hills they stared at, and his reclusive ways—something to break the flow. Maybe that would help the woman regain some of herself. Maybe she would find a way to hold her chin up and finish the conversation with dignity.

The waitress looked at the clock. The train would be there in 5 minutes. This was her chance.

The waitress put down the beer and ceremoniously announced the coming of the train, just as the lady threatened to scream. The American gathered himself and left the table, looking as appreciative for the separation as she hoped the woman felt. With a demure smile playing at the corners of her lips, the waitress faded into the recesses of the kitchen, saying a silent prayer for the woman, so tortured yet so graceful, sitting on the platform alone.*

---

* Editor's Note: This story reimagines the action and setting of Ernest Hemingway's classic short story, "Hills Like White Elephants," first published in the August 1927 issue of the literary magazine *transition*, then later that year in Hemingway's short story collection, *Men Without Women*. This author has given Hemingway's "girl" a much more empathetic witness.

THE CALL

The blood always calls to me.

I always hear it beg for release, a gift I cannot give... I *should* not give. It beckons me do its bidding in the evening, caressing the words, teasing my earlobe with its feathered touch. The darkness masks its face, leaving me defenseless and blind as I reach for it to sate and be sated. Ay, but no, I shall not give in this time. I will not let it manipulate me for its wanton desires. The blood must be controlled even as it threatens to deny my very existence.

I lay covering my ears, denying purchase, but it finds other ways to make me weak. I bend to its will even when I resist. My body does not agree with my mind and falls prey all too easily, each and every time.

On the edge of the bed I sit awaiting the next touch, the next whisper; the next command. I look out of the window at the vast city below, its people sleeping their mindless sleep, reveling in the façade that is serenity, and laugh despite myself.

DENIAL

"Because I don't want to!"

That's the last thing he said before he turned off like a light switch. He was there, still there... awake, if not fully aware. I knew because I could hear him. I knew because there was no reason for him not to be—25-year-old man in good health and fine spirits before he went inside. I knew because he had to be... if he wasn't, the world didn't make sense, would never make sense again.

"Babe, come out," I whispered, even though I heard the world crack open and swallow him whole, body and soul.

ANYMORE

His hands were on her and then they weren't.

He was pawing, prying, panting in anticipation, pressing down on her so she couldn't get up, couldn't move, couldn't breathe...

... but then he wasn't.

He wasn't because he wasn't anymore.

He wasn't hot anymore, not game anymore, not *him* anymore.

He wasn't... anything, not anymore.

He said nobody would notice.

He said even if they did, nobody would stop him because they would be too busy saving their own asses to care what he was doing out there, right out in the open.

Because it was all over.

He laughed at her.

Called her stupid.

Because she didn't see it, didn't believe it would happen, didn't think the world would be wiped away.

As he lay on top of her, tears springing from his eyes like fire hydrant flow interrupted by a big stick, drenching his face as he pulled at himself, tugged at it, flaccid thing that it was, terrified into permanent inaction, but still he pulled and pulled and pulled. With the other hand he squeezed her breast, twisted it like the crank of a Jack-in-the-Box, fingers bruising, digging into her flesh. He heard her squealing, but no, he didn't care because it was over, it was over, it was fucking over, goddamn it, couldn't she see that? Who gave a shit anymore?

When his head split in half, a diagonal slice that looked like it was made with a sword, she didn't cry for him. The squealing that had been issuing forth from her mouth minutes before died in her throat as the sky behind him first went black then blossomed with the most brilliant of reds like Heaven was on fire. She choked on her screams as she heard people dropping around her, falling to the ground dead, dead, so very dead. She could see inside some of them, holes bored through their foreheads to show their brains, through their chests, all the way out of their backs.

Carol from the diner. She must have left food in the window to run out of the place before the lasers came to kill all of them, cold and impersonal like sunlight through a magnifying glass over an ant colony. The beam cut into her body, opening her with the precision of a surgeon. Carol fell right behind where she and Buster, the bastard who died with his limp dick in his hands, lay in the street. Carol fell on her back, her stomach open where she'd been sliced, intestines spilling out like they were too big for the cavity they had been crammed into.

Walker and his wife. Was her name Maggie? Margaret? Misty? Marla? She didn't remember, and it didn't matter, not anymore. They fell next to where she lay under that bastard, Buster, close enough that Walker's arm flung onto her shoulder when he landed, their eyes burned out, burned clear through their heads.

She could hear the hiss of the beams coming from some unseen thing in the sky. Must be a UFO, she thought, but even then, she wasn't so sure. It was just something she would have said twenty minutes before, when all she had to worry about was what she was going to have for dinner.

Aliens.

That's what people thought of when terror came from the sky, right? That's what they said in the movies, like aliens didn't have anything else to do but to mess with the good people of Earth and take over the planet like squatters.

Buster smelled of cheap cologne and his own piss and shit.

She looked left, saw the kid whose only job was to gather up the carts from the parking lot and bring them inside. He couldn't have been more than 16 years old, probably went to the high school down the street from where they both lay. The carts were on top of him—the little ones meant for just a few items; the big ones for Thanksgiving dinner-type shopping.

THE OPEN BOOK UNIVERSE

There was even a cart designed for kids to pretend they were driving sitting on top of him, the handle attached to a racecar cockpit with a steering wheel and everything. This one had landed on his head after the wind that came behind the lasers swept through, wind strong enough to push carts full of food abandoned by their owners across the lot...well, at least partially: some carts still had limbs attached to them, fingers gripping tight in death even as the arms they belonged to were severed at the elbows. The wind was strong enough to uproot street signs and carry them over the highway and up the hill to where she was pinned beneath Buster. Decatur Street. That was at least a mile away, she thought. She wondered what was happening on Decatur Street then, whether or not someone was surveying the aftermath like she was from a similar perch, stuck beneath the rubble and rot.

She looked right and saw more of the same. Downed bodies covered in blood, organs on the ground covered in the dirt that had been pulled loose in the windstorm, innards dredged in viscous fluid and coated in soil like a snack ready to be pan fried and served up to who? The aliens? The gods?

Something stringy and wet flapped toward her propelled by the wind but tethered to something on one side. She recoiled beneath Buster, disgusted because she thought that the pink, fleshy thing was sinew even though she had never seen a picture of sinew to know for sure. She wriggled, desperate to get away from it, single-minded in that effort now that she had convinced herself about what it was. It kept flapping toward her, reaching for her. She was sure that if it touched her, it would consume her, eat away at her like acid, skin ulcering like a canker sore on the sensitive pink of one's lip, falling off in big clumps... flesh-eating disease in the end because why not? She laughed, the prospect enough to break her resolve, to tip her over the edge and send her into hysterics.

And nobody cared.

A thought came to mind as her laughter trailed off, an elaborate picture show forming in her head to display everything in graphic detail.

Maybe the stuff she thought was sinew was really a spore like in that old alien invasion movie. Maybe if it touched her, she'd see it turn *into* her, first morphing from the stringy crap into a blob, then forming a face that looked like hers, a body that was tall and slender, gangly when pressed into action, like her own. Maybe it would open its eyes and stare at her, shoot a fleshy appendage out to touch her face, feel the contours so the replica would be better... more authentic. Then she laughed again, the sound harsh in the deafening quiet. She laughed in part because of the beast made of sinew, the monster after her essence, but mostly because she realized she was going to die beneath that bastard, Buster, after all. She was going die after surviving the fucking apocalypse, managing to dodge hot globs of flying flesh and lasers intent on cutting everyone in half. She was going to die because she couldn't breathe underneath his body anymore, his dead weight feeling like a ton of bricks on top of her thin body. She was going to die because she was afraid to get out from under him, afraid to stand exposed in the crowded parking lot where she'd be utterly alone. The laser would find her if she did.

When the librarian had fallen, she had lost her shoe.

The old guy who picked up trash off the street in town had lost his teeth when his head hit the ground unprotected, unshielded, smacking against the asphalt hard enough to break the thin skin over his skull and spew blood. She had to crane her neck to see him, could have avoided that particular sight, but she couldn't stop herself from moving, from stretching, from trying to see. His mouth was open, jaw permanently set in a surprised 'O'.

It was quiet. Quiet, but not silent.

Fuzzy.

The way one might think static would sound.

She listened to it. Closed her eyes and tried to fall asleep to it. Maybe when she woke up she'd be ready to move, ready to make a run for it, just in case the laser was waiting for her.

Maybe when she woke up, she'd be dead.

She squeezed her eyes shut.

Buster's blood dripped onto her face, into her mouth.

The sinew monster took another swipe at her, getting closer this time.

She shrieked at the thought of it making contact, attaching itself to her skin, sucking at her with toothy mouths that dotted its flesh. She found strength she didn't know she had, pushed Buster's mutilated body over to the side, and stood up on shaky legs.

She was out.

She was out.

She turned around in a circle, surveying the lot.

She was alone.

Bodies strewn around, torsos here, limbs there. Scalps, fingers, livers, hearts—she thought of Humpty Dumpty when he fell off the wall, a grisly puzzle with the pieces lying on a table, some right side up, some upside down. She grabbed at her arms, reached for her legs, looked at her shoes, still on her feet, and wriggled her toes, checking even though she could feel herself, knew everything was still where it should be, but because nobody else around her was intact, she looked at herself anyway, to be sure. Then she looked back at Buster. That asshole, Buster, who always looked at her with kind eyes when he said hello; Buster, who always seemed to be coming when she was going, always happened to be wherever she was; Buster, who she thought was harmless right up until he threw her to the ground to have his way because the world was ending.

Buster, who had saved her life by getting on top of her.

She saw the bodies around them and realized something that made her angry.

He had been right.

Nobody cared.

Carol, the librarian, the garbage picker, Walker and whatever his wife's name was, all the people who had met the laser close by her and Buster, so close they could have touched them, screamed at him, pushed him off of her—none of them cared about what Buster was doing. They were too busy trying the save their own asses to worry about anything else.

But the laser saw.

The laser knew all.

The kid with the carts was looking at her with a smile on his face as a bubble of bloody spit grew large on the corner of his mouth, like gum.

And that didn't matter either.

Because he wasn't anything anymore.

DISCLAIMER

These stories were found at the corner of Eel Road and Rte. 77 and in a dressing room at the community theater in Corelle.

LAB WORK

"It's because you like cryptids, that's why."

When she said that, Cody simply nodded. He didn't know what it meant, didn't know if she was insulting him or singing his praises, so he smiled and nodded noncommittally, the way his mother had taught him to when things went over his head. It was charming, she'd said, makes you look smart, but in a quiet, shy way. The girls will love it, and the guys will envy it, she'd said, and she hadn't been wrong. Cody was popular with people he never thought would give him the time of day, popular without really knowing what he was doing to be that way. It was a blessing and a curse, she'd said, or maybe he'd thought it himself, one of those random thoughts that blinked in neon in his head just before he fell off to sleep. He didn't know which and it didn't matter, because in the end, it was true.

The thing under the microscope squirmed, its pincers opening and closing, looking for purchase. Cody smiled at its tenacity, the desire to grab, to pinch, to crush. The abdomen of a cave cricket, the thorax of a spotted lantern fly, and the majestic head of a praying mantis; Cody's creation was a strange tagmata that he found positively gorgeous. He wanted to share it with someone, a person who could appreciate how high it could jump, how it could cling to the wall and display its red wingspan. But he didn't know anyone who would appreciate its beauty, didn't know anyone who would let it grab hold of their flesh with the pincer perched on its antennae and squeeze.

Cody pushed away from the desk and rubbed his forehead with a gloved hand, feigning frustration before the final two students leaving the lab. To them it looked like he had failed again, had miscalculated or misconstrued, that whatever lay beneath the microscope lens had been wrong, wrong, so very wrong, and he had to go back to the drawing board. They'd empathize with him as they passed, if only to temper their relief at not finding themselves in his shoes. But it would be more than that, and Cody knew it. It would be real sympathy, a real emotional response to his plight because he was him and that's how people reacted to him. They'd feel his frustration, try to catch his gaze so they could show him they cared. But he wouldn't let them meet his eyes. He couldn't run the risk of them offering to help, to fix, to save. He'd keep his head low and his eyes averted while playacting in the lab, and soon they'd be gone, the floor would be empty, and the real work could begin.

The parade would be packed; with the weather slated to be a comfortable 68°, projections were in the thousands. That was good. He needed a large sample to determine what properties were most prevalent. Would it hunt using olfactory means or echolocation? Would it paralyze its prey or poison it? Cody needed to get it into the enhancer as quickly as possible so that levels could be assessed—pheromone, venom, neurotoxins, formic acids, and the like. He needed to get it out of the lab and into the launch space he'd prepared by the rusted cellar doors that hadn't been opened in ages, and he had to do so unnoticed because if anyone saw what he'd created, it would all be over. They'd take it, destroy it, and then turn their sights on him. He had no idea what that might mean for his research, for his future. No, Cody needed it to live, needed it to be free, if only for a few minutes. Even if the original specimen was lost, the data the sensor implanted in its underside would send back would inform his next iteration.

He already had plans for the next one.

As he looked at the enhancer, the model the school had just procured that stood at 7 feet tall and double that in width, Cody realized that version two, his spider-legged butterfly would require a bigger unit. He also knew that the girls, they wouldn't love it, and the last thing the guys would feel was envy, not when his creature tore their throats out to suck at their blood as though it were nectar. And that didn't bother him at all.

SHARE AND SHARE ALIKE

The balloon, let loose to float up, up, up in the sky amid screams of dismay and clammy, clasping digits just missing its string, passed through the atmosphere carried on the wind. Another child cried for it, saw it below, and beckoned it come.

It obliged.

Under a dark sky pocked by the residue of starbursts like fireworks and littered with century rock, a scaled appendage grasped the string tightly and buzzed with joy.

CLARITY OF THOUGHT

He inched closer, fingers reaching like tentacles to graze skin. He didn't know whose skin he might touch, and it didn't matter; he simply needed connection. He'd given of himself before, swore he would never do it again, but here was, wanting, needing, actively seeking... someone.

Anyone.

The door obliged, but that wasn't what he wanted. Stuck half in and half out of the garage as he had been for what could've been hours as easily as seconds, he found the interior of the car suffocating, as if the doors, the headliner with its yellowed light cover and puckered roof, the very upholstery on the seats inched closer with his every breath, closer like a boa constrictor to tighten around him. Closer, closer, ever closer. Something was back there, behind the car. Something he couldn't see.

But it could see him.

He'd walked down the steps in the garage and over to the driver's side door the same way he did every day. It was one of those things people did on autopilot, completing tasks while their minds were otherwise occupied with bills, presentations, dinner plans, everyday worries. He was alone in the garage, which made sense. He lived by himself, and the space was his and his alone, connected to the three-level townhome that he was still furnishing after two years. Being alone never bothered him because he could change that when he wanted to, could go outside and join the throng of people jogging, walking the sidewalks, shopping in big box stores. He could have a conversation with someone at the gas pump, in the supermarket, at the fast-food place if he wanted to use his voice. He could take himself off mute in meetings and actually contribute to the conversation if he really needed to take part. He could do any of those things in his own time so, alone was good, alone was comfortable, alone was what he wanted it to be, when he wanted it to be. Alone never crossed anyone's mind until it needed to, until being so was dangerous. That day was no different.

He stopped in the garage and reached for the car door, ready to get into the car. He had errands to run, solitary ones where he didn't have to speak with anyone at all if he didn't want to. Drop mail in the slot. Top off the air in his tires. Withdraw money from the ATM. He was plotting his route absently as he got in the car, not thinking about the movements actively as much as his body propelled him toward an end, activating to move him toward a path. The buzz beneath his fingers as he touched the door handle didn't register until after he got in the car and started it up, the remnant of the unexpected tingle lingering there to numb his fingers as they curled around the scalloped steering wheel. He looked at his hand, flexed the fingers under his gaze, and placed it back on the steering wheel as the sound of the car engine filled his ears. He pressed the button on the remote to open the garage door, couldn't feel the plastic beneath his fingers. He brought his hand back to the steering wheel. He started the ignition. His hand still felt wrong, false, like rubber, so he took it off the steering wheel again to slap it against his thigh. False, false, like a prosthetic.

Like it was someone else's.

The garage door opening was loud on the track.

He leaned toward his hand, turning his wrist so that he could examine the fingers closely, and that's when it happened. The beep of a vehicle in reverse; the chime of alert when something is detected in the sensor, when something is in the car's path rang in the cabin. A beep that shouldn't be because he had not yet put the car in reverse.

The camera flickered to life as he looked, finding himself eye to eye with the display since he'd bent so low to examine his numb fingers, and he saw nothing that would indicate a reason for concern. The garbage can hadn't been left in front of the garage door where he could hit it this time, nor had a package been left there. He always checked for that now; he'd crushed a gift from his mother years before, a box full of housewarming bits and bobs all mutilated by the tread of his tires, and then there was the box filled with things that spoke of love that he'd all but annihilated under the car's weight, but there was nothing there this time. Nothing there. Nothing at all, until the sensor on the left side of the car began to glow, began to pulse, began to shriek.

He reached for the door with his numb hand, numb like gums injected with Novocaine, he reached for it but didn't want it, didn't want it at all, because it couldn't save him. He would never be able to use it, to scramble to the other side of the car and open it so he could fall out onto the garage floor only to rise to his feet at a run; he'd never be fast enough for that. The sensor positively howled now, long wailing notes like ill-planned chords on a theremin, like the car was begging for help, so he knew that to reach for the door was futile. But flesh would have sufficed. Flesh would have helped him to make sense of the moment, to ground himself in the inevitability of it, and to find and give comfort. Living skin would have provided warmth, solace, and understanding, would have opened him to emotions he might not normally feel, the gooseflesh beneath his fingertips a conduit to an emotional awareness he had never known before. Sex in the senses, appreciated in the final seconds, because the car was wailing, it was mewling, crying like a mother over a child whose first and last breaths were taken within her arms, crying in despair and fear and loss like an animal in a trap.

Crying its warning about the thing he couldn't see.

The thing that inched closer and closer.

He locked his doors, slapping at the switch wildly, hoping for purchase, but he heard them disengage as soon as they had slid home. Beads of sweat sprang on to his brow and he wiped at it with his numb, useless hand. His cry joined that of the sensor, its high-pitched beep seeming to adjust to form perfect harmony with his own. He reached again, across the passenger seat and into the void to touch, to feel, to be made whole for the last time, his mind begging for familiar skin, for commiseration, for flesh of any kind however cold, taut, or gelatinous. But there was only the door. The light streamed in to illuminate it, to wash it with bright sunlight he hadn't noticed before, so bright he would have had to shield his eyes to look through its rays to see the door clearly. Bright light calling him back, to, away, toward. But he couldn't look; he was too afraid to look away from the display, from the benign street shown behind him, cookie-cutter homes with only the colors of the shutters to differentiate them. He was too afraid to look away from the pulsating dot on the screen.

He braced himself for his fingers to meet the door once again, the plastic arm the last thing he'd find, warmed now by the light of the sun to trick him into thinking it was living flesh, flesh that would be impossible to occupy that space because nobody was supposed to be there. Dimensions had taken him far and away from those who cared enough to send him boxes to be crushed under cars, and he occupied his space alone, alone, entirely alone.

So, he reached.

And he reached.

AN AFTERNOON OUT

"Damn it," he said under his breath, realizing too late that he wasn't exactly quiet. It was about to rain. It was about to rain, and he was stuck outside. It was about to rain, and he was stuck outside at a concert he didn't really want to be at—it was just 'something to do.' He hated when she came up with things 'to do,' casual days spent doing nothing, simply finding ways to spend the time. To waste time. He'd rather be sleeping.

Outdoor concerts were almost always given by performers past their prime. The audience was usually made up of people reliving their past, singing lyrics they only kind of remembered loudly, out of key, and with more gravel in their voice than there used to be. There was always a lot of dancing, most of which was hilarious to watch because moves that were done in one's teenage years don't look the same when done in their 40s.. There was much drinking too, but if one really wanted to get a laugh at point number one, they had to keep their own drinking at a minimum, so they didn't miss the cameos. Sometimes there was a hill involved—people perched on a hill with picnic baskets, bottled water, and yes, alcohol. He lived for the moment when someone would combine all those variables for his viewing pleasure: dancing too hard while singing off-key after imbibing for too long while perched precariously on a hill. He would drop money on the first guy to roll down the hill in this state, would make it rain for him.

She told him he was being mean when he thought that way because he didn't just think it would be funny... he wished for it to come to fruition, preferably near him so he'd have a front row seat.

"It'll pass," she said as she looked toward the stage, never turning her head to look at him. The opening act was set to come out soon, and she didn't want to miss a second of it. He had to fight himself not to shake his head. She couldn't see the stage from their spot on the hill, not even if she stood on her toes. The screen was what she'd be watching, and as far as he was concerned, she could do that at home. She didn't have to pay to sit on grass that would soon be soggy and muddy and endure wind that would be too cool to be considered comfortable to watch a screen that didn't catch anything that happened on the far sides of the stage. He used to say that, back when he thought he could win the argument and watch a recording of some other performance—everything can be found online... that was the beauty of technology—in the comfort of his own home, but it never worked. So, he stopped. He sold himself on the fact that he would miss the epic rolling down the hill if he had stayed home. And that was true—it was enough to keep him afloat for the few hours it took to finish the show.

Almost.

It was about to rain, and he was stuck outside at a concert he didn't really want to be at—some cover band with enough of a following that he had to hustle to get a decent spot on the hill. If he hadn't, they would have only been able to see the wooden steeple-like top of the stage. It always reminded him of the structure they set on fire in *The Wicker Man*. He might have pushed to go home if that was all he could see.

He almost said something back to her about the storm, almost bitched about how they don't allow umbrellas at the venue again like it was the first time he'd ever heard of that rule, even though they'd been going to shows there every summer for the better part of 10 years, almost said they should have brought ponchos, but then he remembered that they had. Ponchos in case of rain; blankets in case it got cold; water in case they got thirsty; snacks in case they got hungry. She had thought of everything. So, he closed his mouth and laid on his back. The sky was gray, and the clouds looked angry, but she was right; blue skies were off to the right. It would be over soon if it even happened at all. Great. No chance of the show getting cancelled, no chance of getting out of there without hearing old music through distorted speakers. No chance of a reprieve at all.

He heard the metal bounce off the lamp cover before he saw something glint in the dim light in the distance. Once, twice, three times. Then he felt the wind as it fell from the sky to land in the grass next to him with an audible *whoosh*. He was about to say something to her about it, something about the rain coming down hard enough to cut paper, that maybe there was lightning because he saw something like a flash, but he didn't get the chance. She was pulling on her poncho when he saw her for the last time, the knives bouncing off of it like a shield even as they pierced his upturned eyes in the downpour.

She'd really thought of everything.

HAIR

They say hair doesn't grow after you're dead, that it only looks like it does. Morticians rub cream into dead flesh, scalps and jaws, brow ridges sometimes too, so the skin doesn't dry up, doesn't recede, doesn't pull away from life to shrivel and decay. That's what they say. But here, inside this box that I share with her, some nameless woman erased from the world and left buried alone in a remote wood, I know better. I know because her hair, as long as she, released its hold on her putrefied skin to enfold mine, calming me with jasmine and wet earth, and I succumb, I accept, I acquiesce as my own intertwines, reaches from my broken scalp to greet hers.

HALO

"He knows."

Those words stopped me dead in my tracks.

He knows.

I almost didn't hear the rest of her warning, the part that was most telling about how all this would play out.

Don't go home.

The odd-looking couple, a woman with a shaved head in ill-fitting clothes clinging to a desperate, wild-eyed man who was familiar somehow, kept moving, merging into the crowd, emerging then disappearing as quickly as they came. They were gone in an instant, as if they were never there in the first place. But they *were* there, and she spoke to me. She said the words I hoped I would never hear. As implausible as it was for this random stranger to know anything about my life, I knew, with every fiber of my being, that she did. If I knew what was good for me, I would heed the warning.

The banana peel on the counter.

I nearly fell to the floor where I stood. The gravity of what was about to happen—what would have happened if I had lingered in the store a few moments longer and our paths had not crossed—hit me with such force that I could barely stay on my feet. I dropped the bag in the corridor of the mall. I didn't need those shoes anymore. There was no gift I could give him that would change things if what she saw was true.

I made my way to the car, half running, half walking, looking over my shoulder all the while, afraid that her timing was off, and he was lying in wait among the parked cars. I could tell I was being paranoid, but as irrational as it was, I had complete faith in what the woman said. I had to move, had to run, had to hide. Still, I needed to get control of myself. I opened the car door hurriedly and slammed it shut behind me. *I'm safe in the car, I'm safe in the car... calm down...*

I had to think.

"Damnit!" I screamed and banged the steering wheel. How could I have been so stupid? Leaving the banana peel out was such a ridiculous thing to do. With all of the planning that went into stealing the money, something so utterly avoidable was going to be the thing that got me caught? He must have suspected something already, must have noticed a change. I expected as much. That's why I was shopping for him. Sure, I was using a little of the money I had taken, but that was ok if it bought me a little more time. I only had one more account to work on. He would have told me the access codes, I'm sure of it. All I needed to do was work him a little longer.

A million dollars down the drain because I forgot to throw out the garbage.

It was more than that, really. Having a banana in the first place spoke of money—money he knew I didn't have. The way produce is rationed nowadays, only the well-to-do could get their hands on the fresh stuff. I remember the first time Colin took me to a dinner party and I saw them dropping raspberries in their champagne like it was nothing... like there was more where those came from. I tried not to look too eager as I did the same, popping a few in my mouth when nobody was looking and hoping the juice didn't color my lips and tongue or else I'd be found out.

Did they halo people for theft?

A chill ran through me, causing me to shiver. Would Colin really kill me? I mean, he wasn't clueless. He knew who I was. When we met, I was working a dead-end job making just enough to get by. Surely, he notices how I stare a little too long at all the fine things he has at his house. I should have never let him upgrade my apartment, should have never let him have a key to come and go when he pleased, but I figured it was no big deal. Men like him didn't waste time showing up at their escort's houses. Colin wanted eye-candy, a little pretty on his arm for those stuffy parties he likes to go to. It wasn't love—neither of us were foolish enough to think that... right?

But still, there was a level of trust he expected of me, and I knew that going in. It had been risky taking all that money, but, oh, the rush.

I looked in my rearview mirror to see my frightened eyes. Wouldn't the pre-crime division catch Colin in the act if he tried to kill me? There hasn't been a murder in years—doesn't that mean I'm safe? My eyes pleaded with me to think, for once in my life, think things through.

Even if they could stop Colin from killing me, they might not get there in time to stop him from trying.

With a start, I turned on the car and put it in gear. How long had I been sitting there? Five minutes? Ten? Precious time wasted. I needed to get moving. I didn't know where I was going, but I knew it wouldn't be home. Ever again. As I pulled the car out of the mall parking lot and ascended to Route 302, heading out of the state and away from the only life I have ever known, I said a silent thank you to that strange, almost ethereal woman for saving my life. Maybe one day I can repay the favor.

WHAT'S SEEN IN THE DARK

Under the moon, we watch.
    Stars long dead put on a celestial show.
    How pretty the moonlight on your dark hair.
    Only you don't know, couldn't comprehend that you're everything.
    Ubiquitous.
    Luminous, like the moon that has us so enamored.
    Distracted.
    Beguiled as though we're alone in the world.
    Entranced as we lay prone and cast our eyes upward.
    Soupy, the dark furthest from the moon.
    Caliginous like the inky depths of the night sea.
    And you love it, this darkness.
    Relish it in ways I don't yet understand.
    Exciting, intriguing, tantalizing, if I'm honest.
    Draw me in, take me deep, until we are inextricable.

ACKNOWLEDGMENTS

Thank you, Sean, Bree, and Mike, for helping me find pockets of time to do this thing I love. Thank you, Laura Fasching and MaryAnn David, for your keen eyes along this journey.

Thank you, readers, for travelling along this road with me.

ABOUT THE AUTHOR

L. Marie Wood is a Bram Stoker, Golden Stake, International Impact, and two-time Bookfest award-winning author. She is also a MICO Award-winning screenwriter, an Elgin and Rhysling Award-nominated poet, an Ignyte Award-nominated author, an accomplished essayist, and a playwright. Wood has won over 50 national and international screenplay and film awards.

She has been published in groundbreaking works, including the anthologies *Sycorax's Daughters* and *Slay: Stories of the Vampire Noire*, as well as industry staples such as the *Magazine of Fantasy & Science Fiction* and *Nightmare Magazine*.

Her nonfiction has been published in academic textbooks such as the cross-curricular *Conjuring Worlds: An Afrofuturist Textbook.* She is also part of the 2022 Bookfest Book Award-winning poetry anthology, *Under Her Skin*, as well as Bram Stoker Award® and Shirley Jackson Award Nominee anthologies *Shakespeare Unleashed* and *Mooncalves*.

Her papers are archived as part of University of Pittsburgh's Horror Studies Collection. Wood is the Vice President of the Horror Writers Association, the founder of the Speculative Fiction Academy, an English and Creative Writing professor, a horror scholar with a Ph.D. in Creative Writing and an MFA in Speculative Fiction, and a frequent contributor to the conversation around the evolution of genre fiction. Learn more about L. Marie Wood at www.lmariewood.com.

ALSO BY L. MARIE WOOD

The Open Book

The Tales of Time

Imitation of Life

The Lost Stories

Crescendo

The Promise Keeper

The Realm Trilogy

Mars, The Band Man, and Sara Sue

Telecommuting

The Black Hole

12 Hours

The Unholy Trinity

About Horror: The Study and Craft

The Horror Aesthetic

FRIENDS OF FALSTAFF

Thank You to All our Falstaff Books Patrons, who get extra digital content each month! To be featured here and see what other great rewards we offer, go to www.patreon.com/falstaffbooks.

PATRONS

Dino Hicks
John Hooks
John Kilgallon
Larissa Lichty
Travis & Casey Schilling
Staci-Leigh Santore
Sheryl R. Hayes
Scott Norris
Samuel Montgomery-Blinn
Junkle

Thank You for Supporting Independent Publishing!

We believe that you should be able
to read your books, your way.
That's why this Falstaff Books
print edition includes a digital copy
at no additional cost!

Just scan the QR code with your device,
follow the directions on Prolific Works,
and enjoy!
You can also join our newsletter when prompted,
and never miss an awesome Falstaff Release!

FALSTAFF
BOOKS
WWW.FALSTAFFBOOKS.COM

www.ingramcontent.com/pod-product-compliance
Lightning Source LLC
Chambersburg PA
CBHW050610110726
47899CB00001B/56